Send Me No Flowers

Jenny Tomlin is happily married and living in France. With continuing support from her two children Martine and LJ, she still loves to write and enjoys family life to the full. She champions the causes of those charities that fight to wipe out abuse in all its forms, these include Barnardo's, Refuge, Red Cross and Domestic Violence Units, amongst others. Her first novel, *Sweetie*, was published in 2008 Her other works have been in non-fiction: *Behind Closed Doors*, *Silent Sisters* and *Not Alone*.

Also available by Jenny Tomlin

Sweetie

Send Me No Flowers

JENNY TOMLIN

arrow books

Published in the United Kingdom by Arrow Books in 2009

3 5 7 9 10 8 6 4 2

First published in Great Britain in 2009 by Century

Arrow Books
Random House, 20 Vauxhall Bridge Road,
London SW1V 2SA

www.randomhouse.co.uk

Addresses for companies within The Random House Group Limited can be found at: www.randomhouse.co.uk/offices.htm

The Random House Group Limited Reg. No. 954009

A CIP catalogue record for this book is available from the British Library

ISBN 9780099509844

The Random House Group Limited supports The Forest Stewardship Council (FSC®), the leading international forest certification organisation. Our books carrying the FSC label are printed on FSC® certified paper. FSC is the only forest certification scheme endorsed by the leading environmental organisations, including Greenpeace. Our paper procurement policy can be found at www.randomhouse.co.uk/environment

FSC
www.fsc.org
MIX
Paper from responsible sources
FSC® C016897

Typeset by SX Composing DTP, Rayleigh, Essex
Printed and bound by CPI Group (UK) Ltd, Croydon, CR0 4YY

This book is dedicated to Ken Lettman, a giant of a man with a giant heart and a loving, kind soul. My friend, always and forever

Acknowledgements

As always, I must thank my family for their wonderful support during a difficult time for me. The transition from non-fiction to fiction has not been an easy journey to make, although I have loved every minute of all the hard work it's taken to get me to book two and an increased readership. I must also thank the book-buying public for giving this new novelist the opportunity to write from the heart. You have bought my books, read them, enjoyed them, and, best of all, written to me to say how much you've enjoyed them. It's been wonderful to take my readers back twenty short years to an altogether different era, to relive the music, TV, and overall tone of this expansionist time, the last banquet before the leaner years.

As always, thank you to my publishers for all their support, especially Mark Booth, my mentor and guardian angel, and to all at Random House: the secretarial staff, the sales and marketing teams, press and PR. To the great and wonderful Debbie – you know how special you are, and what a great team player you are now and always will be. Thanks a million! To my wonderful man Alan, and my other wonderful man and great son, LJ. Martine, I can never express what I feel for you and how much I love and adore your wisdom, support and guidance in all I do. I am forever amazed by your beauty, both inside and out. Your fairness, modesty and fresh outlook on life, no matter what it throws at you, leave me spellbound!

To all the rest of my family – sister Kim, nieces, nephews, in-laws – love and thanks. And to all who know and love me, warts and all, I love you unconditionally too. A big hug for the Fennells, Dodds, Conns and Battys. Love to all, and very special wishes to Kim Baker and family. That's it!

Introduction

The content of this book is both shocking and explicit and makes for tough reading. Those of you who have read my previous books will know that I tell my stories from the heart and describe events which I know have really happened. As a writer, I take these facts and weave them into fiction. But to do justice to these truths, the horrors must be described in bald detail. There is no point my dressing up horror in fancy language, just as pulling my punches would in no way make the stories less gruesome.

It is an uncomfortable truth that in January 2008 alone reported cases of domestic abuse were up 28 per cent on the previous year. The key word here is 'reported' because it is an acknowledged fact that most domestic abuse is never recorded. Little wonder when over half the women who are raped are victims not just of people they have known, but people they have loved and cared for. My critics may accuse me of leaving little to the imagination but it is my express intention that such abuse should be shown in its true colours, namely as the worst kind of betrayal of trust that can be visited upon a human being.

I cannot write any less explicitly, for to do so would be to dishonour the victims' experience – these are people fighting for sheer physical survival, leaving aside the mental torture they endure. But I have seen, felt and retain tremendous hope that humans can not only survive but triumph over such circumstances. It strikes me as common sense that the most expedient way of achieving this is to name it for what it is and not sweep it under the carpet, as we are so squeamishly inclined to do.

In a recent interview I was stunned by a conversation I had with a high-profile media figure who shall remain nameless. He accused me of blowing the scale of such abuse out of all proportion, and sensationalising its horrors. I told him, in no uncertain terms, to talk to the victims and their families and see if he still felt the same way after he'd heard their stories of heartbreak and tragedy. Also to look at the figures. On average, two women a week are killed by a current or former partner, and a quarter of all violent crime is domestic, with one incident reported every minute. He remains convinced that I overstate such issues for the sake of grabbing the public's attention, but might it not be instead that such media notables live in gilded cages and have very little idea of what happens when you mix together vulnerable people and poverty? There is still a lot of prejudice out there, especially among the chattering classes, and I believe that my quest is not yet complete.

There is in this novel, I hope, a very definite warning about the use of drugs and how easy it is to get into them. This story starts back in 1986, over twenty years ago, when mainstream drug use escalated with the introduction of ecstasy and the advent of the rave scene. The drug trade today is as healthy as it ever was, and all the time there are profits to be made there will be plenty of drugs available. This is not likely to change in the foreseeable future. I would urge all parents to be watchful and users to beware.

We never think it is ourselves who will get hooked but that it's something that always happens to somebody else. Except it isn't. My message is, say no.

Finally, love. It is an emotion felt by all of us, in one way or another, and has a profound effect on people in a multitude of ways. We love our lovers, families and friends, our neighbours and pets, we can even love a hobby, work or life itself. But what happens when the love we feel takes a turn for the worse? What about the love that turns to envy, jealousy or hate, obsession, control, fear and dependency? It happens, and sometimes without the parties concerned even noticing. The power of love is immense in the way it changes people. I have seen love in many forms and experienced the wonderful feeling of being loved. Now in my life it comes unconditionally. This is how it should be; being loved for yourself is the greatest gift, and one that I personally treasure. It hasn't always been this way. I have deep and disturbing memories of being loved in the wrong way many times in my past.

My daughter's father loved me at first in a healthy, natural way. For our first few months as a couple we were blissfully happy. Slowly, as time went on, his love turned to obsession and I found myself allowing it to happen, feeling powerless to stop the situation I had put myself in. Love for me at that time was blind. I should have seen the warning signs early on, but I was young and totally caught up in it. Despite a cruel and often violent relationship, I would be drawn back into his arms time after time, until my life was no longer mine but his. My every waking moment was spent in dread and fear. I was almost robotic in my behaviour. Whatever he asked of me, I did. It was while drawing on these memories, and the stories of other women who have had the same experience, that I wrote this book.

Never mind that it's fiction, I relate totally to the characters and their experiences on their journey to eventual escape. Some women and men are not so lucky. They never escape an unhealthy, violent relationship. When asked why I decided to get out when I did, again the answer is love – not for my partner, but the deeper, more intense love I felt for my child. In amongst all the chaos and suffering, she was the innocent one who needed me to break free so I could give her what she needed more than anything: a stable, loving home to grow up in, even if it was with just one parent. It's difficult to explain what drew me back time and time again and what finally forced me to make the break. Why then and not before? I don't really have the answer, but something just clicked in my mind that made the choice for me, and once I knew I had to get away, escape became my obsession and need.

I didn't do it completely alone, I don't think anyone can, but it's amazing the strength you can absorb from those who deeply love you, faults and all. Friends and family did their best to help and I will always be grateful to them and to the One Parent Families organisation, the Police and the Samaritans.

There is help available out there, and I urge anyone in a similar situation reading this book never to give up. The human spirit burns so much brighter than we can ever imagine, and help is always at hand. There is no need to continue suffering. The longest journey starts with a tiny step, but the steps get bigger and bigger until eventually you return to the person that you once were, and you are running!

Don't suffer in silence, talk to someone.

Prologue

The girl in the bed lies quiet and still. Gradually, her eyes flutter open. It's difficult at first, they seem to be thick with a sticky substance like Vaseline, but gently she wills them open, blinking to try and make out where she is. She finds herself staring at a white ceiling. It's painful to move her head, and the room is dimly lit, but she can see the white blanket stretched across her body and the metal rail at the end of her bed. To one side there is a window with the blinds down, but she sees there is sunshine behind them, and to the other side of the room there is a door. She tries to move her arms but her hands are attached to tubes and drips, and by the edge of her bed she can hear a monitor, bleeping softly. Her face feels enclosed in something, and her cheeks seem to be squashed, causing her lips to pucker tightly together. They feel cracked and dry.

The effort of taking in all this has been too much. Her eyes flutter closed once more and she falls back into a painless sleep.

Outside the door of the private room sits a female police officer on a plastic chair. Her head is buried in a book to help pass the time until she is relieved by a colleague. Down the corridor in the small waiting room a few people are gathered together with two uniformed officers and a plainclothes policeman. By the window stands a tall, attractive woman, head bowed low and silently sobbing, being comforted by another woman, much younger and very beautiful. A man holds a young boy close to him, shaking with anger and fear which he tries to hide from the child seeking comfort. The family are traumatised by the violent assault that has left their daughter close to death. The policemen are doing their best to piece together the events that led up to the crime.

Once again the girl struggles to open her eyes. Something is touching her cheek, something familiar, soft and safe. Out of the corner of her eye, she spots a pink, furry shape. It's Pookie, the ragged cloth rabbit she's had since childhood. A tear forms in the corner of her eye and she starts to remember things: her family, her home, and her young life shattered. Then there is overwhelming shame and pain. It's too much for her to bear. She feels she wants to die rather than face whatever lies ahead and closes her eyes again, desperate for sleep, not wanting to remember anything. Not wanting to wake up again. Sleep is her only escape. Awake, the memories are all too vivid, and far too much for her to cope with.

Down in the waiting room, a new arrival comes charging in to join the family, her face frantic with worry and exhaustion. Her long blonde curly hair is tangled and matted, make-up is smeared down her face. She looks worn out. She's wearing some kind of fancy dress costume underneath the large man's overcoat which is keeping her warm. She heads immediately for the mother and sister of her friend, desperate for news of the girl who lies critically ill nearby even though she has clearly been through some kind of recent ordeal herself.

They speak in quiet, muffled tones. The girl leaves the waiting room, despite being informed that the police want to question her, and walks briskly down the hospital corridor towards the side room, a million thoughts racing through her head. The girl in the hospital bed, her best friend, has sustained injuries so severe that the doctors have warned her family she may not make it. Her best friend needs to see her, though, to let her know that she is with her and always has been.

Nothing could have prepared her for what she sees. The once beautiful girl in the bed is swathed in bandages, her face unrecognisable. Her friend takes a deep breath and slowly approaches. She pulls up a chair and sits by the bedside, resting her head on the crisp, white sheet and blanket covering the broken body. She cannot fight back the tears, but as her friend stirs she wipes her eyes and paints on a smile.

'Hey, babe, it's me. Don't try to speak, everything will be all right, but you have to promise me that you're gonna fight, mate? I need you and miss you, and I'm here.'

The girl in the bed looks at her friend as she starts to open her eyes. 'Where am I? What's happened to me?'

Tears flow freely down her face, wetting the bandages that are holding her face together. The friend feels ashamed and useless.

'I'm sorry, mate, he found you. But don't be afraid, the old bill will get him this time, and he'll be out of your life forever. I'll always be here for you. Together we will get you better, and the memory of all this will fade away in time.'

The girl in the bed manages a thin smile, acknowledging her friend, and as the years roll back in her mind she remembers all too well every moment of her short life.

'Don't you dare give up, Donna, stay with me, mate,' her friend implores. But Donna has closed her eyes again and slid far away, back to the beginning.

Chapter One

The sun streamed through the window and lit up the pink bedroom, casting its warmth over the crumpled bed. Young Donna Stewart stretched out her long limbs and smiled to herself. This was the day she had been waiting for. She giggled to herself with a mixture of nerves and anticipation, hoping she would be able to achieve what she had worked for so hard. She looked at Pookie, her scruffy pink cloth rabbit, grabbed him and kissed him on top of his head, stirring up the safe, familiar smell of her childhood.

She had worked hard to get good grades in her A levels, but the nagging doubt that she had maybe bitten off a little more than she could chew blunted the edge of her excitement. Four difficult subjects were all necessary to satisfy her conditional offer from Sussex University to study Sports Science and Donna felt slightly apprehensive. She got herself out of bed and went to the window to greet the day. Taking a deep breath, she decided that what would be, would be. She was sure she had done her best.

After a long shower, Donna towelled herself dry and slipped into her jeans and a T-shirt before she brushed her long, thick, dark hair. There was no doubting the fact that Donna was a real beauty in every respect. She had not only a sweet and winning personality, but a slender yet curving figure, naturally olive skin, large blue eyes, and a pouting full-lipped mouth with beautiful straight white teeth. Her mother Joyce and her never-ending nagging about health and hygiene was partly responsible for Donna's looks. Maybe this was why she was so keen to enter the world of health and fitness.

Donna checked her light make-up in the mirror and made her way downstairs to join the rest of her family. As usual Joyce was getting breakfast ready, and Brandon, Donna's young brother, had his nose deep in a football magazine, loudly complaining about Argentina's victory in the World Cup that summer. 'Hand of God, my arse,' he mumbled. 'Lady in Red' was playing on the radio and Joyce was singing along tunelessly.

'Morning, Mum. Morning, monster,' said Donna as she ruffled Brandon's curly mop of dark hair.

He grunted at his big sister and Joyce greeted her back by saying, 'Big day for you today, babe. Your dad had to go early but he's left you a card, and Jane has called already, wanting to know if you've any news. I told her she was too early, but you know your sister. She never did have much patience.'

Donna took her usual seat at the kitchen table and, pushing aside Brandon's pile of West Ham magazines, opened her card. 'Good luck to our beautiful princess,' it read in Dad's writing, with love from him, Mum, Jane and Brandon. She had always been called 'princess' by her dad, Ian. He was so proud of both of his girls. They had always been clever at school, and with Jane already away studying Economics and Languages at university, he hoped that Donna would follow in her footsteps.

Not many families in the East End waved kids off to higher education, and to have two of them in the same family was no small source of pride to the Stewarts. Brandon wasn't as academic as his sisters, but he was a sporty boy and very popular. They were proud of all three of their children. It wasn't unusual for kids in the neighbourhood to be brought home regularly in a squad car, but the Stewarts had always made sure that their kids worked hard at school and kept their noses clean. They led by example. Ian had worked himself up to a managerial position in the local council, and Joyce had taught at a local primary for over twenty years. They constantly stressed the importance of hard work and honesty, drilling this into their children. By any standards, they had done a good job.

'What time are you going down to the school?' Joyce asked Donna. 'Make sure you eat your breakfast before you go.'

'I'll just have a quick cuppa now and get something later. I'm off to meet up with Shaz and Nic and then we'll go to the sixth form. They're posting the results there this morning. After ten, they said.' Donna smiled at her mum, a look of apprehension briefly crossing her pretty face.

'You're going to be fine, darling,' Joyce said as she put Donna's tea down in front of her. 'Your dad and me will be proud of you, no matter what happens. But don't think you're leaving this house with just a cup of tea inside you. Try and eat something.'

Glancing at the kitchen clock, Donna gulped down the last of her tea. 'I can't eat, Mum, not now, I feel a bit sick, but I promise I'll grab something on the way. Gotta dash, don't want to keep the girls waiting. Have a good day at school, Brandon. You too, Mum, keep the little brats in check. I'll call and leave a message in the staff room for you.' She kissed her mum on the cheek, and made her way to get her jumper off the banister in the hall, leaving Joyce muttering something about nothing good happening to anyone on an empty stomach.

As a teacher at the local infants' school, she had strong feelings about kids receiving regular meals. Theirs was a poor area and many of her pupils came from homes where good food was hard to come by. She was convinced that failure to learn in some kids came down to something as simple as not having a good breakfast inside them before school. Still, the opportunities to learn were there and she was pleased to be part of an education system that offered even these kids a chance to get on.

Jokingly tapping Brandon around the head, Joyce told him to get a move on for school or he would be late. Drying her hands on a tea towel, she paused for a moment to gather her thoughts. She remembered when they had first moved into this house, how they had managed to become home-owners through the local right-to-buy scheme. She remembered the girls as toddlers then, and how for a few years afterwards they had struggled, but onwards and upwards was Joyce's motto. She would repeatedly tell her girls how important their schooling was. All that nagging and encouragement had paid off and now she allowed a wave of pride engulf her. It was 1986 and they had come a long way. With a lot of hard work and a drop of luck, they had done better than they could ever have imagined when they first started their married life, living in the spare room at Ian's mum's. Joyce felt profoundly grateful for her life today, and the chances given to all her family.

Suddenly snapping out of her thoughts, she reprimanded herself for daydreaming. She too would be late if she didn't get a move on.

As Donna made her way down the road, there was a slight skip in her step. It was a beautiful day and the sun shone high and bright. The roads were as busy as ever, with cars, lorries and buses all crawling in the morning rush-hour. As she reached the pelican crossing, she could see Shaz and Nicola waiting for her on the opposite side of the road, outside the local sweetshop. Donna sighed to herself. She knew this was so that Nicola could buy her cigarettes. Donna wished she wouldn't but it was her friend's choice. Donna and Shaz had tried to talk her out of it, but Nicola was now hooked. She needed her fags. Donna hated the smell of stale tobacco, but the more she nagged Nicola, the more defiant she became.

Nicola had always been the live wire in their group, ever since they'd first met and became friends at infants' school. Their early friendship had lasted and together they had shared the formative experiences of growing up. Nicola had grown into the real party animal of the three of them, always the first to try something new. Donna was hardly an innocent, she had smoked a few joints and had a few lines of speed in her time, but Nicola could really let her hair down in ways Donna didn't always approve of. But, as her best friend, she knew it was not her place to judge, merely to support and always be there for her.

Nicola's brother Freddie had followed the predictable path of falling in with local gangs and doing their bidding in order to finance his habit for hard drugs. Her parents were finally about to embark on a divorce, but it had come too late for Nicola. She had had to fight hard all her life to make any headway, and whenever she seemed to be getting anywhere, memories from childhood which told her she was worthless and would never amount to anything would always return to trip her up.

Shaz was totally different from both Donna and Nicola. Of mixed race, she was very petite. Too petite, she would say. She was eighteen but still had trouble making people believe she was old enough to drink, to get into clubs or watch an X-rated film. Shaz had grown used to carrying identification around with her, but secretly longed for the day when her breasts would develop and her legs would lengthen. With Shaz standing just five feet tall, Donna and Nicola towered above her.

'Come on, Donna, hurry up!' Nicola shouted across the busy road. Donna pressed the button and waited for the green man to appear, to allow her to cross. Nicola and Shaz always teased her for being such a goody-goody, perfectly adept themselves at dodging in and out of moving traffic, but Joyce liked to quote accident statistics to her kids and, despite sometimes wanting to be more like her friends, Donna was too much of a conformist at heart. Safely across and united with them, she giggled and laughed with her friends, each nervous about the A-level results. As the one who struggled the most with her academic work, Nicola smoked three cigarettes on the short walk to the sixth-form college. As they reached the gates, the three girls linked arms and then raced into the grounds, cheering and shouting.

The sixth-form common room was packed and the air inside fairly crackled with tension. The students milled around, chatting amongst themselves, all nervously casting occasional glances at the clock, waiting for the seconds and minutes to tick by to ten a.m. As the big hand approached the hour, the room fell into an uneasy silence until Mary, the senior prefect, said, 'OK, everyone, it's time.'

After filing into the main hall, the students formed a queue and waited in line while the staff laid out boxes of brown envelopes on the wooden table. As each student approached and gave their name, an envelope would be passed over. Donna edged her way forward in the queue. She could feel her palms getting sweaty and her heart thumping loudly. Falteringly, she gave her full name and an envelope was pressed into her hand. Looking up, she caught the reassuring smile of her science teacher and allowed herself a moment's hope. With the envelope gripped tightly in her hand, Donna made her way over to a quiet corner and tore it open with her eyes closed, praying to God she had passed.

Three As and one B! With her mouth hanging open but no sound coming out, Donna ran from the room and made her way down the stairs and out into the grounds. Suddenly a scream erupted from her mouth and she danced on the spot with delight. Within minutes Shaz and Nicola had joined her and they hugged each other and cried. All three of them had passed, Shaz with two Bs and a C, and Nicola three Cs – not what she'd been hoping for but enough to get her on to a top-flight training programme at the Savoy Hotel, with day release to catering college. The girls were ecstatic, exchanging kisses and congratulations and promises to meet up later. Donna made her excuses to them and said she needed to call her family. Before parting they arranged a time to meet up later, to go to a local nightclub to celebrate their news.

With her envelope gripped tightly in her hand, Donna walked jauntily along the familiar road home, thoughts and dreams of university racing through her head. She was a picture of radiant youth, a girl on the crest of a great future, with the sun making her long dark hair gleam and joy and beauty shining from within.

In her excitement, she fumbled her keys and dropped them twice before finally crashing through the door where she dumped her bag and jumper in the hall. With trembling hands Donna picked up the phone to call Mum and Jane. She saved Dad until last. When she heard his familiar voice at the other end of the line, she said, 'Hi, Dad, it's me. Your princess did well.'

Chapter Two

The family had gathered around the dinner table in a jubilant mood. Joyce had persuaded Donna's sister Jane to take the coach down from Manchester as a special surprise, and now together with Nicola, whom Donna had had the foresight to invite, knowing there would be no special celebrations in her own home, the three girls shrieked and giggled as they talked about future plans.

Joyce was having a hot flush in the kitchen as she laboured over the pots and pans, pushing her blonde fringe off her forehead with the back of her hand. She had thickened with age and wore clothes two sizes larger than she would have preferred to, but she was still pretty for forty-five, with deep dimples to either side of her smiling mouth.

Jane was a strikingly attractive girl, just like her younger sister. Her trademark long dark hair was pinned up to reveal a lovely oval face with huge almond-shaped blue eyes, a petite nose, high cheekbones and pouting lips that always stayed red. With her height, long legs, and trim but womanly curves, she made a striking figure that turned many heads. The Stewarts had been blessed with three gorgeous-looking kids. Not only did Jane have beauty, she had brains too. She desperately wanted to recommend

Manchester University to Donna, if only because the club scene in the city was so up and coming.

'There's this place called the Hacienda . . . it's completely mental, you could lose days in there!'

'You're supposed to be studying, young lady, not dancing the night away,' chided Ian with a wry smile. 'Anyway, never mind university, help your mother and lay the table.

Ian Stewart was still a very handsome man. The children had taken their dark colouring and piercing blue eyes from him. Despite going slightly grey at his hairline, at over six foot two and with a great physique due to regular visits to the gym, he was an impressive figure but a naturally gentle man, who loved his family and his home life.

'Yeah, but Dad, we work hard and then we play hard – fair's fair,' Jane pleaded.

Ian just shook his head and said to her, 'Have you seen this?' pointing to the TV. 'Honestly, no girl's safe out there any more.' The report about missing estate agent Suzy Lamplugh had really affected him.

Joyce, who hadn't been able to stop smiling in the three days since the A-level results were announced, instantly sided with her daughter.

'Oh, Ian, stop worrying. They've got good heads on their shoulders and their feet on the ground, they'll be fine.' She drained some potatoes through a colander and the steam rose up, enveloping her. 'None of our kids has ever come home in a police car or got mixed up with drugs . . . we should thank our lucky stars.'

Nicola and Donna widened their eyes at each other at this comment as Nicola had managed to get hold of a bit of speed for their special night out tonight. They weren't druggies, but they liked a good time. Ian just mumbled something under his breath about kids having it easy these days and went off to the front room to get some bottles of cream soda and lemonade out of the cocktail cabinet.

After dinner the girls had planned to meet up with Shaz and go for a night out, dancing and celebrating, at a local night spot called the Limelight Club. It was a bit scruffy and could have done with a refurb but the dance floor was huge, the music excellent and the bar stayed open till one. Officially it had an over twenty-ones-only door policy, but Nicola knew the bouncers and the girls never had any trouble getting in. They hadn't made it out as planned on the night of the results as Ian had insisted that Donna stay home, it being a week night. She may already be eighteen, but all the time she was under Joyce and Ian's roof there were rules and a code of conduct they expected her to comply with. Donna's protests that school was finished now fell on deaf ears. Her dad made her stay put and have a quiet night in with her parents and Brandon. She hadn't minded much, truth be told. Donna was a home-loving creature at heart and had happily whiled the evening away with her mum, watching an episode of *Dynasty* which they'd recorded the previous Saturday, with Joyce sighing and saying, 'Isn't Blake Carrington gorgeous?' and Ian and Brandon rolling their eyes at each other as they played a few rounds of three card brag and pontoon.

Life in the Stewart household had always been tranquil and happy, apart from the usual sibling arguments. Donna dreamed of one day meeting somebody and recreating it for kids of her own but first there was so much she wanted to do, so much she wanted to experience. Settling down could wait. For now, Donna was determined to pursue her immediate plans – a gap year in which she'd work and save some money, followed by university. There was the additional matter of her netball which she played every weekend with Shaz – Mile End Ladies had scooped the regional cup three years running. They knew they were the best and practised hard to maintain their position at the top of the East London District League.

But for now there was fun to be had. After they had all complimented Joyce on her chicken and mushroom pie and mucked in with the washing up, Donna and Nicola headed for Donna's bedroom upstairs, leaving Mum, Jane, Dad and Brandon watching the TV. Saturday nights were always good for telly, and the four Stewarts who weren't preparing for a night on the tiles settled down happily with a large bar of Fruit and Nut for the new episode of *Dynasty*.

Up in Donna's bedroom the two girls giggled with excitement. They had the stereo on full blast. Nicola danced round the room to James Brown's 'Living in America'.

'God, I love this tune, Don, it makes me all fired up and right in the mood for a good dance. Can't wait to get out tonight and let me hair down.'

When that record had finished playing, Donna put on Madonna's 'Papa Don't Preach' and the girls sang along loudly and tunelessly until Ian bellowed up the stairs for them to keep the noise down.

Nicola started to unravel the rollers from her long blonde hair. It fell well past her shoulders, glimmering in the evening sunlight. There was no doubt that she was a striking young woman. Her beautiful green eyes held sadness, though, and for all their high spirits Donna knew her best friend was facing some harsh realities in her own home.

'Things any better at yours, Nic?' she asked.

'Nah, the usual shit, I can't wait to get out of there. I

start at the Savoy on the twelfth of September and it hasn't come a moment too soon. I get accommodation and day release for Westminster College so I won't have to see them at all if I don't want to.'

Donna's face fell slightly. Catching this, Nicola quickly followed up with, 'But I'll be coming back all the time to see you and Shaz.' She paused while she ran her fingers through her curls, arranging them around her shoulders, and tactfully moved the conversation on. 'Your grades were fucking fantastic though, Don, I can't believe you're gonna wait a year to go to uni.'

They had hotly debated this topic many times. Ian had always provided well for his family, but also felt it was important for the kids to sweat a bit and earn for themselves. It had been drummed into Donna that she had to make some money of her own. And, besides, she liked the challenge. Donna was adamant that she was sick of studying and just wanted to work and save some money for a year before she went on to do her Sports Science degree. Nicola was keen for them both to move away at the same time, progressing their lives in tandem. She thought someone as bright as Donna was mad to want to hang around the East End, taking any old job, just to save money for a year.

'Just think, we may end up together one day, you with your sports and leisure complex and me with my very own café! I could do healthy foods actually, in the Sports Complex. What do you reckon?'

Donna started to laugh. 'We'll always be together, Nic, but I'm not sure where Shaz will fit in with her art and weird painting. Perhaps we can exhibit her work throughout the complex and offer painting and pottery classes?' They fell about laughing at the thought.

Donna had already decided on her outfit for the night. It

was a really short denim skirt with a lace frill all around the hem. A tight-fitting white bodice went with it perfectly, and blue strappy cork platform shoes set the outfit off to perfection. With large silver hoops in her ears and showing a bit of cleavage, she looked a knockout.

Nicola wore dark blue denim jeans with brown cowboy boots underneath, and a white boob tube with glitter all around the edges. Her pert bosom defied gravity, and with her blonde curls cascading over her shoulders, she too looked a million dollars.

'Did you get the Thunderbird, babe?' she asked.

'Of course, silly. Get some cups from the kitchen and I'll pop it open. Don't worry, Mum and the others won't hear you, they're all too wrapped up in that new colour TV.'

Drinks were a bit steep in the Limelight Club, especially for unwaged teenage girls, so they cut the cost in time-honoured fashion by getting a few down them before they went out, to put them in the party mood. Nicola arrived back with three paper cups, knowing Shaz would arrive at any minute. Right on cue the doorbell rang and Donna opened it to find little Shaz jumping up and down on the spot with excitement. The three girls swallowed two bottles of Thunderbird wine, an experience not dissimilar to drinking vinegar, but the more they drank, the better it tasted. They danced around the bedroom as they added the finishing touches to their make-up. Shaz looked cute in her strappy summer dress patterned with blue flowers. Despite the make-up she still looked too young to be clubbing, but the three of them set off into the warm August evening, making their way to the Limelight.

The girls arrived early, around eight, to find the club pretty empty, just a few groups of people huddled at the bar, but it gave them the opportunity to bag a good table, right near the dance floor. The Limelight Club was definitely the best place to dance in East London. Its music was a mix of old and new, with the time-honoured tradition of the slow-dance records always being played at the end of the night. The walls were lined with woodchip paper painted purple and lemon and hung with posters advertising various DJs who would be playing in the forthcoming months. The toilets were pretty grim, with only three loos in the Ladies, one of which was always out of order, but by arriving early the three girls had the chance to empty their bladders of cheap drink, touch up their make-up and put on a final squirt of perfume.

Slowly the other punters filed in and the club began to fill up. By pub closing time the whole place was heaving with people talking, dancing and drinking. Smoke hazed the air. People had to shout into one another's ears to be heard. The whole club stank of stale perfume and sweat.

The girls threw themselves into dancing the night away, handbags piled up in the middle as they danced. With the help of a few more drinks, cheap lager and lime, and a few lines of the speed supplied by Nicola, they were flying and having the time of their lives! They were totally oblivious to the envious stares of other girls, as well as second glances from more than one man. Sitting directly opposite them was a group of men. Nicola spotted her brother Freddie among them. She smiled at him but made no attempt to go over because of the guys he was with. She hated his druggy crowd. Among them was a well-known face in the area, known as Lucky Danny Lester.

Nicola noticed that Danny Lester spent a lot of time gazing at her and her friends, and only just resisted the temptation to go over and ask, 'What are you staring at?'

She couldn't stand the guy, but thought it best to ignore him. Only gradually did she work out that it was Donna who had caught his eye. She saw him and Freddie pointing and talking and knew that her hopeless brother would be telling Danny everything he knew. Donna danced and laughed and twirled around and around, oblivious to Danny's attempts to catch her eye. Nicola had to smile to herself. Danny Lester really fancied himself as a ladies' man and usually had no problem getting a woman's attention, but tonight Donna was so wrapped up in her friends and having fun with them that she failed to notice him at all.

The evening was drawing to a close when at last Donna sat down. The slow records had started to come on. The DJ kicked off with 'Unchained Melody' and it wasn't long before tall, blond, very handsome Danny Lester was standing in front of her, his hand outstretched, asking her to dance. Without thinking, Donna found herself placing her hand in his. As he held her close, she could smell Kouros on his neck and found herself drifting away, her body pressed close to his. She had never been held this way, it felt safe somehow, and she was amazed that this man had chosen her when there were so many beautiful girls standing around, just waiting for the opportunity to pull a man. One slow dance gave way to another, and the two of them stayed locked together for half a dozen songs until the lights came up at 2 a.m. Donna found herself staring into his cornflower blue eyes then, waiting for something, anything.

Finally, he said, 'It's too early to go home yet. Come with me for a drive around. My name's Danny. And don't worry, you'll be safe with me.' She knew instinctively that he was telling the truth; that this man she had never laid eyes on before tonight would take care of her.

Nevertheless, she glanced over at Nicola and Shaz, a flicker of indecision on her face. 'I'd love to, but let me tell my mates.' As an afterthought she added, 'I'm Donna, by the way.'

He held her gaze for a few seconds before answering, 'I know,' and she was secretly thrilled.

Nicola, wired on speed and feeling a bit snappish, was not happy to hear about it. 'Don, I know about Danny Lester. He hangs out with Freddie and his loser mates. They're all bad news. Let's head home together. Besides, he's too old for you. He's about thirty!'

But Donna was still looking at Danny when she said, 'Honestly, Nic, I'll be all right. He's so lovely, and just a drive won't hurt.'

Nicola's eyes pleaded with her to stay but Danny had quickly moved in and put his arm around Donna's waist, leading her away. Looking back over her shoulder, she called to Nicola and Shaz, 'I'll call you first thing in the morning, honest.'

'I don't like this one bit,' muttered Nicola to Shaz, biting her thumbnail.

Three hours in the car with Danny passed like minutes. Every time Donna caught his eye her stomach flipped over and her insides felt as if they would melt. His dirty-blond hair flopped sexily over his forehead, and he had the most intoxicating smile. In the early morning, some time around five, after they had spent the small hours driving round the East End, just cruising and chatting, Danny finally stopped the car to kiss Donna.

Parked outside her parents' house, she felt she didn't want to leave him. They had talked about everything: her life at school and hopes for university, her family, her friends. Danny had spoken softly to her about his own life, how he had virtually grown up on the streets, and he'd told her truthfully that he had never met anyone like her in his life before. He had no real family to speak of, his parents having split up when he was fourteen. His mother quickly met a man from Manchester, fell pregnant within months, and had relocated up North before the baby was born. She'd offered to take Danny with her but he was adamant that his life was in the East End and refused to go. The arguments raged for several weeks until finally one day she walked out, leaving only a twenty-pound note on the table, never to return.

Donna felt shocked and saddened by Danny's story and they held tight to each other, she feeling strangely protective of this big, rugged man. She asked what had happened to his father but Danny answered dismissively that he'd died two years later, knifed in a pub brawl in South London. Donna, with her cosy, secure home, could not imagine the hardship this man must have suffered. Somehow he had managed to stay in the small pre-war flat his family had lived in by lying to the council about his mother's absence and fending for himself. From such beginnings he had fashioned the basic philosophy that being able to look after himself, having respect and money, was all that counted. Donna gazed at him in wonder, awed and moved by his story. Danny was incredible.

He told Donna that she was everything a girl should be: pure, innocent and sweet. He whispered that he was totally taken with her beauty and freshness, how clean and unspoiled she was compared to the other girls he knew. He confessed he was no angel; that he had had to be a thief to survive. He could handle himself, too.

Far from putting Donna off, it only made Danny more fascinating to her. When he kissed her again, she melted in his arms. His tongue searched for hers, and he held her even tighter than before, desperate to go further but knowing he had to respect her youth and naivety a little longer.

'You need to go in now, babe,' he said finally. 'I'm losing control here. I respect you, though, and want to see you again. Can we meet again later?'

Donna readily agreed. She kissed him again, this time even more intensely, holding on tightly. But he got out of the car, opened the passenger door and helped her out.

'Let's meet at the White Lion pub, seven-thirty sharp. Is that OK?'

Donna just nodded and looked at the ground, not wanting him to leave her. She watched him drive away and then made her way to the door, let herself in and crept up the stairs to her room. The sun was just coming up. In a dream-like state, she undressed and felt herself below. Her knickers were wet, and her whole body ached for the man she had just left. She had never had these kinds of feelings before. She lay under a single sheet in the warm morning and drifted off to sleep, images of losing her virginity to this wonderful man drifting in her mind. She had always known it would have to be someone special. Finally he had arrived.

Chapter Three

Later that morning Donna heard a tap on her door. Joyce looked in at her daughter who was gently waking up, stretching her arms above her head. She had a beaming smile on her face, puffy as it was from a deep sleep.

'Late one, eh, babe?'

Donna smiled back, nodded her head and yawned. 'Any chance of a cup of tea, Mum?'

'You might want to come down and get it. There's a delivery arrived for you. Come and have some brekkie and tell me all about it.'

'Delivery of what?' Donna sat up in bed, suddenly alert.

'Come and see for yourself.' Joyce smiled and made her way back down the stairs, humming a tune. Half a minute later her daughter came thundering down after her and wheeled round the bottom of the banister to find an enormous arrangement of Cala lilies and white roses lying on the kitchen table

'God, they're gorgeous!' said Donna, searching for a card which she eventually found buried in the deep green foliage. After tearing open the small envelope, she read, 'Can't wait to see you later, Danny xx'. Donna clasped the card to her breast and sat down in a dream-like state, remembering his kisses and their tight embrace of only hours before. She felt her stomach knot and a tingling in her loins. The toaster popped and Joyce, feigning indifference to the identity of the bouquet's sender, started to butter it for her. 'Jam or Marmite, babe?'

'Marmite. Oh, Mum, it's all such a dream! I never expected this. I can't believe it.'

Donna just stared into space as Joyce placed a steaming mug of tea in front of her and her plate of toast. 'Why don't you eat something and tell me all about it?' She wiped her buttery fingers on her apron and sat down at the kitchen table, facing her daughter expectantly.

'Well?'

Joyce and Donna were close. Despite their younger daughter being a bit of a Daddy's girl, it was to Joyce that she confided the intimate stuff. Dad was good for unconditional adoration, new clothes and shoes, but Joyce had always been the practical one, ready with sound advice. She had lovingly steered all her children through the traumas of school, friends and exams, with a firm but fair hand. She took a more realistic, hands-on approach to her children than her husband did, especially when it came to Donna. To Ian, she would always be his little princess, never to be refused. Joyce took the more balanced view that somebody had to keep her feet on the ground.

As Donna dreamily ate her toast the phone rang and Joyce answered. It was Nicola.

'Hi, honey, how's you? Just a minute, I'll get love's young dream for you.'

Donna rushed out into the hall to take the call.

'Hi, Nic . . . yeah, I'm fine and everything's great. You wouldn't believe the flowers that arrived this morning . . .'

Joyce took herself back into the kitchen, fighting the urge to hang about and listen in on their conversation. She was very fond of Nicola and, despite the fact that Donna's best friend could be a bit of a one for the men and smoked liked a chimney, took an indulgent view of her. Spending time with the Stewarts had provided Nicola with the only normal family life she had ever known and Joyce took care to be affectionate and accepting with her. Besides, she was a faithful friend and ally to Donna, who, in turn, helped keep Nicola on the right side of the track. Joyce was proud of Donna for sticking by her friend when other people, who weren't aware of her situation at home, were quick to label her. The two girls supported each other through thick and thin. Although they'd had their squabbles over the years, they'd remained tight.

Donna entered the kitchen again and slumped down into her chair, looking downcast.

'What's up, babe?' asked Joyce.

'Oh, nothing, just Nic moaning because I met some man last night . . .'

'Obviously,' Joyce interrupted.

'She isn't keen on him. It's OK, though, she's popping round later.'

'What's not to like?' asked Joyce, eyeing the flowers.

'Nothing, Mum, honest. He's so handsome and such a gentleman. I suppose you could say he swept me off my feet.'

'Well, if he sends flowers and makes you feel so happy, that's OK by me.' Joyce smiled at her. 'Best get dressed, babe, or you'll miss half the day.'

'I'm meeting him again tonight, Mum, and I can't wait! Bring us up a vase, will you? The nice cut-glass one that Auntie Jean got you for your anniversary, not that horrible yellow thing with the daisies painted on it.'

Donna scooped up the flowers and ran up the stairs to her room. For a while, she lay on her bed and thought of Danny. The tingling feeling returned and this time she touched herself, wondering how it would be to lose her virginity to a man like him. She had thought of this moment many times, and at eighteen realised she was a bit behind other girls, but with Danny, she believed, her moment had finally come. Afterwards, safe and dreamy in her warm bed, she fell back into a contented sleep for another hour. Joyce arranged her bouquet in the cut-glass vase and left the arrangement next to her bed, smiling broadly to see her daughter's contentment. She was pleased for her. Donna had worked hard at school all these years. She deserved a nice boyfriend.

By the time Nicola arrived, Donna was washed, dressed, and eager to tell her friend all about her marvellous time with Danny the night before. Nicola kept a sour-puss expression on her face the whole time she was talking, though. 'Honestly, Nic, I thought you'd be pleased? He's gorgeous, and just so different from any boy I've ever met before.'

'That's because he's not a boy, Donna, he's a grown man at least ten years older than you. It's not right, he's too old for you. Besides, he's a bloody criminal.'

Exasperated, Donna turned on the stereo and flicked through her albums, looking for something suitable. She took a Prince record out of its sleeve before thinking better of it and slipping it back. Nicola drew a deep breath.

'Listen, Don, I don't know him well, but there are always rumours about that bloke. I mean, he's into all kinds of trouble. He got my Freddie hooked on coke and all sorts, and those low-lifes he hangs around with are dodgy as fuck. Believe me, I want you to be happy but not with him. He's a bloody drug dealer!' Nicola stared at her friend, pleading with her to listen.

'So is that where you get your speed from, Nic, and your

puff ? Honestly, you can be such a hypocrite. Last night we were hoovering up lines of sulphate and today you've gone all prim. I'm not as naive as you think. And as for Danny . . . he looked after me really well and made no move on me at all.'

The two girls stared uneasily at each other for a few moments in a tense stand-off before Donna softened her tone and pleaded with her friend, 'I really like him, Nic, and I want you to be my mate and trust my decision. It's not a lot to ask, I've always been there for you.'

Nicola looked down at the floor. It was true. Donna had always stuck by her, even during the times when Nicola couldn't bring herself to tell her what was going on at home or why she was so upset.

They dropped the subject of Danny and spent the rest of the afternoon returning to the safer ground of playing records and chatting about outfits. Just as Nicola was leaving, Donna put her arms around her.

'I know you're worried about me, Nic, but honestly, I'll be fine. Whatever you've heard about Danny, it's not the same person as the guy I was with last night. I will be careful, I promise!'

Nicola shrugged her shoulders non-commitally. Donna tried again. 'Let's meet up tomorrow. We can sort out some time to talk about what flipping job I'm going to get, and I can let you know how I got on with Danny. I'll be able to put your mind at rest then. Is that OK with you?' She beamed hopefully at her best friend.

Nicola smiled. 'Yeah, 'course it is, silly. Love ya.'

Donna took particular care over choosing her outfit for the date with Danny. Many clothes were jettisoned in a pile on the floor as she struggled with various combinations of clothing, trying to strike just the right note.

Eventually she hit upon the best look. As she stood in front of the mirror, she liked what she saw staring back at her. Her dark hair hung down her back and over her shoulders in thick ringlets, and she wore a gold headband to lift it back from her face and show off its perfect shape. Her gypsy top was pillar-box red with gold ruffles, and the sleeves dropped off her shoulders, revealing her tanned olive skin. Her short black ra-ra skirt emphasised her long brown legs, and large gold hoop earrings finished off the outfit perfectly. As a last- minute touch, she fumbled through her jewellery box and slipped on the gold bangle her parents had bought her for her eighteenth birthday. With her high cork shoes on, small black clutch bag and a dab of Joyce's Chanel No. 19 behind her ears, she was ready.

Outside the White Lion, she drew in a deep breath. All sorts of silly fears ran through her head. Would Danny be there? Would he remember her? Would he just ignore her? Would everybody laugh? But as she entered the saloon bar, all heads turned and the pub fell momentarily quiet.

She instantly spotted Danny at the bar, talking to two men: one young, one middle-aged. They looked like they could be father and son. The young man was handing a large sum of money to Danny who was pointing a finger in his face, almost like a warning. The older man looked worried and was clearly trying to calm things down. As if sensing Donna's presence, Danny turned and stared at her with hungry, appreciative eyes. He waved the two men away, and they backed off without any protest. Donna moved towards him bashfully.

'You look stunning,' he said, looking her up and down. She could only murmur a thank you. Inside, her heart was pounding, and her mouth had gone dry.

'Let's get you a drink, sweetness.' He signalled to the

barmaid to come over. Donna wasn't a hardened drinker, and as it was early decided on a Coke while Danny had a pint of lager. They made their way to a small table and sat down. As he sat close to her, she caught an intoxicating whiff of his aftershave, woody and deep. 'I've got plans for tonight, sugar. I've arranged for a Chinese meal – you do like Chinese, don't ya? And then I thought we'd go to a club for a few drinks. Does that sound OK? If you wanna do anything else, I don't mind, just as long as you're with me.'

He tenderly kissed her on the cheek and Donna blushed. 'No, I love Chinese, it sounds fantastic.' She gazed into his sultry eyes which held hers for a long time before he broke away.

'Listen, babe, there's just something I gotta do quickly then we'll be on our way. I thought we'd go up West. Wait here, I'll be two minutes.'

Up West . . . Donna had thought it would be the local Chinese restaurant. Up West sounded really glamorous. She'd never eaten in the West End before, only been shopping on Oxford Street for jeans before Jane left to go to Manchester.

Leaving her to her thoughts, Danny rose from the table and eyeballed the two men he had been speaking to earlier, indicating that they should join him somewhere quiet.

It was a lovely summer evening. As they drove out of the East End on their way into town Donna felt like a true princess, with her knight in shining armour by her side. Danny's hands on the wheel were broad and strong, his forearms well-muscled and covered with dark-blond hair. He was very manly and she felt safe and protected. With the convertible's roof down, a light summer breeze whipped her hair across her smiling face, making her look like a gypsy. Danny loved it. Occasionally, between gear changes, he would reach over and squeeze her hand. His touch sent shivers through Donna's lovely young body. At traffic lights, she was aware of the admiring glances of other men as they stared at the beautiful young passenger. She and Danny laughed and talked all the way, and after eventually parking the car made their way to Chinatown where Donna had the time of her life.

She had never seen a fortune cookie before. At the end of the meal, when she snapped hers open and read, 'Life changes direction, follow your heart,' her happiness was complete. It seemed Danny was well known to the owners. Everything he asked for, he got. At the end of the meal, when he went to pay, the owner dismissed him with a wave. He was clearly a regular and very popular. Donna felt like the Princess of Wales. After the delicious meal and more wine than she was used to, she felt light-headed and on cloud nine.

'Mr Danny, Mr Danny, you got two minutes to spare?' asked the waiter.

'For you, Foo, anything,' said Danny obligingly. He excused himself and disappeared into the kitchen behind the beaded curtain. He was back within minutes and the two of them said their goodbyes to the beaming staff, left the restaurant and walked around Chinatown in the fading evening light, the shop windows illuminating the young couple as they paused to kiss and cuddle.

'I've 'ad a thought, babe,' said Danny, as if it had just occurred to him. 'Let's go find a fabulous hotel and stay in town overnight. We can get a few more drinks and then, tomorrow, go shopping. I fancy a bit of retail, and what better way to spend my money than on my very own beautiful girl?' He suddenly pulled her to him tightly. 'You are my girl, aren't you, Donna?'

She felt the same tingling as she had before and her heart beat faster. At that moment, she knew she could not deny this man anything.

'Of course I'm your girl, Danny. Let's go.' Thoughts of anyone else . . . her family, Nicola . . . left Donna's mind. All she could think of was this man who held her in his arms so tightly. Mad as it seemed, she was in love. It was quick and sudden and had come from nowhere, but she didn't care. Nothing had ever felt this right before. This was where she wanted to be.

The Berkeley Hotel was beautiful. Their suite of rooms overlooked Hyde Park. As Danny poured two glasses of vodka, Donna perched on the edge of the bed. She was a little afraid and he could read her thoughts it seemed. 'Danny, I need to tell you something.' She hesitated and sighed, her fingers fidgeting with the edge of the bed-spread. 'It's my first time with a man. I mean, I've kissed other boys, but I've never . . .'

'It's OK, baby, I know and I understand.' He stared into her eyes. 'Don't be afraid of me. Never be afraid of me.' He cupped his hands around her delicate face and kissed her hungrily. 'I would never hurt you.' He lowered her gently on to the bed and slowly started to remove her clothes with a gossamer touch, light and assured, as he took in every inch of her perfect body. He wanted to please Donna in every way he could. Danny was an experienced lover and knew all the tricks to make a woman come, over and over again.

'You're my baby woman, Don, I'm gonna look after you. You're priceless, baby,' he said, staring into her eyes as he stroked her body. 'I've never had anything as pure and untouched as you before.' He gently spread her legs, kissing the inside of her thighs, causing her to sigh and moan. When he reached what lay between, he caressed her with his tongue, exploring every part of her, licking and sucking gently while his hands moved up to caress her breasts. He ran his mouth up and down her body, sucking her nipples – softly at first, and then a little harder to make her moan louder. He teased her with wet fingers, slowly moving them inside her. First one, then two, pressing in hard and sucking her clitoris at the same time. He knew she had climaxed more than once. Now it was his turn for pleasure.

He moved his now naked body on top of hers and guided his hard penis towards her mouth, instructing her to kiss and suck it. 'Pull the foreskin down, baby, and put as much in your mouth as you can. Then suck me hard.'

The wait was not long as Donna seemed to thrill him instantly. He turned himself around. Guiding his penis with his hand, he pushed it gently into her vagina. There was pain at first and Donna grimaced. 'Don't stop now, babe, it's in and we're ready.' Slowly he withdrew, only to push himself in again. Donna forgot the pain for the pleasure was far greater. As Danny thrust into her, deeper and faster, she felt an electric pulse run through her body, and a craving for him not to stop. The whole experience was magical for her, and Danny whispered that it was the best sex he'd ever had.

That was just the beginning of their night of pleasure and excitement for no sooner had they climaxed than she wanted to feel him inside her again. After hours of lovemaking, the two of them fell into a deep sleep.

After a sumptuous breakfast they made love again then Donna headed for the shower, to get herself ready for the day. She could hear Danny on the phone, but paid little attention.

'Fuck me, I'm away one night, Trippy, and you fuck things up! Listen, I ain't got long, I'm taking Donna shopping, but I'll be back later this afternoon. Don't do anything till I get there.'

He put the phone down as Donna appeared with a towel wrapped round her. 'Is everything OK, Danny?'

A broad leer spread across his face as he opened his arms and pulled her down on to the bed, still wet from the shower. 'Come 'ere, baby. With you around, everything's great.' After kissing her for a few moments, he affectionately patted her bum. 'Now let's get out of here and hit the shops.'

They had the perfect day. The shopping was brilliant, and Donna found herself laden down with bags full of dresses, shoes and perfume. As they drove back in the car, she could only gaze at her man in a state of wondrous love, oblivious to anyone else. As they pulled up outside her parents' house, they kissed passionately.

'Tonight then, babe, about eight at the White Lion?' he said eventually.

Donna looked towards her front door. It suddenly dawned on her that she should have called home.

'Listen, my mum will be a bit pissed off with me for staying out all night and not calling. Maybe we should leave it until tomorrow?' She could see that Danny wasn't pleased. She didn't want to leave him, not even then, or wait until tomorrow, but she needed time to sort things out with her parents.

'OK, babe, whatever you say, but no later than tomorrow. I'll meet you at the White Lion at eight. And, remember, I love you. I really do!'

Donna smiled.

'I love you too, Danny.'

*

Joyce was not at all happy when Donna came into the house. 'Where the bloody hell have you been, young lady? You had us all worried sick! Your father was in a right state. What do you think the phone is for?' Donna knew she was in the wrong, but no one could spoil last night for her, not Mum, Dad, anyone. 'Nic's been calling all day, asking where you were,' Joyce said crossly.

'I'm sorry, Mum, it's all been such a whirlwind, but I'm safe and fine and really happy. Let me put my stuff away and I'll tell you everything. I'm in love, mum, really in love. Please say you understand?'

Joyce looked at her daughter's luminous smile.

'You've slept with him, haven't you?'

Donna flushed.

'Yeah, but Mum, I love Danny and he loves me. I know it's all happened very quickly but you'd only known Dad for days when you realised he was right for you. The way Danny is right for me. Please, just trust me. When you meet him, you'll love him too.'

Fighting back a mother's natural instinct to worry, Joyce told herself she had to trust her daughter's judgment on this. Silently she hugged her. The two of them held on to each other for a while until Joyce released Donna, brushed her hair from her face and said, 'Right then, let's have a look in all those bags. What did he buy you?'

Chapter Four

Nicola was none too pleased that Donna kept letting her down. She'd called several times, trying to make arrangements to meet up, but Donna kept putting her off, leaving her in no doubt that she was now in second place to Danny. All Donna could talk about was Danny. Danny, Danny, Danny. The arrival of a second bouquet of flowers even bigger and more impressive than the first, only made matters worse. Donna had made a promise to meet up with Nicola for lunch in the week and assured her friend that nothing between them had changed. But, just for now, all she wanted was to concentrate on her new relationship and make sure she saw Danny as often as possible.

On the phone she explained. 'Listen, Nic, I wanna tell you everything but I haven't even had a minute to breathe. I'm just so happy, and I thought you'd be happy for me too. If I didn't know you better, I'd think you were a little bit jealous.'

Nicola guffawed at her down the phone.

'Don, I'm not the least bit jealous! It's just that you, me and Shaz have plans. We need to crack on.'

'Don't worry, I've not forgotten our plans, and when we meet up in the week, everything will get sorted. Listen, mate, I gotta go, I'm meeting Danny in an hour and I need to get ready. I'll call you later in the week.'

As Nicola replaced the receiver she knew her friend was lost to love. Freddie glanced at his sister's face as she put the phone down and said, 'Looks like Dan's got your mate well and truly hooked. You gotta hand it to him, she's a right looker. Not second-hand goods like you, eh, sis?' He lurched to his feet then and leaned on the table for support, starting to giggle.

'Shut up, Freddie, you're as high as a kite. You make me sick, you and your poxy gang. You're all fucking druggies!'

'Oh, listen to little Miss Innocent. Butter wouldn't melt, eh?' Freddie sneered. 'What you need is to get out and enjoy yourself. You take life so fucking seriously with all your training course crap. You need to live a bit.'

'What I need is to get the fuck away from you and this place.' And with that she stormed out of the flat with such force that the glass pane in the door rattled for several seconds afterwards.

The hours, days and weeks seemed to speed by for Donna, who had little or no time for anyone but Danny Lester. Jane had returned to Manchester University in disgust at the end of October, after making a special effort to come down bringing her new boyfriend to be introduced to all the family. Donna missed his visit. David Taylor was quite a catch: twenty-one and doing his Master's in chemical engineering, as well as being a broad-shouldered, six foot four rugby nut. Joyce and Ian were thrilled for Jane and thought they made a lovely couple. David was just the sort of bloke any parent would wish their daughter to find. Both their daughters, in fact.

But Donna hadn't even bothered to turn up for the

special meal that Joyce had spent all day preparing to welcome David, and hadn't thought a phone call necessary either. She came home in the early hours to find her exasperated mother standing on the landing in her dressing gown, demanding to know where she'd been and what on earth she found to get up to for all that time.

When Joyce tried to wake Donna the following morning to say she was off to work, all she got was a grunt and wave of the hand. Joyce was furious. Despite her daughter's fulsome apologies when she finally got out of bed the next afternoon, she knew that Danny had subsumed the family in Donna's affections. It was normal for girls her age to become wrapped up in their boyfriends, Joyce wasn't so old she couldn't remember how it felt, but Donna spent every day she could with Danny, stayed out most nights, and slept in until late the next day. There seemed to be room for nothing else in her life. Joyce hadn't minded that Donna wanted to take a year out before going to university, but wasn't she supposed to be looking for a job?

Ian and Joyce decided it was time they had a little chat with Donna. The opportunity arose when they sat down to a Sunday roast. Ian was agitated; he hated any confrontation, especially with Donna. Joyce, less scared of challenging her kids, went into teacher mode and demanded some answers from Donna about her plans for her future and education. As Ian carved the leg of lamb, casting furtive glances in the direction of his wife and daughter, Joyce dived straight in.

'Listen, babe, me and your dad have been talking and we think it's time you started making some decisions about uni. As far as I'm aware, you haven't even formally accepted your offer for next year from Sussex. You need to get cracking or they'll strike you off their books and then you'll be back to square one. All the paperwork and booklets have been lying around for ages. You need to address what you're gonna do.'

Brandon poked his greens with his fork, slyly enjoying his big sister's dressing down since it was usually him getting the lecture. Donna stared at her mother in disbelief. Where had this suddenly come from?

'I'm in no rush, Mum. I'm just not ready at the moment. It's no big deal. Anyway, I'm gonna work for a while before I go anywhere. I'm sick of studying. '

At that Ian clattered the carving knife down on the table. 'What do you mean, no big deal? It's all you've ever talked about . . . all you've ever wanted to do. How can you say it's no big deal?'

Donna just glared at him.

'For Christ's sake, Dad, stop trying to live my life for me. I'll do it when I'm ready, OK? I don't wanna think about it right now.'

Picking the carver back up, he pointed it at her.

'It's that bloke, isn't it? It's all about him now, and everything else has been thrown out the window. You don't even see your mates. We've had Nic on the phone again, in tears this time because you keep blowing her out every time you arrange to meet her. You can't blank your best friends just because you've got a boyfriend. They'll be around long after lover boy has buggered off.'

'For Christ's sake, I'm eighteen. I can make my own decisions,' Donna said indignantly. 'Besides, Danny's not like that. He loves me.'

'Yes, but that's the trouble, love, what exactly is he like? You're spending all your time with some bloke we know bugger all about. You can't expect us not to be worried sick, we're your parents, we still have a say all the time you're living under our roof,' said Joyce, putting the gravy jug down in the middle of the table next to the mint sauce.

'That's it, I'm outta here! What's the bloody point talking to you two? You just don't get it.'

Donna jumped up from her chair and stomped out of the kitchen. After grabbing her coat off the banisters where she'd tossed it in the early hours of that morning, she slammed the front door.

'Well, that went all right,' said Joyce. 'Anyone for extra roasties?'

Donna wandered around the streets for a while, feeling furious, and ended up at Nicola's house. She was lucky to find her in. Not wanting to stay at home with Freddie's greasy and emaciated form sprawled out watching TV, Nic suggested they take a walk, get a Coke somewhere and have their first real girlie chat in ages.

Donna was worried that Nicola might be a bit frosty with her after all the recent let-downs but she was as good as gold and said nothing, just pleased finally to see her friend. Once settled in the local Wimpy Bar, Donna opened up and told her friend all there was to know. She seemed in a dream-like state as she spoke of Danny, their first real night together, and all the wonderful things she had experienced since.

Nic puffed hard on her fourth cigarette in fifteen minutes as she listened intently to Donna's tale of romance.

'You know, Nic, I think he'll propose soon. Only yesterday he asked me if I'd ever been to Paris. I mean, me in the city of true romance!' Nicola stubbed out her cigarette

'Don, do you really know Danny? I've not wanted to speak out before, and trust me, I've had to struggle to keep my gob shut on more than one occasion, but you really don't know this bloke like I do!'

Donna met Nicola's gaze indignantly.

'Listen, Nic, all you have to go on is rumour and hearsay. I'm sick of people telling me about the man I love and how bad he is when all I see is kindness and caring.' Donna was in defiant mood, but Nicola wasn't afraid to challenge her.

'Let me have my say, Don, and once I'm done that'll be an end to it. Just think about it. Where does a man like Danny get his money? Fast new car, rolls of cash, the latest phone . . . He ain't got a proper job, has he? No, he deals drugs, hard drugs, and I know that for a fact because it's where my slime-ball brother gets his from. Freddie is Danny Lester's lackey, and I can tell you, he's not a nice man.'

'Well, of course I don't know everything that goes on, but no one is responsible for Freddie but himself. Nic, I'm not stupid, he's nearly ten years older than me, but he loves me!' Donna spoke with all the certainty of first love. Nicola just shook her head.

'Babe, he's not the man you think he is. Sooner or later you're gonna get drawn in right over your head and you won't be able to handle it. He's bad news, Don. I'm telling you all this for your own good.'

'Christ, Nic, you sound like my bloody mum.'

Why couldn't Nicola understand? Donna knew that what Danny did was wrong, she had heard all the same gossip, but that was just business. When she was with him, he was different. That was the real Danny: loving and kind, generous in and out of the bedroom.

They never spoke about his work; she didn't ask and he didn't tell her, it was like an unspoken agreement between them, and what Donna didn't know couldn't hurt her. He didn't want her worrying about money, that was his job. With her Danny she was safe. She didn't care what other people thought. If they wanted drugs and Danny could supply them, who was she to question it? If it weren't Danny selling them, someone else would be. Why shouldn't he make a living, the same as anyone else? It wasn't as if he'd had the benefit of an education, as she and Nicola had done.

Nicola realised that she wouldn't get through to her friend. No matter what she said, nothing would change Donna's mind. It wasn't going to stop her trying, though.

'What about uni, Don, and all our plans? You're so wrapped up in Danny you don't even know my latest news. It happened over a week ago. I've started my job at the Savoy with day release to Westminster College. It's unbelievable, the most exciting thing that's ever happened to me! There's staff accommodation, but it's just a poky little cell next to the boiler room so I'll only use it when I'm working nights. But at least it gives me a break from that dump.' She nodded in the direction of the block of flats where she lived with her mother and Freddie.

'Oh, Nic, I'm so happy for you,' said Donna, reaching across the table and squeezing her best friend's hand. Nicola shrugged,

'It'll all be dogsbody stuff to start with, chopping veg and what have you, but in two years' time I'll be a qualified sous-chef, cooking at one of the best hotels in the world! My dreams are coming true, Don, and I want yours to come true, too. I thought you wanted do Sports Science at Sussex so you could be a fitness instructor or netball coach, run your own classes all over the area, even open your own leisure complex one day? What about that dream, mate?'

Donna looked a little saddened and chewed her thumbnail thoughtfully for a moment, but she had Danny now and all those old plans had paled into insignificance. Lying, she said, 'Well, I can resume my plans for all that whenever I want to. I've got the grades I need to go to university, I can use them any old time. Right now, I'm thinking wedding dresses and kids.

'My life has changed for the better, Nic. When you meet that someone special and know they're the one, you'll feel what I feel right now. That love is the most important thing in the world. You gotta grab it with both hands when it comes along.' Donna's eyes implored her to understand.

Nicola sighed inwardly but smiled gently at her friend, her own eyes filling up with tears. 'It must be wonderful. Look, whatever happens, I am always here for you, Don. You're my best mate, and I really hope it turns out well, honest I do. I'm not trying to piss on your parade.'

She took another sip of Coke, lit another cigarette, and resigned herself to the fact that her best mate was on a hiding to nothing.

Donna walked home in a thoughtful mood. She knew that Nicola didn't have any axe to grind and was genuinely concerned for her, but her friend had never known proper love and had no idea of its power to change lives. One day she would meet somebody and feel about them the same way Donna felt about Danny. Only then would she truly understand. As she put her key in the lock she could hear the TV blaring. She slipped past the front room unnoticed and went up to her room. She only had two hours to get ready before she met Danny. They were off somewhere special again, and already Donna could feel the excitement tingling in her body as she thought of the pleasures she would share with him.

She loved speeding along in his XR3 Cabriolet car, with the top down and the wind in her black curls. She loved the goose bumps that formed on her body as she sat waiting in anticipation to see where they would be going next. Danny liked to surprise her. She was always excited to receive flowers from him. They arrived every couple of days, at around the same time, and as Donna gazed at the latest bouquet, deep purple irises and blood red roses, which Joyce had left on her bed, she dismissed Nicola's concerns from her mind.

She applied her make-up carefully, wanting to look her best for him, to please him. At eighteen she was already woman enough to know the power her beauty had over him.

They had arranged to meet at the usual place and time. Donna always arrived at the White Lion at eight o'clock. A three-minute walk from her house, it was easy for her to get there and convenient for Danny as it was where he concluded his business for the day. Danny's routine was to rest in the afternoon, then have a bath and shave before serving up for the evening clientele.

Donna came through the doors of the pub to find him at his habitual end of the bar, by the fruit machine and men's loos, with Trippy, Stevie and Johnny. Unlike some men who felt the need to play it cool, Danny never made a secret of how pleased he was to see her. He would hug and kiss her and always ask his beautiful girl to do a twirl for him as he admired her latest outfit. Any other man would have looked like a pussy-whipped wimp for wearing his feelings on his sleeve, but on Danny it seemed masterful and passionate. Here was a guy so sure of himself that he could eat his dinner with a shovel and make it look stylish. Money was no object as far as Donna was concerned either, and after many expensive nights of passionate lovemaking in some swanky hotel, he would take her around London's best shopping districts and shower her with expensive gifts, including shoes, bags and make-up. Nothing was too good for his girl!

The other men in the pub would just stare and drool over the beautiful eighteen year old, envying Danny Lester for his good luck in finding such a gem.

But tonight Donna could tell straight away that Danny was agitated. He was no less pleased to see her than usual, but from the way he was drumming his fingers on the bar and chewing the inside of his cheek, she could tell he was nervous. He bought her a drink and handed her a brochure.

'Do me a favour, babe, sit tight for ten minutes while I finish up a bit of business. 'Ave a look at this brochure I picked up today and let me know what ya think?'

Donna just smiled and did as she was asked. Three sharp-suited men entered the pub then, men Donna had never seen before, and Danny visibly relaxed, a broad grin stretching across his face as he slapped them on the back, offering to get the drinks in. She wasn't deliberately eavesdropping but Donna couldn't help but catch snippets of their conversation.

'Danno,' said the tallest of the three as he shook Danny's hand. 'How's it going, mate. That your bird over there?' The man cast an approving glance at Donna which made her feel strangely uncomfortable. She was used to men giving her the eye, but there was something predatory and menacing about this one. She shifted nervously in her seat, pretended to concentrate on her brochure. 'Fit as a butcher's dog, ain't ya, babe?' Donna smiled vaguely. She could feel her face burn as she stared unseeing at the brochure.

'Let's just get to business, eh, Tony? You holding enough?' Danny steered the conversation to matters in hand and diverted the man's gaze from his girl.

'Yeah, mate, 'course I am. Let's adjourn to the men's room, shall we?'

*

Their suite at the Imperial Plaza was stunning, with views overlooking the Royal Victoria Docks where the sinking sun cast a golden shimmer over the calm water. From where she stood, Donna could look out over a wide swathe of London. She loved just to stand and gaze, and sometimes pinch herself at this new reality she found herself a part of.

'Come 'ere, babe,' motioned Danny, 'I've something special for both of us tonight.'

Lying on the glass-topped coffee table were two white lines of powder. 'I want us to take this together, babe.'

Donna looked at him, amazed. 'Danny, is that cocaine? I'm not sure, really . . . I've had a couple of lines of sulphate with Nic and Shaz before, but nothing like this. I don't know.'

Danny walked over to the window to take in the view himself.

'It's OK, Don, if you don't trust me, I won't push you. I wanted us to have a special night, a real, relaxing, lovemaking chilled night, that's all. It's been a bastard of a day for me. But if you don't feel safe, it's OK, I understand.' Donna was confused.

'I just don't see why we need it. We have a good enough time together without it, don't we?'

Danny put his hands over his face.

'I've fucked it up, ain't I?' he said. 'I'll clear it away.' He moved towards the table, watching Donna from the corner of his eye. He held his head low, looking for all the world like a man defeated. That did it for her.

'No, Danny, stop! Look, if it's that important to you, we can try it. After all, it's only once. You'll have to show me what to do. It won't make me ill or anything, will it?'

'Trust me, babe, it'll be fine. You do it just like speed,

only it's better, not so bumpy, it's a much smoother ride. It's clean and pure, not like that shit you do with your mates.'

Rolling up a ten-pound note, Danny carefully showed Donna what to do. The few times she'd tried to snort sulphate it had ended up going everywhere, and in the end she had just swallowed a bit wrapped up in a fag paper. Danny took a little himself at first and watched Donna take hers. He then snorted the rest of the powder up his nose, tilted back his head, sniffed loudly, and smiled at her.

The effects hit Donna immediately. She felt a little sick at first, but as the nausea subsided and Danny made her a strong vodka and coke, she began to relax. They stripped off their clothes and Danny found some slow tunes on the radio. Before long, Donna was feeling more aroused than she had ever felt in her life. She found herself begging him to fuck her harder, and after climaxing twice Danny lined up two more lines of gear and another drink. He made her relax on the bed, licked his fingers, wiped them through the cocaine, and rubbed the powder around her vagina and anus. As numbness took effect, Danny proceeded to insert first one finger and then another in her anus. Donna made no complaint, the drink and the cocaine cocktail only forced her to want more.

In minutes she was on all fours and Danny was getting what he had wanted for a long time. He continued to bugger Donna for most of the night and she never complained. She was in heaven, loving the way the drink, drugs and sex made her feel. She felt bolder and more alive than ever before. By the time morning crept around, they had strength enough only for two large drinks before falling into a deep sleep, naked, sweating, exhausted and deliriously out of their minds.

Chapter Five

Joyce and Ian had given up their nightly vigil of waiting for Donna to come home. Joyce was simply too tired to lie awake each night, waiting for the sound of her daughter's key in the lock. There was no way humanly possible that she could be a worried mother and do her job of teaching twenty-four bouncy six year olds every day. The months of sleepless nights were stacking up and taking their toll, not just on her work but also at home where she was becoming unreasonably snappish with Brandon and exasperated by Ian's refusal to do something about the situation.

'She's eighteen, Joyce. Short of chaining her to her bed there's not a right lot we can do. We'll just have to lump it, love.'

They had grudgingly accepted that their younger daughter now came and went as she saw fit, occasionally calling them to let them know she was OK, but mostly not. Other than when she slept in her bed from time to time, changed her clothes and prepared herself for going out, they barely saw Donna. The mother's time-honoured phrase, 'You can't just come and go as you please, treating this place like a hotel,' fell on deaf ears at best, and more often than not provoked another round of door-slamming, widening the gulf in their already strained relationship.

Like many an indulgent father, Ian just kept his head down and hoped the whole thing would soon blow over. He'd heard the whispers about Danny Lester and secretly hoped that he'd be caught out with another woman soon and break Donna's heart. He'd hate to see his princess upset, but at least that way she'd be at home where they could keep an eye on her.

The Donna they once knew – loving, bubbly, family-oriented and full of schemes for the future – had disappeared in a few short months, to be replaced by one who seemed to have little interest in anything except the new man in her life. Their last heated argument, a humdinger, had started out innocently enough with Donna complaining that the best jeans she'd wanted to wear for a date with Danny hadn't been washed. When Joyce responded sharply that she wasn't a servant, and why couldn't her daughter wash them herself, this had resulted in Donna screaming that she hated her and storming out of the house, not to return for three days. When she did, she looked tired and agitated, wanting only to have a bath and go to bed. Fearing a repetition of their last row, Joyce was now wary of engaging Donna in any kind of discussion, but worry finally got the better of her. One afternoon, after dropping Brandon at Football Club, she found herself alone with Donna in the house. It seemed as good a time as any.

Joyce called her daughter into the kitchen where a fresh pot of tea and some buttered teacakes were laid out on the table. Donna didn't seem to have much of an appetite these days and Joyce was worried that she wasn't eating enough, but she knew how partial her daughter was to a teacake. Donna came in and slumped down into a chair.

'All right, babe?' asked Joyce tentatively. 'You look a bit pale. Get a bit of grub inside you.'

'Yeah, I'm fine thanks, mum, just a little under the weather. I think I might have a cold or something coming on.' Donna started to pour the tea, sniffing. Joyce handed her a piece of kitchen roll to blow her nose on.

'Listen, babe, I don't want to keep going on but it's been months since your results. We're well into autumn now and if you're going for a place at uni next year you need to get those acceptance forms in. I understand that you needed a break from education for a year, but I'm starting to think you don't want to go back to it at all.' Donna said nothing but stared at the plate of teacakes, tracing a pattern in a pool of melted butter with her finger. At least she didn't flare up. Joyce pushed on. 'As your mum, I just need to be sure you know what you're doing. You'll be nineteen soon, Christmas will be here before we know it, and if you don't want to go to uni, what are you going to do instead?' Donna sighed deeply.

'Mum, I've always done what you asked, always worked hard at school, always been what you wanted me to be. Just like Jane! I'm *not* Jane, though, and I've found something more to do with my life. I don't want to keep going over and over the same old ground.'

'Yes, sweetheart, but you were supposed to be getting a job and I haven't even seen you looking. It's not good for a relationship to spend all your time together, you know. You need something of your own, your own little bit of money and independence, I don't care how much in love with this Danny you are.' Joyce took a big bite of teacake and swallowed it down with a slug of tea.

'But, mum, there's no point. Danny says I don't have to work, he'll pay for everything. He says I deserve a break after all those years in school.'

Joyce rolled her eyes at this one, she wasn't standing for that.

'Donna, you're eighteen years of bloody age! You don't need a break, you need a job. *I'm* the one that needs a bloody break . . . twenty odd years of bringing up kids and working, but you don't find *me* complaining. Going to work is a fact of life, love. You'd better get used to it. Your father supported me when you children were small, but there's no way we'd manage on just his wage from the council. Anyway, I like my job, it makes me feel good about myself.'

Mother and daughter looked at each other awkwardly for a few moments before Donna spoke again.

'I know Danny will ask me to marry him and I'm sure it's going to be soon.'

Joyce sipped at her mug of tea, feeling utterly deflated.

'Marriage is a big deal, babe, and you've only known him for a few months. Are you sure he's the marrying type? Does he even want to settle down? From where I stand, I just see a bloke with more money than sense, and trust me, dodgy dealings don't make a good foundation for married life. Me and your dad . . .'

'Oh, for God's sake, Mum, stop there! I'm not you either and Danny isn't Dad. Just leave it out.' Donna slammed down the cup and put her head in her hands. 'Why are you all so against him?'

'We're not against him, love, we don't even know him. He's doesn't come in the house when he picks you up, just waits outside in that bloody car of his, revving the engine. Any decent bloke would have introduced himself at least.'

'I can't bring him in here because you're all so bloody hostile!' Joyce bit her lip, sensing it was pointless to contradict her daughter while she was in this state. 'Look,

I don't wanna talk any more about it. I'll be away over the weekend. Danny's taking me to Paris.'

'Paris! When was this arranged?'

'The other night. It's so romantic, isn't it, Mum?' For a moment Joyce saw a trace of the old Donna, the one who'd sought her mother's approval and wanted to share every bit of happiness.

'Blimey! Your father's never taken me to Paris. You kids, honestly!' Joyce managed a smile. It did seem romantic. He must think a lot of Donna. She wasn't ready for what was coming next, though.

'And I'm thinking of moving out. I need some space, and me and Danny need a place of our own.' Donna cast a nervous glance at her mother but Joyce's face remained impassive, not betraying the rising panic she felt inside. 'I was gonna talk to Dad about pulling a few strings at the council, to see if he can sort out a place for us. He's in with the housing bloke, isn't he?'

Joyce got up from the table, turned away from her daughter and rattled some cups in the sink. She could feel herself choking up and didn't want Donna to see. Her greatest fear was being realised. Donna wanted out. Joyce was all for her children getting their independence, but it was more halls of residence she'd had in mind. As much as she didn't want Donna to go, she knew Ian might see things differently and give his daughter and her young man a chance at going it alone. Joyce's sinking heart began to bow to the inevitable.

'Yeah, I'm sure he could sort something out. Besides, you know what your father's like, he could never say no to you anyway.' Joyce wiped her hands thoughtfully on the tea towel. 'I just want you to be sure, Don, that's all I ask. And maybe we could meet this knight in shining armour first? At least see what he looks like.'

She attempted a laugh but it sounded hollow, full of fear and uncertainty. Donna stood up and came over to stand with her mother at the sink where she gave her a big cuddle. Joyce couldn't remember the last time she had felt her child in her arms and squeezed her tight. She had a physical memory of how Donna's tiny head had felt against her face when she was a baby and kissed it now as she had then.

'I just worry about you, love, that's all,' she whispered in her daughter's ear.

'Honestly, Mum, I know what I'm doing. Trust me, I'll be fine.'

Upstairs, in the privacy of her bedroom, Donna examined herself in the mirror. Her skin seemed a little sallow and there were the beginnings of dark circles under her eyes, but she put this down to erratic sleep patterns and long nights of endless passion. Danny had been right about cocaine. The drugs and drink sent them on to a new plane of pleasure and sexual gratification, which frequently lasted all night. She remembered their sweating bodies, locked together, slipping and sliding, the drips of perspiration on Danny's face and the vein that bulged on his brow as he continued to fuck her for what seemed like hours. However long they went at it, she always wanted more. She had grown from being a shy virgin to an insatiable woman in a few short months.

Danny was careful never to come inside her for fear of her getting pregnant. She wouldn't have cared, carried away on a tide of love as she was, but he had said that the time wasn't right for them to take unnecessary chances. Donna was becoming his willing sexual slave. The minute she took the white powder, she was ready for action of any kind, and when it wore off, she wanted more and more.

She was his supplicant, his willing concubine who loved to be dominated, the passive partner to Danny's sexual master. It made her feel safe and she loved to please him.

Their romantic weekend got off to a surprise start. At the last moment, Danny told Donna there had been a change of plan and they were heading for Amsterdam instead. She was a little disappointed as she had hoped for romance and fine dining, but nevertheless was excited at the prospect of visiting Europe for the first time. Family holidays had always taken place in Margate or Herne Bay, except for two years ago when they'd travelled as a family to visit Ian's brother who lived in Australia. That had been her only trip abroad and she had loved it.

As they sped away from Schipol airport in a taxi, Donna thrilled to the new sights around her. Amsterdam was beautiful and so different from London. There were far fewer cars and thousands of bikes. The day was fresh, crisp and clear as she opened the doors to the balcony in their hotel, overlooking a flower-lined canal where tourist boats chugged up and down. The sun shone brightly overhead as Danny led her out into the streets for a walk around. There were flowers everywhere and lots of lovely little cafes. He indulged her, letting her look in as many tourist shops as she liked and buying her a pair of wooden clogs and a massive great armful of tulips for their room.

Donna had never seen so many cafes and bars. Danny asked her to choose one for them so they could grab a drink and *Broodjes*, a kind of traditional sandwich.

'I've some great plans for us tonight,' he said. Donna was pleased at his thoughtfulness in making all the arrangements and glowed with love for him, hanging on his every word. 'I thought we'd go for an early dinner, have some local cuisine along with some wine followed by

Jenever – it's a fabulous gin. After that, we can visit De Wallen.'

'The what?' asked Donna.

Danny looked at her and smiled naughtily. 'The red light district, babe. You can't come here and not expect to go and visit the red light district – it's a hive of fun, dancing and sex. As it happens, I know someone there who can get us into a real sex joint. It's all live on stage . . . it'll be a blast. Got some white powder too, babe, just to move the night along.'

Donna felt a little put out, having hoped for something more romantic, but Danny assured her all would be well and that they would have a great time.

'It's the norm 'ere, babe, everyone does something. Much more chilled out than the English, these Dutch. When the sun goes down in Amsterdam, the place really hots up! You wait and see, it'll be a night to remember, and it's all for you, babe. I want us to experience everything together. You ain't disappointed, are you? I mean, I've done it all for you!'

Donna felt ashamed when Danny spoke to her this way. He was doing everything he could to make this weekend special for her and now she felt really ungrateful. Swallowing her disappointment, she smiled and laughed out loud.

'It sounds great, Dan, I'm sure I'll love it all.' Danny's momentary look of defeat turned again to one of triumph. She was his, totally his, and it made him feel ten feet tall.

After lunch, he took her on a glass-topped canal boat. Donna thought it was the most romantic thing she had ever experienced as they gently chugged along the water. She waved to people on the canalside as the boat meandered over the water. Danny made up a joint and the two of them smoked it together, hanging off the back of the boat. He watched Donna visibly relax and knew his plans for the evening were falling into place. At the end of the boat ride they stopped at a *Matjes* that served herring and smoked eel, and washed it down with Amstel beer. Danny wanted Donna to absorb all that was Dutch and traditional.

Back in the hotel room, he ordered some more drinks and booked dinner for seven-thirty. 'I thought we'd eat early, babe, then get the party swinging.' This gave Donna only an hour to get ready, but she was immaculate by the time they went down to the hotel restaurant for their meal. Before stepping out into the night she went back to the room with Danny, to fuss over her make-up a little more and get a good nose-full of cocaine. Usually Donna only liked to do it at the end of an evening, before they went to bed, but Danny insisted they take the gear before they went out tonight. He knew it would put her on a real high. He had told her he had quite a few wraps in his shoe, as he had done the deal when they arrived at the airport. It was always there if you knew where to look and there was no point taking the risk of crossing borders with it in your luggage. With a potent mixture of strong puff and the devil's dandruff inside them, they were set for a stomping good few days ahead.

The streets were already heaving when they left the hotel. Within five minutes, they walked over a bridge and found themselves right in the heart of the red light district. Donna's mouth fell open as she gazed into shop windows, barely able to believe her eyes. There were vibrators for sale, of all colours, shapes and sizes, anal penetration tools, clitoral stimulators and battery-operated inserts for women or men. The magazines were more explicit than anything she had ever seen before, and there were all kinds of videos and outfits and accessories that she just could not work out! Danny led her into one of the shops and she browsed uneasily, feeling embarrassed as he busied himself buying some things he wanted for later.

Prostitutes lined the alleys of De Wallen, swaying enticingly, trying to attract custom from inside their glass-fronted windows. All sizes and colours of both sexes were available to anyone, male or female, young or old. Groups of lads on stag nights were pushing and cajoling one another to participate, and many did. Donna was shocked to see even some women entering the doorways. She knew that men went in for this kind of thing but just couldn't imagine herself being so bold! It seemed to Donna that anything and everything went on in this street.

When they reached the top, Danny hailed a cab. 'C'mon, babe, enough of this tame stuff, let's hit the real thing.'

Donna had no idea where they were going and felt a strange sense of anticipation and fear as the cab turned down dimly lit streets, away from the main thoroughfares. It took only a few short minutes to reach their destination. 'C'mon, babe, this is it.' Danny held his hand out to her as she got out of the cab and, once on the pavement, had a quick word with the doorman.

Donna hovered nervously by his side, looking up and down the street before the two of them were ushered in at a side door, not the main entrance. A gloomy corridor lit by a single red bulb opened into a large, smoky room heaving with people. Donna thought she'd never be able to stand up all night in her high heels but Danny slipped some money to a guy and the two of them were quickly shown to a small intimate table near the side of the stage.

Donna scanned the room; everyone here looked so ordinary, she couldn't understand all the secrecy over getting in and why the small room should be so interesting that a mass of people should all be squashed together in it like sardines. At the back people stood on chairs and there was not a spare inch of space. Suddenly the lights went down and the crowd began to whistle and cheer as the opening bars of Donna Summer's 'Love to Love You, Baby' blared out of the speakers.

The curtains on the stage opened to reveal two very large beds, a few chairs, and a couple of padded rugs on the floor. In one corner was a step ladder and in the other an ottoman. After a delay of about thirty seconds, as the crowd called for action, three women entered the stage, each in fancy dress. One was in bra and knickers and sported a mortar board on her head, a whip in her hand and a pair of the highest-heeled boots Donna had ever seen. The other wore a nurse's uniform with a very short skirt and carried what Donna thought was a church candle. As she squinted in the darkness she could see that it was in fact a vibrator, and a very big one. The third girl was young, only about sixteen, and she wore a typical school uniform. Then a fourth girl made her entrance. Taller and broader than the others, she also had a massive bosom and chunky, strong thighs.

As the music gathered tempo the girls all began to play with themselves. Breasts were cupped and massaged, fingers licked and rubbed across the outside of their crotches. The teacher lay spread-eagled on the bed and the tall girl stripped off to reveal male genitalia. Donna's hand involuntarily flew to her mouth in shock. A gasp went up in the audience with some beginning to chant, 'Fuck her, fuck her!' The half man, half woman, threw himself on top of the school mistress while the other two gathered at the sides to watch. There was so much going on, such an assortment of limbs and body parts, that Donna wasn't sure what to look at next. The cocaine had taken hold and she could feel herself becoming more and more aroused by what she saw. She felt slightly ashamed, but Danny squeezed her hand and kissed her cheek.

Within minutes a man was called up on stage by the schoolgirl. He was old and fat, but the schoolgirl beckoned him with her finger, coaxing him on to the stage. It wasn't long before a host of men had joined the women and everything was happening at once. The nurse had been thrown on the other bed and two men were positioning her to have double sex. One penetrated her vagina from beneath while the other pushed his penis into her anus. Donna's hand flew up to her shocked face again, but this time because she couldn't believe that the girl was crying out for more.

She looked on as more and more punters climbed on stage until large gaps began to appear in the audience. It was a mass orgy. A woman was flung across the step ladder and had sex virtually standing upright, men and women were fucking each other on the duvets, and two men were having sex with each other on the ottoman. After a short time, they all moved round and took over from each other. The whole spectacle seemed to go on for a long time, but it could only have been minutes. She looked at Danny as he laughed and pointed at the scene before them. Men were coming to their table, trying to grab Donna to go on stage, but Danny told them to fuck off and himself declined with a polite smile when women beckoned him on to the stage.

At every table people were sniffing cocaine or rolling joints. Booze was being knocked back at a fast rate, everyone in the rhythm of the orgy. Danny lined up two lines of coke. Although Donna felt she'd had enough, she sniffed the powder straight up like a pro. Despite her shock at what she saw, she could not help but feel aroused and wanted nothing more than to get out of this place, get back to the hotel and be fucked senseless by Danny. She leaned towards him and whispered in his ear. He grinned at her then dragged her out of her chair and pushed a way through to the exit.

In the back seat of the cab, he opened her legs, pulled her pants to one side and smeared coke all over her genitals and anus. All Donna did was laugh. She was completely high and oblivious to her surroundings. The cabby took no notice at all, neither did the concierge as they stumbled into the hotel in a state of disarray. They had seen it all before.

Once inside the room Danny lined up another two lines of coke and poured some very strong drinks. 'Let's play a different game tonight, baby. I'm gonna double fuck you and, like the tramp on stage, you'll ask me for more. I've got it all ready.'

He went to the brown carrier bag he had been clutching to him all night. From it he produced a tiny silver spoon and miniature silver tube. 'We'll take the coke in style, baby.' He then produced a large tube of lubricant and unwrapped a huge plastic vibrator from its box. 'Let's go, girl. Spread 'em wide, here comes your Danny boy!'

It was mid-morning before the two of them fell into a drunken, drug-addled sleep. Donna had become restless from all the gear so Danny had made up a large joint to help her wind down. With the help of two very big vodkas each they had fallen asleep, glued together in a sticky combination of sweat, a little blood and lots of KY jelly. They came round in the late-afternoon and woke up starving. Danny rang for room service while Donna attempted to tidy the room and get a shower. Under the hot water, she had memory flashes of what she and Danny had done together. The cocaine, drink and wacky baccy made it all so easy, but as she washed the traces of their night away, all she could think of was her love for this man who had opened up a whole new world for her. She felt no shame for this was true love. She was having experiences that she knew she would never share with another. Danny could ask anything of her and she would do it.

As she reappeared in the room, a tray had been set with a light dinner for them both and a large pot of coffee.

'Do you fancy going out again, baby, or d'ya want more of what we've had?' Danny smiled at her.

'Let's just stay in, Dan. I feel a little sore and tired. Besides, we have to go back tomorrow. I wish we didn't have to, though.'

Donna just welled up with love then for the man who sat there pouring coffee for her. She walked over to him, straddled her naked body across his lap, and kissed him passionately.

Chapter Six

Donna passed the journey back to London on Monday morning in a sombre mood. She spent the short flight home gazing out of the window of the plane, feeling let down that Danny had not taken the opportunity to propose to her. Before they'd left for Amsterdam, she'd felt certain that this was the purpose behind their trip and that at some point he would go down on one knee and ask her to become Mrs Lester. She rationalised that they had only known each other for a couple of months and that he would ask her to marry him when the time was right, but still her heart felt heavy and tears pricked at the back of her eyes. Be patient, she told herself, all in good time.

Joyce was cock-a-hoop to see her daughter and desperate to get Donna to talk about her weekend, but she just said everything had been marvellous, that she'd had a wonderful time but not much sleep, and would speak to her about it after getting some kip. Joyce could tell that something else was on her mind but decided not to push it. Donna had to be handled with kid gloves at the moment and she was desperate not to fall out with her again.

Ian had been looking forward to seeing his daughter, too, but she was fast asleep in her room when he came back from work. He had spent the weekend endlessly discussing with Joyce the pros and cons of helping Donna get her own place to live in with Danny. There was plenty of hard-to-let housing stock in the borough, and his friend in the Housing Department told him that if you knew what to write on the application forms, getting a place wasn't difficult. Ian could understand Joyce's reservations about Donna taking such a big step so young, though, and her fears that she was losing her daughter. He, too, was disappointed that Donna's university plans had been put on the back burner, but as he explained to his wife, 'We're either for her or against her, Joyce. She's our girl and we've got to support her. If we don't, she'll just distance herself from us and we'll lose her anyway. I want to get a proper look at this bloke first, though.'

And so it was that the following Sunday, Danny Lester crossed the threshold of the Stewarts' home for the first time. Joyce had spent the morning flapping about with the Hoover and getting out her best china plates and linen table cloth, which she used only on special occasions. As Donna led Danny into the kitchen to say hello to her mum and dad, Ian was standing by the sink revving his electric carving knife. 'Hello, I've been looking forward to meeting you, son!' he said. His tone was matey but his stance was stiff and awkward. Danny didn't really get the joke and for a few minutes a kind of dumb awkwardness prevailed, with Danny standing with his hands stuffed in his pockets defiantly and Donna rolling her eyes at her father as if to say, Give it a rest, Dad! When Joyce started talking a mile a minute out of nervousness, Danny began to relax and recovered his composure

Eventually, as lunch progressed, he moved into top gear. He'd come prepared and won round his hosts with a large bunch of flowers for Joyce and bottle of single malt for Ian. Even Brandon, who had hung back in the front room watching telly and refusing to shift from the sofa, changed his mind when Danny produced a West Ham football shirt for the Hammers-mad youngster. They chatted easily about the team's recent form, the best season in the club's history, and Brandon was totally seduced when Danny offered to get tickets for West Ham v Spurs at the home ground at the end of November. When he then proclaimed that Joyce's pork with crackling and crispy potatoes was 'the best roast I've ever eaten', he was home and dry.

The Stewarts, having expected to meet the wide boy of local legend, had been thrown by Danny's apparent affability and affectionate nature. He obviously thought the world of Donna and didn't mind getting stuck in with the washing up after the table had been cleared away. He joked around, wearing Joyce's apron, making Ian laugh. Donna relaxed totally, seeing the man she loved getting on so well with her family. It was going to be all right. Joyce and Ian obviously thought so, too. Danny really did seem a lovely lad. True, he was older than Donna and a bit rough around the edges, but he'd had it hard growing up on the street. For all his swagger his manners were superb, and all this talk of him being such a bad boy was obviously just rumour and hearsay. As he hugged and kissed Donna, he assured the Stewarts that she truly was the only girl for him. He played the part of the prospective son-in-law to perfection.

With a few whiskys inside him, Ian was expansive and optimistic about their chances of finding a small flat in the borough, and said he would do everything he could to help. The forms were duly completed by the end of the following week and Donna and Danny were able to leapfrog to the top of the waiting list.

Donna was overwhelmed by the thought of moving into a new flat with Danny. In all her dreams, she'd never thought she could get what she wanted so quickly. She felt that they were really getting somewhere and that living together would eventually prompt a proposal. Danny said he was over the moon that they had a place to call their own. The flat was a small two-bedroomed property in Crisp Street, Poplar, which had been lying empty for over a year. It was close to her parents who were pleased that Donna would at least be within easy walking distance. Situated on the first floor, at the end of a long balcony, the flat was the usual bog-standard council affair, but part of just a small block with no one above them. The flat next-door was also empty, making it perfectly positioned for privacy. The front door was painted royal blue and had the number sixteen on it in brass, with matching door knocker and letter box. The flat had obviously been looked after by the previous tenant and was clean if a little careworn. Nothing that a lick of paint wouldn't see to, Ian reassured them.

Donna looked around, picturing how it would look once she and Danny had made their own mark on it. The kitchen was lovely and bright with a sparkling new stainless steel sink and plenty of cupboard space. All she needed was a nice cooker and fridge freezer and it would be perfect. There was even enough room for a small breakfast table and a couple of chairs. The front room was quite spacious but the carpet was a little worn and grubby and would need to be ripped up. The previous tenants had painted the walls a peculiar shade of pink – not Donna's taste at all – and that would have to go too.

The day they moved in she was wandering about, surveying the bedrooms and bathroom, when she heard voices coming along the landing. Standing there with paint pots and rollers in his hand was Trippy, Danny's best friend.

'Hiya, Don. Dan's been a little held up on business, but

I've brought this lot up for us to get started. The other blokes will be 'ere soon and Dan says he'll catch up with us later.'

Trippy pushed past into the hall, pausing to give Donna a quick peck on the cheek, and headed for the front room. 'Blimey, babe, your old man did all right for you with this, didn't he?' Trippy stood admiring the flat, nodding as he surveyed the front room. 'Very nice, yes very nice indeed.'

Donna was a little disappointed. She had hoped that Danny would be with her so that they could settle in on their own, but no sooner had they unloaded the boxes from the van than he had said he had to go out for a bit. Still, it was thoughtful of him organise the lads to help get it done quicker. He really did take care of everything.

Within half an hour, his mates Johnny and Stevie had arrived with a few six-packs and they started to remove the old carpet and get the front room ready for painting. There was dust everywhere. Donna had to open all the windows to air the place out. A radio blared in the kitchen and the flat was soon a hive of activity, with ladders, rollers and paint pots scattered everywhere. A few hours passed. Donna had nipped out to get some groceries so that she could make some sandwiches and hot drinks. By the time she got back, Danny was there.

'Where you been?' he asked suspiciously.

'Just to the shops, babe, thought you might like something to eat while you work and a cuppa, that's all.'

Danny pulled her towards him. 'Let me know where you're going, honey, I don't like not knowing where you are. Anyway, the boys and me are gonna 'ave a beer and a little livener, to get us working quicker.' He started to laugh.

Donna felt a bit deflated, she wanted it to be just the two of them together, but Danny had other ideas. 'Get the beer open for the lads while I line them up a little something. You want some gear, babe?'

'Not right now, Dan, I've still got bits to pick up from Mum and Dad's. Maybe later, eh?' He made no argument. 'Don't be long, princess, I want you here with me to let me know what you think of the new colour. Oh, and by the way, I've ordered the carpet, it'll be here tomorrow with the cooker and fridge-freezer. And, best of all, I've ordered two beds, a king size for us and a smaller one for the spare room.' Danny smiled triumphantly but sensed Donna's mood. 'What's up, babe? Thought you'd be pleased.' He seemed to scowl a bit.

'No, it's nothing, I just thought we were going to pick them out together, that's all.'

Danny scratched his head. 'Well, I was owed a few favours and thought I'd call 'em in. It's all good quality, brand new stuff – you'll love it. Anyway, you can go out tomorrow and get some lovely bed linen and curtains, how about that?' Donna smiled weakly and nodded, chastising herself for not being more grateful. 'Right, you pop to your mum's, but 'urry up 'cause I miss ya already!' Donna hugged him. He really was a man in a million and all this was for her, she had to remember that. She kissed him and left the boys to do their bit together.

She made a quick trip to her parents' house and her dad helped her bring over a few boxes of personal things, dropping her off at the foot of the stairs to her new flat.

'Not gonna ask me up then?' said Ian.

'Not now, Dad, I'd rather you see the place when it's done. Besides, it's like a madhouse at the moment. Danny's got all his mates in there doing the painting, there's not enough room to swing a cat.' Ian looked at her enquiringly, as if to ask if she was OK. She smiled in an attempt to reassure him.

'I'm all right, Dad, I'm just a bit knackered, that's all. I'll be back later anyway, for my last night at home, so see you in a bit.' She waved her dad off and climbed the flight of stairs with her two boxes. Danny and the boys were in full swing and already had the ceiling and three of the walls painted a lovely creamy colour. Donna loved it. The boys seemed enthusiastic to carry on, so Danny lined them up some more cocaine and, laughing, said, 'The whole place will be finished by tonight babe.'

Donna placed her boxes down and felt a rising sense of panic in her chest. 'Be careful with that stuff, babe,' she said, eyeing the lines of coke on the table.

Danny suddenly glared at her. 'Are you fucking telling me I don't know what I'm doing?'

Donna recoiled, frightened by his response. It was a real slap, in front of his mates and all, and she felt the sting. Tears filled her eyes.

'No, babe,' she told him. 'I just didn't want the lads off their heads, that's all. I never meant anything by it, honest.'

Trippy had obviously heard and saw the confrontation. Her eyes welled up with tears and Danny softened. 'Baby, I'm sorry I shouted at you, I never meant to. One thing about me and this stuff you gotta understand, though, is that I know what I'm doing. You gotta trust me, little girl. I won't never harm you, but don't cross me or question me. Now, come 'ere and give me a cuddle.'

Donna obliged but there was a new fear inside her. She had never heard Danny talk to her that way before and hoped it was a fluke. As far as that white stuff was concerned, she would never question him again.

Within a week the flat looked beautiful. No expense had been spared and the place was soon looking like a palace. Everything was gleaming new. The chocolate brown suite with cream trim and round wooden legs fitted perfectly in the front room, and matched the walls and other fittings exactly. Heavy embossed cream and gold curtains hung expensively from the large windows, looped back with gold ties. Everything was lush and top of the range. A new TV and video took pride of place in the corner, and in the other there was a well stocked bar.

Their bedroom was a dream. Again, lovely cream walls set off the white and gold semi four-poster to perfection. Danny had bought Donna Tigger, the most enormous white teddy, to sit in the middle, but secretly she still preferred the tatty old rabbit, Pookie, that was always perched on her side of the bed. Fitted wardrobes with gold handles lined one wall, and the cream dressing table and gold-velvet-cushioned chair with gilded legs looked perfect. Donna's bits and pieces added the personal touch to the bedroom and she was thrilled with the result.

The spare bedroom was a little more garish. With red walls, cream carpet and a red bedspread, Donna thought it looked like a tart's boudoir, but kept her feelings to herself. There was no point in goading Danny when he was trying so hard to make her happy. The entire flat smelt clean and mint and spoke of new beginnings.

Now that they were living together, Donna realised how hard Danny worked and how little he would be around. Somehow she had imagined things differently. Their first week together he was hardly home, and even though he always left a bundle of notes for her to buy whatever she needed each day, she missed not having him around. But Donna loved to shop and it gave her the opportunity to see Nicola and Shaz. She had really missed the girls lately, tied up as she'd been with the move, but they'd been busy, too, pursuing their new courses and jobs. It seemed as though the once inseparable trio were splitting off in different directions. It was nice for them to meet up and spend some proper time together, talking about anything and everything, just as they had during their schooldays. Nicola was guarded on the subject of Danny and whenever Donna launched into one of her speeches about how wonderful he was, just smiled weakly and kept quiet. She felt a little isolated for she would never betray Donna by saying anything to Shaz, and it seemed the whole Stewart clan had been won round by Mr Golden Balls. As much as Nicola wished Donna would see the light, she had to concede that now they had set up home together this was unlikely. She wanted so desperately to tell her friend a few things, but with Shaz around and everyone else singing Danny's praises, she knew Donna would not believe her.

Employed by Danny to do his running around, her brother Freddie had lost a ton of weight recently. Often he would come home on a real downer with a bruised face and Nicola knew that Danny was behind it. One night while Nic was out in a club with some girls from catering college, she had seen Danny with his mates. There were few clubs he could not get into. A backhander to the bouncers was usually all it took to get Danny through the door to conduct his business. Nicola watched him for several hours, slowly getting more and more wound up. After a good few drinks and with the resentment inside her boiling up, she could take no more.

'Happy in your work, are ya, Danny? Does Donna know where you are and what you're up to?'

'Fuck off, Nicola,' was his reply, but she continued.

'You got any pity for anyone or any morals?' She pointed at a bedraggled Freddie. 'Look at my brother. Look at the state of him. All thanks to you and your drugs, that is!' Danny looked around him before grabbing hold of Nicola's arm with a grip that told her he meant business. He led her to a dark corner of the club.

'Now listen 'ere, you. You keep yer fucking voice down

and yer big nose outta my business! As for your brother, what he does is up to him. If it's not me supplying him it'll be someone else. Now you've a pretty face, and according to Donna you're a nice girl, but you ain't no innocent. Want a twenty-pound wrap or an E to share with yer mates?' he sneered. 'Now fuck off and stop bothering me.' He gripped her arm tighter until it really hurt and began to twist it up her back. 'You say a fucking word to Donna, and that loser of a brother of yours'll be found amongst the dustbins. Do I make myself clear?'

Nicola nodded her head painfully and Danny released his grip. She felt tears fill her eyes, not just because Danny had hurt her physically but because Freddie had looked on, unable to help, and she felt his shame. She realised then that he was lost to her, and that the same thing would happen to Donna.

Danny had been right in one way, Nicola could party with the best of them, but she knew when enough was enough. There was a time for work and a time for play, and she never got the two mixed up. She was too bugger-minded ever to let a drug get in the way of her life, and the only habit that enslaved her was her cigarettes.

Nicola never mentioned this incident to Donna and the three girls spent a spirited afternoon, gossiping and laughing. It had been lovely spending time with her friends again and Donna felt a chill of loneliness run through her when the other two made their excuses and had to leave. It was Shaz's evening class in pottery and Nic had to dash off to the Savoy. Only Donna had nothing more pressing to do than getting home to Danny. She had to squash the worrying thought that maybe she was making a mistake by giving her whole life over to him. It was getting cold now in the evenings. Winter was beginning to bite.

Hugging her coat around her and lifting its collar to shield herself against the sharp wind, Donna made her way back to the flat with her shopping bags.

Danny still wasn't home when she got back so she decided to set about making a nice evening meal and perhaps open a bottle of wine. Candles would look perfect on the table, too, making the occasion more romantic. But the clock ticked away. Slowly the hours passed, the candles burned down, and the lasagne in a low oven turned to a crisp. Donna blew out the candles and went to run a bath, trying to banish her sense of disappointment. After a long soak followed by a careful massaging with body cream, she took herself off to bed. Tucking Pookie up under her arm, she grabbed a magazine and flicked through it, looking at the wedding dresses. Just as she felt herself drifting off she heard the key in the door. 'Danny, is that you, babe?' She waited for his voice.

'Yeah, babe, it's me. Do me a favour and make me a drink, I've had a hell of a night with some right fucking idiots and I'm totally wound up.' Donna climbed out of bed and made her way into the front room, but when she got there he had already taken himself off to the bathroom. 'Danny?'

'I'm just 'aving a wash, babe, be with you in a bit.'

After several minutes he emerged from the bathroom and walked into the front room, looking refreshed and smelling clean. 'Sorry I'm so late, babe. I got caught up with a client, and it just went on and on.' He didn't look at Donna.

'Don't matter, babe,' she said, draping her arms around his neck. 'Dinner's ruined, but as long as you're safe, that's all that matters.'

'Let's take a few lines,' he suggested, kissing her neck. 'I've been missing you all day and need you real bad. There's nothing on tomorrow, we can just chill out tonight and sleep in late.' He grabbed her around the waist and pulled her on to his lap, massaging her breasts.

'Sure, baby, whatever you say.' Donna was pleased he needed her and the coke would wake her up. She loved it when it was just him and her.

It didn't take long before the two of them were locked into each other. Danny was playing hard-core tonight and any way he could take Donna he would. As he buggered her from behind, he whispered in her ear, 'What would it be like to have another man fucking you at the same time, babe?' Donna, flying by this point with several big lines inside her, was a little shocked but assumed it was all part of their fantasy game.

'Anything you want from me, you can have, baby.' Danny smiled, reached for the vibrator, and gave her what for, only this time he was rough and hard. It didn't stop there; he flipped Donna on to her back, inserted his penis in her anus and used the vibrator to do the double again. When he'd finished this he asked Donna to get on top. He penetrated her anus roughly, intent on pushing harder and harder. As much as Donna had learned to enjoy being buggered by Danny, it was beginning to get painful.

'Dan, you're hurting me a bit.' She started to swerve a little with the headiness of painful sex, too much coke and far too much vodka. But Danny was intent on his own pleasure and wouldn't be distracted. 'Keep it up at bit longer, and do me a favour . . . hold them tits of yours, they're swinging everywhere and I like them kept straight.'

He bent forward and bit one, not hard, but it hurt Donna a little. He carried on for another twenty minutes, just pushing, pushing, all the time. The coke meant that he couldn't come and he was getting really wound up as he sought his release. 'Tell me you want another bloke in with us,' he ordered her.

In her delirium, she whispered, 'Yes, yes.'

*

Donna awoke to a messy flat and a terrible hangover. She felt muddled and cloudy, could remember sniffing loads of white powder. Mixed with too many drinks it had given her the headache from hell. She made her way to the bathroom in an attempt to get cleaned up and was shocked by her appearance. Her eyes were bulging, her face was swollen and her genitals and anus were stinging like crazy. She climbed in the shower to wash away the coke, KY Jelly and semen that covered her body. She felt terrible but kind of great, all at the same time. It was a real feeling of being free and alive and doing all the things she'd never thought she would. She was living on the edge and she liked it. It was all part of being with Danny, and if it was part of him, she loved it.

She recalled the sex they'd shared the night before. It was unlike any they'd had up to now, with no love or passion, just an urgent need to get their rocks off. He had used toys on her more violently than before and was also demanding about the position of her body during sex. She remembered his comments about another man being involved and his complaints that her breasts moved about too much. She must do something about her heavy breasts. She examined them in the mirror and thought, Danny is right as usual, they do tend to move about a lot. As for the toys and his roughness, she figured it was all part of pleasing the man you loved. If that involved a bit of pain, then so be it. She knew Danny loved her.

She went into the kitchen to make him some coffee, to find that he had already left to go to work, leaving on the table a bunch of the biggest, deepest red dahlias she had ever seen next to a generous bundle of money.

Chapter Seven

The café was a seedy place, filled with cigarette smoke and the strong smell of Turkish coffee. Danny sat with three other guys at the corner table by the door. Trippy, a tall lanky twenty-four year old, was rolling his habitual joint – hence the nickname, which he much preferred to his christened name of Jeffrey – while Johnny Wisten and Stevie Blakemore sat waiting for their instructions from Danny on the distribution of the latest batch of white powder, due to hit the streets the following week. Danny was waiting on a call and was impatient with the delay. It was twenty minutes late.

Trippy broke the silence. 'How's that little cracker of yours, Dan? She's a real looker, that one, you lucky bastard.'

Danny raised his eyes from the little black notebook he was looking at and stared at Trippy, then smiled.

'Yeah, she's something really special, and I won't take any jokes or dirty talk about her, so you lot keep your filthy fucking mouths shut!' At that moment the pay phone rang and Danny instantly got to it.

'Yeah, mate, no worries. 'Course I got the dough, all of it. I told you, I'm holding good at the moment. It ain't been cut about too much, has it? I need it in block. Cool then, man, see you at five in the usual place.' He replaced the receiver. 'Right, we're on.'

Stevie looked at him. 'Listen, Dan, Mickey wants back in, says he has a guy who wants a whole ounce. What d'ya think?'

Danny hesitated. 'How's the idiot's face?'

Stevie looked down at the floor.

'He ain't gonna cross you again, Dan, he was just a bit late with the money, that's all.'

'OK, Stevie, I'll take your word for it. Now, you all know what territory to cover. Get out there and get the orders in. We've got a lot of shit to shift, and if we're clever there'll be a little bonus in it for all of us.' Danny sniffed the air. 'Get what I mean?'

The four of them all left together, laughing, before they got into their cars and went their separate ways.

Business was thriving and Danny's list of clients growing by the day. In order to cope with demand and keep his head above water, he delegated more and more of the local distribution to the other three lads and used his own time to secure the really big deals among a widening circle of contacts. It wasn't just the East End any more. He was serving up in North London too and it looked as if a bit of business might be coming his way from South of the River. Lucky Danny Lester could do no wrong. His ability to get what was needed and fast was appreciated by his customers, and he never stinted on the quality. In fact, Danny was fast making a name for himself. You got what you paid for, it wasn't cut to fuck, and his reputation for being able to handle himself with a knife didn't hurt either. The wacky baccy brought in pennies compared to the powder, but to keep Freddie in he allowed him to deal with the softer side of the business. Freddie was rarely paid in money, he was too hooked on the coke, and Danny had to keep a close watch on him as he was beginning to make mistakes. But for now Freddie was still in, though Trippy for one wasn't very happy about it, as he told Danny later that day.

'I'm telling you, Dan, he's a fucking liability. He can't function through the day without a few grams, and if he fucks up he's gonna harm our reputation and maybe even take us down. He ain't like the rest of us, who can sniff and get on with the job.'

Trippy really wasn't happy. Getting caught because you made a mistake yourself was one thing, but when someone else dropped you in it through sheer carelessness it was maddening. For some reason, Danny was reluctant to give Freddie the shove just yet.

'Look, Trip, if he gets to be too much of a problem, I'll deal with it, I promise. But, trust me, we've got bigger fish to fry at the moment. The next consignment's our biggest so far. We stand to make a mint.'

Donna tidied herself up, took her bundle of notes from the kitchen table and hailed a cab all the way into the West End where she had a proper spend-up. The events of the previous evening retreated from her mind as the balm of retail therapy took hold. She was soon able to turn her mood around, tell herself that it wasn't so bad after all. If Danny didn't love her, he wouldn't give her all this money to spend. She was lucky, she told herself. She didn't have to work, had all day to please herself, and no shortage of money to buy anything her heart desired.

She came home laden with bags and couldn't wait to show Danny what she'd bought. She hoped that by wearing sedate silk camisoles and French knickers she could coax him into making love to her tenderly, to undress her slowly and hold her close. But Danny was working late again and when he finally got back around eleven he was wired to the gills and wanted more of the previous night's action.

Donna was dismayed when he ripped off her delicate silk underwear, but a few lines of coke soon got her in the mood and she found she could not refuse him. It had become a pattern. His passion had developed a hard edge and soft caresses always gave way to rough sex. Again and again Donna tried to get their lovemaking back to how it used to be, but the more coke she sniffed – and they never had sex without it any more – the more she allowed herself to be taken by Danny, in any way possible.

In the morning she would wake up feeling dirty and used, but the flowers arrived without fail and Donna took this as proof of his love. She was still convinced that he was the only man for her, but there were times when she started to question these feelings. The sex was beginning to feel out of her control, but when she took the drugs and the booze all she felt was a desperate need to satisfy Danny.

Donna was spending more and more time alone. There was only so much shopping and cleaning that she could do. She waited patiently every night for Danny to come in, and when he did he smelt more heavily of alcohol and it was always apparent he had taken some kind of drug. Donna was concerned for her man, and at times even a little afraid of him. His mood swings were becoming more extreme. Each time they made love, he insisted on her taking not only coke but a new drug called ecstasy which came in little tablets with a dove stamped on to them. 'Love-doves' he called them, and it was true that they intensified passion and kept them both flying for hours.

And so Danny made his plan. He made sure that Donna

got as much coke and ecstasy in her as he was taking, and during the height of their sexual games he asked her if she wanted someone else to fuck her. She had developed a taste for dirty talk by now and loved it when he said those things, readily agreeing. Once he had her consent, the only thought was who to include and the obvious choice was Stevie. Danny had always admired him, especially the time he'd served three years for dealing and never grassed up his mates even though he could have got himself a shorter sentence by doing so. Stevie was sharp-suited, cool in a crisis and always up for an adventure. He had never made any secret of his attraction to Donna and had often asked Danny to bring her along the next time they had a threesome. Not that Donna needed to know about those. The other girls were just slags, not like her, and there was no point upsetting her.

Most of the women they used were addicts. It was all too easy, though, and Stevie wanted a challenge, something with a bit more class. He loved Donna's looks and figure, especially her long legs and pert bum. He would often daydream of fucking her arse, and when he was out of his head, fucking some other poor woman, would say to Danny that he wished he could have the chance with Donna. Stevie was an expert. He would be a perfect introduction to threesome sex for Donna.

And maybe, once Donna got used to it, Danny could introduce other elements: another woman, maybe more. His ultimate fantasy would be to have Donna in an orgy. Amsterdam was still fresh in his mind. He would have loved to have jumped up on stage and joined in, but he knew then as he did later that these things had to be taken slowly. Despite all the fun and games they had at home, Donna was still an exclusive sort of girl. She would have to be broken in gently.

*

Danny sat in the café in his usual place. He had just completed a great deal that had earned him an absolute bundle and was feeling like a king. He had moved into other drugs at just the right moment. The rave scene was beginning to kick off and demand for ecstasy had gone through the roof. He was knocking out the pills at twenty quid a pop and making a very healthy profit. Trippy and Johnny had gone off to do a bit of local distribution and Danny was left alone with Stevie.

'Listen, mate,' said Danny, grinning from ear to ear. He took a long drag of his coke and wacky baccy roll-up and continued, 'You still interested in my Donna . . . you know, a threesome?' Stevie grinned lasciviously.

'What do you think?'

'I reckon I could pull it off if we plan it well,' said Danny, handing the joint to his friend.

Stevie, equally off his face, slapped his mate on the back. 'Just name the time and place. You know I'm up for a bit of that.'

'Hold your horses, Stevie boy,' laughed Danny. 'Like I said, it will take a little organising and planning, but 'ere's what I 'ave in mind. Don wants the bathroom re-tiled. I can arrange it for Saturday night, say that you and the others are willing to do it all in one evening. Then I'll get rid of Trippy and Johnny. We'll have a drink, a little bit of this and a little bit of that, and we can take her from there. What d'ya reckon?'

Stevie, chuffed as monkeys, nodded emphatically.

'Sure, mate, sure, that sounds fantastic. I can't wait.'

'Keep your trap shut, though, eh? If you say anything to the others, the deal's off.'

Danny stared intently at Stevie.

'No sweat, man, you 'ave my word.'

'Now, I've more gear than ever to shift, so we need some more punters. You get yourself out and about. Make your way over to Hackney, see what business is like there. Also, check the local gyms, I've got some steroids to offload. And while yer at it, call in at York Hall, a promoter friend of mine by the name of Willy the Wager needs some stuff too. Just get 'is order. I'll sort 'im out about money later myself.'

Donna decided not to wait in all day for Danny to get back and gave Nicola a call to see what she was up to. 'Hi, mate, fancy meeting up in a while? I've got to go shopping for some tiles and thought you might like to come with me.'

She could hear Nic hesitate for a moment. Then she replied, 'Well, I've got a few classes later in the afternoon, but I could meet ya now. I tell ya what, I'll meet ya at the Blind Beggar. There's a great new tile shop in the high street, it's bound to have something ya like.'

Donna agreed, said her goodbyes and quickly changed into some jeans, a pair of furry boots and a padded jacket. She'd lost a lot of weight and didn't want Nicola questioning her. The jacket filled her out, and with her scarf and hat on as well she was sure Nic wouldn't notice. She knew it was the drugs that took her appetite away. At her mum's the other week, Donna had picked at her food while Danny ate the whole lot of his Sunday roast and most of hers. She didn't know how he could take drugs all night then get stuck into food the next day like nothing had happened.

Nic was waiting outside the pub when she got there and the two of them decided on a quick drink before they headed off to the shop. It was freezing cold so they decided on double brandies to thaw themselves out and settled down with them at one of the tables.

'This will warm up the ol' cockles,' said Donna.

'You OK?' Nic asked. 'You look a little drawn in the face. Is everything all right?'

'Sure, mate, everything's fine. Just had a few wild nights lately. You know, bit of the ol' rampant sex and what have you.'

'It's the what have you that concerns me,' replied Nic, sharp as a blade. 'Listen, Don, I know it's your business but you gotta go careful with that shit – it hooks yer before yer know it. Look at my Freddie. Started out as a puffer, but as soon as he got on the powder he was gone beyond all recognition within months. He's a fucking shell of himself these days.' She stared at Donna, waiting for a response. Donna laughed.

'Look, babe, I know you worry, but honestly it's all under control. The shit doesn't affect me. I'm fine with or without it, but I'd be a liar if I said it didn't improve things . . . if you know what I mean?' She started to giggle.

Nicola knew she was getting nowhere and decided not to pursue it but her friend's appearance scared her. Despite the padded jacket Donna looked thin and pale. Her legs were like stick pins; her hair greasy and unkempt under her fluffy hat. The Donna she knew, who took so much pride in her appearance, was gone. This was all Danny Lester's fault.

'I just hope he's looking after you, that's all. Danny's an animal, Don, he can handle it. It's different for women.' Nicola leaned across the table and took her mate's hand.

'Nic, please leave Danny out of this,' she said, drawing it away. 'I'm fine, I really am, and I don't like you accusing my man of things all the time. It's not on. Danny loves me to bits and I don't get why you can't understand that. He treats me like a queen. I don't 'ave to work. I never go short of money or anything. He gives me everything I need. Please, let's just drop it.

'Come on, drink up. I wanna get these tiles and get back, it'll be getting dark soon.'

Nic knew she was on a hiding to nothing. Donna refused to see what Danny was doing to her, but Nicola was not so naive. Things would get much worse for her before they got better. The thought made her shudder.

When Danny arrived home to find the flat empty he was not happy. He'd expected Donna to be there waiting for him. She hadn't said she was going anywhere. He paced around irritably for a bit before sniffing two lines and pouring himself a large vodka. He was not alone for long, though. Ten minutes later Donna arrived back, carrying a large box. 'Where ya been, babe?' asked Danny, more than a little put out.

'Sorry, babe,' she replied, slamming the door behind her. 'I met up with Nic and we went tile shopping for the bathroom. They're beautiful, you wanna see? I didn't expect you back this early so I thought I'd catch up with Nic and get these at the same time.'

She noticed the way he was swigging down his drink. He slammed the glass down on the table.

'Come 'ere,' he said, motioning to her. Donna placed the box down on the table hesitantly, fighting a flurry of panic in her chest.

'What's wrong, babe? I didn't think you'd mind.' Danny grabbed her by the arm and she could feel his fingers digging into her thin flesh. 'Dan, you're hurting me! Please . . .'

Danny pulled her close. By now his face was almost pressed against hers. 'I don't like you being anywhere without me knowing, d'you understand? Not at the shops, not at your mum's, and especially not with that trollop Nicola. I can't stand the bird, she's nothing but trouble.'

He released his grip and Donna backed away, rubbing her arm.

'I'm sorry, Dan, I just thought it would be OK.' Tears welled up in her eyes and Danny realised he'd got a little out of control again.

'Look, babe, leave me a note in future or give me a call. You know how to contact me. I was just worried. Your flowers are in the kitchen.' Donna made her way through and on the table found a colossal arrangement of pink and white roses.

'Danny, these are lovely. I'm so sorry I worried you. I'll make it up to you, I promise.'

He smiled at her and picked up his empty glass. 'Make me a drink, babe, and one for yourself. There's a nice big line of gear for you there too. Hurry up, baby, my dick needs sucking.'

Donna sighed, took the coke and made the drinks.

'Anything for you, babe.'

As she knelt down on the floor in front of him she started to unzip Danny's jeans.

The next morning Donna woke feeling quite perky. Last night the sex had been much more loving than she had recently been used to. As usual, he'd made her feel wonderful, and whatever he did to her, she enjoyed it to the full. Danny stretched out in the bed. As Donna pulled the covers off he leaned over and tickled her nipples with his tongue.

'You were fantastic last night, babe,' he said, nuzzling his face against her chest. 'Make some coffee, honey. I got a real busy day today, and I wanna make sure that all business is settled before Saturday night. Want to get that bathroom tiling done for ya.' As Donna stood up, he slapped the bare cheek of her bottom playfully.

She switched on the radio in the kitchen and sang along to the Pet Shop Boys' 'West End Girls' while making the coffee. She carried the two mugs into the bedroom and placed them carefully on their separate bedside tables, then jumped back into the bed and cuddled up to Danny.

'Blimey, girl, you've given me another stiffy. Jump on top, let's 'ave a quickie. Nothing like an early-morning romp to get ya started for the day ahead.'

Donna obliged, thoroughly enjoying herself; it was almost as if she was in control.

'Bloody 'ell, Don,' he started to grumble, 'since you've lost weight, your titties really swing about the place. It's a bit off-putting! I've told ya about them before. Can't you hold them steady?'

Donna cupped her breasts but it affected her rhythm so Danny tipped her over and finished the job. As he went to have a shower, Donna went back to the kitchen to fix some food. She had a huge appetite for a change and made bacon and scrambled eggs for both of them, plus extra toast for Danny. He sat at the breakfast table with just a towel around his waist and devoured the lot.

'You gotta eat a bit more, babe. You need to pad out a bit. Don't want you losing that famous figure of yours, now do we?' Donna looked towards the floor. 'Tell ya what,' said Danny, 'why don't you go and get your hair done, buy some new sexy underwear and just treat yourself?' He left the table to get dressed.

After Donna had washed up she went into the hall where Danny was getting ready to leave. ''Ere, babe, a few quid for you to spoil yourself and make yourself sexy for me. Be back by the time I get home, though, and I'll see ya for dinner. Better still, let's go out, just the two of us? How about Chinese?'

Donna's face lit up. 'Really? Oh, Danny, I'd love to.'

'Right, be ready for eight, princess. See ya laters.'

The door slammed behind him and a jubilant Donna headed for the bathroom with a song in her heart. Princess. That's what her dad always called her, and now Danny had too. It felt so good.

Danny almost skipped down the stairs, laughing to himself. His master plan was working perfectly. Last night he had gone easy on her during sex, and this morning with the money he'd given her to spend and his ace card dealt about dinner, he knew she'd be putty in his hands when it came to the weekend. He had toyed with the idea of buying her a ring too, but thought he'd save that one for when he really needed an out. He did love Donna. She was a real beauty, the envy of all his friends, and she still managed to turn heads, young and old, despite her weight loss. But something about her was changing. If he couldn't get her to toe the line he'd lose the respect of his peers and he could never allow that to happen. Danny convinced himself that sharing her was not a problem because, at the end of the day, Donna was really his. After all, it was just sex. That had nothing to do with love.

Danny made his way to the café and waited for the three other lads to join him. Business was brisk. If he cut the gear just a little he found it went further and bumped up profits. It was all working out perfectly. Danny's new line of selling pills was going down a storm, and not just ecstasy either. Women were buying slimming pills by the dozen, steroids were booming at all the local gyms, and with four nightspots now allowing him exclusive access to sell whatever he wanted, the money was pouring in. He availed himself freely of all his stock because it was important he knew exactly what he was selling. Or that's what he told himself. A little bit of this and a little bit of that and quite a lot of the other.

He planned Saturday night in his head, down to the last detail. Donna would be flying, and with him and Stevie joining in, it was certainly going to be a night to remember. Who knows? he thought to himself. Maybe if Donna continued to play ball, which he was almost sure of, he would introduce a few more of his friends, and next time another woman. He'd had threesomes before, but with Donna as his main partner, and her so beautiful, the possibilities were endless. He rolled himself a coke joint and puffed hard on it to get psyched up for the day ahead.

The lads arrived on time as usual. Danny's boys were good timekeepers as they had learned to their cost that tardiness could result in one of his increasingly famous outbursts of temper. Each was given their jobs for the day, and a little gear to get them on their way. The lads were all doing really well out of the business. They had never had so much money before. Trippy, Johnny and Stevie had good cars, great clothes and a string of women on hand. Only Freddie was still a loose cannon. Danny gave him the odd wrap for delivering the wacky baccy, but he would never give him the more important clients.

Danny secretly harboured a soft spot for Freddie, felt a bit sorry for him. The gear had really taken over his life. He spent his time looking paranoid and shiftless. Danny had the feeling that Freddie would not be around forever, but for now he was their joker, loyal to a fault and easily dealt with. The boys took their stashes and left the café, but Stevie hung back a bit and Danny knew why.

'Before ya ask, it's all planned and everything is sorted.' Stevie just grinned and left the café a happy man.

*

Donna waited patiently for Danny. She looked fantastic in her new clothes, hair falling in thick black ringlets around her beautiful, more finely chiselled face. Danny was only a little late arriving. In his arms he carried a fantastic bunch of bright orange and yellow rununculus.

'Blimey, babe, you look stunning.' Scooping her into his arms, he kissed her gently. 'Do you know how much I love you? You're the best thing that's ever happened to me and I am so grateful.'

As he stared over her shoulder he grinned broadly. Tonight he would spoil her rotten. He would wine and dine her, and make love to her in a wonderfully romantic way. She would be his totally. He knew exactly how to work her. Tonight there would be no drugs, just him and her, and he would pleasure her in the way he knew she loved.

Donna gently broke away from him. 'Danny, the flowers are gorgeous! Have I enough time to put them in some vases?'

He laughed. ''Course you have, babe, take your time.'

The Peking Garden on Roman Road was the best Chinese restaurant in the East End, some would argue in the whole of London, and looked beautiful. Already people were preparing for Christmas and the restaurant was softly illuminated by twinkling lights. As Danny led Donna through the door, they were greeted immediately by the manager. Danny used the place often and was as well known in Bethnal Green as he was in China Town.

The restaurant was busy, mainly with couples, but there was a group of about eight lads on one long table. Danny had clocked them straight away. He knew a few of them well. Donna's entrance caused the usual stares of admiration and a few of the lads whooped and whistled. Danny stared in their direction and all of them except one instantly looked away.

'Wang, take my girl to the table,' said Danny to the manager. 'Donna, I won't be a minute.'

As he approached their table all the lads but one looked at the floor. The loud one had obviously had too much to drink. He tried to stagger up out of his chair. Danny pushed him back down into it.

'Do you know who I am?' he asked the loud lad.

'I don't give a fuck who you are, I was looking at yer bird. You take a bird like her out around 'ere and everyone will look. She's a cracker!'

Danny lifted the guy from his chair with ease. Without saying a word he frog-marched him to the men's toilets, returning calmly a few minutes later. He leaned over the lads' table and spoke to one of the guys he knew.

'Your mate needs a little help. He seems to have cut himself. Don't forget to remind him of my name.'

Danny sat down next to Donna, gave her a kiss, and they looked at the menu together.

'Is everything all right, Dan?' she asked.

He smiled. 'Of course, baby, it was just a little misunderstanding. The bloke's drunk. They'll be leaving soon.' True enough, the now subdued lads began to pile out of the restaurant, leaving one behind to pay the bill. The others were propping up their friend who was holding a blood-soaked napkin to his face. The guy at the cash till nodded over to Danny, as if to accept what had happened, and left without another word.

'Danny, why was that man bleeding?' But Donna knew why, and could feel her insides contract.

'I don't know, he must have cut his head open or

something when I pushed him against the sink. Don't worry about it, babe.'

'But you can't go around hitting people just because they wolf whistle. It doesn't bother me, really.' She looked past Danny's shoulder and out of the window of the restaurant to see the wounded man surrounded by his concerned friends, blood having soaked the napkin through by now. Even Donna knew this was no bump to the head.

'People need to know that I won't have you treated like that, Don. You're my angel, remember, I don't want blokes thinking they can leer over you like some old slag.' Danny's face softened as he reached for her hand. 'I just love you so much, Don, and I want to look after you.'

Donna gazed back at the man she loved and thought how wrong people were about him. If they could see and hear him like this, they'd understand why she loved him so much. Never had she felt more looked after and protected. It was how she wanted to feel: possessed and cared for. The rest of her evening was fantastic. Everything was perfect. The flowers on the table were beautiful, and as the champagne flowed Donna's tongue began to loosen and she broached subjects she otherwise found awkward.

'Danny, I've been thinking . . . about Christmas. Could we see my mum and dad and spend the day with them?'

He thought for a while, and very quickly got a plan in his head.

'Yeah, 'course, hon. Why not? Not 'aving parents, it doesn't really occur to me to think about who I'm going to spend it with, but I think it will be great. A real traditional Christmas Day, why not? I'm happy to see them. Is your sister coming down too?'

'Oh, yeah, Jane'll be there, it'll be lovely. Thanks, Danny.' Donna leaned across the table and kissed him. He smiled, feeling pleased with himself.

'Well, that's that sorted. 'Ave to get you out Christmas shopping, mind, I want them all to have something really fantastic. And they get you Christmas Day, but you're mine for the rest of the holiday and New Year. Is that a deal?'

'Absolutely,' said Donna. 'Wonder if it'll be a white Christmas?'

Danny laughed. 'Oh, it will be, babe. I can guarantee that.'

The week flew by. Saturday, the day for tiling the bathroom, soon arrived with Donna busy preparing sandwiches and snacks for the lads. She carefully set out a little buffet, arranging it to look as attractive as possible. She wanted to show Danny that she wasn't just a pretty face but a good homemaker too. Christmas was coming and what better time for them to buy a ring? By early-evening the lads had arrived and work had started on the bathroom. With all hands to the pump it was done in record time and afterwards the guys sat and relaxed while Donna ran back and forth, fetching beers, ashtrays, and clearing plates. She surveyed the bathroom and had to admit that it looked mint. She was thrilled. Their home was now complete and shiny as a new pin.

Johnny and Trippy finished their food and made their excuses to leave. Danny had work for them that evening, apparently, but he asked Stevie to stay behind as they had some business to talk through. Donna busied herself in the kitchen and tidied up until the flat looked immaculate. She could hear Danny calling to her from the front room and appeared in the doorway with a tea towel in her hands.

'Put your feet up, babe, I've made ya a real nice drink.' Danny tried not to smirk.

'Oh, thanks, babe, I could do with this now.' Donna swigged the drink back. The cleaning fluids she had used in the kitchen had made her throat dry and she was thirsty anyway. Danny quickly made her another. As the cocktail of drugs laced in with Donna's drink started to take effect, he lined up the coke. There was line after line which the three of them demolished easily.

By now Donna felt easy in Stevie's company and, like Danny, she had a lot of time for him. He was easy to talk to, always made her laugh with some story or other, and, though she would never say as much to Danny, he was a very good-looking man. She hoped that Danny had not noticed the way she always seemed to giggle a lot when Stevie was around. She'd caught Steve giving her a look from time to time so she knew that he found her attractive too.

After half an hour or so of relaxing in their company, Donna became aware of a strange floating sensation in her head. She had never felt so spaced. The drink had made her head swirl and she was having trouble focusing. Reading the signs, Danny moved to the stereo and put on some upbeat dance music. Donna began to dance around the living room, in a world of her own, oblivious to the meaningful glances that Danny and Stevie were exchanging

'Why not give Stevie a slow dance, babe?' asked Danny, changing the music then cutting out some more lines. He also slipped a crushed up ecstasy tablet into Donna's vodka and grapefruit. Feeling strangely uninhibited, she didn't mind dancing with Stevie, feeling his body pressed close against hers. She could feel his hard penis in his trousers, but didn't panic. She looked across at Danny who was smiling broadly. Didn't seem to mind a bit that one of his best friends and his girlfriend were getting so close.

Stevie started to kiss her, gently at first and then with more urgency. 'Let's strip off, babe. I wanna take a look at that beautiful arse of yours.'

Donna felt aroused but looked at Danny, fearing his reaction. He seemed completely relaxed, just nodded for her to continue.

Stevie lowered Donna on to the chocolate brown sofa, and began undressing her. She giggled, thinking they were mucking about. Soon, however, she was completely naked and Stevie was getting ready to penetrate her. As she realised what was about to happen she opened her mouth to speak, but Stevie just leaned down and kissed her hard. She responded hungrily, and as she did so he entered her forcefully and began thrusting hard. Oblivious to what was really going on, all Donna could see was the shadowy figure of Danny somewhere on the periphery of her vision and Stevie's intense sweating face as he pushed into her, harder and faster. Before long, Donna's legs were over her shoulders, exposing her vagina and anus.

'Can I, Dan?' asked Stevie, delirious with pleasure and still with a rock-hard penis.

'Yeah, mate, just save some for me.'

All Danny's dreams were coming true. He watched Donna intently, and smiled as he saw her wince with pain as Stevie inserted his penis into her anus. Danny was more and more excited. He asked Stevie to move over and give him a turn. It continued this way for an hour and Donna just went with the flow, not knowing who was inside her and who wasn't.

Danny took over once again. 'Line up more drinks, Stevie, and more gear. This is fucking fantastic. I told ya what a good lay she was and she'll do anything for us . . . anything!' He held the glass of laced vodka to Donna's mouth. She almost choked as she swallowed the lot in a few gulps. Danny positioned her to take more coke up her nose, and when she had done it, smeared more on her genitals and anus, to help numb the areas.

Within minutes, Donna had both men on her and was taking them at the same time. After several minutes of double penetration, Danny wanted them to change around so that Donna could go on top of him and Stevie push from behind. As she bounced up and down on top, however, Danny could only focus on her titties, swinging and swaying. He lifted her off him and rolled out from beneath.

'Keep going, Stevie, I've got an idea. Her fucking tits are driving me mad.'

He left Stevie to continue fucking Donna in any way he wanted and staggered into the kitchen. Rummaging in the drawers there, he found what he needed. Returning, he patted Stevie on the back. 'Give her some breathing space.' But as Stevie tried to withdraw, Donna only pulled him back to her.

Danny whispered in her ear, 'You're loving every second, ya filthy bitch, ain't ya?' She stared at him through glazed, semi-conscious eyes and just nodded.

With Donna lying flat on her back while Stevie satisfied her with his mouth, Danny lifted her tits. 'Hold these up, baby?' Donna obeyed and felt something wet applied to the creases under her breasts. 'Now push them down and hold them still for a while.' Soon Danny had Donna on top and her breasts moved no more. 'That's better,' he murmured as they both continued to take her in every way imaginable.

The night moved on until the morning sunshine broke through the drawn curtains. Two bodies lay sprawled across the sofa, both of them delirious. Donna had passed out before them, to be carried to the bedroom in her unconscious state.

*

When she finally came to, it was dark outside and she realised she had slept the day away. Struggling to get out of bed, her head thumped and she felt completely disoriented. She made her way hesitantly through the flat but found nobody there. Danny must have gone out.

The previous evening swam into Donna's consciousness in a series of flashbacks. Shame flooded her as she remembered not only the things she had done, but the fact that she had been a willing participant in the degrading sex-fest. She struggled to the bathroom and turned on the shower. She slipped a few times and had to steady herself on the rail. Her reflection in the mirror shocked her. Her face was smeared with dirty make-up, and semen had dried around her mouth. Her nostrils were caked with white powder. Her skin was dry and grey. Once under the water, Donna just let it run over her skinny aching body for a long time. As she looked down at herself, she could see bruising and fingermarks that were still red and blotchy. She reached for the shampoo and felt a tearing sensation under her breasts. She tried to lift them both but nothing would happen. All she could feel was tearing skin.

She sank down in the shower cubicle as the water splashed around her and attempted to ease her breasts away from the skin of her ribs. After what seemed like an eternity of massaging herself with a thick body wash and easing the folds apart, she freed her breasts. Her skin was red-raw and stung like crazy but what hurt her most was the realisation that Danny had glued her breasts to her ribs, to stop them from moving.

Slumped in the bottom of the shower tray, she sobbed uncontrollably until the water ran cold. Finally, she wrapped herself in a big bath sheet and tiptoed through the trashed living room to her bed where she pulled Pookie towards her and fell into a deep sleep.

She stirred sometime in the night and felt the heat of Danny's body next to hers. He was snoring loudly. She glanced at the clock and saw that it was after midnight. She turned and slid her arms around him. Whatever had happened, it didn't matter. It was all her fault anyway. Danny had told her on more than one occasion that her tits irritated him, and she had readily agreed to sex with a third party when it had come up during one of their sessions. She should know by now that when Danny said he wanted something, she had no way or even right to deny him. Remembering the events of the previous evening repulsed and excited her in equal measure. It was some time around three before she was rescued by the oblivion of sleep.

Chapter Eight

After her night with Danny and Stevie, Donna was quiet and reserved. She continued with her daily routine of shopping, cleaning, cooking and waiting faithfully for Danny to come home at night, but he noticed the change in her. In the days that followed, she held herself with the wariness of a whipped animal and stepped in a wide arc around Danny. She wanted to tell him how upsetting she had found the whole incident but couldn't find the words, especially when he seemed so grateful for the experience.

'You were amazing last night, Don, world-class. No one can hold a candle to you.'

It was true, too, that at the time she had been a more than willing participant. Less wide-eyed and childlike now, she wore the expression of a woman who had just stumbled across an uncomfortable truth. She felt older, wiser, and no happier for her discovery that the drugs made her do things she wouldn't dream of when straight.

Danny's usually unshakeable confidence that he was in control temporarily left him. He worried he might have overstepped the mark, especially when Donna undressed at night to reveal wadding taped to her torn and raw breasts. His response was to lay her on the bed and tenderly kiss the ravaged skin while she lay there, wet-eyed and morose. He never apologised or even spoke of it except to say, 'I love your tits, Don.'

He knew he'd have to go the extra mile to get her back on side and showered her with tenderness and flowers, to show his appreciation for the wonderful experience they'd shared. Aware that their wild night had left her shaken, he pulled out all the stops to make sure she felt safe and secure once more. He was patient and didn't push for sex, instead making an effort to come home on time and just curl up beside her, watch TV, hold her tight throughout the night and stroke her lovely hair.

Privately, he admitted that they'd been a little rough on Donna; her legs and backside had sustained heavy bruising and there were welt marks from where Stevie got carried away when he was slapping her backside. She'd seemed to love it at the time, but Danny had to remind himself that Donna was still an innocent compared to the women he'd been used to. He knew he'd better bide his time before their next adventure which he'd decided would include a woman; not as hard on Donna, and in many ways more interesting to watch. Off his face on coke he'd loved watching Stevie bang her, but there was still that part of him that wanted to be her only man, the only one to make her cry out when he fucked her hard.

He knew he could rely on Stevie to play ball. The guy had been on cloud nine for days afterwards and would go along with whatever Danny said; he'd even suggested he had the perfect girl to join in, a junkie and therefore willing. She wasn't bad-looking, a slightly older type with brown hair, lovely tits and a nice fat arse. Stevie thought she'd be perfect. Danny just had to name the day. Danny reflected that Stevie was game-on, a brother under the skin, and knew he could rely on him to keep schtum. If it weren't for his loyalty to Trippy, Danny would have made Stevie a permanent partner in the business, but as it was he was a foot soldier par excellence. He was a Danny Mk II, worked at the same speed, liked the same games. A man you could trust with your life.

The weeks went by. With the help of a few good meals and some high-intensity sun beds Donna began to look like her old self again. She asked Danny if it was all right to start some early Christmas shopping and he threw a wad of notes on the table without blinking.

Bolstering this demonstration of generosity, he said, 'Listen, babe, I thought we'd go up town and take in a show. Have a real weekend together, just the two of us. Whaddya reckon? ' He paused to smile at her. 'I want it to be special. I've got something to ask you.'

Donna knew this could only mean one thing. She leapt up from the kitchen table and threw her arms around his neck like a child on Christmas Day.

'Oh, Danny! Can we go and see *Phantom*? That would be a dream.' She kissed and kissed him all over his handsome face. Gently, he peeled her off,

'Steady, babe, you're like an excited little girl. You're my little girl, though, and I love you.' He kissed her hard. 'Now look, you've given me a stiffy already, and I gotta get out on the streets and make some money. You turn me on so much, Don, that's why I get carried away sometimes.' He squeezed her tight against him and she felt the strength of his arms engulf her. Now was the time to ask.

'Dan, is it all right if I pop round to Mum and Dad's? I've not seen Brandon in ages.' She looked at the floor, waiting for an answer, while Danny swallowed his first impulse to refuse.

'All right, babe, but 'ave me dinner ready for seven. And,

listen, I don't mind yer family, but stay away from that Nicola. She'd do anything to break us up.'

Donna felt angry that he was being so mean about her friend when he didn't really know her, but now, on the brink of getting a proposal of marriage, was not the time to tackle him about that.

He held her face in his hands and stared into her eyes intently. His grip tightened almost imperceptibly. 'You're all mine now, Donna, and I'm not gonna let anybody take you away from me, do you understand? You're the first good thing I've ever had to call my own.' Her face held fast, she could manage only a tight nod of agreement. He released her, smiled and kissed her again, and headed off to work.

Donna sat at the kitchen table and cupped her mug of coffee in her hands. The draught from the open door whipped around her thin legs. She looked at the box of cream cakes that Danny had brought home the night before. 'Get them down ya,' he'd said. She wasn't really in the mood for eating but scoffed the lot anyway and made herself feel sick. Unbeknown to Danny, she had arranged to meet Nicola and Shaz later that morning, desperate to see them and catch up on all the gossip. Now she wasn't so sure.

Nervously she dialled Nicola's number but it just rang and rang and she knew that her friend had already left to meet her. There was no way she could get hold of her to cancel. She'd just have to be careful. It was only for a quick coffee and a chat anyway, it was harmless. She told herself to stop panicking, put her coat, boots and hat on, and tucked the money safely away deep in the pocket of her jeans.

It was late-November and bitter cold. The wind blew

along the high street and it was all Donna could do to walk straight. Giving up the struggle, she got to the bus stop just as a number nine turned up to take her to Bethnal Green. The girls were already waiting in the Wimpy Bar when she arrived, windswept but smiling. Her pale skin was flushed red from the elements and her hair had come loose from her hat.

'Christ, it's bloody freezing out there,' she said, lowering herself into a chair opposite Nicola and Shaz and peeling off her expensive sheepskin mittens, which the other two clocked immediately

'Hot chocolate, babe?' asked Shaz.

'Mmmm, yes, please,' replied Donna, getting her breath back.

'You look like you need a Special Grill as well, girl. God, you've lost weight,' Shaz remarked innocently. It wasn't a criticism, just a statement of fact, and she shrugged when Donna shook her head at the suggestion of food. Nicola made no comment. The hot chocolate arrived along with the other girls' burgers.

'You sure you don't want nothing?' asked Nic.

'No, really, I've just scoffed three cream cakes with my coffee earlier, before I came out. I'm stuffed.' Donna turned away from Nicola, careful not to meet her eye. 'So, Shaz, how's things going?'

'I can't tell ya, Don, I'm in heaven. I play with paints and clay all day, and I've just got day release for, wait for it . . . Selfridges!' Shaz beamed. 'I'll be a dogsbody in the design department to start with, but I'll be learning interior design, window dressing, and can spend time in their art department whenever I like. They're a really great bunch of people too.'

Donna watched her friend happily munch her burger and felt a twinge of something. It wasn't jealousy, she was pleased for Shaz, but something didn't sit right.

Shaz put down her burger. She wiped her mouth with her paper napkin and asked, 'What about you? How's semi-married life? Is it all it's cracked up to be . . . you know, lots of sex and shopping and staying at home with your man?'

Donna just smiled.

'Something like that. But, yeah, it's great. I'm in love, and I don't want for anything. I'm really great.'

Nicola eyed Donna steadily when Shaz made her excuses and headed off for the loo.

'So, how're things really, Don?'

'Fine. I just said so, didn't I?'

'Well, you don't look fine. You've lost so much weight, and you're all pale and tired-looking. What the fuck's going on?' Nicola looked down the restaurant to keep an eye out for Shaz, coming back from the loo. She wanted to keep this private.

Donna steadied herself and took a deep breath. 'Look, Nic, I love ya and I know you care, but you 'ave to stop all this Danny bashing. There's nothing wrong with us. We're better than ever. When you gonna get it through yer head that I'm happy?

'I want different things now. I'm really made up that you and Shaz got what you wanted, why can't you be happy for me? It's ruining our friendship, Nic. You gotta stay out of my business when it comes to Danny. You don't understand how he . . .'

'Well, talk of the devil.' Just then Nicola peered over Donna's shoulder at the figure of Danny walking past in the street with a person she didn't recognise. Female, quite old – in her thirties at least, maybe a relative.

'Fuck!' said Donna. 'I'm off to the Ladies, I don't want him to see me.' She bolted just as Shaz returned

‘Get the bill, Shaz, I’ll be back in a minute,’ said Nicola, rising to follow Donna to the toilets. Inside, she was splashing her flushed cheeks with water drawn from the cold tap.

‘You don’t think he saw me, do you?’

‘No, calm down. What’s the problem anyway? It’s only a hot chocolate with yer mates. Fuck me, Don, has he told you that you can’t see us, is that what all this is about?’ Donna looked desperate, and Nic caved in straight away.

‘Look, it’s all right, just stay calm. I’ll check it’s clear and come back and get you. I won’t go on about it, but if you ever need me, Don, you only ’ave to pick up the phone.’ She cuddled her friend close to her for a moment. ‘It’s cool. If this is what you want that’s fine, but promise me you’ll call if ever you need me?’

Donna nodded, starting to cry.

‘I’m sorry, Nic, it’s just that Danny knows you don’t like him and he thinks you’re trying to split us up. Things will get better and he’ll come around soon, I know he will.’

Nicola gave her friend a smile to cover up the sinking feeling inside her.

Back out on the windy street Donna watched Nic and Shaz walk away from her, arm-in-arm. She felt very alone in that moment and in her desolation wondered what might have been. University was out of the question now. No way would Danny stand for her going off to Sussex for three years. He did his nut if she went out shopping without telling him. Love had come early and she’d had to abandon her childhood hopes and ambitions to meet its demands. Danny was the sort of man you had to commit yourself to – no half measures. He expected his woman to be at home where he needed her. Donna loved Danny needing her, and you had to make sacrifices for love, she reasoned. The thought of the weekend ahead lifted her spirits and she vowed then never to look back, only forward. All thoughts of her friends and their shared dreams in the past must be laid to rest so that she could step fully into her new life. When they fell in love they'd understand.

She dawdled around the shops for an hour or so, choosing a few gifts, and then realised that if she wanted to see her family, too, she'd better get her skates on. At her parents' house it was a hive of activity and she welcomed all the noise and bustle that was once so familiar. The flat could be terribly quiet sometimes with just her at home, waiting for Danny.

She slumped down at the kitchen table, casting her heavy shopping bags all about her. Joyce hadn't long been in from school and was trying to get the tea going before Brandon emptied her fridge and fruit bowl, muttering to herself, 'That boy never stops eating, he's got bloody worms or something . . .'

Brandon was running through the house looking for his football, ready to join his small gang of friends outside, and Ian had just got off early and walked in with a pile of paperwork to go through after dinner, obviously pleased and surprised to see his princess.

Donna lifted her arms over her head in a big stretch, revealing the protuberance of her ribs. Ian and Joyce exchanged worried glances. Donna just smiled.

'What's up with you two?'

'Babe, you're like a stick insect. When was the last time you ate a proper meal?' asked Joyce.

'God! Not you two as well. It's bad enough listening to Nic. I am not thin, I'm a standard size eight, Mum. Besides, it's all the fashion to be so slim. It's great for clothes, and Danny likes me this way.'

Ian stared blankly at his daughter.

'Spit it out, Dad, if you've something to say,' she said defensively.

'All right, young lady, I have. For starters you look bloody ill, and if Danny likes you like that there's something wrong with the bloke. Since you've left home, we hardly see you. Danny's been a few times to visit with you, but it's days and sometimes weeks before you phone us. We've called in at the flat several times, just to chat, and Danny has always said that you're either out, in bed with flu, or else no one answers at all. You look half starved and you expect us not to worry!'

Joyce saw her opportunity to jump on the bandwagon and took it. 'Jane's been down twice and on neither occasion have you even bothered to call round for a cup of tea and see her. You're always busy, away on weekends or staying at some posh hotel. We're not stupid, Donna, we know what you're up to.'

'Meaning what?' she said, her voice climbing dangerously.

'We know how Danny makes his money. You'd better not be mucking around with drugs or I'll bloody kill you – and him as well.' Joyce slammed a saucepan of water on to the gas ring to boil.

Donna's face was puce with anger. She was outraged by the way everybody spoke about Danny.

'Well, ain't this great? I come to see you 'specially to ask if it's all right for me and Danny to come on Christmas Day. I have had the flu actually, and was on a diet before that, but I *don't* take drugs. I can't believe you don't trust me and Danny. He's the best thing that's ever happened to me.'

Donna couldn't keep it up. A few angry tears turned into a fit of sobbing.

That was it for Ian. He was at her side in a second, holding her and saying sorry, over and over again. 'We thought all sorts of things, baby. We thought you 'ad that slimming illness at one point. We never see ya, and Nic's been phoning too, wondering why she can't get hold of you at the flat . . .'

Through her sobs Donna answered back.

'I might 'ave known *she'd* be on the blower. Don't take any notice of her, she's just jealous. Everyone wants me to be away from Danny and living their lives. Well, I gotta live *my own* life.' She got up to leave.

'C'mon, babe, we're sorry,' said her mum. 'Stay and at least 'ave a cuppa?' Donna looked at her tired but lovely face, reading every trace of disappointment in its lines.

'I'm sorry, Mum, I've got dinner to get ready and shopping to put away.'

She looked down when she said this and the kitchen fell quiet. Brandon suddenly burst through the door, breaking the silence.

'Wow! You should 'ave seen that goal, it was a belter.' Ian moved swiftly to pick up Donna's bags and hustle her out before her little brother saw that she'd been crying.

'C'mon, little 'un, I'll give you a lift.' Donna accepted sheepishly and they drove the short distance in silence. Parked outside the flats, Ian looked at his girl. She was still a beauty, but there was no denying the change in her.

'Is there anything you want to tell your ol' man, babe, anything at all?'

'Dad, I love you and Mum and Jane and Brandon, but you have to believe me when I say I'm OK. Danny does everything for me. I want for nothing. I am so happy, Dad. I just want your blessing, that's all.'

Ian went quiet. He couldn't quite give her that.

'Well, at least let me help you with your bags?' he pressed her.

'No, Dad, I'm fine. And besides, the flat's a tip and I need to clean up a bit.' Donna gathered her numerous bags and got out of the car. The wind had picked up again and was whipping her like a lash.

'See ya, Dad,' she said, making her way to the stairwell.

'Donna!' Ian shouted out of the car window. 'We will see you at Christmas, won't we, babe? You and Danny, the pair of you?' He was giving her the clumsy thumbs up sign he always did when he wanted them to make-up with each other. Donna had to smile.

'Yeah, 'course you will.'

The flat was quiet and still as she unlocked the door and made her way to the kitchen. They were all against her: her friends, her family, just about everyone. She unpacked the food shopping, put the large steak in the pan, and turned the gas on low. Danny liked it well done. By the time she'd put the other bits away in the bedroom, she'd still have plenty of time to peel the spuds and do the salad.

While the dinner cooked slowly, she examined the new underwear she had bought. Danny would just love this. The red and black bra held her breasts firmly, and the tiny matching knickers were cut out across her bottom, revealing the cheeks of her arse. The gusset was so small it showed off more genitalia than it covered. Pulling on thigh-high black boots, she looked into the mirror and knew she looked good. Her body didn't have an ounce of fat on it. There were a few blemishes on her skin but nothing that the sun bed wouldn't sort out. She carefully wrapped the items back in tissue paper and packed them away for her weekend to come.

As usual the hotel was fantastic. Danny had changed his

booking from the Savoy when he found out that Nicola might be around the place and switched it to the Dorchester. Donna bounced on the bed for joy at the luxury of her surroundings. The carpet was so thick and springy that her feet sank into it, the bed was as wide as it was long and the bathroom the size of her front room at home. She'd never seen so many fluffy towels.

She spent the afternoon preparing herself for whatever the night might bring. She applied a face pack, put a conditioning treatment on her hair and carefully painted her nails the shade of deep crimson which Danny favoured. He had been cagey about their plans and she smiled to herself, thinking that this was the night he was going to ask her to be his wife.

That evening she wore a tight-fitting black cocktail dress and high stiletto heels. Around her neck was the diamond cluster necklace that Danny had given her before they set off for the hotel. Another box lay on the bed as she came out of the bathroom.

'For you, baby,' said Danny.

She slowly untied the ribbon and lifted the lid off the large box to reveal white tissue paper covering a chocolate brown mink coat. She slid effortlessly into its rich satin lining to find that it fitted her perfectly. She looked stunning in it. For a moment the pair of them were speechless. Finally Danny whistled approvingly.

'Now you're Danny Lester's girl for sure!'

As they stepped out of the hotel into the windy night to hail a cab, Donna was walking on air, though at the back of her mind lurked a vague sense of disappointment that he still hadn't asked for her hand in marriage. Diamond necklaces and mink coats were great, but they were not quite the solitaire she'd had in mind.

The show was no disappointment, though, and as they

walked slowly away from the theatre afterwards she glowed with happiness, hugging her coat close to her. Danny looked so handsome in his tuxedo and pure new wool Crombie coat. They made a striking pair.

Back at the hotel Danny ordered three bottles of their best Champagne from room service while he waited for Donna to finish in the bathroom. She vaguely wondered why he'd ordered three when two would have done, but thought little of it. He tipped the waiter ten pounds and asked with a wink that they not be disturbed until the next day. Donna finally appeared in the bathroom doorway, posing in her erotic new underwear and boots.

'You look fucking good enough to eat! As a matter of fact, I might just eat you all up, starting with that crack between yer legs. Come to Danny.' He licked her briefly before a better idea occurred.

He lined up the gear and poured Donna her Champagne, laced this time with 10mg Valium, not as strong as the opiate he'd used on her with Stevie. By the end of her second glass Donna was swaying. She wasn't at all anxious about how out of control she was, but felt she could fly.

On the dot of midnight a loud knock on the door was answered to reveal Stevie with a small, demure-looking girl hiding behind him. 'Surprise!' said the grinning Stevie, clutching a bag of booze. Danny eyed the girl and pulled him to one side.

'Is that the best you could do?'

'Sorry, Dan, the other bird was off her tits at eight o' clock tonight and Little Jen here was all I could find. Don't worry, though, mate, she's tried and tested. Although there's not a lot of her, she can give a fantastic fuck and go all night. She's just needs a little something to get her going, don't ya, babe?'

The young girl nodded eagerly as she spotted the lines of coke. Donna, so out of it that their arrival was not even noted with surprise, lurched over to Stevie and kissed him hard on the lips

'Hiya, babe, you come to join the party?' she asked. Stevie looked at Danny as if to say, Wow, she's already loaded.

'Listen,' said Danny, 'you get reacquainted with Donna and I'll take this little thing over there and get her jump started.' Before long, Stevie was writhing with Donna and she welcomed him in any way he wanted. The two of them were soon thrusting and moaning. Danny eyed his mate and Donna together. His erection was rock-hard so he left the baby woman on her knees on the floor, where she'd been sucking him, and pushed Stevie to one side. He needed to get his first fuck out of the way.

When he'd finished he took two more lines and instructed the girls to do the same. Once they'd swigged a bit more of their Champagne, Danny placed his arms around both of them and pulled them in close to whisper, 'Now I want to watch you two eat each other out. And make sure I can see your arseholes while you do it.'

The girls lay on the bed and did as they were told. Donna was a little nervous and giggled to start with, but young Jen seemed at home with another girl's body and was able to arouse her out of her inhibitions.

Stevie and Danny watched while they sniffed more cocaine. When their erections could wait no more, they joined the girls on the bed and spent the night alternating sex between the four of them, each bringing something new to the events. Neither Danny nor Stevie had experienced anal sex before but couldn't refuse when the girls turned the tables and used the vibrators on them. It was new, exciting, painful, but exhilarating!

The drink and drugs kept coming and Donna was growing more sexually assertive, demanding Danny do this but not that. Their lust was unstoppable. Little Jen even showed them a trick with a Champagne bottle. She was a real sort, that one. Nothing seemed to make her squeamish. When the two guys and Donna all hit on her at once, she surrendered to it totally and allowed them all to penetrate her. Danny had experienced a threesome fuck plenty of times, but this kid was taking the two men and Donna using a vibrator. It was wild, sick at times, with an inexhaustible desire to rage on. The scene lasted until late the next night when the drink and drugs ran out and all four of them collapsed on the bed and finally slept.

When Donna awoke, Stevie and the young girl had gone. Danny sat eating breakfast, just out of the shower, wrapped in a towel. The sitting room had been tidied and he smiled at Donna with the radiant well-being of a man who had rested and eaten well.

'Get yourself showered, babe. I ordered breakfast. You need to eat before we make our way back.'

The journey passed quietly, Danny just turned the radio on and hummed along to the tunes being played. Donna sat, reliving the experiences of the weekend, feeling muddled. She'd thought it was supposed to be just the two of them, whereas in fact Danny had planned something very different down to the last detail. She felt horribly let down, not just by him but by herself. Danny loved his drink, drugs and sex, and now she had become an integral part of that there was no going back. He was not a man to take no for an answer and her role as willing partner was set. She wondered if it was always going to be like this from now on.

Then she looked at his happy, handsome face and chided

herself for being selfish. It wasn't as if she hadn't enjoyed it at the time. And, more importantly, she was loved and adored by Danny. If he occasionally wanted to share her, it just meant he was proud of her. Once inside the flat, Donna felt weak and tired and collapsed on the sofa, but Danny's energy was undiminished.

'Listen, babe, I gotta get to work, but why don't you just relax and sleep today? Don't want you getting poorly. It's snowing outside now, so you stay wrapped up in bed. When I get in later, I'll fix you a nice cuppa and bring home a takeaway. How's that sound?'

Donna beamed at him. He was just so caring.

'That sounds fantastic. Dan, it is just you and me tonight, isn't it?'

He wrapped his arms around her.

'Don, don't worry. The weekend was just a one-off, to show you how spreading love around makes everyone feel good. And, of course, I wanted to please you too. But tonight it's just us, I promise.'

But in Danny's mind it was never just them any more. Even when he was riding Donna for all she was worth, he was finding it increasingly difficult to come. To bring himself along he would fantasise about different people all fucking each other, and eventually his imagination would get him where Donna alone no longer could. He briefly entertained the thought that maybe the gear was affecting him before dismissing it out of hand.

Chapter Nine

It was Donna's favourite kind of evening, just the two of them at home, some good food and a bit of telly – *EastEnders* followed by a repeat of *The Good Life* which she loved. When the football came on Donna busied herself on the floor of the lounge, wrapping presents and showing Danny what she'd bought, bubbling with excitement about spending Christmas with her family. Their first Christmas together; a very special time. She never knew what surprises might lie in store.

Danny nodded and smiled distractedly as she chatted on, without ever averting his eyes from the screen. He was more thoughtful than usual but Donna thought he was just relaxing for a change. During his busy day Danny had in fact met up with Stevie again and been introduced to the woman he recommended: Christine. A robust, well-endowed woman with a substantial rear end, Danny found her unexpectedly arousing. She'd been drinking at lunchtime and snorting coke with Stevie, and wasted no time in letting Danny know she'd fuck his brains out whenever he wanted, and take on his silly little bird too.

He'd been a bit offended by her forthright manner, one which assumed he would want her, and was a little put out that she had ridiculed Donna, but he'd stayed cool enough to say he'd think about it.

He did want her, though. She was too good a chance to miss.

After their recent excursion to the Dorchester, Danny knew it was too soon to plan a repeat performance. He needed to play for time and keep his ace up his sleeve. The two-carat solitaire diamond ring was still in his sock drawer, ready for when the moment came. If he could just keep Donna sweet for the next week or two and get through Christmas, he'd be playing with a good hand. And so he planned to indulge her taste for all things Christmassy by taking her on shopping trips followed by quiet bistro dinners and lavish displays of tenderness. In the meantime, he would meet up with Stevie and try out Christine, a kind of dummy run, before definitely putting her on the guest list. He wouldn't mind another pop at Little Jen, the young kid, either. Johnny would be up for it, too, and the orgy he planned could take place at Danny's flat, under his control and watchful eyes. They would all see in the New Year, Danny Lester-style!

The weeks leading up to Christmas were the happiest of Donna's life. Danny was spending more time at home and, even though he still had a few lines in the evening, he'd slowed down on the coke. Occasionally she joined him in a line but there was no pressure for her to get completely off her face and she revelled in their domesticity and togetherness. What she didn't realise was that Danny was now taking coke during the day as well as the evenings, because he found it shifted the hangovers and he could get more done that way. He knew it wasn't good to keep sniffing it, so he'd taken to rolling it into joints for daytime use; it was less obvious.

The day before Christmas Eve an enormous arrangement of holly and pine cones with saucer-like red dahlias was delivered to the flat and Donna lost an afternoon trying to find the right place to arrange it in the flat. It was too big for the kitchen table, and really needed a table all its own to be displayed properly. Eventually she covered the wide stool from the bathroom with a white linen cloth and placed that in the corner of the front room, next to the television. You couldn't miss it when you came into the room.

In the other corner she had decorated a six-foot pine tree in silver and red, its wider bottom branches supporting an avalanche of presents. She had even made some homemade goodies, just to get her in the Christmas spirit. Danny loved her mince pies, and Donna was proud of the way the flat looked and how she was spending her days. She felt womanly and mature, caring for her man and their home. Things seemed to have returned to how they used to be – there had been no nasty surprises, just her and Danny. Donna also found time to call Nicola, get back on better terms with her, and was in regular phone contact with her parents. Everyone was happy.

Business was booming and Danny Lester was a busy boy. Trade was at its seasonal peak and he was fast selling out of everything, but his regular supplier just kept it coming and ounces of the stuff arrived in time for the party season. The bookies were offering terrible odds for a white Christmas, but it was snowing hard in East London. As well as coke, they were pushing out amphetamines and something known as Rohypnol, a tranquilliser which left the user with no memory and which Danny had used on Donna to good effect in the past.

In order to spend more time at home with her, Danny had begun to delegate more of the work to the other lads. The first few times they took delivery of big orders he was nervous that they would cock it up somehow or get ripped off or start creaming a profit off the top. But they were all too keen to get to his party to try anything on. Danny should have trusted more in their loyalty to him, especially the devoted Trippy. Danny sometimes wished that his old mate was a bit more like Stevie, more up for a wild time and getting stuck into the gear, but he still hadn't changed a bit, the same boy that he had always been, in jeans, with the lazy smile and messed up hair, who liked his home comforts. Danny had known him since he was in short trousers.

Trippy's ties to Danny ran deeper than blood. Both boys from broken homes, they'd spent their childhoods like a pair of lost feral dogs on the streets of the East End. Family life had already taught them what it was like to live with fear and so they negotiated their new environment well, keeping on the right side of the big guys and not getting mixed up with the nutters. Danny had always been the more dominant of the two, certainly the more vocal. Trippy, more reserved and laid-back by nature, was slow to anger and kept his cards close to his chest, but never failed to come through for his mate. The two boys forged an intense bond, through many acts of bravery and brotherhood, but Danny could still pinpoint the exact summer when he'd decided that Trippy was the one person he could always count on.

That scorching summer of 1965, the boys were only around eight or nine but were already streetwise. They enjoyed fishing down by the canal, pulling bits of old prams and shopping trolleys out of the water instead of fish. One day down the towpath they spied Ian Downey, much-feared eldest son of alcoholic Irish parents. Mother Downey would occasionally be seen in her nightdress, walking down the road, shouting at nobody as she went off to find more drink. Ian Downey must have been around 14, an angry little bastard who was always up for a fight. If he couldn't find one, he'd start one, so Trippy and Danny kept their heads down and voices low as Downey came closer to them along the towpath.

They could hear him muttering loudly, something obscene and challenging that they couldn't quite make out. As he passed behind them he took a swing at Danny's back with his boot and completely winded him, sending him rolling over on to the bank, unable to move.

Trippy was up in a flash. He screamed, 'Fuck off, you midget Paddy!' and promptly landed two clean punches on the older boy's jaw. Downey wasn't hurt, but the shock of somebody actually retaliating put him on the back foot. After looking at both boys unsteadily for a few moments, he continued along the towpath, shouting threats of retribution. But they knew that they'd seen him off. That was Trippy all over; quiet, but right there when you needed him.

Recently he had been keeping a lower profile than usual, only seeing the others for work and keeping himself to himself on his days off. In his paranoid moments Danny suspected there might be some skulduggery going on. What he didn't realise was that Trippy had his eye on a girl.

On Christmas Eve Danny took Donna to the local pub, the White Lion, where they always used to meet in the early days. After a few quiet weeks with just the two of them at home, Donna was up for a night out and had dressed to the nines. The pub was heaving with people and from her place at the bar, where she chatted with a few of the locals, she could see Danny's progress around it, pumping handshakes and winking. She knew that he was busy doing some last-minute dealing, but she didn't care. She was with him now and everyone knew she was Danny Lester's girl. A few women eyed her enviously and it made her feel wonderful. She had landed the biggest, best-looking fish in the neighbourhood and glowed with pride. Not only was Danny with her, he really loved her. Tomorrow the pair of them would be with her family and she couldn't wait.

She hoped Danny would like the presents she had bought him, she'd been more adventurous than usual. One day, shopping in the West End, she'd found a sex shop tucked away in St Anne's Court, between Dean Street and Wardour Street. It sold all sorts of grotesque sex aids, but she found a tasteful silver straw and spoon for his coke, some raunchy videos and a new vibrator that was 'specially to be used on her. She'd read in one of her magazines that men got turned on when women took the lead in sex sometimes.

She bought him lots of normal things too: a jumper from Marks and Spencer, a Fred Perry shirt, some aftershave and a book about boxing, but she knew he would be thrilled with the sexy stuff most of all. It had become a way of life to Donna and felt no different from buying him socks or pants. She had revelled in their recent togetherness and wanted to keep things that way. She couldn't deny to herself any longer that she disliked a lot of the things Danny wanted to do sexually, but if she could give a little and meet him halfway, she might be able to keep it just between the two of them. This way at least the situation was manageable and she felt slightly more in control.

It never occurred to her that Danny controlled everything, including letting her take the lead occasionally; his terms, not hers.

When the pub finally turned out around midnight they weaved their way happily back to the flat, both a bit pissed and in high spirits, particularly Danny who had made a bucket-load of money. Tomorrow would be his day off with Donna. Tonight he would let her open his gifts to her, and he would open hers to him. As soon as they got through the front door Danny poured more large drinks. It was Christmas Eve after all.

His presents to her, naughty underwear and a couple of saucy outfits, were no less than she'd expected and Donna dutifully modelled them. He made all the right noises about the clothes and aftershave she'd bought him, but was really over the moon with his sex-shop presents.

'Blimey, babe, this is fantastic,' he said, examining the spoon and silver straw. 'A lot longer than the one from Amsterdam – let's try it out.' Donna looked down before saying softly, 'Dan, I don't want to go mad, we're due at Mum and Dad's tomorrow quite early and I want us to have a really special day. That stuff can make me feel rough, like I've got a bad cold, and I don't want to turn up at home with red nostrils.'

Danny's expression changed to one of anger,

'*This* is your home, Donna, here with me.'

'Well, of course it is, Danny, but you know what I mean.' He looked crestfallen and she felt guilty and knew she had to soften him up a little. 'Well, maybe just a small line.'

Danny's answering smile reached from ear to ear.

'Don't worry, babe, I've got the answer. Drop your drawers and bend over the sofa.' Donna just stared at him and laughed out loud.

'No, seriously, Don, just try it. This way it won't make you feel rough and everything will be great tomorrow. This is something totally new, trust me.' Donna obeyed. 'Pull the cheeks of your arse apart for me . . . that's it, nice and wide.' She felt the coldness as a straw was inserted into her anus followed by a cold shot of air. 'It's OK, babe, it's the coke. It enters the bloodstream more easily this way, and there's no running nose.'

Donna couldn't believe it, but within minutes she felt the effects. 'You're right, Dan,' she giggled, 'it works. Do it again!'

More coke and drinks followed, and Danny performed his ritual sex on Donna, the double entry that was his preference. The new vibrator was thicker and bigger than ever, and with that up her front and him shagging her from behind, her arse tight as a drum, the pleasure was amazing.

After a few hours of energetic fucking, the two giggling lovebirds had another large drink and a big joint to help them wind down and get some sleep before the next day.

In the morning the two of them awoke, happy and fresh. Donna felt no ill-effects from the previous night and got herself up and ready for the day ahead. She was desperate to get to her parents and Danny was happy to get excited with her. As they stood at the door ready to leave, he pulled her close. 'Merry Christmas, babe. Hold up a sec, I've got something else for you.'

Out of his pocket he produced a red leather box trimmed with gold ribbons and embossed with a Hatton Garden address. Donna just stared in amazement. 'Well, go on then, open it, you prune!' he urged her.

Carefully she unwrapped the box, and as she pushed its lid back on stiff hinges her jaw almost hit the floor.

'Will you marry me, baby?' asked Danny, staring at her intently. 'I love you and want the world to know how special you are to me. I want you to be my wife.'

The emerald-cut diamond was bigger than anything Donna had ever imagined. Lost for words, she fell into his arms.

At the Stewarts' house the atmosphere was hectic with activity. Joyce was in and out of the kitchen, busy getting lunch prepared and complaining at Brandon and Ian as they tried to assemble his new Scalectrix set in the front room. 'I'll break my flipping neck on this lot!' Jane was flicking through the record collection, looking for something Christmassy, and the phone was ringing off the hook with various friends and relatives getting in touch.

When Danny and Donna arrived they came into a house blaring with music and a rush of people coming to greet them. Danny had never met Jane before. As he eyed her up and down he could see a startling resemblance to Donna. Slightly taller than her sister with her hair cut into a short bob, Jane had a much bigger bust. Dan was impressed. She had his number immediately and wasted no time introducing her man. 'This is David, my boyfriend.'

'Pleased to meet you,' said Danny, shaking his hand, eyes still on Jane. What he couldn't do to her, given half the chance! Donna was so excited she was hopping from foot to foot. She could contain herself no longer than it took them to get in the front door and take their coats off.

'Mum, Dad, everyone . . . we have an announcement. Danny and I are engaged!'

There was a brief silence, but then everyone politely

whooped for joy. Privately, they felt a sense of disappointment, but her parents knew it was what their Donna had been hoping for and hugged the happy couple hard.

Joyce stared at the huge diamond on her daughter's left hand. 'Good grief, it's bigger than Liz Taylor's!' Everyone started laughing.

Dinner went off without a hitch and everyone loved their presents. Crackers were pulled, carols played, and even Brandon ate Brussels sprouts! The rest of the afternoon saw the girls chatting away together while Danny smoked big cigars with Ian and David.

'I'm glad you've decided to make a real go of things with my Donna,' said Ian.

'Mr Stewart . . . umm, I mean, Ian . . . I love your daughter with all my heart and she means the world to me. I'm sorry we don't get round very often, but we will try to see you a bit more. It's just that work must come first. I like to keep my Donna in the luxury she deserves.'

Ian was far from satisfied with this explanation as he knew damn well the source of his daughter's dubiously luxurious lifestyle, but with the help of a few glasses of Harvey's Bristol Cream and a dollop of seasonal goodwill, he managed to smile politely. Ian Stewart was a wise man. He knew that if his daughter really wanted to marry this character, the die was cast. He simply had to accept it.

By tea-time Danny was eager to get away. For all his hail-fellow-well-met manner, he really hated the family thing. It brought back hateful memories of his own childhood. But he played the game, for Donna's sake – and his own. Hiding a bad motive under a good one, he played it well. Now that he'd done his bit, though, he just wanted to get back to the flat and try some more experiments with his new fiancee. He hadn't had any coke all day and could feel himself starting to grow agitated. He didn't want this to show in front of the family.

When night started to fall, he pulled Donna to one side and said, 'We need to get back now, babe.' She wanted to stay longer, but today had been more than she'd hoped for and so she easily gave in.

Donna still could not stop looking at her ring. It was slightly too big, but she didn't care. She loved to touch and feel it and experience the warmth and glow of being officially engaged. Back at the flat she switched on the tree lights while Danny headed for the bathroom to take his fix. From time to time he would hide the extent of his drug use from her, but Donna knew he was snorting coke and didn't care. It was part of who he was and she had to accept him totally. He could have had his pick of women, but Danny was her man and she was the chosen one. That night she dressed up for him in a cute bunny outfit that he had bought her and urged her to try on. Coke was inserted as before and Danny was ecstatic that he had found a way to get the gear into Donna and make her feel like everything was perfect.

The whole plan was coming together, the thought of New Year never far from his mind. With bendy Christine and Little Jen lined up, it was really taking shape. Johnny was hung like a donkey; Stevie would perform brilliantly. The thought of what lay in store kept him hard all night.

The next few days went by quickly. Donna's spirits were soaring and Danny took the opportunity to tell her that he'd invited some friends round to see in the New Year, knowing that she would not protest. Donna made no argument but busily set about planning a buffet and getting the place looking lovely with candles and flowers. Danny couldn't help but laugh to himself. She was a cracker, his Donna, but so stupid at times.

He was almost wild with excitement at the thought of it all. Couldn't wait to get the boring shit out of the way and reach New Year. He'd been lucky to have a try-out with Christine and Stevie some weeks ago. They'd had a brilliant time. That bird was like rubber. She could take doubles up the front and back, and he knew she would not disappoint at his party. He'd even picked up his new trick from Christine. Her use of a straw to blow coke up his arse had been a magnificent piece of ingenuity, which had worked brilliantly on Donna too. He'd also decided to give the young kid another seeing to and she'd proved OK, though not a patch on the more experienced Christine. At one point Little Jen had screamed when they both had her, but Danny had to accept that they did put her through her paces and make her bleed. Considering she was only fifteen she'd coped well with the pair of them and he was happy to put her on the guest list for New Year. In total, there would be six of them. Not a mass orgy, but enough for now.

The days leading up to New Year were hectic for Danny, what with party orders to complete. In the evenings he just came home, ate his dinner and got in a few early nights. For Donna, if this was what life was like being engaged, she was extremely happy.

She managed to see Nicola and Shaz briefly and give them their presents. The girls desperately wanted her to join them for New Year's Eve at the Limelight Club but Donna declined their invitation and they didn't push it. They wished her a Happy New Year and said they would all catch up soon. Donna felt really guilty about it; they had shared so much in their younger days, and she still felt a strong connection with Nicola, especially when she thought about the past and all they had gone through together.

Donna had always had Jane as her big sister, teaching her and guiding her through typical teenage problems, but Nicola had had no one to turn to when things got rough at home and simple everyday things were difficult. The girls had shared intimate secrets with one another.

For a few moments, Donna had a flashback to the girls' toilets at school where, in separate cubicles, they had both tried to insert a tampon. Nicola walked out doing an impression of John Wayne, whereas Donna, having asked Jane about it, had managed to do it easily at her first attempt. The two of them had fallen about in fits of laughter! Now that all seemed so long ago. Donna couldn't believe it would soon be 1987. Time had flown. Within six months she'd gone from being a schoolgirl to a woman who was engaged to be married. She was a changed girl, but a happy one.

New Year's Eve arrived at last. Danny finished up work as quickly as he could and got home early. Donna was absorbed with her preparations in the kitchen and he took the opportunity to get things sorted in the front room and bedroom. Within a short time, the lethal cocktails were prepared, toys were hidden in both rooms and he'd already lined up the coke for all the visitors. Not wanting to run out, he'd made sure they had sixteen grams. Two per person should do the job. Donna sensed what lay ahead as she walked in the front room to see the glass-topped coffee table full of lines of coke.

'Blimey, Dan, let's not go too mad, babe.'

He grinned. 'In the bedroom, you, and drop yer knickers. Let's get you happy and relaxed before anyone arrives.' Donna knew better than to argue and before the first guests arrived had already downed one of Danny's special cocktails and was as high as a kite.

'God, Dan, this is really strong and it's got a weird taste, babe.'

'Knock another back in one, sugar, and you'll feel great,' Danny assured her. She did as she was told and as she started to feel herself drifting there was a knock at the door.

Two women arrived with Johnnie and Stevie and Donna welcomed them into her home. She'd met little Jen at the Dorchester. Still a teenager, she was sweet and childlike with a rounded face and tiny body. Donna had never met Christine, the elder of the two. She had an intimidating presence, heavily made up with her curvaceous body barely dressed in provocative clothing. After two of Danny's knock-out cocktails Donna didn't really care. The guests fell on the coffee table like wolves and lines of coke were snorted up before the drinks had even been poured. Cocktails were downed in one when Danny toasted, 'Come on 1987, bring it on!' and the night got off to a quick start.

He put a porn film on the video and hands were soon stroking, teasing and undressing other bodies. Within the hour all six were entwined in a sexual mass, pausing only to copy moves from the video. Christine, the older woman, took whatever was going while Jen, the young kid, seemed to be struggling to accommodate two men and Christine, who was trying to insert a vibrator as well. Donna could sense that something wasn't right, but the will to help the young girl had left her and she downed more drinks until Little Jen's protests faded completely from her mind. Everyone was taking turns with anyone who had a free hole, and the various forms of intercourse went on and on.

At one point Donna saw Johnny leaning over the older

woman, thrusting his penis deep into her throat. Despite her gagging, he thrust all the more. At one point Donna looked at Danny, fucking Christine up the arse ecstatically, and felt nothing, not a twinge of jealousy or even curiosity. In some dim recess of her mind she thought that maybe she ought to be feeling a bit pissed off, but nothing more. She went into blackout with Johnny inside her.

When Donna came to several hours later there were limbs everywhere. She rolled herself off Johnny and tiptoed to the kitchen for a glass of water. Danny was in their bedroom still having sex with the older woman who seemed to have the vitality of a horse. The rest of them were sprawled throughout the flat, in the spare room or crashed out on the sofa. The sight of them all was too much for Donna. She crawled into bed in the spare room with Little Jen, closed her eyes and fell into a fitful sleep, hoping they would all be gone by the time she woke up again.

Donna drifted in and out of consciousness for two days before she felt able to get up. Her body was covered in bruises, there were deep welts across her buttocks and her anus and vagina were throbbing with pain. She found it difficult to walk, but slowly staggered to the bathroom where she climbed under a hot shower.

Agony hit her like a lightning bolt as the water fell on to her swollen bottom. As she slowly examined herself she found scratches and bite marks all over her body. She stayed in the water for as long as she could bear to. When she climbed out and wrapped a towel around her she felt the pain anew as the soft terry cloth touched her raw skin. She checked the rest of the flat on her way back to the bedroom and found it empty. She had no idea what day it was or where everybody had gone to. Her mouth tasted foul, but before she brushed her teeth she needed to drink.

She made her way to the kitchen and had to down four glasses of water before her thirst was quenched. Her stomach was doing somersaults with hunger and she felt the need to eat anything she could lay her hands on. The flat was a complete tip, but there on the sideboard was the stale food she had prepared almost three nights before. Like a starving animal she devoured sausage rolls, stale pizza, nuts and crisps. As she surveyed the room between mouthfuls, flashbacks overwhelmed her. She had to fight down a wave of nausea. In that moment Donna knew she couldn't do this any more. She started to cry.

She slumped on to the sofa and didn't move for hours until she heard a key in the lock and a wave of panic shot through her.

Danny came in. 'So, you're finally up, are ya?' he asked abruptly. Donna knew something had upset him and almost flinched when he came close to her. 'Fucking 'ell, Don, look at this place. Can't you get your fucking act together and clean this shit hole?' He swept the paper plates and other stuff from the sideboard with one stroke of his hand. They fell to the floor. 'You can be a fucking lazy bitch sometimes.'

Donna was afraid, but replied, 'I'm sorry, Dan, I feel terrible. I don't know what happened on New Year's Eve but I'm covered in bruises and my head and throat are killing me. I'm so tired.'

Danny threw back his head and let out a demonic laugh. Grabbing her by the arms, he pulled her up from the sofa and pinned her against the doorframe. With one hand under her neck and a look on his face she had never seen before, he squeezed her throat. 'Dan, you're really hurting me!' She attempted to free herself, but his grip tightened even harder.

'Listen, you soppy bitch, we're all out working and getting on with our lives. It was a fucking party, that's all! All you do is swan around the place, lying in bed all day and doing fuck all. If you want out, you can fuck off.' He released his grip and threw her to one side. 'I'm sick of your moaning and whining. You wanna leave, then make sure you're fucking gone before I get back.'

The door slammed shut behind him. A dumbstruck Donna stayed on the floor where he'd thrown her and gave in to uncontrollable tears. What did he mean, leave? Where had that come from? Fear motivated her to get moving immediately. She decided that she had to toughen up and get herself organised. Within an hour she had rallied herself, dressed and started cleaning the flat. She had to have it all looking fabulous. When it was finished she would pop to the local shops and get some fresh groceries to make them a lovely supper.

She had to make it right with him. The fear of losing Danny was worse than anything she had felt on drugs and drink. He was her life.

Chapter Ten

Danny felt fit to burst as he made his way back down the stairs and out on to the street. He was furious with Donna, and the gear he'd smoked that morning had not lifted his spirits but made him edgy and cross. He was beginning to discover that, more and more, it didn't always make him feel how he wanted, but put that down to the quality of the gear.

New Year's Eve hadn't been all he had hoped it would, apart from Christine who'd performed like a trouper. Donna and the young kid had been a pain and kicked up a fuss, although they'd done as they were told eventually. Danny got a kick from slapping them about a bit, but the silly kid had gone and landed herself in hospital by falling down the stairs when she'd left the flat.

There had been a bit of a commotion trying to get the skinny bitch to Casualty in Mile End as everyone was off their faces and it had been the last thing they'd needed. Finally Stevie had agreed to drive and they'd dumped her unceremoniously at the entrance to Casualty, thinking she'd just sprained her ankle, but Danny had since heard the kid had a fractured skull and also sustained some internal injuries. Maybe they'd been a little too rough on her after all.

Somewhere deep inside Danny nurtured a vague hope that she would be OK. But this sort of thing came with the territory. You couldn't carry those kind of worries around with you, especially when you had other fish to fry and business to attend to.

Barry, his usual supplier in Bow, was late on delivery and stocks had nearly run down after such a booming Christmas and New Year. The guys had worked the day after New Year's Day, and so had Danny to keep up with demand. He'd bumped into Christine who was as bright as a button. Danny couldn't understand what made Donna feel so tired and shitty when everybody else managed to bounce back to normal within a day or two. Maybe it was because she had too little to motivate her and needed to be kept occupied. For some time he had been getting anxious that his regular safe house was becoming a little too well known and, not for the first time, thought of moving some of his operations back to the flat. Donna was bright. She could count cash and even do a bit of dealing here and there to help him out. It would keep her busy and she could start earning something to pay back what she put up her own nose. Or what he put up her arse.

After giving the flat a thorough clean and throwing open all the windows to air the place out, Donna wanted to get into the fresh air for a while and down to the shops before Danny came back. It had been raining hard that morning and showed no signs of letting up, but there was no way that Danny could come back to a house with empty cupboards so, in the absence of any transport of her own, she decided to sprint it. The shops with their bright lights and chattering customers and colourful displays were soothing to Donna's frazzled nerves. She realised with a sense of shock that she felt safer on the street than she did at home. It was something of a sickening realisation.

As usual she bought far too much food and, laden down with heavy bags, trudged back to the flat in Crisp Street in torrential rain, arriving home soaked to the skin and feeling shivery. She really was under the weather and needed a hot bath and a nap. Always a miserable month, January was proving harder to get through than usual this year and she was still feeling little battered and bruised after New Year's Eve. She kept gazing at her engagement ring, reminding herself that she had to take the rough with the smooth. She'd got what she wanted, after all.

Desperate to get into the warm, she put the key in the lock and pushed open the door, dumping her bags in the small passageway, their contents spilling on to the floor. 'Bugger,' she muttered to herself, but left them where they fell as she kicked the door shut and made her way to the bathroom to get a towel. As she dried her long black hair, she could hear the front door open again and the familiar sound of Danny's voice as he spoke to someone else. Donna closed her eyes, and took a deep breath. What was he doing back so early? And who did he have with him? She looked at her hands which had started to shake. She decided that she must be coming down with a chill. Quickly she dragged a brush through her hair and went to greet him.

'Hi, babe, this for me?' he asked as he retrieved the cucumber that had spilled from the carrier bag and lay on the floor. 'Or is it for our old mate Christine?' he said, stepping aside to reveal the heavily made up woman she remembered from New Year's Eve. Today Christine was dressed unseasonably in a halter-neck top, short skirt and stilettos. Her eyes were glazed and she was grinning inanely as Danny stroked her barely covered backside. She must be in her thirties at least, thought Donna. She smiled weakly by way of a greeting but her heart sank. What was that woman doing here? Oh, God, please, not again.

Danny was swaggering about the place, talking far too loudly with his eyes shining wildly. Donna was used to seeing him coked-up but he was higher than she'd ever seen him before and she felt her heart beat faster in her chest with a rising sense of panic. She could tell by the look on the woman's face that Christine had been at it too. Danny had left angry and upset that morning. This was obviously his way of dealing with it. He seemed happier now, though, and bragged to Donna that the morning had gone better than he'd hoped and his worries of earlier were sorted. Danny had known that Donna would be there when he got back. Of one thing he was sure: all the time she had that rock on her finger and the hope of marriage and babies alive in her mind, he knew he had her safely wherever he wanted her.

They both stood there, giggling for a while, until Christine pushed her way past Danny and looked at Donna. 'So,' she said slowly, 'you're my competition again, are ya? She's a good-looking girl, Dan, but that's no substitute for experience, babe.' She looked at Danny and laughed hard. He placed his arm around her and roared with laughter too. Donna failed to get the joke.

'Make some drinks, Chris,' he said, 'you know where they are.' Seeing the worried look on his fiancée's face, he slid an arm around her shoulders and said, 'Donna, c'mon, babe, let's get some gear into you and have some fun.' He led her into the kitchen where he placed a coarse white rock on the table and began to crush it. 'This is fab stuff, babe, totally uncut pure gear. You're gonna love it.'

Methodically he shaved the rock and then chopped and slit and ground it down into powder form until he had three long lines. Taking a ten-pound note out of his pocket, he said, 'This'll do nicely.'

Donna retched inwardly at the thought of taking more drugs; she still hadn't got over the last time, but she knew as soon as that first line went up her nose and hit the back of throat she'd keep at it until it had all gone. Not only could she not refuse Danny, once she got going she couldn't say no to coke either. Their life had taken on a certain predictability, and it wasn't just the drugs that were part of their routine. Danny made no secret of the fact that he found group sex more of a turn on than being alone with Donna, and she knew that tonight she would have to submit to whatever he wanted to do with her and Christine. He loved watching another man having sex with Donna, and tonight it would be Donna's turn to watch him go at it with Christine. Anxiety fluttered in her chest as she watched Danny roll up the ten-pound note and hand it over for her to take the first line. She placed one end up her nostril and the other on the line of powder on the kitchen surface. As she inhaled deeply, she felt a sharp pain at the top of her nose and recoiled instinctively.

Danny grabbed her head and tipped it backwards, ensuring that nothing came back down and that all the cocaine was fully absorbed. 'Don't want you wasting this gear, Don, it don't come cheap.' As she brought her head back down to its resting position she felt the cocaine going down her throat and the terrible taste it left in her mouth. She pulled a face, and Danny laughed. 'Told ya it was powerful shit. Chris, c'mon, babe, I've cut a line up for ya,' he shouted. 'And bring the drinks in 'ere, Donna's got a nasty taste in her mouth.' He laughed again.

Christine entered the kitchen carrying three very large vodkas. 'Got any ice, babe?' she said to Danny, with a wide toothy smile framed by frosted pink lips. He moved to the fridge and took out an ice tray, starting to push the cubes from the tray into the drinks. Donna stared at Christine. She was undoubtedly a good-looking woman. Top-heavy but with a small waist, she looked sexy in her halter-neck top and blue denim mini skirt, although she did have that horrid fat arse. Her mid-length blonde hair curled at the bottom, resting neatly on her shoulders. Donna was drawn to the large crucifix that hung down into the cleavage of her ample bosom.

'Got great tits ain't I, girlie?' she said, catching Donna staring at her breasts.

Donna looked down, embarrassed, but managed a smile. Christine looked tough, she wouldn't want to get on the wrong side of her. The coke was kicking in now and Donna knew from experience just to go with it and relax. If she fought the feeling it would only make her uptight and the day was only halfway done.

'Drink up, baby,' Danny said as he pushed the drink into her hand. 'I wanna get started.' Turning to Christine, he grabbed her breast and squeezed it hard. Looking at her with a leering grin he said, 'Come on, I'm horny as fuck.'

Danny stood at the kitchen door and, like a waiter, waved the girls through. As they passed by he made a sweeping bow. Donna moved out into the passage to make her way to the bedroom, glancing at the bags and their contents abandoned in the small hallway. She had bought a steak for dinner. It would be going off by the time she got round to unpacking it. She let out a resigned sigh and made her way with Christine into the bedroom. Even with the coke inside her, she couldn't muster any enthusiasm.

As Christine started to undress she looked around the room, all decorated in cream and pink. She started to laugh.

'Right girlie room this is! If I remember rightly, last time we all crashed in the front room.' She swept the scatter cushions and cuddly toys from the bed and on to the floor. Donna glanced at her beloved Pookie along with Tigger, the teddy that Danny had bought for her when they first started going out with each other, and her mind went back to when he had given it to her. Holding it hidden behind his back, he had made her choose an arm to see where her gift might be. That seemed like a long time ago with a different man altogether.

Both girls were now naked and Christine was eyeing up Donna's body. 'Bit pear-shaped, ain't ya? But then, I love a good arse to smack,' she said dispassionately. Donna just nodded in agreement, and looked towards the door as Danny came in.

'That's what I like to see, two lovely girls, just waiting for my dick. Let's hope I can please you both,' he said, rubbing his unshaven chin. 'Tell ya what, you fuck Donna first, Chris, and I'll watch.' Christine stared at him. 'With what? You got something behind yer back?' she replied. Danny grinned.

'It just so happens, my woman went out shopping this morning.' And slowly he produced the cucumber along with a large tube of KY Jelly.

Within seconds, Danny had pushed Donna on to the bed and spread her legs. With him kissing her breasts and stroking her private parts, Donna became reluctantly aroused. The cocaine was kicking in and the drink had made her relax. Christine inserted the cucumber and began to fuck her with it, all the while rubbing her clit. Danny watched the two women together from the end of the bed as he massaged his balls and penis to keep it hard. Before long, Donna had an orgasm, and Christine took out the cucumber and placed it on the side of the bed.

'My turn now,' she said. She pulled Danny on top of her and arranged herself so that he could enter.

'Watch me, babe,' he ordered Donna. She lay on her side, at eye-level with their hips, watching him thrust in and out of Christine. She felt strangely detached from the spectacle before her, the sight of the man she loved having sex with another woman having lost its ability to shock her. Danny instructed her to speak dirty. She did as she was told, but in a robotic fashion, and began to feel cold and slightly sickened. The first time she had willingly engaged in a threesome, had even enjoyed it, but now it made her feel a cool disgust. The cocaine was not doing a thorough job this time, and she knew she would need more to get her through this ordeal.

Danny had already thought about more gear. Before long it was time for more cocaine, more vodka, and then more sex. Donna slipped into a mist of unknowing, vaguely aware of what was happening to her but without the wherewithal to fight it. The threesome had sex in a variety of positions all night until she was exhausted and sore. Even Christine had collapsed into a deep sleep and Danny took a few more swigs of vodka before he slipped into unconsciousness on the floor of the bedroom.

Donna willed herself to get up and go to the bathroom. As she greeted her reflection in the bathroom mirror the tears rolled freely down her cheeks. Mortified and shaking with humiliation, she grabbed the sink for support. She asked herself over and over again how she had come to live like this. It was never supposed to be this way.

When the tears slowed she opened her eyes and gazed at herself once more. The eyes were red and swollen and her whole face was looking bloated, her complexion sallow and greying. The booze and cocaine had started to take their toll on her. Although still very beautiful, she knew her skin, hair and eyes were dull and lifeless. Having previously been so conscious of what food she ate and what beauty routines she followed, she couldn't believe she had let herself go so badly. She clenched her teeth together. They looked dirty and discoloured, and there were dried white clumps of powder around her nostrils. She turned on the tap, washed her face and brushed her teeth, contemplating her next move.

Grabbing her clothes from the bedroom floor, she tiptoed out into the passage and hastily dressed herself. Picking up the shopping from the morning before, she glanced at the clock in the kitchen. It was 10.30 a.m. A whole day and night had vanished. She paused by the bedroom door and looked at Danny's crumpled, naked body on the floor. Her heart still lurched when she looked at him, but there was disappointment there as well. Donna needed to get some air.

She opened the door and went out on to the balcony, gulping in deep lungfuls as if she could swallow it like water. She could still smell the cocaine powder up her nose and the strong aroma of stale alcohol was seeping out of her pores. She felt poisoned by substances and the memory of Danny and Christine fucking each other ecstatically. Having willingly participated in all they had asked her to do she felt she had no right to feel violated or like a victim, but she felt tainted nonetheless. The drugs and the drink had made her give herself to both of them, whenever and in whichever capacity they'd asked. Now all she could feel was a deep sense of shame. She turned from the balcony back into the flat and, grabbing her coat and keys, was seized by a need to get away from the scene of the crime. Briefly, she paused. Danny would go mad if she left without telling him where she was going. He always liked her around when he was coming down from the high of drugs, but today even her fear of him could not persuade her to stay. Shutting the door behind her quietly, she made her way down the stairs and into the street below. She began to walk, not knowing where she was going or why.

Donna wandered the streets for hours, looking at all the ordinary people getting on with their lives, doing ordinary things. It made her feel all the more ashamed of what she'd done and the direction her life was taking. She thought of her mum, herding all those young kids around every day, trying to teach them how to read and write and giving them a window on the world. What did Donna do for anybody these days? Wouldn't it be nice just to do normal things, like go to work and have friends and maybe a day out on Sundays? To achieve this would mean sacrificing the thing she loved more than anything else in the world, though, and she knew she could not let Danny go.

As she sat on the bench in the grounds of the local church, she heard the clock strike six. It was as if someone had suddenly woken her up from a deep sleep. She had no idea how she had got to the church, why she was sitting on the bench or how long she'd been there. All she knew was that she had to get back. Danny would be up by now, would have discovered her absence, and she would be in deep trouble. Her mind searching frantically for suitable alibis to account for her absence, she wrapped her coat tightly around her and turned back for the flat.

She reached it in a state of high alert, still searching for the right excuse. She opened the door to silence within and tentatively walked towards the bedroom, whispering Danny's name. She peered around the door and was surprised to find it empty. The room was in a terrible mess from the night before and still reeked of the pungent odour of stale bodies and booze. Without thinking, Donna began to tear the sheets off the bed and throw open the windows to let in the cold January night air. Bundling up the filthy stained sheets in her arms, she knelt down to pick up Tigger and Pookie and placed them in the centre of the bed before turning off the light and leaving the room.

Making her way to the kitchen, she paused as she passed the living room. There on the table was a massive bouquet of white roses, her favourite flowers, with a card attached. Before she opened it she already knew what it would say: 'Sorry, Danny XX'. Donna held the card to her chest and went back into the bedroom where she placed it in the bottom drawer of her unit with the many others she had kept. She knew that Danny truly was sorry. It was just that once he got the gear in him he became a changed man and no longer accountable for his actions.

Smiling to herself, she went into the kitchen and started the washing up and cleaning up. She had to consign last night to history. All that mattered was that Danny still loved her. He'd sent her flowers, hadn't he?

Chapter Eleven

Danny arrived home later that evening to find a spotless flat and all traces of debauchery removed. Donna looked tired but was clean, fresh and smelt gorgeous with her freshly shampooed hair falling in curls around her fine-boned face. She stood by the cooker, stirring a Bolognese sauce, his favourite. 'I missed ya when I woke up, where were ya?' he asked. He sounded more inquisitive than angry and Donna found the lies rolled easily off her tongue.

'We needed fresh groceries so I went to the shops, that's all.' Danny nodded his head, not really interested. Donna wasn't sure what time he'd got up or what time Christine had left, and didn't like to ask. He hadn't made a fuss about her absence so there was no point provoking him with questions that would only make him angry.

'I'm gonna 'ave a good soak in the bath. That bitch's smell is still on me and I need to get clean and put new clothes on. I got a lot of business to do tonight, so I'll eat dinner and go out a bit later.' Danny headed off to the bathroom. Usually Donna felt disappointed when he went out at night but for the first time that sense of disappointment was replaced by one of relief. She leaned against the work surface and drew in some deep breaths. Maybe this evening, just for a change, she could chill out, phone her parents and Nic, and get a well deserved early night. A small struggle went on inside her. She had always wanted Danny there close to her, to be with him wherever he went, but tonight she relished the unaccustomed sensation of freedom. Not so free that she still didn't need his permission, though.

As Danny kissed her goodbye for the evening she asked, 'Do I need to wait up or is it OK to get an early night?'

'You could do with a bit of beauty sleep, Don. You're looking a bit jaded lately. Get an early night, I'll see ya laters.'

Danny smirked like a man with the world at his feet, looking as dapper as ever and smelling fantastic as he took long confident strides to the car, knowing he had hit Donna where it hurt. Hopefully she'd try a bit harder with herself now because the partying was definitely taking its toll. Maybe he'd let up on her for a while. There were plenty of birds more than happy to do what he wanted them to do, and when he did share Donna he wanted to make sure other men were envious that he had the best-looking bird in the area. Knowing that his business associates were desperate to shag his bird was a power position that Danny liked a lot. He thought it all through as he sped along in his car. He'd put Donna through her paces recently, worked her hard sexually, and now he felt the need to ease off her a little, bring her back to championship form. He'd have some more fun with her when she felt refreshed and better.

More importantly, in the short term he needed her input in the business. He was totally overstretched with his lads serving up all over London, and she was bored at home. He could start her off doing a bit of weighing up, then move her on to a bit of dealing from the flat – only the more trustworthy punters, though, he didn't need any idiots turning up on his doorstep drawing attention to the place. This way he'd be sure where she was at all times. He laughed hard to himself as he thought of setting up a timetable for her, with just a few free slots for shopping and sun beds. The sheer control he would have over her gave him a real buzz. For good behaviour, he would let her visit her parents!

The guys were waiting for him as usual at the café. Stevie, usually chipper, was a little sulky. 'What's up with you, Stevie boy?' he asked.

'Nothing really, just saw Christine a little while ago and she said she'd had a real good time at yours the other day.'

Danny's face clouded over with anger. He felt for the knife in his pocket, then held his hand. Stevie was a mate, but Danny wouldn't be questioned by anybody.

'Come 'ere, Stevie, I need to whisper in your shell-like.'

Stevie moved closer and bent down. In a rasping, firm voice, Danny told him, 'That fat slag has no business telling you anything. If I hear another word, I'll do her and you. Now, what I do, and when I do it, is my business. You get it, *mate*?'

Stevie went white. Not easily frightened, he had nonetheless seen enough of Danny's handiwork with a knife to know not to push it

'I'm sorry, Dan, I meant no harm.' He cast nervous glances at the others, looking for support. Trippy looked on impassively. He was away in his head, thinking about Margaret, the girl he had liked for a long time. They had been on a few dates and things were working out well. Could it be love? Snapping back to reality, he rejoined the scene.

'Sit down and let's 'ave no more of it,' said Danny with finality. 'When something's going on that you can be a part of, I'll let you know. Right now, we have business to sort out.'

He explained his new strategy for moving some of the business to the flat and getting Donna weighing up and dealing to a carefully chosen set of customers. 'It'll take a bit of the day-to-day pressure to deliver the small stuff off our shoulders, leaving us free to concentrate on the bigger fish. I've 'ad some enquiries to deal on a big scale with some blokes in Hackney and South of the River.'

He leaned back in his chair and placed his hands behind his head, in a gesture of supreme self-satisfaction. Smiling widely, he said, 'Word's spreading that our shit is the best, and because of that we've got a chance to make some serious money. We're moving up a league, boys. Johnny, you'll cover Hackney. Stevie, I'm taking you to the new clients over the water for an intro. You'll be their contact. Right, let's 'ave a nice coke joint and get this show on the road.'

Back at the flat, Donna stood looking in the mirror. Danny was right; she was looking a little rough around the edges and the time had come for her to lay off the coke and drink and get herself back to normal. Easier said than done! She could cope with Danny on their more subdued nights but the orgies and threesomes were really showing on her. Her petite body was bruised and battered, her skin mottled, and dark circles were forming under her eyes. She was determined not to let her man down, though, and made a vow to eat as much good food as she could, drink loads of water and start up her skin routine again. She would make a point of buying some vitamins and some decent products for her face and body. Tonight, she would soak in the bath, cleanse her skin thoroughly and eat another portion of spaghetti Bolognese.

Donna put some music on the stereo and started her pampering. By eleven o clock the need to sleep took over and, although she wanted to wait up for Danny, tiredness won. She slipped into the fresh clean sheets with Tigger and Pookie and fell into a deep sleep. She had no idea what time Danny came home but as she woke up the next morning she could feel the heat of his body next to hers. Creeping quietly out of the bed, she left him to sleep. After breakfast she left Danny a note to say she was off for a sun bed and some shopping. In her note she apologised for looking so bad, told him she would only be a couple of hours, and that all he needed for breakfast was in the kitchen.

Donna thoroughly enjoyed her shopping trip and scoured the chemists looking for hair products, facial treatments and vitamins. The sun bed made her feel fantastic and some of the blemishes could hardly be seen. She'd even found a cream that helped her bruises heal quickly. Laden down with bags, she made her way home. It was only eleven-thirty. Thinking that Danny might still be asleep after a late night, she tiptoed into the flat. But when she moved down the passageway she heard the shower running and knew that he was up and about. A small shiver of fear went through her. Danny left the bathroom and looked at her like she'd been a naughty girl.

'Now, what you been up to?' he jested.

'Oh, Dan, I hope you don't mind, I was only gone for a bit. After what you said yesterday, I wanted to get myself looking good for you again. I'll make your breakfast, babe. I've bought loads of good things, and lots of great groceries. I spent ages picking out all the right stuff. You know, the ones with added vitamins.'

'Of course I don't mind, sweetheart, I saw your note. Anyway, none of that healthy stuff for me, I'll 'ave a fry up.'

Donna laughed. 'OK, honey, I'll do it straight away.'

She started to cook Danny's breakfast while he dressed. As usual, he entered the kitchen smelling and looking like an Adonis. She gazed at him and felt a swell of pride and love for her man. She started to twist the engagement ring round her finger, just to remind herself that he *was* her man and nothing was too much trouble for him.

'Sit down, Don, I wanna talk to you.' She obeyed. 'I've been thinking about something for you to do. I know I've been a bit aggressive with you lately. It's because I've got so much work on I can't cope, not even with the lads helping me full-time.' Danny paused, head down, smiling. He knew how to play this girl like a fiddle. 'Baby, I need your help. Will you do a few things for me?' He put down his knife and fork and rubbed his face with his hands, making his face appear blotchy and tired. Donna was out of her chair in an instant, cradling his head in her hands.

'Baby, of course I will. I love the fact that you need me. That's what I'm here for.'

Danny coughed a little.

'I'm sorry, babe, think I've got a bit of a chest infection, too, but I can't turn business away and . . . well, if you could 'elp out, it'd make all the difference.' He explained to Donna what she needed to do. 'It's so simple, babe, and I don't trust anyone else. I'll teach you how to do everything, and I promise it'll make a real difference to us. We'll get to spend more time together, rather than me being out on the street all day.'

Being a drug dealer was not Donna's idea of a job, but

she had no choice. Her man needed her and that was the bottom line.

Donna picked up her duties easily. Within days she was capable of weighing and counting out pills without thinking too hard about it. She learned how to tell the difference between coke and speed and what you could cut each with. With Danny at her shoulder, guiding and teaching her, she turned from novice to expert in a very short time. She loved the sense of togetherness it gave her. This was their business, their foundation for the future, and the rules were pretty simple really. If in doubt, do nothing and wait until Danny got home. Never let any buyer inside the house, serve them their gear with the chain on the door at all times, and never, ever give anything without payment first. There were to be absolutely no exceptions.

Donna was impressed with herself. After a few days off the coke and drink she was bouncing back and feeling good. With a responsibility to get it right, Donna was completely focused. Her beauty treatments and the odd sun bed had really made a difference and she was thrilled when Danny told her how fantastic she looked one evening before he went out to work. She was hoping now that their lives had turned a corner and she was firmly back in a safe relationship with the man she had fallen so deeply in love with.

Danny was on his best behaviour. It was an integral part of his game plan and he played his part to perfection. Cutting down on the coke he snorted had perhaps proved difficult, but with Christine on hand to blow it up his arse, or by smoking it in a joint, he was able to fool Donna that he had really cut down. He certainly wasn't racking the lines out on the table as soon as he got in, like he used to.

They would have the occasional drink on their own and perhaps the odd line, but it was nothing compared to before. Donna's new regime of eating well, taking her vitamins and doing her beauty regimes was paying off, and Danny made sure he remarked on her appearance at every opportunity. He put effort into making her feel special again by having normal one-on-one sex, though he always had to imagine there were other people involved to get himself turned on. All this good behaviour was killing him, though, and he knew he would have to plan something soon or he'd explode.

With immense self-control he allowed things to continue in this vein for several months until he slowly upped the tempo as winter turned to spring. The longer days and general upswing in mood helped in his bid to encourage Donna to have a drink and a few lines when she'd finished work for the day, saying he was on his way and that she should get relaxed for the evening ahead. He wasn't sure how much she was using but she was often pretty high when he came home.

She was certainly on top of the job, though. Everything was meticulously weighed and counted and the accounts always tallied at the end of the week, so Danny had no complaints on that score. He loved to take control when he got in and always had regular new toys and other implements to play with when he took her to bed. As long as he kept whispering endearments about her being the only woman who really turned him on, he found he got his way. In the end, Donna would be the one asking for more.

There was only one night she refused him when he came home to find her glued to the television watching the unfolding drama of the Zeebrugge ferry disaster. There were tears in her eyes and she just kept saying, 'A hundred and eight people dead, Dan, can you imagine?' He placed a protective arm around her and slowly slid his hand down her shoulder and on to her breast. He tried not to get angry when she pushed his hand away, saying, 'I can't, Dan, I'm too upset.'

But the time was drawing near when he knew that she would be in the palm of his hand, willing to go along with anything he asked. He already had a gang of blokes lined up from his dealings South of the River. He'd mentioned to the new crew that if they were interested in some real hard-core shagging he could arrange it, and they were all were straining at the leash. When the subject of orgies came up, the gang leader, Sean, mentioned that his dad, Sid, who was around sixty, was partial to a youngster and that if Danny could arrange it, it certainly wouldn't hurt their business relationship. And so it was that Danny invited Sean and Sid together with two other gangland big-hitters, Bobby and Darren, to be at his flat the following Friday at midnight. Danny also enlisted Jen, the young kid, now fully recovered from the horrors of New Year and back on the gear, together with Christine. She promised to bring along a young black girl she knew called Maddy who liked a nose-up and would be game-on for a night of filth. And so it was all arranged. Four girls, five blokes and a variety of nasty toys seemed like a perfect night's entertainment.

Danny had thought it through carefully. He would let old Sid have first choice and when he wanted to move on, he could have any one of the others. It was important to treat the older generation with respect. He'd make it a surprise, though. No point giving Donna time to think about it.

For Donna, Friday started out like any normal day. She'd been out for her sun bed and gone shopping early as Danny had asked her to stock up on booze. She was incredibly busy all day with punters calling from midday onwards and didn't finish with the last one until ten-thirty, managing only a quick cheese and pickle sarnie all day. She'd had a few lines and two very large drinks to keep her energy up and was just fixing herself a third when she heard familiar footsteps coming down the corridor outside. She could tell it was her Danny but there were other voices and she knew that he wasn't alone and wanted to party tonight. She'd suspected as much when he'd asked her to lay on more booze.

She quickly sniffed up the big line of coke she'd prepared on the kitchen table and resigned herself to what lay ahead. She'd half expected that this night would come round sooner or later. Danny had mentioned another orgy a few times during their lovemaking, and out of her head and in a sexual frenzy she had willingly agreed, only to dismiss it from her mind by the time morning came round.

The front room filled up quickly. There were five men including Danny, the other four she'd never set eyes on before. Christine was there, of course, with Little Jen and a very beautiful black girl Donna had never laid eyes on before, though apparently she'd grown up locally and gone to the same school only three years above Donna. The music went on, the gear was lined up, the drinks were flowing and a dirty video was playing in the background. Sid had no hesitation in grabbing Donna. She was gorgeous.

Donna wrinkled her face at the prospect of the old man and turned it away from his as he started to undress her. With very little by way of a preamble, he mounted her on the sofa and was soon riding her as fast as possible. At first the others just looked on, but before long couples began to peel off and the sex began in earnest. Bobby, a huge, sweating giant of a man, had no partner but soon flipped

Donna over and both he and Sid shagged her together.

It didn't take long before anybody was anybody's and the predictable double and triple shagging unfolded. Sweating bodies entwined with each other and toys were being used, not just on the women. Darren liked to be fucked hard and didn't care whether it was a bloke or a woman with a dildo. Encouraged by this brazen display of homoeroticism the other blokes were soon emboldened enough to try it too. On Darren it didn't look in the least bit effeminate; on the contrary, it made him look hard as nails. The women were allowed short breaks to wash while the video was being changed, only to be used again and again on their return. There was an endless supply of coke and line after line was being taken, either snorted or blown through a tube up vaginas and backsides alike. The booze was being guzzled down at a fast rate, and the first to pass out was the skinny kid. She was dumped in the spare room without anyone even bothering to put a blanket over her, but the orgy continued for nearly two days.

By Sunday lunchtime Donna was wrecked. As she sat perched on the old man's lap, he pinched her nipples hard, just for the fun of it. She was tired now and her head was drooping. As well as the pain she felt from the old man twisting her nipples, she had to contend with a wave of nausea which tore through her body. Pushing herself away from Sid, she managed to get to the bathroom where she spewed up thick white liquid. Her hair was matted with dried semen and the stench from the toilet was almost unbearable. To her utter horror there were long lines of shit down her legs where the rough shagging had made her lose control of her bowels. It was the final humiliation. She locked the door shut, even when Danny demanded that she open it. She fell unconscious to the floor and into a drugged sleep.

*

When Donna came to, she had no idea what time it was or how long she'd been lying there naked on the bathroom floor. The flat had an eerie stillness. As she gingerly opened the door, the first thing to hit her was the smell and then the mess. She must have been asleep for a long time because everyone had gone and all was silent. Still dazed and not feeling at all well, she knew that she had to clean up not just herself but the flat too. By now, she knew she was expected to fulfil her role and that was to have the place spick and span, and to deal with customers.

The clock on the kitchen wall told her that it was eleven in the morning but she had no idea what day it was. She switched on the radio. Listening to the DJ, she realised it was Monday morning. The whole weekend had disappeared in a haze of drugs, drink and sex. In an attempt to get herself together quickly, she rushed into the shower and cleaned every last inch of her body, feeling humiliated, distraught and ashamed. She had never been put through such an ordeal before. This time Danny had gone too far. The filthy old man, with his hands all over her, pushing relentlessly into her vagina, and that massive brute who had taken her from behind . . . it was almost too horrific to recall. Flashes of what had happened came back to Donna in waves. Not even the drugs prevented her from remembering every last detail this time. She grabbed her towelling robe and left the bathroom to go to the kitchen. As usual after brushing her teeth, her thirst needed quenching and she made her way to the kitchen and drank down glass after glass of water.

Suddenly, she heard a noise, more like a groan, coming from the spare room. She went to look. As she opened the door, the child-like woman inside stirred. Jen was covered in blood and shit from the waist down. What the fuck had they done to her? Her small body was covered in bite marks and bruises.

Donna approached and touched her gently. The girl opened her eyes wide, looking like a frightened rabbit. 'It's OK, everyone's gone,' said Donna. 'It's only me here and I'll help you.'

She helped the girl out of the bed and led her to the bathroom.

'Get yourself showered, there's a towel and a spare robe on the back of the door. I'll make you some tea.' The girl looked grateful.

'Could I borrow a toothbrush?' she asked.

Donna pointed to the cabinet.

'Of course you can, the spares are in there.'

Donna made her way into the kitchen which was piled high with dirty glasses thrown hastily in the sink. She put the kettle on and then went through to the sitting room to make a start on the clearing up. Soon Jen was out of the shower. She came into the kitchen and awkwardly offered to help. The events of the weekend were too shameful for them to discuss and neither of them knew what to say to the other so Donna just offered Jen some clean clothes. Once dressed, the girls got busy with tidying and made quick work of the flat. They hadn't eaten for days and by the time they'd finished cleaning were both ravenous.

'Fancy fish and chips?' said Donna.

Jen nodded eagerly. 'Yes, please, I'm starved.'

With the chippy only two minutes away, Donna was back in no time and the two girls fell on their food like a pair of wolves, washing it down with several cups of tea. An uneasy silence fell between them then. Jen started to make her excuses to leave.

'You can stay a while, if you like?' Donna offered, but Jen seemed agitated by this and eager to get away. Donna went to the bedroom and grabbed a jumper. 'Put this on then, it'll keep that chill off you. The sun's shining, but there's a real nip in the air.' Again, Jen looked grateful.

'I don't know what to say.' She was looking down at her feet. 'You've been so great to me. I'm so sorry for everything, but it's the gear, I can't get by without it.'

Without hesitation, Donna went to the drugs cupboard in the bedroom. 'Look, here's a few wraps to get you by. But try and cut it out, it's the only way to climb back up.'

'I ain't going nowhere, Donna,' said Jen, matter-of-factly. 'I'm at the bottom and there's no way up for me. Thanks for the freebie, though, I won't forget it.'

The rest of the day passed in the usual fashion with Donna serving up wraps and tablets. The phone hadn't rung all day, and she was beginning to wonder if everything was all right or whether Danny was punishing her for something she wasn't aware that she'd done, by not calling. The flowers had arrived, as they always did, but they meant little to her now. The vague cravings for a regular life she had been having for months were growing stronger. Afternoon turned to evening and there was still no sign of Danny until the phone rang at nine-thirty.

'Hi, babe, you OK?. Did ya get my flowers?'

Donna thanked him as enthusiastically as she could manage but he wasn't really listening. He sounded as high as a kite. 'Thought I'd get you the big roses you like as you were so fantastic at the weekend. I hope that little slag has left?'

Donna bit her lip and tried to think quickly.

'Um, yeah, she went ages ago. The flat's all cleaned up. What time you heading home?'

'Well, that's why I'm calling, babe. I won't make it back tonight, I'm on a bit of a bender with the South London lads. Fuck me, can they party! I might make it home by tomorrow night with any luck but I got business going on, too, so you'll have to look after things at that end. Treat yourself to a sun bed, 'ave some gear and chill out. I'll see ya soon.'

'Oh, OK. Well, if you have to, take care. I'll be waiting for you. Love you.' She said it automatically, without even stopping to think if it was still true.

'Love you too. Be a good little girl for your Danny, and I'll be back, never worry.'

Donna revelled in her freedom and the relief that she wouldn't have to encounter Danny or his friends for the next twenty-four hours. She was troubled that she'd lied to him, though, by not telling him that she'd given Jen the wraps. She'd always been honest with him before and this was a new departure. OK, she'd tricked him once or twice so that she could meet up with Shaz and Nic, but she had never stolen his property before. She had crossed a line.

She sat at the kitchen table, thinking and thinking until her brain hurt. She had to get away, not just out of the flat, which now felt sordid and wrong and not at all the cosy home she had hoped to build with Danny, but from the man himself. The realisation that her whole life was now drugs, drink and orgies was followed by the strong impulse to escape. She went to the bedroom where she packed a small bag with just a few essential items. All the beautiful clothes and jewellery he'd given her stayed where they were; Donna wanted none of them. She was, however, drawn to the bedside cabinet where all the wraps and pills were kept. Could she make it through without any help at all? She battled with herself for a few minutes but finally stashed a wrap in her sock before grabbing the small bag and heading for the door.

She had no idea where she was going but eventually found herself standing outside Nicola's flat. She didn't even know if her friend would be there as she seemed to spend most of her time at the Savoy these days. However, it seemed the only other option was going back to her parents and having to listen to their endless questions, and that was something Donna couldn't face.

She rang the doorbell and within a few seconds Nicola opened the door, a look of shock on her face. 'Fucking 'ell, mate, you look awful. What's happened?' Donna, though ashamed, wasn't too proud to ask for help.

'Nic, can you put me up for a few days?'

Nicola took her small case, and without asking any questions took her upstairs to the flat.

Chapter Twelve

Danny rolled on for another twenty-four hours with the South London lads before crashing out in one of their safe houses. Remarkably, Christine and Maddy kept going, managing to please five men by doing whatever was asked of them, with the help of a lot of cocaine. Every person present at the orgy had been completely off their face until eventually, one by one, they fell by the wayside and crashed out on the floor, exhausted and desperate for sleep.

Danny had his usual eight hours and woke up fresh as a daisy, with only a slight hangover. Soon the others began to stir, and by mid-morning everyone was awake and sorting themselves out. The girls went off to shower and the men sat around talking over the previous few nights' events, laughing and rolling joints. Danny spoke business with Sean and Sid who placed a major order with him – his biggest yet – and Danny knew it was all down to the good time he had given them. Business was flying. With the major outlet South of the River tied up, he was on a buzz.

'My guys will be over later today with your merchandise, gentlemen. Of course, I'll need my regular retainer but you can pay the balance to them.' Handshakes were exchanged and the deal was done.

*

Flush with success and in a benevolent mood, Danny decided to drop off the two slags in Mile End on his way home. Before long he was back in his own manor, meeting up with his little gang at their usual table in the Turkish café. The guys were given their orders for the drop off in South London and all agreed readily to their new tasks, except for Trippy who hung back, saying very little.

'What's up with you?' Danny asked eventually.

'Nothing. I just wondered how well you really know these guys, Dan? They're pretty heavy, from what I hear, always tooled up, and the amount you're shifting their way . . . well, it's a lot to take on trust, ain't it?'

'You questioning my judgment, Trippy?' Danny stared hard at his best friend and the others coughed nervously and twisted in their seats. Trippy returned the stare and said nothing for a few seconds before he finally replied.

'As long as you're sure.'

'Well, of course I'm sure. I've just spent the last three days getting off my nut with them. They're as sound as a pound.' Danny looked at the others for agreement and they just shrugged in deference to his superior wisdom. None of them had the bottle to query Danny except Trippy, who again said nothing.

'Well?' asked Danny, his face growing red.

'Well, what?' replied Trippy steadily.

'Are you in or are you out?'

Trippy slowly stood up, put his jacket on and methodically checked his pockets for keys, cash and cigarettes before finally saying, 'Yeah, I'm in.' And with that he left. Nobody knew what to say. An awkward silence prevailed until Danny dismissed the incident with a wave of his hand.

'Don't know what's up with him, must have got out the wrong side of bed this morning.'

The others agreed heartily. The exchange with Trippy still nagging at him, Danny decided to turn his attention to business by making a few personal stop offs, just to make sure everyone was happy with the service they were getting. He called Donna but there was no reply. He thought nothing of it and went about his business as usual. She was probably out shopping or lying on a sun bed again. Lazy slag.

Nicola waited till she got back from work the following day before putting the kettle on, sitting her friend down and waiting for an explanation. The night before she'd run her a bath and made up the sofa bed, but didn't push it as Donna had looked totally done in. It was obvious that she'd experienced something awful. Nicola hadn't seen her for nearly three months – an eternity when you considered that they used to meet up every day. All her calls had gone unanswered, and the Stewarts weren't able to enlighten her either as they'd had very little contact with Donna apart from a quick call here and there, but no visits since Christmas.

Now Donna clutched the large mug of tea her friend had given her. 'I really don't know why I came here or why I left home in the first place. I should probably be getting back, Nic.'

Nicola put her arm around her.

'Do you want to talk to me about anything? Whatever you want to say, I'm happy to listen. I'm not going to judge you, Don.'

She twirled the engagement ring around her finger and stared into space. After a long pause, she sighed heavily and said, 'I do love Danny, Nic, and I don't want to be without him, but these last weeks have been hard. I'm not gonna lie to you, things have got pretty heavy.'

Nicola looked closely at her friend.

'You're well on that shit, ain't ya? I can tell, you're all skin and bone and you've dark circles under your eyes and . . .' But Donna interrupted her.

'Look, Nic, I don't need a fucking lecture. And besides, I love the odd line 'ere and there. It's just that Danny is full on it and it's affecting everything. I don't want to give up the coke, I enjoy it, and I love a drink. Anyway, that's not the problem. It's just that I don't really feel loved any more. You know, I feel a bit . . . a bit taken for granted. I packed my bags to teach him a lesson. I need you to put me up, not turn me against him.'

'I haven't mentioned Danny, I just said you were looking like shit.'

'Same difference, Nic.'

Nicola knew then that it would only take the slightest persuasion from Danny to get Donna back. She would return, and things would improve for a little while, and then it would all kick up again. Same old, same old. Nevertheless, she was still Donna's best friend and wanted to be there for her, to catch her when she fell. If this was what Donna needed, then Nicola would be the friend she wanted her to be. She wasn't silly. Like everyone else in the neighbourhood she had heard about the goings on at the flat, with visitors calling all day and wild parties and loud music at night. Even Freddie, usually too out of it to notice the time of day, had made mention of orgies at Danny Lester's flat, and Nicola knew that Donna was in it up to her neck. But she kept quiet and just listened when her friend wanted to talk.

Slowly Donna started to tell her a little of what had been happening. She began by going on about her nights in the West End and all the kind things that Danny did for her. She proudly showed Nicola her ring and described the wonderful hotels they'd visited and her fantastic new fur coat. Nicola listened patiently, waiting for the real story.

Then Donna began to open up about their drug-induced sex, her own semi-conscious willingness to do whatever Danny asked her, and the sense of shame she always felt the next day. If Nicola was shocked she didn't let on, just kept nodding for Donna to continue. Nicola was no angel herself, had had her share of men, but for her sex had to be one-on-one, no exceptions.

Donna continued talking until it was all out and found that she felt better for having told Nicola. She tried to describe that, as well as feeling shame, there were times when she'd really enjoyed what had happened and said that maybe Danny had a point when he went on about sharing love. Nicola made no verbal judgment on her friend, but was quietly appalled at the lifestyle she had slipped into. The Donna that she'd known was gone, to be replaced by this passive zombie, completely under the spell of Danny Lester. A combination of drink and drugs and the sheer force of his character had brainwashed her. Nicola sensed that now was not the time to take action, though, and kept her thoughts to herself.

Donna shuffled in her chair, and looked sheepishly at her friend. 'Listen, Nic, I could do with taking a line, if that's all right with you? I feel a bit edgy and nervous about what to do next and . . . well, d'you mind?' Nic shook her head and asked if she wanted a drink to go with it.

'I've got some voddy and lemonade?'

There was no point in refusing Donna, it would do more harm than good, so Nicola went along with it. The two girls shared some coke and a few drinks, but eventually Nic called a halt to matters as she had to get some work done for college the next day. After making up the sofa bed for Donna again, she put her arms around her friend.

'Try not to stay up too late, babe. Whatever happens, you can stay here for as long as you like. Now get some sleep.'

Danny spent another night away from home after an unexpected invitation from the rubber woman, Christine, and didn't make it back to the flat until the following morning. It had been an opportunity he couldn't refuse as she'd just happened to be in the right place at the right time, and as always was gagging for it.

Christine really was the ultimate shag. She never complained about anything and thoroughly enjoyed being fucked, any way and with anything that came in handy. Danny used her well and made sure she was completely satisfied in every way possible. She had loved the various vibrators, vodka bottles and even the old broom handle. What a great bird she was!

When he reached the block of flats in Crisp Street he was surprised to find a few people waiting outside the door. This wasn't good. It attracted all the wrong type of attention, which he'd been seeking to avoid by setting Donna up at the flat in the first place.

'Fucking silly bitch is probably having a bloody sun bed,' he muttered under his breath.

As he put the key in the lock, he had the strange feeling that all was not well. He got the required gear for the punters waiting outside and, once he'd got shot of them, looked around the flat. Nothing seemed to be out of place and everything was how it should be. Then he noticed the bedroom was intact except for the two stuffed toys that Donna usually kept on the bed. Alarm bells started to ring in his head. He opened the wardrobe to see that all her clothes were still there. All the drugs were in place, nothing else was missing, and everything appeared normal. Then, as he was leaving the bedroom, he noticed the small overnight bag that Donna used for their weekends away was missing.

He went to the phone and called the Stewarts but there was no answer. Of course, they were all at work. Wherever Donna was, she'd better get her arse back pronto as he needed her for the South London boys to whom he'd already promised a re-match. Quite apart from that there was the day-to-day stuff that he relied on her for. She couldn't have gone far because she didn't have any money and he knew that he had enough of a hold over her to get her back, but the point was that she had caused him inconvenience and that really pissed him off.

He called his lads and instructed them to ask around, find out if anyone had seen Donna, but also to get their arses out on the street and continue with their sales for the day. Fortunately there wasn't much in the way of big money to be made that week, but he needed the bitch back by the weekend as a party had been planned over in South London and he knew he couldn't afford to lose face with that crew.

He had already lined up a couple of his lads, plus the usual girls. The South London boys had found two other women, and lovely they were too by the sound of things, but Sid had insisted on having Donna involved and Danny had given his word. Donna had proved to be a big hit with Sid and it was important for Danny's future prospects to keep him on side. Donna might not have the stamina of the other birds, but she was tight-arsed and Sid loved her shape and her vulnerability during sex. He loved the way she screamed when they doubled up on her and how eventually she stopped fighting and just moaned and groaned with sheer delight.

*

Within the hour Johnny was on the phone. 'No sweat, Danny, she's with Freddie's slag of a sister. Got her phone number for you, too.'

Danny thanked him and promptly called the number. Donna answered the phone as Nicola had already left for college. She was startled to hear Danny at first but thrilled that he'd taken the trouble to track her down. If he didn't love her, he wouldn't have bothered. She listened with a lurching heart as he told her of his frantic search for her and how he'd been worried sick. Within ten minutes Donna had been promised the earth and was on her way back to the flat at Crisp Street. Her ploy had worked and she was walking on air. He'd learned now not to take her for granted and was sorry for what he'd put her through. It wouldn't happen again. She quickly scribbled Nicola a note, saying that all was well and she would call her soon.

Nervously, she put her key in the front door of the flat. Danny stood waiting for her in the hall, holding a large bouquet of spring flowers including freesias whose scent filled the air.

'Baby, thank God you're back! Why did you leave me? I love you so much. Please, never leave me again.'

Tears rolled down his face and Donna threw herself back into the arms of the man she loved, wondering how she could have been so silly. They lined up some coke, took the phone off the hook and Danny made love to her, tenderly and carefully.

Just to make sure all bets were covered, he pulled another ace out of his sleeve. 'Baby, now that you're back, I promise things will be different. I want us to start a family soon, and I want us to get married. It can't happen right now because I want to make sure we get a nice place first, but it will happen soon, I promise.'

Donna fell into his arms, whispered how much she loved him, and then into a blissful sleep, dreaming of white wedding dresses and bridesmaids. Once Danny was sure that she was asleep, he called Sean over in South London.

'Hi, mate, the delivery is sweet for Saturday, 'ave you got the money?' He smiled at the answer and added, 'By the way, everything's still on for the party at your place. Make sure the gear is flowing and there's plenty of booze. There are quite a few of us this time, it's gonna be the best yet. See ya Saturday.'

Danny replaced the receiver. With his cock rock-hard and ready for more than Donna could give him, he called Christine and arranged to meet her at her seedy flat in Brick Lane.

Donna woke up the next morning to an empty flat. Nestled next to her were Pookie and Tigger, and she smiled as she realised Danny must have placed them at her side, before going out. The sex between them had been lovely. There was no anal, no toys and no surprises, just straightforward intercourse in the most normal and natural way possible. She roused herself and stretched her slim body.

She made her way to the kitchen and by the phone saw the note that Danny had left her: 'Off to do a bit of work. You were fantastic and are the love of my life. Can't wait for marriage and babies. Be back soon and will ring you when I'm on my way.'

Donna clasped the note to her chest and smiled broadly. Her leaving him like that had given him just the shock he needed. Danny had learned his lesson. Her little stay away had obviously made all the difference.

He called her as promised, arriving home late and tired. The two of them went straight to bed. Donna had taken no gear and was tired herself, so they just cuddled up and once again Donna fell into a deep sleep in his arms. Danny, completely fucked by Christine, was knackered but happy and satisfied. He drifted off to dream of filth, lust, and a rip-roaring night on Saturday.

Over breakfast the next morning he told Donna that he had a very important meeting over in South London on Saturday. That it was big business.

'Now, I want you to look your very best, babe, so get that tan topped up and buy something really nice to wear. It's major league stuff from now on, and I want you with me. You're my biggest asset.' He kissed her passionately. 'I'm lost without you, Don. I need your input. You OK with that?'

Of course she was OK with that. At last they were the inseparable team she'd always dreamed they would be. Danny went to work, leaving Donna dreamily washing up the plates, singing along to a Wham! song and dreaming of her wedding day.

Chapter Thirteen

Danny was happy and content. Now the king pin of Poplar, Hackney and a big chunk of South London, all those years of scratching a living on the streets had finally paid off. Being handy with a knife, and quick and unafraid to use it, had gained him the respect he needed. He enjoyed seeing the look of fear on people's faces when he confronted them, and having a bird that every geezer wanted to fuck didn't hurt his reputation either. Donna was his to control and offer out, as and when he pleased.

He could only laugh inwardly at her conviction that marriage and babies were on the cards. He still felt a lot for Donna but, Christ, she could be a dopey prat sometimes! She'd also lost that certain magic for him, especially in the bedroom where she wanted him on top all the time when all he wanted to do was fuck her up the arse. Sometimes she would play ball, but she was too wrapped up in her girlish dreams of romance to be a real player in the sack. But, for the time being, he had to keep her sweet. And in between times there was always the ever-dependable Christine

Donna went about her day, happy as a sandboy, managing to squeeze in a quick sun bed before the first of the day's customers arrived. Coming back from the

Electric Beach she had gone a little dizzy and had to grab the balcony rail outside the flat for support. The girl at the tanning shop had said that could happen sometimes but she hadn't mentioned the nausea that rose up in Donna's throat, which she was barely able to restrain until she got inside the flat. All she brought up was the tea that Danny had made her and she cursed herself for going out and having a sun bed without getting some breakfast inside her first.

She just had time to clean herself up and get some tea and toast inside her before the first customer arrived. It was one of those relentless days when no sooner had she seen out one customer than the next arrived. Danny would be pleased with the takings, and she'd even managed to shut up shop for long enough to nip out for some saveloy and chips around lunchtime. Once she'd been sick, her appetite had returned with a vengeance. She wolfed the lot down, even mopping up the grease on her plate with a large slab of bread and butter. The last customer didn't leave until ten-thirty that evening when Donna finally collapsed on the sofa. She eyed the vodka, instinctively turned away, but in the end decided she deserved one. After all the food she had stuffed her face with today, she could do with a drink to wash it all down. She swigged her drink rapidly and then decided that a couple of lines might liven her up while she waited for Danny to come home.

By one-thirty she was just about to give up waiting and go to bed alone when the phone rang. 'Sorry, babe, been a bit held up with some of the guys in Hackney. Don't wait up. Get some sleep and I'll let myself in quietly.'

He could tell she'd had a few lines and smiled to himself, knowing she wasn't exactly the innocent she sometimes made out. It gave him more ammunition when she started up one of her regular rants about them cutting down on the gear. He knew it didn't really suit Donna as, unlike himself and his mates who bounced back the next day, she just hung about with a face like a slapped arse, feeling miserable and jaded. He'd have to try her on something else. Maybe that would sort her mood out.

The South London boys had recently put him in touch with a man who supplied large quantities of crack, and when he'd sampled a little of the goods Danny couldn't believe the high it gave him. It was the most sexual of all the drugs he'd ever tried. Made him want to fuck all night, in a much more urgent way than coke ever had. He'd been warned that it was highly addictive, but Danny could handle anything. No worries on that score.

Perhaps a combination of crack and ecstasy could be the cocktail that finally got Donna eating out of his hand completely. God knows, he was getting bored with having to play house and be romantic with her. Could be the magic combination that would come up trumps on Saturday when he needed her on top form.

He told Donna that he loved her, replaced the receiver and went back to fucking Christine.

The week passed quickly and the day of the party, as Danny liked to refer to a mass orgy, came round fast. He was both excited and nervous at the thought of what was to come that night. The South London crew were a heavy posse, they'd made no secret of the fact that they fed their enemies to the fishes, but who could blame them when so much was at stake? Small-time they were not; he was really running with the big guns now and didn't want to let them down.

The pretence with Donna had worked like a dream: he continued to spin her a line, and on the morning of the party sent her off to get some new clothes and enjoy a little spend-up. He'd been concerned that she might not be on form for the party as she'd seemed a bit pale and lifeless that week, though happy enough in herself and continuing with business at home at usual. She took the odd line here and there, when she felt really tired, and made a good attempt to perk up their sex life. She knew sex was important to Danny and that he had his preferences. These last few days she had allowed him to have whatever pleased him.

Danny was happy to take over the clients for the day while Donna was out, and he also had his new gear to play with. He knew he should hold off until the evening came round but couldn't resist putting a few of the small greyish rocks in his pipe and smoking them. He prepared a few strong hash joints laced with crack for him and Donna to smoke before they went out that night, just to make sure she was in the right mood when they arrived. Donna would think it was just a bit of puff but he hoped the buzz she got would make her a sure thing for the night ahead. After a couple of drinks, she should be primed and ready for use immediately.

He smiled to himself, snorted a couple of lines of coke for good measure, and laughed out loud at the thought of how clever and shrewd he was.

When Donna arrived home Danny was happy and in the mood to get out as soon as he could. She'd had a great day, had bought a lovely dress which looked stunning on her, but had experienced a few more dizzy spells. Despite her stopping for a decent lunch, the dizzy spells continued and there were moments when she thought she was going to be sick. In all honesty, she'd have preferred to stay home and watch a bit of telly but she knew how important this occasion was to Danny and wouldn't let him down. If he needed her to be on his arm while he did business, then she would be right by his side, making him as proud as she could.

When Donna stepped out of the bath and was putting her make-up on, Danny poured two large drinks and lit the crack joint for her. Donna was happy to have a drink and a mild smoke. The taste and the smell of the joint seemed different but she thought little of it until she became possessed by a feeling of incredible strength and invincibility. This high was like nothing she'd ever felt before, and apart from a brief moment when she thought she might be sick, she'd never felt so horny or ready to party!

The house South of the River was a large, detached, white-painted, double-fronted property behind heavy iron railings bordering Wandsworth Common. Two large bay windows were covered with thick curtains and nothing of the inside of the house could be seen from the road. Danny held Donna's arm tightly as he led her to the front door, a gesture she mistook for nerves on his part. She had smoked another joint and taken quite a bit of coke on their journey over the water. Danny could see a real difference in her attitude. Donna had talked non-stop in the car, and as they walked to the front door she was giggling and struggling to balance on her high heels.

After they'd rung the brass bell and waited for a few minutes while Danny tapped his foot impatiently, the door was opened by Sid whose face broke into a huge smile when he saw Donna. Her heart sank at the sight of the old man and a flicker of fear ran through her, but she managed to convince herself that if Danny had said it was business, it was business and she wouldn't be expected to perform. Anyway, she was in a great mood and that filthy old man wasn't going to ruin her evening.

They crossed the threshold into a large entrance hall stuffed with antiques and expensive furniture. Like a stately home on a smaller scale, it betrayed no sign of what was going on in the reception rooms on the ground floor. Sid led them into the drawing room where it immediately became obvious the party had already started.

Naked bodies were entwined on overstuffed couches, and couples and threesomes were shagging everywhere. Another room, which looked to Donna like some kind of study, also held naked bodies in various attitudes of sexual play. A woman dressed in a rubber corset was laid across a large oak desk on her stomach, with one man thrusting his penis into her mouth and at the other end a second man riding her arse. A quick headcount revealed about twenty people in total, engaged in various combinations of group sex.

Donna was shocked to see three guys having homosexual sex in another part of the room, and a lone girl taking real punishment from three others, her screams muffled by a hand placed firmly over her mouth. In her mind Donna knew that she ought to be feeling shocked or afraid but instead she just watched with detached interest as she was handed another joint and a large glass of Champagne.

Within minutes, she had been approached by two total strangers who began to peel off her dress. One man crouched beneath her to study her crotch in detail before laying her across a chair and fucking her. The other guy pushed him out of the way and penetrated her roughly, all the while kneading her breasts hard with his big hands.

Sid's face took on a thunderous expression as he observed the scene. He quickly went over, threw the second man off Donna on to the floor and roughly pushed his penis up her arse without bothering to lubricate her first. Donna felt strangely disconnected from what was happening to her and, rather than fight it, welcomed everything that came her way. Video equipment had been set up in each room but no one seemed to mind. Donna was going with the flow, not enjoying herself exactly but, after more crack joints, coke and booze, happy to please anyone in the room who wanted her. At one point she shocked herself by going up to a man she'd never seen before and asking him to please fuck her hard.

Through glazed, drugged eyes she recognised a few familiar faces. Johnny and Stevie along with Danny were giving Christine the ride of her life, to the extent that even she begged them to ease up a little. Jen was being kept busy by two men old enough to be her grandfathers, and the beautiful black girl Maddy was being thrusted with vibrators by two women dressed in dominatrix uniform.

She recognised a few others, including the large brute who had been with old Sid at her flat. He was doing something with an older man which involved inserting small plastic bags into his bottom. Donna felt she was not a participant, just someone on the outside looking in. Whatever it was she had taken, it flew her to a new level and, despite being abused in every way possible, she seemed to be above everyone else. No matter what was done to her physically, she was feeling no pain.

Donna stirred in her own bed at home with little recollection of what had happened to her. She awoke fresh and clean, having obviously been washed before being put to bed. Danny was snoring next to her, it was dark outside, and she had no idea that two days had passed since Saturday when she had been a willing participant in a mass orgy that had been captured on film.

Confusion nipped at the edges of her consciousness. Still sleepy, she cuddled up next to Danny and went back to sleep. The next thing she was aware of was the smell of frying bacon and the sound of Danny whistling happily in the kitchen. She called his name and he appeared in the bedroom, carrying a steaming mug of coffee.

'Blimey, Dan, what day is it?'

'You've been sleeping for Britain,' he replied. 'It's Tuesday morning.'

Donna held her head, confused and a little frightened as she couldn't remember anything. 'I don't remember the last few days, Dan. I must be ill or something. I remember getting to the party, but not much else.'

Danny seemed his normal, cheerful self and casually reassured her that everything had gone well, he'd been really pleased with her. Inside he was euphoric that the crack had worked its charm.

'You did get a little dizzy at the party, babe, and you did have a lie down in one of the bedrooms, but I brought you home the next day and gave you a little wash and put you to bed. Don't you remember anything else?'

Donna tried to remember something, but nothing came to her apart from that feeling of dizziness when she'd first arrived there.

'God, Dan, have I let you down? I felt a bit ill when I was shopping on Saturday, but I was fine when we left here. I must have picked up a bug or something.'

Danny turned away and tried to control his laughter.

'You didn't let me down at all, you were fantastic. The South London boys loved you and business was great.'

Leaning back on her pillow, Donna tried to recall something, anything, but nothing came back to her. Her mind was a complete blank.

'C'mon, babe, don't fret yourself, it was probably just a

bug. Now, how do ya want yer eggs? You haven't eaten for days, you must be starved.'

Donna spent Tuesday in bed recuperating, but it was business as usual the following day and she had to deal with a steady stream of customers. Danny had been out and about a lot, doing big business, and had been getting home late and just crashing out after eating his dinner. She was pleased that things were getting back to normal, but dogged by strange flashbacks that seemed disconnected in time and space, like snatches of dreams that made no sense. They were always about sex and faceless people, images that felt threatening until she woke up and realised that she was safe at home. She was also experiencing strange cravings she didn't understand, like she needed something but didn't know what.

Danny knew he had finally hit on the magic combination that would make Donna a willing participant in anything he could dream up. Coke and booze were good, but add crack and you had the makings of a dream come true. It made her what he needed her to be: willing, able, and with no apparent side effects as yet beyond the almost total loss of memory. He liked the crack himself and had found the high incredible, sexier than he'd ever felt before although he had puked the first lot up when he'd tried it with Christine. Sean had told him that it wasn't unusual to react like that first time around, but after that the buzz just got better and better. Danny still preferred his coke and booze for everyday use, but for special occasions crack was king!

Unlike Donna he hadn't taken so much that he couldn't remember things. He wanted to hang on to every little detail of that party and all that he had experienced. The whole thing was on film and he was eagerly awaiting his personal copy. Once he got it, he would try Donna again on a crack joint at home, just the two of them, see what happened when she watched the film. He got stiff at the mere thought.

Business had boomed after the orgy. The lads in South London were now not only business colleagues but friends, brothers-in-arms with a taste for outrageous sex. Danny wanted to get some of the Hackney lads involved soon; they were a game bunch and would love it. He fancied that a few black cocks would add a new dimension to their orgies, and it would be exciting to see the girls put through their paces by a few of the big lads.

By Friday Donna was still not feeling herself, but business continued as usual and when the doorbell went, just as she was sitting down to her mid-morning coffee, she was surprised to see the shrivelled figure of Little Jen at the door.

Donna knew the girl was no threat and she could break her no-punters-in-the-house-rule and ask her in for coffee.

Inside Jen wasted no time. 'Look, Don, I need a favour. I'm desperate for some gear but I've no money. Can you 'elp me out, just for now? I've had nothing in days, not since that big party at Sid's, so I'm feeling really rough.'

Donna had a memory rush. She recalled seeing Jen there, but not much else. Feeling deeply sorry for the young girl, she went and sorted her out a few packets, to keep her going for a little while. As she gave them to Jen, she made her promise not to let anyone know she'd had a freebie.

Jen lined up almost immediately. Once she'd snorted her coke, she looked instantly better. Along with the change in her appearance, her true personality seemed to return. She chatted busily while sniffing hard and washing away the foul taste of the cocaine with her coffee.

'Well, that was some weekend, wasn't it?' she said eventually.

Donna was a little puzzled. She explained to Jen that she remembered little of it as she'd been a bit poorly and Danny had obviously had to bring her home early. Jen was getting high now, very loose-tongued, and poured out all the events of the mass orgy, in particular Donna's willingness to please.

'Girl, you were fucking anything and anyone in sight. God knows what you'd taken but you made us all look like amateurs. You could easily be a porn queen on that performance.'

Donna felt a cold shiver of sickness run through her as she struggled to recall anything at all of the party, but it was obvious that she'd been heavily drugged and involved in something she was pleased she couldn't remember. Her heart sank as she realised that Danny had used her again: drugged her, lied to her and served her up on a plate. Worst of all, she had fallen for his deceit all over again. After sniffing yet another line and finishing one of her packets in no time at all, Jen continued to chatter, oblivious to Donna's distress.

'Don't worry,' she said as she wiped her nose across her sleeve, 'it's all on film. The whole thing was videoed, close-ups, the lot. Apparently all the guys are getting a copy, so if you do wanna see yourself up there on the small screen, babe, you can.'

Picking up the rest of her freebie packets, she made her excuses. 'You know what, Donna, you should get yourself down the doctor's, you look really peaky!'

When Jen had let herself out, Donna sat frozen to her chair in the kitchen. Burying her face in her arms, she fought back tears and tried to convince herself that Jen was just an unreliable junkie. That she shouldn't believe a word the girl said. She didn't want to believe that Danny would really do all the things Jen had described, but knew deep down that it was probably true. She felt as if her mind was playing tricks on her and that she was going crazy.

She decided to call the doctor's for an appointment, and after that she would have a joint to calm her down.

Donna dragged hard on the joint, feeling the tension leave her body. The joints had been ready made up and she had just helped herself as usual. She didn't want any coke, just a nice bit of puff, but this joint had a peculiar taste, the same taste they'd had on Saturday before the party . . . and suddenly she experienced the same sensation she'd had at the weekend, a state of high arousal, a need so urgent that she wanted Danny to come home now and sort her out.

Time seemed to pass in a daze. Although she was able to function and deal with the odd client who called, by four o'clock she decided to shut up shop, have another joint and get some vodka down her. Danny arrived home around eight o'clock to find Donna off her tits and drunk. Never one to miss an opportunity, he got the toys out of the cupboard and got to work. Leaving those crack joints in the drawer was a stroke of genius. He could kick himself for coming home alone as Donna would have been able to take on more than one person in her current state, but it was a good time to play the video and let her see what a star fuck she really was.

There were two ninety-minute films and throughout the full three hours of footage Donna just giggled and laughed, any trace of the shame she had felt earlier with Little Jen vanished. It was almost as if she was watching someone else. There were even times she asked Danny to rewind the film so that she could get a second look at particularly enjoyable sequences. He loved the reaction he was getting from her and thanked his lucky stars that he had finally found the drug that worked her so well to his advantage. They fucked long into the night before collapsing into each other's arms.

Donna awoke feeling drowsy and with little recollection of anything that had happened the night before. She cuddled up to Danny and put all thoughts of what Jen had told her out of her mind. Proof of her wisdom if it were needed arrived when Danny woke and, reaching for her, pulled her close, saying she was the moon and the stars to him.

The doctor looked at Donna with some concern. He had been the Stewart family's GP for many years and had known her since she was a baby. It took some time to get her to list all her dizzy spells, nausea and episodes of memory loss. He advised her to eat better and drink plenty of water and most definitely cut down on alcohol, for she had obviously been drinking heavily. She had been open with him and confessed to thoroughly enjoying a drink. And when he asked her if she indulged in recreational drugs, she admitted that, yes, occasionally she did. What was the point in lying? Everybody was doing drugs these days and she was young and strong so why shouldn't she enjoy herself?

The doctor was casual and accepting, saying that as an adult she had the right to do what she liked. But, after a brief internal examination, he put it to her that it might not be the best thing for her unborn child. Donna was disbelieving until the nurse came back in with the results of her urine sample and confirmed that Donna was indeed pregnant. The doctor estimated she was about three months into her term but said that exact dates wouldn't be available until after a scan.

Donna was in a daze. She wasn't sure whether to jump for joy or panic about all the poisons she had put into her body recently. Once she'd recovered from the initial shock, she felt pleased. At last things were moving on. She and Danny were going to be parents, and she couldn't wait to tell him. He might be a little shocked to start with but she was certain he'd be cock-a-hoop about the news afterwards. She left the surgery with a broad grin across her face, patting the tiny bump of her tummy. It was all meant to be. This pregnancy explained everything: the dizzy spells, the weird cravings and restlessness, and of course the nausea. Now, with a baby to think about, Donna was positive in her own mind that things had to change, and that the drink, drugs and group sex would have to stop. She knew Danny would continue for a while, but she believed that a new baby would change him. After all, hadn't he said that marriage and babies were what he wanted?

Chapter Fourteen

Danny had aroused the interest of rival dealers in Hackney who'd sent word via Trippy that they wanted a meet. Wary at first, he prevaricated, not wanting to tread on the toes of his new allies South of the River, but Trippy persuaded him at least to go along for a chat. Even if they couldn't do business, they could agree not to queer each other's pitch.

'They're not hostile, Dan, they just want to know if you can supply ecstasy in big enough quantities at the right price. They're going round getting quotes like housewives after a decorator.'

Usually cocksure, Danny was hesitant about this proposal, knowing the two ringleaders, Tyrone and Yellow Man – so-called because of his albino colouring – by reputation as men not to be trifled with. He took Johnny and Stevie with him for back up, fearing some kind of trouble, but the outcome proved surprisingly favourable.

With the advent of ecstasy there was a new spirit abroad, a sense of brotherhood among former rivals – one little pill could turn a Godfather into a Gandhi, it seemed. They informed Danny that he wasn't the cheapest supplier they had spoken to, but he had the benefits of being local and a known quantity. Came highly recommended, in fact.

Danny was puffed up with pride to learn that he had such a reputation among the drugs fraternity. After a few drinks and lines to cement the deal, all concerned were pleased with the new arrangement. Danny had Tower Hamlets, a big chunk of South London, and now Hackney firmly in the bag. In his excitement about the new business partnership, he had suggested a party to celebrate, leaving them in no doubt about the kind of party he favoured.

Yellow Man readily agreed. 'Bring it on, guy.' Tyrone just smiled at the prospect.

Danny was jubilant. He, Stevie and Johnny raced back in the car to their regular hole-up at the café. Danny felt he had just struck gold – Hackney was a real peach to supply, and he liked the two black guys he had just joined forces with. If the stories were true and they really did have huge cocks, then he couldn't wait to see them in action with his girls. He took a lot of coke that day and the idea of a party consumed his thoughts.

Danny was beginning to feel untouchable, like he could walk on water, and thought only of pleasing his new colleagues, fucking everything in sight and enjoying the high life that only big chunks of cash could bring. After years of working the streets, finally he was the main man. He'd made it from the pavement to the penthouse.

Stevie and Johnny were trustworthy companions and always up for after-hours of fun, but Trippy showed little interest in his orgies. No angel, he'd had his share of wild times on the gear but had grown tired of the recovery time involved after every session. As Danny's right-hand man he needed to be on the ball at all times, didn't need to be wigged out and paranoid. Drugs were Trippy's job, not his life. Besides, he was becoming very fond Maggie, the girl he'd been seeing for the last few months, and his outlook was beginning to shift. For the first time in many years, he was seeing family life again. He loved their Sunday roasts when he joined her and her family, and often they would meet up at the local pie and mash shop and Maggie would bring her little sister, Tracey. Trippy would look at the kid, scoffing her pie and mash, thinking she was only two years younger than Little Jen and yet their lives were miles apart. Maggie had brought out another side of him. He liked the warm glow that filled him when he was with her, and the way her family made him welcome. Sure, he liked a few joints, and so did Maggie, but she wasn't a powder and pill girl and he didn't see the point in getting off his face alone.

Quietly, Trippy had reservations about Danny's mood swings brought on by the coke, sharp changes in attitude that never used to be his style. Danny had always seemed the most unaffected of them by the gear, a real animal who could just take it in his stride, but recently Trippy had seen his normally excitable character turn unpredictable and wild. He was keeping a close eye out. In his heart Trippy knew that Danny was venturing into a different drug culture, one of drug rape, lethal cocktails, and, worst of all, crack. He was still faithful to Dan, though, and was waiting as usual for the other guys to arrive back at the café. He had a stash of money and a lot of deliveries to make.

Danny and the others entered, high but really happy. Danny sent Johnny and Stevie on their way to make some urgent drop offs and sat there with Trippy, telling him all the news from the meeting in Hackney.

Trippy stared at the floor the whole time Danny was talking, and when he mentioned yet another orgy shuffled uncomfortably in his chair.

'Oi, mate,' said Danny, 'you've been really odd lately. What's up?' Trippy drew hard on his joint. 'Nothing really, Dan, just bothered that we might be taking on more than we can deal with if we start mixing business with pleasure. Those 'ackney boys ain't to be messed with.'

Danny laughed out loud.

''Ere, see this,' he said, showing Trippy the palm of his hand. 'They're all eating outta it, and with a special party and more to come, they'll stay loyal. No worries, my friend, no worries.'

Trippy didn't know whether now was the right time to speak or not, but he drew breath and said, 'Dan, these parties, mate . . . they really cost a lot of dough, and are they necessary? I mean, occasionally it's OK, but they're becoming something of a regular event. What about your Donna, don't she get a bit pissed off?'

He couldn't help but think of Maggie and how he would do anything to protect what they had together. No amount of drugs or money would ever change that. Danny just looked at his best friend with sheer incomprehension.

'You've gone soft, you 'ave, since you met that bird. And, nah, Donna loves it. Besides, she does what I say . . . like everybody else.' Gripping his friend by the arm, he continued, 'We all know who the boss is around 'ere, don't we, Trippy?' Danny's face now wore a look of menace. 'You got a problem with that, Trip, just let me know.'

Trippy shook his head from side to side.

'No, 'course I ain't, mate. I just want the business to run smooth, ya know? And, yeah, I do really like this new bird so I wanna back off the parties, Dan, keep my head down and the money rolling in.'

Danny's menacing expression turned into a smile. 'Is it love?' he asked his friend. 'You watch out for yerself. If you don't wanna party, that's cool, man. I'm happy for you to carry on as my lieutenant and keep the business ticking over while I'm 'aving my bit of fun. Now, I gotta dash. If you change ya mind about the party, it's cool. It's scheduled for a fortnight Saturday. 'Ere, Trip, bring the bird if ya like!'

Trippy barely managed a smile. He would no more take Maggie to one of Danny's parties than he would his grandmother. No respectable girl did that kind of thing unless she had no choice. He started to think about Donna then and wondered what she really made of it all. Danny was being a fool there. Trippy disliked the way he talked about Donna, the way that he used her. He knew that his friend had taken a sweet, innocent young girl and turned her into a whore; he had an overpowering hold on the kid now that no one could break. But a part of Trippy still felt disloyal to Danny for even thinking these things – at the end of the day, Danny was his mate as well as his income, and he had been there for Trippy all through their difficult teenage years. If this was what Danny wanted out of life, who was he to question it?

As the two men said goodbye they hugged each other uncomfortably then Danny jumped in his car and raced off. Trippy walked away to make his usual drop offs, eager to be finished and spend the evening with Maggie, but he had a bad feeling about the way the business was going. It wasn't good. Not good at all.

Danny arrived home to find Donna cooking happily in the kitchen. She seemed a little different, more excited than usual, fussing over him as he came in the door. He noticed the kitchen table was laid for a special dinner.

'What's all this babe?' he asked her.

'Oh, I just thought we'd have a nice romantic dinner for two, for a change.' Donna beamed at him. He assumed it was just her being a girl and having a go at romance. If it kept her sweet before the party with the Hackney boys then he was happy to go along with it. It didn't do to come between a girl and her silly daydreams. Not if you needed to keep her sweet – you had to give a little, see? The dinner was really good, spring lamb with roast potatoes, and Danny knew Donna had gone to a lot of trouble.

Easter was coming up and she mentioned wanting to go and see her folks and drop off Brandon's egg. He just nodded and smiled. Say yes now, but find some excuse to blow it out when the time rolled around. He did what was expected of him then and told her over and over how much he loved her. As they cuddled up on the sofa after they had cleared everything away, he went and lined up the coke as usual and poured a few drinks.

'Fancy a joint?' he asked.

Donna hesitated. 'To be honest, babe, I don't think I will.'

'You ill or something?' Danny asked in all seriousness.

'No, not ill, but I made a visit to the doctor's this morning and . . . well, I just don't think it's a good idea.' Donna started fidgeting with her hands, spinning the ring around her finger. Danny didn't seem too bothered.

'Well, you've had a little cold or bug or something, but it's not serious. The gear will make things even better, not worse.'

Donna didn't know how to say it, and so she just blurted it out.

'Danny, I'm pregnant.'

Silence hung heavy in the room between them. Danny bent down and snorted two lines of coke before turning round and asking, 'What did you just say?' He looked at her strangely, not quite believing what he'd heard.

'I'm pregnant, babe, isn't it wonderful? I know it's a bit earlier than we planned, but we've always said it's what we want . . . you know, a family, children.'

Donna looked down at her ring again. She sensed rather than saw Danny's approach. The punch he delivered hit her square on the side of her head, sending her off balance and reeling backwards over the side of the sofa. Before she had a chance to sit up straight, she felt herself being hauled up and thrown across the room. 'You fucking stupid bitch! You complete fucking idiot!'

She lay on the floor, disoriented and stunned. The pain in her head was intense. She could feel it starting to swell almost immediately. Danny leaned over and picked her up by her hair, using both hands to tug her to her feet. He pushed her against the wall, smashing the table lamp and sending the drinks and contents of the coffee table across the living-room floor.

'Danny, please . . . Danny!' Donna was screaming. He pressed his fingers and thumb to either side of her mouth and stared, wild-eyed, into her face.

'Now you fucking listen to me, and listen hard. If you know what's good for you, you'll get back down that doctor's and get rid of the fucking bastard you're carrying, 'cause it ain't mine! I've never come inside you, you silly slag, I save that for your fucking arse. One of the others has spunked in you and it's someone else's bastard child you're carrying, not mine. Do I make myself clear?'

Donna, terrified and in pain, nodded her agreement but nothing could keep the lid on Danny's anger. He head-butted her straight in the face, her nose and mouth spurting blood everywhere, and then threw her like a rag doll on to the sofa. 'I'm fucking out of 'ere. And when I come back, I want you sorted.'

As a parting shot he kicked her in the stomach and she felt sickness surge into her throat. She opened her mouth and blood and food spurted out all over the carpet. Through a blur of pain she heard the front door slam.

Pulling herself up to a sitting position she started to sob, heavier and harder than ever before, holding her tummy and rocking backwards and forwards, lost in pain and despair.

Donna managed somehow to clean the flat and herself. She stared in the mirror at her hugely swollen face, cut mouth and black eye. Not knowing what to do next, she found herself drawn to the bedroom cabinet, to get a joint, and then to the front room to pour herself a large drink. She lay on the sofa, a wet flannel against her face, her brain and body aching. Not prepared to suffer the pain, she helped herself to some coke as for some reason the joint hadn't helped. It didn't seem to have the same taste or effect as the others Danny had given her recently. In a drunken, drugged state, Donna fell into a restless sleep on the sofa.

The morning after proved even more uncomfortable. The swelling around her face had turned a nasty black and yellow. Donna stood chewing her nails, staring at the phone and wondering what to do next. She had never felt more alone. What a fool she had been! Of course the child wasn't Danny's, she knew now it couldn't have been for he was right, he had never once come inside her. What an idiot she'd been to allow herself even the thought of babies and marriage. She had to make some clear decisions now, and she needed to call the doctor, but more than that she needed her friend.

Slowly, she picked up the phone and dialled Nicola's number. Her friend wasted no time in jumping into her new second-hand car and racing round to Donna's, to pick her up at the bottom of the stairs to the block of flats. Donna was nervous and agitated as she waited for her friend, fearing Nicola's reaction, but there was no way she could face the next few days alone. She'd made every attempt to cover her face, but it was impossible to conceal the bruises and Nicola could not hide the shock she felt when Donna at last revealed her injuries.

'My God, Donna, what has he done to you?'

Donna kept her eyes down.

'It's my fault, Nic, I pushed him too far. I thought I could make him happy, but I've failed him.'

Nicola sighed heavily. The usual lament of the battered wife, it was so fucking predictable. She was just waiting now for Donna to say how much she loved him. Nicola knew there was nothing she could say that would convince Donna that perhaps the blame did not lie with her and so decided to keep quiet and get her to the doctor's straight away. From the surgery she was immediately referred to the local Casualty department to deal with the uterine bleeding that had already begun. Upon examination, an immediate D&C was arranged. Donna didn't need an abortion; Danny had already done it for her. While she lay on the trolley, waiting to be taken down to the theatre, Nicola stood by her side, holding her hand

'It'll all be over soon, babe, it's for the best.'

Donna looked up at her friend from a bruised and swollen face.

'I know Nic, but I'm never gonna forget, am I?'

Nicola saw a small glimmer of hope there. The drugs were out of Donna's system now and she was clear-headed.

'Can I come to your place when this is all over? I've got a lot of thinking to do,' said Donna.

Nicola squeezed her friend's hand.

'I will be here when you wake up, when you need to go home and whenever you need my help with anything.'

Donna's eyes fluttered shut as the pre-med kicked in.

Nicola wept as they wheeled her friend off down the corridor and eventually out of sight.

Danny sat in the café and rubbed his knuckles which were still bruised from the beating he'd given Donna. He couldn't say anything to anyone, even Trippy. It would shame him and show a lack of control on his part that could easily lose him respect. No one liked a woman beater, but the silly bitch had needed to be taught a lesson. He couldn't believe she'd allowed herself to get pregnant. Not once did it occur to him that he might bear some responsibility. One of his fucking mates had come inside her, but who? He had warned them all, especially in Donna's case, either to come up her jack or in her mouth. Obviously one of them had lost control. He couldn't face seeing her now, not marked and bruised as he had left her and with some fucking bastard kid inside her. It would do her good to know who was boss, who called the shots, and that she couldn't take the piss out of him.

He would send one of the new youngsters round the flat to take over the sales and day-to-day customers, but would make sure the only gear left there was for sale. The rest he would stash somewhere else. Danny knew that by now Donna would have gone to Nicola's, and for the time being she could stay there.

The bush telegraph went into overdrive. Everyone knew Donna had been in hospital and was shacked up with Nicola. No one uttered a word to Danny or asked why she was in hospital, but rumour was rife. Danny kept schtum, concerned only that the bastard had been got rid of and that soon Donna would be back to her old self, reinstated in the flat for work and ready to be fucked senseless by the Hackney boys.

He knew he had a bit of fancy footwork to do to get her back on side, but it wouldn't take much to have her eating out of the palm of his hand once more. He still needed Donna. She was the best-looking bird in the brothel, the best performer once on the gear, and the punters loved to make her scream and then eventually give her a slap and make her moan with pleasure. Everyone rated Donna. Christine was good but never screamed, just took it all. Little Jen was OK, but a bit boyish to look at, and Maddy was robotic and predictable. But Donna was the real star, and she belonged to him.

After a few days he called Nicola's. Donna fell silent when she heard his voice.

'Did you get my flowers, babe? Look, I'm sorry. I was off my head and mad with jealousy. I didn't mean to hurt you. Don, please come home.'

Donna had waited for this call and had steeled herself to stay strong in the face of a charm offensive. But still the sound of his voice left her speechless and her heart flipped over. Despite everything he'd done, she missed him. More worryingly, she also missed the drugs and drink. She wasn't going to cave in straight away, though.

'I can't, Dan, I'm still not well and I don't want the life you offer me any more.'

There, she had said it. Even though her heart was racing, she continued, 'I can't be the girl you want, Dan. I'm just too fucked up at the moment and I need you to leave me alone.'

She could almost feel his anger at the other end of the line, but his voice was quiet and trembling with apparent remorse.

'You can't leave me, babe. I've been off the gear, and I'm trying to do the right thing. I've been haunted by what I did. You've just got to give me another chance. I can't face life without you because you *are* my life. I've been so lost. At least see me, you'll know then that everything's changed. Please, Don?'

Donna listened to his promises and wanted more than anything to believe him. And how could she know whether or not he'd changed if she didn't go back? She was listening but Danny knew he needed to pull something a bit more persuasive out of the bag.

'Donna, I swear, I'll do something to myself if you don't come back, I mean it. I feel so lost and empty without you that I don't want to carry on.'

She felt panic rise inside her; she had never heard him talk this way before. Hesitantly, she whispered, 'OK, I'll see you, but that's all at the moment. I'll pop round the flat tonight. But I'm not staying, Danny, I mean it.'

At the other end of the line, a huge smile appeared on Danny's face.

'OK, babe, whatever you say. About half-seven all right?'

Donna agreed and hung up.

Chapter Fifteen

Donna arrived home to an immaculate flat with enough flowers in it to stock a florist's. The kitchen table was set for dinner, with candles burning and Champagne chilling in the ice bucket. A Welcome Home banner was strung across the kitchen door, and soft romantic music filled the air: Sade singing 'Your Love is King'.

Danny pulled Donna to him, kissing her face tenderly and holding on to her as if his life depended on it. 'I'm so sorry, Don,' he whispered. He smelt beautiful and Donna felt herself kissing him back and cuddling him close to her. She pulled away briefly to stare into the eyes of the man she loved and saw real tears there. She could feel the remorse coming off Danny in waves and felt a profound connection with him. It wasn't easy for him to say that simple word 'sorry', she could see that it had cost him. Her own eyes began to fill with tears as he spoke.

'God, Don, I thought I'd lost you there. I was an idiot, babe, I was off my face. It's no excuse, but I'm just so pleased to see my beautiful girl in one piece.'

Still clinging on tight to him she nodded as if to say, It's OK, I understand.

'I didn't mean to hurt you so much, Don, I just lost it. I'd 'ad such a bad day, and when you said you were pregnant I knew it couldn't be mine and it sent me mental.'

By now Donna was shushing him as if he was an upset toddler, and stroking his hair. But he still hadn't finished.

'Look, I know it was all my fault, with the mad parties and all, but I promise, I won't ever let anyone put you in that position again.'

Donna could feel that this experience, however awful at the time, had actually strengthened the bond they shared. Pain had brought them closer and made Danny realise how much he loved her. She interpreted his words as a promise of exclusivity, his guarantee that no other man would ever touch her again, and the overwhelming need to believe him led her straight back into his arms. Let Danny straight back into her heart.

Donna woke up the next morning with a clear head and a sense of profound gratitude to be back home in her own bed where she belonged. Danny was in the kitchen making coffee and toast. From the bedroom she could hear him whistling a happy tune. She wrapped herself in the silk robe that he had presented her with the night before and padded into the kitchen to satisfy her rumbling tummy. For a while they sat together contentedly, munching their toast, talking and laughing, before Danny's voice took on a more serious tone.

'Don, I want you to go on the pill.'

She stared at her coffee mug, trying to reconcile these words with his statements of undying love and desire for them to have children, which he'd definitely said the night before. Reading her thoughts, Danny instantly knew what he had to do to head her off at the pass. 'I've got a surprise for you, babe. Business is going well so I thought about what it would be like to have a house and a garden . . . fit for a family, when we're ready. It's not forever, Don, you going on the pill. I just want everything to be right before we do it.'

She looked up into his face. His eyes were glistening with tears. He smiled lovingly at her before going to the kitchen drawer and pulling out a wad of house details that he'd picked up from local estate agents. 'Look through these and let me know what ya think. Once we're settled with a proper house and a garden, then we can have two or even three little sods running around.' He gave her an imploring smile, willing her to do what he wanted. Donna clutched the house details to her chest and grinned from ear to ear.

'Do you mean it, Dan, really? Our own house, a real home, for you, me and some kids?'

He pulled her up from the chair then and the house details slid to the floor as they held each other in a close embrace.

'Of course I mean it. I love you more than anything. But I also mean it when I say I want to do it right. I don't want any kid of mine growing up in a council flat. So for now, Don, things 'ave to carry on as normal. We need all the money we can get if we're going to buy a house. It'll mean that you and me are gonna have to really pull together, to make it all happen. Now, can I trust you to be a good girl and do as you're told?' he asked, cupping her face in his hands.

Donna, already lost in a tide of thoughts about houses, decorating and babies, wasted no time coming to heel.

'I'll be good, Danny, I really will. I'll get on to the Family Planning and get the pill sorted out today. I'll need to go to Nic's to pick up a few things I've left there, though, is that OK?'

Danny frowned.

'Yeah, but don't be long. I've got a young lad, Tommy,

who's been filling in for you here. We need to keep him on the pay roll for now, babe, so he can cover when you need to go on appointments or for your sun beds. He's a good kid, only young but trustworthy. Don't worry, he won't get in your way.' Donna smiled.

'No problem, babe, that's a really good idea. I get a bit knackered sorting it out all on my own here.'

'Well, of course you do, that's why I've organised a bit of help. You know, take the pressure off a bit.'

Danny smiled again, this time to himself. He'd ordered Donna to be watched at all times. He would know exactly when she went out, where she went and to whom she spoke on the phone. Her every move was now being monitored and all information reported back to him.

Within a fortnight Donna was back on form. She had been to the Family Planning clinic to get the pill and even managed to take a few sun beds. Danny had spent a fortune on expensive eggs for her family at Easter and they'd turned up at the Stewarts' unannounced with their booty. Joyce and Ian had been thrilled to see her, though Joyce noticed the faint residue of bruising across the bridge of her nose. 'What happened to your face?' she asked Donna in the kitchen while Danny chatted to Ian in the front room.

'Oh, that,' said Donna dismissively, 'I was trying to move some furniture around and ended up bashing myself on a doorframe, silly moo.'

'Oh, right,' said her mother. 'Looking after you, is he?'

''Course he is. Treats me like a queen.' Donna plastered a broad smile across her face.

'Glad to hear it.'

Donna and Danny only stayed long enough for a cup of tea. Danny didn't even want to hang around to see Brandon who was on his way back from a mate's house.

As they waved them off from the doorstep Joyce turned to her husband and said, 'I hope I'm wrong, but I think he's been knocking her about.'

As spring turned to summer Donna recovered from the miscarriage. With the help of good food and a lot of expensive beauty treatments, she was beginning to look like her old gorgeous self – a fact that had not escaped the attention of Tommy, Danny's new gofer who worked from the flat. A nice lad, no more than twenty, Donna found him quiet, polite and easy to be around. Occasionally she would feel him staring at her, though, and it made her feel a little uncomfortable. But Danny would never compromise her safety by putting someone in their home who wasn't safe.

In fact, Tommy knew about the orgies and was desperate to be initiated, but Danny was making him wait. The more he wanted it, the better he'd perform. Besides, Danny wanted to keep home life normal before his big party in the middle of August. He had already christened it Summer Madness and was gearing up for a big one.

Danny was by now receiving regular orders from the Hackney boys and, true to their word, they spent bundles. In return, he made sure they got the cream of the gear. If he had learned anything in business it was that it was important to look after your big clients. Tommy was becoming better at cutting the gear for the small-timers, but the big boys got the best and always had Danny sorting them out. It impressed the big dealers. They didn't like to see the monkey, they liked to be dealing with the organ grinder.

Danny made a monumental effort to keep evenings at home low key but couldn't resist getting Donna to have the odd line of coke and occasional crack joint. In order to convince her that he was cutting down, he would do most of his gear before he came home. She was convinced he was truly making a massive effort for her so didn't mind indulging him with the occasional treat. He really did want to make a better future for them.

On the nights she smoked the crack, Danny was able to ease her into different positions, using a variety of methods to get her to take his penis and toys at the same time. Even with the drugs inside her she just couldn't manage it, and he assumed she had tightened considerably during her recovery from the D&C. Rather than force her, Danny would ease her gently round, assuring her that she would be able to please him in this way eventually, just as she had before. As it was just between the two of them, Donna didn't see the harm; she had no idea she was being stretched and groomed for the oncoming party, where she would need to provide a three up, no matter what! Danny had already planned to lace her drinks with as much muscle relaxant as he could give her, shy of her passing out. The Hackney boys swore by it. With that and a couple of crack joints, he knew she and the rest of the girls would put on a good show. Tyrone and Yellow Man had promised to arrive by nine-thirty and said that they were going to bring two women with them who would add a little more colour to the party.

The day of Danny's Summer Madness party arrived: 19 August. No sooner had she pulled on her jeans that morning than a huge bouquet of exquisite white and yellow flowers arrived for Donna. Attached were estate agent's details for a substantial house in Kings Square, a lovely little corner of Tower Hamlets. It was a beautiful detached Georgian house with steep steps leading up to a shiny black door with a brass number plate. Double-fronted, it offered two enormous bay windows at ground level and four more sash windows on the next two storeys. Donna read the details unbelievingly: a fully fitted kitchen, two reception rooms, four large bedrooms and two family bathrooms. It was dreadfully expensive, but she loved it instantly. At the bottom of the page was a message in Danny's familiar writing: 'Plenty of rooms for nurseries! Love you. Dress up tonight for me. Love, Danny.'

Donna clutched the paper to her. He *had* meant what he said.

By eight-thirty that evening, Donna was flying. She had spent the day glued to the telly, watching the unfolding horror of the Hungerford Massacre. Michael Ryan had managed to bring total carnage to the sleepy Berkshire town by killing sixteen people before turning the gun on himself. She barely looked up when Danny said that he had invited a few mates over for a drink, just grunted in agreement. In recent months there had been such evenings when a few of the lads popped round for a beer, but none of the outrageous antics that went on before her miscarriage.

Danny occasionally watched the events unfolding on the TV over her shoulder and made comments along the lines of, 'Just goes to show, life's too short to worry. Party today, babe, for tomorrow may never come.'

She agreed with him completely. She'd been mad to worry the way she did and was now determined just to forget about all the horror in the world and enjoy herself. Life was short, love was precious and we only had today. She knocked back a few cocktails and the drugged drinks entered her blood stream with immediate effect. Danny handed her a toke on a couple of crack joints as she applied her make-up in the bathroom mirror and by the time she'd finished dressing she was ready to rock and roll. When Johnny and Stevie turned up she welcomed them with open arms, but when Christine and Jen appeared five minutes later her heart sank. It could mean only one thing. She'd thought all that shit was behind her now. When the Hackney boys arrived with two other women, one obese and the other drugged out of her mind, Donna knew her fate for the evening was sealed. She was angry with Danny but too out of it to put up a fight. Besides it never did to tackle him in front of his mates. He wouldn't stand for it.

Danny sidled up to Yellow Man. 'Fuck me, mate, how much fat do we have to wade through to get to her arse?' he asked, nodding in the direction of the big girl. Yellow Man just grinned and showed a top set of gold teeth.

'It's no problem, my man. Cynthia 'ere is a true performer. Now let's get this party started.'

He took out a rock of cocaine and began to shave it into long lines on the kitchen table. Danny fixed drinks for his new friends and joined them in a few lines. Within minutes the group of men were laughing and joshing each other about who was going to have who first. Danny felt unaccountably shy in front of these guys and for the first time found himself holding back, looking to them to take his cue.

Yellow Man headed straight for Donna and Danny watched as he stroked her face and kissed her gently for some minutes. Danny wondered what he was playing at, it was beginning to look like a seduction scene and not a party, but the gentleness didn't last long. Danny was pleased to hear Donna yelp as Yellow Man bent her over a chair and pushed his penis up her backside, ferociously muttering, 'You ain't never had a dick like Yellow Man's before, baby!'

He slapped her cheeks as he rode her like a horse, getting faster and faster. Impeded by the height of the chair, he pushed Donna on to all fours in front of a wall, gripped her hips tightly and just pounded at her for an eternity. As he did her head hit the wall, but she was oblivious to it all. She had the sensation that it was happening to somebody else and that she was watching from about four feet above the room. People in various states of undress stood around watching until two other men joined Yellow Man. With the help of lots of lubricating jelly mixed with coke powder which was spread across her genitals and bottom, all three took it in turns to fuck her.

Meanwhile in the bedroom Christine was her usual bendy self. Not only did she want three-ups but a penis down her throat at the same time. With not enough men to go round, the girls began to amuse themselves and Cynthia promptly strapped a huge black vibrator on and started on Little Jen. Danny, who'd been busy watching Donna perform with Yellow Man and now Johnny and Stevie, spotted Cynthia out of the corner of his eye and went to join in with the girls. Seizing his opportunity while Cynthia was busy riding Jen, he decided to spread the cheeks of the huge fat-arsed woman, found her hole and rammed his penis into her. She didn't flinch. It was as if he wasn't even there. He could feel someone behind him and turned to see Monica, the black girl, positioning a vibrator ready to insert up his arse. Danny, shocked at first to find himself on the receiving end, began to surrender to Monica and even cry out for her to do it harder. If a penis wasn't available, then the girls would take the initiative to fuck each other, or, if they could, they would give the men a taste of what it felt like to have their arses fucked. The girls were taking control and the men liked it.

*

Danny scanned the room for Donna but his view was blocked by the back of Yellow Man who was forcing his penis down Little Jen's throat, despite her choking and obvious distress. After several minutes the struggle seemed to bore him and he roughly pushed her, spluttering, to the floor. Danny was fascinated by Yellow Man; he both feared and admired him, watching with complete concentration as he went to join Stevie and Johnny to fuck Donna in a three way yet again. A part of him wanted to shout at them to get off her, but he'd never go up against the likes of Tyrone and Yellow Man. He knew their form and that they'd put people in the ground for less.

The pressure was all a little too much for Donna who had been ridden hard for hours. Urine was now trickling down her legs. Danny panicked that they might express disgust but it seemed to turn the guys on even more. Donna, exhausted by it all, began to drift into a state of unconsciousness which angered the men. They liked noise. They liked a struggle. Even Danny winced as he watched them cast Donna off, pushing her to the floor, before continuing with Christine, Little Jen, Cynthia and Monica. Danny pulled his penis from Cynthia and staggered to his feet to pick Donna up and put her in the bedroom. She was like a rag doll, all floppy and virtually unconscious. He would leave her to sleep, knowing she would be out for a day or two. She had taken some punishment that night. The guys had not been gentle with her at all. Despite all her protests, they had continued to ram her, but she was gone now and the night was still young!

He quickly returned to the willing females. After topping up again with more coke, more crack and more booze, they continued their orgy into day and then another night.

*

Donna came to with the sickening realisation that she had let it happen again. Her recollection was patchy and she couldn't work out what had happened or in what order, but she could remember the faces of the men and her genitals and bottom felt sore. From beneath the covers, the stench of stale semen, blood, piss and shit filled her nostrils. She pulled the bedcovers gingerly away from her to find her lower body soiled and bruised. The waves of shame and remorse she felt were dreadful – how many times did this have to happen? Would she never learn to say no?

She tiptoed out of the bedroom to find the flat empty and looked at the clock which told her it was four-thirty. The sun was shining so it was daytime, but which day? In the bathroom mirror she examined the love bites all around her tits and the top of her inner thighs. Her arms had fingerprints indented into them. As she examined her back view in the mirror, she saw that her bottom was black and blue.

Donna felt tears prick her eyes and her throat close with them. But then she noticed another feeling growing within her. A thin sliver of anger began to expand into something approaching cold fury. She was angry with Danny, but more than that she was angry with herself. Was this what her parents had sweated to raise her for? So that she could be a pawn on Danny's sexual chess board? Donna's anger turned then into determination to get out of the state she was in. She ran herself a bath and went into the front room where, to her amazement, everything in the flat was spotless. She spied the back of someone's head, sitting in an armchair. Pulling her dressing gown tightly around her, she made her way over to the chair where she found Tommy, cutting and slicing.

'Hi, Don, you all right? Dan said you were a bit under the weather and not to disturb ya. I didn't wake ya up, did I?'

'What day is it, Tommy?' Donna stared at the coffee table, laid out with drugs on a production line. Without looking up or even pausing in his chopping, Tommy replied,

'It's a fine sunny Monday afternoon and the start of a good week's business. Been rushed off me feet, I 'ave. You must have been poorly, you've been out like a light. The doorbell hasn't stopped all morning, I don't know how you could have slept through that.'

Finally he looked up at her. 'Blimey, Don, you look rough. Better go back to bed, I'll look after everything.' Tommy's face had real concern on it. Donna, suddenly uncomfortable to be witnessed in the state she was in, walked out of the room, calling back over her shoulder, 'No, it's OK, Tommy, I'm gonna take a bath and then do some washing. I'll be fine, you just crack on.'

By seven-thirty that evening, Donna was bathed, the bedding had been stripped and washed, the windows thrown wide open and the bed remade. She had lain for a long time in the bath, thinking while soaking her wounds in salt water. The details were still hazy but there were definite flashbacks of Yellow Man fucking her as she cried out for him to stop because she was wetting herself. She indulged in a fantasy of holding a knife to his throat and seeing how *he* liked feeling powerless. She felt she wanted to punish them all, hurt and humiliate them and use them as they had used her, but right now she needed to feel clean. She scrubbed herself once more.

Danny came home to find her propped up on the sofa with a blanket over her, watching TV.

'Tommy gone?' were his first words to her. Donna just nodded and carried on watching TV. Danny perched on the edge of the sofa and stroked her legs under the blanket. 'How's my girl? Feeling rested? Left ya to sleep. You were fantastic again on Saturday. The money is pouring in and it's all thanks to you, my lovely girl.' Donna still couldn't look at him. "Now about that house . . . when shall we take a look?'

Donna finally turned her head. She studied the contours of the face she loved, that was so familiar to her, but felt as if she was seeing him for the first time. She was hit with a wave of certainty then that she had been living in a fantasy. She had no doubt that Danny wanted nice things, a house, maybe one day babies, but they certainly were not in the equation yet. All that really mattered to him were drugs, parties and money. Donna saw for the first time what had been staring at her in the face all along. It wasn't love or need that Danny felt for her, it was the thrill of possession and co-dependency.

She had to do some fancy footwork when he asked her again, 'Don, you listening to me or not?'

'Yes, babe. Sorry, I was miles away, I'm so bloody tired. Yes, I'd love to see it. When do you reckon we can?'

Danny made himself a large drink.

'D'you want one?'

Donna hesitated. 'OK, but not too much. I feel a little delicate, especially after the party. I'll 'ave a small line as well, if that's OK?' She was thinking on her feet. She would play the game, the normal game, until she'd had time to work out her next move. Danny looked at her and grinned.

'That's my girl, a real party animal. You right enjoyed yerself, didn't ya?'

Donna forced a smile.

'Yeah, the black blokes were fab, but I still just love it with you, babe.'

Danny looked pleased. He'd been given the best possible answer.

'I'm glad you see things my way, sweetheart. It's so much easier knowing you're behind me every step of the way, enjoying the same things, loving the gear, the drinks, and now the big cocks, eh, babe?'

He started to laugh loudly and Donna laughed with him. She surprised herself by how easy it felt to be fake, how easy it was to laugh and lie, and it suddenly dawned on her that it was easy because everything in her life was shallow, everything no more than a sham, a game, a pretend life. Even deep inside, Donna had played her part perfectly.

'Let's see the house on Saturday, babe. Give you a few days to recover and get a sun bed and that. I want you to look lovely when we go to see it. Don't want no bird of mine shaming me, now do I?'

Donna snorted her coke and took a swig of her drink, grimacing out of his line of vision.

'I'll be ready, Dan, don't worry.'

She was starting to feel like Donna Stewart again.

Chapter Sixteen

When Saturday rolled around and they went to look at the house Donna was really getting into her stride. She was finding it surprisingly easy to say and do the things Danny liked, all the while keeping her plans and thoughts private, playing for time, playing the game. The house on Kings Square really was beautiful and both she and Danny loved it. Despite knowing in her heart that she would never live in the house with Danny, she giggled and laughed as she moved from room to room, admiring the space, the height of the ceilings and décor of the rooms. Danny told the agent, he'd give the place some thought and get back to him. With off road parking and the house set back somc way from the street, it afforded Danny all the privacy he needed for dealing, collecting and delivering. Best of all, it was perfect for the parties he loved to throw! He was a legend now. And so they spoke at perfect cross purposes, she going along with him, saying all the things he wanted to hear, and he saying all the things about their future together he thought she would want to hear.

In the days that followed Donna began to make loose plans in her head. It wasn't easy as Danny had Tommy there every day, checking that she was OK, staying on top of her every movement. A strong instinct told Danny that he still needed to keep an eye on her. On the surface nothing had changed – their nights were still filled with coke, drink and sex – but he'd catch her occasionally staring out of the kitchen window at nothing and it made him feel strangely uneasy. Nothing changed his behaviour, though, and on the nights when the thought of going home to Donna bored him he would either go to Christine's or, if he was really lucky, get himself invited to join in a threesome or foursome, usually arranged by Johnny and Stevie who had found new willing women.

The Hackney boys had wanted a rerun and he made plans with them to go over to their safe house. Tyrone and Yellow Man wanted everything videoed and even mentioned the idea of copying the films to be sold on the street. The South Londoners were always up for something special and, keen to keep up with his new friends and business partners, Danny began to formulate a plan. He'd organise a massive orgy, involving everyone and anyone, a kind of bringing together of the tribes, that would seal his reputation as the main man.

All these ideas put Danny in a generous mood and he decided the time had come to let Tommy have a bit of fun. He arrived home early one evening to find the boy finishing up for the day. He was wiping his scales with disinfectant and kitchen towel, sorting the wraps into bundles of ten for the likes of Freddie to distribute around the pubs and clubs, tidying and placing everything methodically in the shoebox which housed his operation.

Danny offered the lad a drink and a few lines by way of saying thank you for all his hard work and asked Donna to join them. She knew immediately what she was being asked to do. Tommy was young and inexperienced and clearly awkward but Danny told Donna to dance with the lad. He put on Massive Attack's *Blue Lines*, his favourite album, and told Tommy he could kiss Donna and rub her tits.

Danny then told Donna to strip and invited Tommy to watch how to do things properly if he wanted to please a woman. Placing Donna on all fours, he told her to lift her arse high in the air. He used some cushions from the sofa to prop her up. Slowly, he exposed her arsehole by spreading the cheeks of her bottom and then ordering Donna to spread them herself with her own hands. She willingly did what was asked of her. She'd had a few drinks, a crack joint, and knew she could get through this. Tommy was going to prove easy. He wasn't a big lad, and his penis was quite small compared to what she had taken before. Danny started to probe her arsehole with his fingers, two then three, and then a vibrator. He eased her hole wide open with the toy, swirling it around inside her and showing Tommy how to finger her fanny at the same time. Eventually Danny let Tommy fuck Donna's arse.

The boy had never done it before. When Danny suggested a double fuck the lad seemed to be in heaven. With the help of cocaine they managed to keep going for a long time, with Tommy instructed minute by minute on what to do and how to do it. By the end of the session, the boy flopped on the couch, Donna went to clean up, and Danny poured himself a very large drink, smiling broadly.

Alone in the bathroom with only her reflection for company, Donna knew that she had got off lightly on this occasion. She had done exactly what Danny had asked of her and she needed to play the game. It was all about timing, careful planning and keeping herself strong.

In the days that followed the session with Tommy, Donna continued to spend most of her time pleasing Danny and doing nothing out of the ordinary, continuing to chat with Tommy as if nothing had happened. But something *had* happened and she knew it. Tommy's previous interest in her, confined to stolen glances and awkward conversation, had now assumed the added dimension of intimate knowledge. When he looked at her, he would hold her gaze for longer than necessary. His eyes would plead with her and she knew it was only a matter of time before he made a pass at her. Donna knew exactly what she was going to do when that time came. She let him have her again, but this time without Danny present. She let him fuck her as before, giving him untold pleasure with her arse, fanny and mouth, making sure that Tommy stayed firmly under her spell. She made sure he knew that if Danny ever found out he would be a dead lad, but if he wanted the occasional fuck when they were alone, well, what could it hurt?

She had her reasons. Donna knew the lad was a little in love with her and that she finally had someone on her side who was going to come in very useful one day. You couldn't just up and leave a man like Danny; he'd find you. Then there'd be hell to pay.

Work continued as usual, a never-ending succession of punters looking for something to take the edge off their dull lives, Donna serving her ladies while Danny went about his business oblivious to what was happening at home. On the surface nothing had changed but Donna's mind was going a mile a minute. She was already putting a few of her less noticeable plans into action.

When Tommy left for the day, she would set about watering down one of the bottles of vodka, making sure that she used this bottle each time she made herself a drink. Danny preferred the high-proof blue label and cared little if she preferred the inferior brand. She also found the time to shuffle the packets of coke around. Danny kept the pure stuff separate from the cut gear and after a few lines with him she could help herself to the ones she knew she had tampered with. Danny was none the wiser. Small details, like adding lots of ice to her drink and slipping into the kitchen to get a glass of water down her, helped too.

She continued to oblige Danny but with full awareness now. Although what she endured sickened her, there was a sense that she was playing for time and a determination to win through in the end. She would leave when the time was right for her, when she'd had time to siphon off enough cash to keep her going for a while after she'd bolted. It wasn't like she hadn't earned it. And so in her knicker drawer she stashed fifty-pound notes, paying them into a bank account registered at her parents' address, every couple of weeks. With all her experience of cutting and weighing the gear, it was easy to make it stretch and cream off the surplus.

Home life had settled into a predictable pattern. On a good night Danny would be so drunk he would just leave her for more exciting company, but even when she did have to play the sex game at home, she treated it as a means to an end. He couldn't hurt her any more. Summer rolled on into autumn and, as the nights drew in, Donna's plans began to crystallise in her mind. Many was the night she sat home on her own, thinking she should just pack a bag and go then and there, but a strong survival instinct told her to bide her time.

She'd overheard Danny on the phone bragging to Trippy about an upcoming party to end them all, though in front of her he was being cagey about the exact date. Danny, feeling hurt and betrayed by Trippy's refusal to be part of these scenes, would make emotional pleas to win him round.

'Come on, Trip, it's always been the two of us, ain't it? We're brothers, we gotta share stuff.'

Trippy stood firm; he would continue to act as Danny's right-hand man and consiglieri in the business, but work and home were separate these days and he wouldn't budge. He couldn't say so directly to Danny because of the slur it would cast on Donna, but Maggie just wasn't that kind of girl. They tore it up all right when they got together, but it was always just the two of them.

Trippy was finding a peace and contentment with Maggie in his adult life that had eluded him all his childhood. He finally felt like he had a home. Maggie was his equal and worked hard to put money in the bank even though he had enough to care for them both. She wasn't some daft tart who just wanted to get off her face. She was strong and told Trippy exactly what she thought, but never stopped him from doing anything. 'You're your own man, you gotta do what you gotta do. But remember to come home, Trip, only 'cause I miss ya.' She was his golden girl, he loved her to pieces. They'd started talking babies and Trippy looked forward to being able to give all the things to his child that he'd never experienced himself: love, security, maybe even a private education.

Danny's approach to relationships, on the other hand, had not moved on at all. Women were there purely to please him. The only warning Donna would get that she was expected to perform was when her usual bouquet of flowers arrived. She noticed they were always the same flowers these days, yellow and white roses, like he couldn't be bothered to think of anything different. Unlike the old days when she would rip off the cellophane wrapping immediately and spend a long time arranging them, they tended to get dumped in the sink for hours before she finally got a vase out of the cupboard and cut the stems. She spent the day going through her usual routine, knowing that later she would be off God-knows-where to do God-knows-what to who. Her heart felt heavy but she knew she had no alternative but to follow Danny's lead, act like everything was still OK. She thought of the beating he had given her and of the threats he had made, and a shiver ran through her body. His temper was like a hair trigger and becoming steadily worse.

'If you ever leave me, I'll kill you,' he told her one night. It wasn't just a turn of phrase with Danny, he meant it. She could never relax and always had to tread carefully, like an animal that sleeps with one eye open. Thoughts of flight were never far from her mind but for the time being she was the bound property of Danny Lester. She needed to take her time and plan her escape right down to the last detail. She knew that when she eventually got away she would have to go somewhere completely different, perhaps up North or even abroad.

She knew only too well the extent of Danny's reach and contacts and how he used them. Apparently he was branching out further afield. He told her that he was off to Manchester for business in a few weeks.

Donna would feel overwhelmed at times, become disheartened by the seemingly impossible nature of what she was attempting. But on other days she would straighten her shoulders and back, look at herself in the mirror, and find that, for all the damage that had been done to her, she was still a beautiful woman. It was harder to heal the scars in her head, but she was using the memory of all her ordeals to make her strong. If she could survive this, she could survive anything. And no matter what the eventual outcome, anything had to be better than this life she led now.

Not that she didn't have her moments of sadness. She looked back to the time they had first met, the times he had loved her so gently, so sweetly, and so totally. It wasn't so much a question of what had gone wrong as wondering now had it ever been right? Why hadn't she seen the signs earlier? Why was she so blind to what was obvious to everyone else? But her love for Danny had blinded her to the truth. Danny himself was a drug of a kind, a leech that sucked the essence out of her and made her feel that being Danny Lester's girlfriend was enough. She remembered their beautiful lovemaking. The time when she'd felt empty when he was no longer inside her, and how her whole being had ached for his touch and his caress.

But she could no longer feel any desire for him. Her body had been given away as if it was nothing, robbing her of her sense of self. She knew she had to get the old Donna back. Her family, too. She had started to miss all the things that her loving and giving family had provided for her, like a sense of trust and security. She felt deeply ashamed that she hardly saw them, that she always put Danny first and her only contact with them was the odd phone call. She had let them down so many times. Dinners, shopping trips with her mum, and most humiliatingly of all Brandon's football awards, when she got off her face and failed even to show up.

When Donna had gone missing one night after a row with Danny and had stayed with Nicola, Danny had taken Brandon from the school gates to watch a football game. Nobody else was told and Ian and Joyce had reported him missing to the police before the pair of them finally turned up on the doorstep late one evening after a match at West Ham. It was a warning to Donna and she knew it. Danny played the innocent with Joyce, said he thought that Donna had told her it had all been arranged but Joyce had seen through him and taken the incident as a deliberate threat to the family. 'I'll stick a bloody knife through him if he hurts any of my kids!' she'd said to Ian.

Thankfully, Brandon had taken it all in his stride like

most young lads and just raved about the game. But Danny had fired a warning shot over the bows: to her family, keep out of his and Donna's business. And to Donna herself, watch your step. Like a portent, the following day a massive hurricane ripped across the country leaving a trail of destruction in its wake. It was the same day as Nicola's birthday, 16 October, and Donna couldn't get out to meet her or even call her up because the phone lines were down. Trees had collapsed and roofs come off houses. Debris was scattered far and wide. The whole house of cards was tumbling down.

Donna picked her time to take a gamble and trust Tommy to lie on her behalf. She instructed him that he was to say she was at her sun bed sessions or down the Family Planning clinic should anyone ask. She had finally established contact with Nicola from a phone box down the street, requesting that they meet up secretly. They decided on English Martyrs, the Catholic church a ten-minute bus ride from Donna's and close enough to the tanning shop to make that an excuse if she should be spotted. Set back from the high street, it gave them the privacy they needed. Donna waited and watched on a bench in the graveyard for Nicola to arrive. It was now late October, but the sun still cast a warm glow and the leaves were drifting gently from the trees before settling softly on the ground.

Nicola arrived just five minutes late. 'Fucking number nine is always so unreliable, and I didn't want to bring the car 'cos I thought it might be noticed by someone. That fucking gobby brother of mine, tells your Danny and anyone stupid enough to listen to him what I've got . . . where I live and work . . . the trappy soppy git just never shuts up! But I don't think he saw me. It's all that fucking shit he puts up his nose, makes him talk for Britain.

'Anyway, I'm 'ere now, what's the score, mate?' Nicola sat down breathlessly on a bench and reached into her pocket for her cigarettes. Now she was done with her little speech she could relax. Donna smiled at the familiarity of it all and took a deep breath.

'I'm getting out, Nic. I'm going to make a run for it and I'm gonna need all the help I can get. I know what you're thinking, and I know that look on yer face, but hear me out and give me the time to explain. You can say whatever you want to after I'm done.'

Nicola lit her cigarette with one hand squeezed her friend's hand with the other.

'You talk, babe, and I'll listen.'

It took about half an hour and a couple of packets of tissues, but by the time they'd said their tearful goodbyes a plan had begun to crystallise.

The purchase of the new place on Kings Square in the nicest part of Tower Hamlets went through quickly with no problems. The house was vacant possession and Danny paid in cash. It needed very little doing to it besides a good sweep and dust, and now seemed an ideal time to have a house-warming party. 'Might as well have a big bash before you start filling it up with furniture and kids!' Danny had joked to Donna, who just smiled.

With plenty of rooms to spread everyone around, Danny could afford to be generous with the guest list and specially printed invitations went out far and wide. He invested some money in new metal toys and even got hold of some medical clamps from a friend of his at the local hospital, knowing they'd go down well. A visit to a recommended sex shop in Kings Cross had provided him with his most explicit videos yet which would be played on the big screens he planned to have installed in every room. With coke, crack and heroin available for anyone who wanted them, the party couldn't fail to be a winner.

Danny spent days preparing for it, even to the point of neglecting business and getting irritated phone calls from Trippy about deliveries not collected and so forth. He rubbed his hands together with glee every time he thought of his big night. A large order of selected beers, wines and spirits was made. He had his own variant on Pass the Parcel planned. Only, in his version, the person who unwrapped it had to have it used on them in any way possible. He'd loved this idea; it made him laugh every time he thought of it.

Although she dreaded the thought of the party, the timing was in some ways ideal. In the busy lead up, Donna had plenty of opportunities to get out and meet Nicola. Danny was so busy and distracted he barely noticed her movements and only once recently had he come close to rumbling her. Pissed, and stinking of sweat and perfume, he had pinned her against the wall when she came home at eight one evening.

'Where ya been? Trippy saw ya 'anging around near the church, as if you were waiting for someone. Was ya?' he asked her menacingly.

Donna smiled at him as if nothing was wrong. She knew he'd been with another woman or maybe at yet another sex session of the more ambitious kind, but she answered him without hesitation. 'Don't be silly. Who would I be waiting for? Babe, it's Thursday, my sun bed day, and they were running a little late, that's all. So I just sat in the churchyard and read my magazine for twenty minutes.'

She kissed him on the mouth, ignoring the foul taste of old coke that clung to his lips in dry white blotches, and slipped from under the arms that pinned her to the wall.

'Fancy some dinner, babe? Got a lovely piece of steak from the butchers, if you want.'

Danny followed her into the kitchen, thrown by her confidence.

'Nah, I don't want nothing, I'm off out again shortly, got a big party to finish planning. You're gonna love this one, babe. All the old gang will be there plus a few others. Got lots of surprises for you, and some really good films and brilliant new toys . . .'

Danny was totally off his tits and speaking freely in front of Tommy for once. 'Eh, Tommy boy, I nearly forgot – 'ere's your invite. Time to join the big players now, mate. You think Donna's a good fuck, just wait and see what's in store for you then.' Tommy smiled as he accepted the envelope. 'By the way, baby,' Danny told Donna, 'there's an even bigger surprise in store for you at this party, but I'm saving the best 'til last.'

He laughed his way up the hallway and opened the door. 'Be good, you two, and I'll see ya laters, Don.'

After waiting for his footsteps to retreat along the balcony outside the flats, Tommy approached Donna and placed a reassuring arm around shoulders, drawing her close to him. 'Don, leave him, come away with me, I'll take ya away from all this and I promise to look after ya. I love ya, you know that. I'm prepared to go wherever you want.'

As Tommy held her close, Donna closed her eyes and thought what a sweet lad he was, but he would never be able to free her from Danny, she knew that. Tommy kissed her tenderly, took her into his arms and laid her on the bed. He made love to her in the way he wanted. No buggery, no rough stuff, just gentle, sweet lovemaking. He murmured tender words but Donna stared into space, thinking of the time when she wouldn't need him, Danny, or any part of this life.

Chapter Seventeen

No expense had been spared and the house on Kings Square looked amazing. Danny had spent time and money getting everything just so: TVs and video equipment were set up in every room and a central sound system serviced each one, all courtesy of Bang and Olufsen. There were new beds in every room, each covered in expensive linens laid over rubber undersheets. A main bar had been set up in the large drawing room at the front of the house, but each bedroom had its own mini-bar and full drugs cupboard with everything that one of Danny's parties might require: heroin, top-grade smoke, Rizla papers and KY Jelly. Various toys were displayed in the rooms, and discreetly placed cameras had been set up to capture every moment. There were even balloons scattered about the place and a complex system of coloured lights to give the house a club atmosphere. A clothes rail held a variety of dressing up clothes from bunny girls to ape man fancy dress. Nothing had been left out and all tastes had been catered for. There were handcuffs and ropes for bondage, whips and canes for beatings, and strawberries, chocolate and cream for the sweet-toothed guests.

Danny had invited forty people in total – any more and

there would have been more spectators than performers. Keen to satisfy his main clients, he wanted to make sure that everybody got a proper go. The afternoon before the party he wandered around the house, adding last-minute touches to the preparations, finally knowing that anyone would have to go a long way to beat what he had created. He knew he offered the best in entertainment, providing what no one else could – flexible women, willing gays, bisexuals, and brutal men with a taste for hard painful sex that they could inflict on anyone. Danny really was the king pin. He knew that with this menu of delights to offer, life for him would only get better, money could be made very easily, and that there was a queue of punters just waiting for their turn to get some of the action.

He was most pleased with his own attention to detail. Knowing that the Hackney boys, Tyrone and Yellow Man, had a taste for the burgeoning rave scene, he had hired, at great expense, one of the best club DJs on the circuit to play the latest garage and rare grooves. It was these kind of small touches that gave him the most satisfaction. He was pleased by his own thoughtfulness.

When the great occasion rolled around Danny insisted that Donna smoke a joint and take some lines of coke before they left, then quickly hustled her out of the flat so that he could be at the house early to get any last-minute problems ironed out. Donna wasn't so off her face that she couldn't feel fear. As Danny drove them too fast to the house she gripped the side of the passenger door, a sick feeling in her stomach, knowing what lay ahead.

At the traffic lights, she fought a strong impulse to jump out of the car and run as far and as fast as she could, but hesitation robbed her of the opportunity. By the time she thought she might just do it, the lights had turned green and they sped off with a squeal of tyres. It was probably for the best. Danny was in a strange mood. He was edgy and careless and hit the kerb several times, causing the car to swing across the road. Donna just closed her eyes.

When they finally came to a stop she opened them to find herself outside the house in Kings Square, the place he'd ostensibly bought for them to start their lives together as a family. She cringed inwardly at her own stupidity for believing him. It was just another flop house, an expensive one, mind, but just a den. There would be no babies and prams in the hallway for her and Danny. Lost in thought, she lingered in the car until he barked at her to get moving.

'For God's sake, what the fuck's up with you? Get yer boney arse out and into that house right now.' Donna quickly obeyed. She hadn't seen Danny so agitated in a long time. 'This is a big fucking night for me, Don. You perform, don't moan, and you'll be all right. You're my hostess. You do the rounds and refuse no one. Do you understand?'

With a sinking heart Donna nodded obediently and walked up the few steps to the front door, eyes brimming with tears. Ordered to put on the bunny costume, she changed and stood at the door with glasses of laced Champagne, waiting for the first guests.

By the time people began to arrive Danny had seen to it that the films were on, the windows blacked out, and disco lights whirling in all the rooms. Donna recognised a few of his associates. Yellow Man took his Champagne glass in one hand and gently massaged her groin with the other. 'Later, baby, later,' he whispered in her ear. Donna grabbed a glass and downed it in one.

The front door was opening with increasing frequency. The usual people arrived: a smirking Christine; Little Jen, looking desperate; Big Cynthia laughing out loud and Fat

Monica joining in almost immediately. The sound of laughter coming from the main drawing room made Donna feel sick. The men had nearly all gathered by now and, with coke up their noses and heroin injected or smoked, everyone was ready to party.

Danny ordered Donna to put down the tray, smoke some heroin and then drink one of his famous cocktails. A large black man grabbed her arm and led her away into a room where a few other men had gathered and were putting on a full display of anal sex between three gay men and a girl Donna had never seen before. Her instinct was to go over and push off the three men who were pounding the girl, but she knew that to do so would be to risk turning Danny's fury on her. So she just bit back the tears and hoped the drugs would soon take effect. Donna could see one of the men stopping the girl from screaming by covering her mouth with his hands while they relentlessly fucked her from all angles.

Grabbing a large bottle of vodka, Donna swigged a good few mouthfuls and sniffed another line of coke. If she was going to get through this, she knew she would have to hit the drink and drugs harder than ever.

Tonight was different from any scene she had been part of before, on a far bigger scale. She had no idea what would happen to her or who would rape her next. Her dazed eyes took in revolting scenes of abuse and sexual depravity. A woman had her legs up in stirrups as if in readiness for a medical examination. A clamp was being used on her vagina and anus, widening her entrances. The woman screamed but smiled at the same time as all sorts of objects were inserted inside her. Donna stared, horrified, until the black man appeared at her side again and grasped her arm. She was dragged into another room, this one empty, where she was laid on a bed on her tummy and handcuffed. Once he had finished positioning her, he took a long whip and began lashing her backside, harder and harder with every stroke. Donna moved beyond pain to a place where nobody could hurt her any more. When two other men came to join them, she registered neither fear nor surprise, knowing exactly what was coming.

Donna lay where she was on the bed, being turned this way and that like a rag doll, disconnected from what was happening to her, listening to the screams of pain, squeals of delight and whoops of joy coming from all corners of the house. Her senses had shut down from overload. She had frozen under the assault of dazzling lights, blaring TVs, and the coming and going of nameless people, wandering into rooms and joining in with whatever took their fancy. It was horrific. Every time she thought it had to stop, somebody else climbed on to her back, oblivious to the tears which streamed down her face. When she was finally released, she wandered round in a daze until she came across an incongruous gathering. In the large conservatory in the back of the house where the DJ had set up, a solid core of about eight fully clothed people, oblivious to what was going on around them, were just digging the music and smiling at each other.

Danny wandered past and snorted happily, 'Look at that lot, they're right on one.'

Donna had come to recognise the phrase as code for having taken ecstasy, and wished that she too was part of their joyful, almost innocent scene; clothed, dancing, happy, not interested in the scenes of depravity all around.

Occasionally there would be a lull in the proceedings as people took breaks for more drugs and drinks and visits to the bathrooms to clean up before the next round. Donna witnessed one man slapping Danny on the back then and congratulating him on his excellent party. 'Fuck me, mate, anything goes at your raves!'

Danny just smiled as if to say, You're welcome. At one point Donna thought she was going mad. She could hear a dog yapping. It was only as she was led by the hair on to a bed that she saw a man on all fours, a small dog licking his anus.

By two in the morning, Donna was battered, swollen, bruised and completely done in, despite the large quantity of coke she'd taken to keep her strength up. Outside the November sky was a dark navy blue and stars filled the heavens. A huge moon shone down like a spotlight. When she tried to make an exit out of the back door and into the garden, just to take a breather, Danny suddenly appeared. Donna froze with terror. His angry face was scarier than anything she had endured that evening. He was wide-eyed and wild-looking, obviously drugged out of his mind, and in his paranoia had convinced himself that she was trying to escape via the back garden.

Before she had a chance to explain that she was simply stepping out for some air, Danny was on her. Her hands flew up reflexively to cover her head but the punch came too quickly. In her weariness Donna lost her balance and fell down a few steps, catching herself on the low railings to one side as she did so. At first she felt no pain but looked on, bewildered, as blood started running down one side of her naked body. She curled up in a heap at the bottom of the stairs, too tired to move or put up a fight. Danny began to kick her, first in her head and then in her body, as if she were no more than a football. The last thing she heard before slipping into unconsciousness was a man's voice shouting at him to get off.

*

The little room was bare and smelt of antiseptic. Donna blinked her eyes open, aware of other people present around her. Nicola was there, smiling down at her, and a nurse was fussing with a drip. Her friend spoke to her gently. 'It's OK, babe, you're safe, and I'm here.' Donna couldn't focus properly and her vision was cloudy.

'Where am I, Nic, what's happened to me?'

Nicola explained briefly that Donna had been found abandoned on the steps of the Casualty department and taken into hospital as an emergency. She had found this out via a very drugged up Freddie who had heard on the bush telegraph about the orgy the morning after and boasted to his sister that things there had got a little out of hand, resulting in Donna being dumped unceremoniously on the steps of the London Hospital.

Nicola had rushed to her friend's side immediately, not knowing what she would find. The nurses had informed her that Donna had several broken ribs and concussion. They were also concerned about her left eye and the extent of her internal injuries. Very gently, Nic explained that objects had been inserted into her that would need to be removed surgically, but that with time the internal stitching would heal and she would be back to normal.

Donna went into a fit of hysterical sobbing. Not only had she endured a severe beating, but even while she was unconscious things had been done to her inert body. How could Danny allow that to happen to her? Hovering in the doorway waiting to speak to her were two policemen and one WPC. The police had been alerted by the hospital due to the extreme nature of the assault. Even though they were gentle when they spoke to her, Donna was filled with dread nonetheless about possible repercussions for her family if she volunteered any information.

The police allowed Nicola to stay by her friend's side the

whole time, gently holding Donna's hand and stroking her hair. They asked Donna about her whereabouts, what she could recall of the night of the attack and who had been present. She closed her eyes, fighting back tears, and refused to answer any questions. Nicola nearly bit her tongue off with the effort of keeping silent. She would grass Danny Lester up in a heartbeat if it were her. The WPC took Donna by the hand and, sitting by the bed, tried to coax her into answering.

'Donna, you're obviously very frightened and you've been through an awful ordeal, but the people who did this to you need to be punished. It's known fact that you are Danny Lester's fiancée because we have been watching him for some time. We know what he does. If you help us, we can arrest him and his gang, and offer you protection. I don't expect you'll find it easy to speak freely to us, and I know you are in a mess right now, but promise me you will give it some thought? I'm going to leave my details with your friend. When you're feeling better, call me. We can meet anywhere and just talk.'

The WPC smiled at her and watched Donna nod her head slightly. She'd got all she was going to get for one day. The three officers mumbled something quietly to Nicola on their way out. She sat down next to Donna again, saying nothing but holding her hand. The two friends sat like this for hours, Nicola knowing now was not the time to talk and Donna feeling safe with Nic's hand in hers, drifting in and out of sleep.

The house in Kings Square was eerily silent. Naked bodies lay everywhere. Apart from Danny and one other lost soul, wandering about the place, everyone was still sleeping the party off. When the bell rang Danny opened the door, knowing Trippy would be standing there. It was now late in the evening the day after the party.

Trippy entered the house, looking distraught.

'Well, did you get her there?' Danny challenged him.

'You're one crazy fuck, Dan. That kid was in a right old state, and it wasn't easy dumping her like that. She's your woman, for Christ's sake, man, what the fuck did you do to her?'

Danny looked at Trippy, indignant at being questioned like this but knowing his friend deserved an explanation after carrying out Danny's instructions. He had summoned Trippy from his bed at four in the morning to come and collect Donna from the house and take her to hospital. Trippy had tried to insist that he should stay with Donna, but Danny had been adamant that she should just be left outside Casualty so that they could not link her condition back to him.

'She tried to fuck off, ya know, split, and she was so high she could 'ave ended up anywhere, or the cops might 'ave found her or something. Besides, the little bitch wasn't playing ball . . . she just caught me at a bad moment. Needed a lesson. No one walks out on me!'

Trippy was cautious but determined to say his piece.

'Dan, you're my best mate, but she had all sorts of injuries. Word on the street is that the old bill have paid her a visit. Why the fuck did you 'ave to go so far?' He looked into his friend's eyes, searching for some reason he could understand.

'Man, I was sailing. I mean, really pumped up and flying, and there was a guy there who liked the thought of playing about with an unconscious body . . . so I just let him take over. I don't remember, Trip . . . just let it go! Donna won't breathe a word, I know that much, she's too scared. And, besides, there's no link to this place.'

Shrugging it off as just one of those things, he turned his

mind to other matters. 'Now you're 'ere, Trip, do me a favour and get this lot up and off the premises and all the drugs cleaned out. I need to get back to the flat and lay low in case anybody starts looking for me. You can start with young Tommy. I need him to come back with me. I've got customers to deal with!'

With that Danny was out the door with his car keys in his hand. His best friend could only stare after him, in a state of utter disbelief.

A week passed before the doctors would allow Donna to go home. Her face looked different. The blows to her head had ruptured a blood vessel in her left eye, which was still very swollen, and the scars around it would remain permanently, although the doctor had assured her that they would fade with time; under make-up they would be barely visible. She still had strapping around her rib cage and found it difficult to walk with the stitching around her anus and vagina, but she was ready to leave hospital.

Nicola had come to pick her up, and hated the thought of driving her back to the flat but Donna had insisted on it.

'But, Don, why not just bolt now? He doesn't know you're due out today. You could be stashed away somewhere up North with your sister by the time he finds out. Why go back for more of the same?'

'Because I know he'll only find me, and he's such a mad bastard there's no telling what he'll do then. Honestly, Nic, it's safer this way, trust me. Better to keep playing the game and stashing the money away than take a risk by running off and him coming after me.'

Nicola just shrugged, started the engine and pulled away from the kerb.

*

Danny hadn't visited Donna once in hospital. Although she knew he was avoiding the police, she was hurt all the same. Did he not even care enough to find out how she was doing? With no firm plan of escape organised, though, she felt it would be foolish to try anything just now. In her heart and mind she was certain that any love she'd once felt for him had gone, and in a way that would make it easier. It was the clinging on to false hope that had kept her down for so long. Despite her injuries, her will was as strong as iron. She knew it wouldn't be long before a plan would be put into action for her to get away for good.

The only sign that Danny felt anything at all had been the bouquet that had arrived at the hospital, without a note or card. Donna had known it was from him and had told the nurse to take it away and give it to someone else.

She arrived back at the flat to find it overflowing with flowers. How the hell had he known she was coming out today? His reach was truly scary – he must have a source in the hospital. Tommy answered her gentle tap on the door and tried to hide his shock at her appearance. He helped her inside and gently put her to bed. The bedroom too was stuffed with blooms. Donna felt as if she were lying in a funeral home, and in a way she was. Large helium balloons with 'Welcome Home' written on them were everywhere, and by the bedside table was a small box. She opened it to find a pair of diamond stud earrings and a note attached to the ribbon which read, 'Sorry, forgive me, I love you.'

Donna chucked them carelessly in the bedside drawer, feeling indignant that Danny thought she could be bought off so cheaply. She was pleased that she had gone with her instinct and chosen to return to the flat, though; if she hadn't shown he'd have been after her like a shot.

Tommy brought her a hot cup of tea and two lines of coke. 'Drink yer tea, babe, and here's a little something for the pain.' He set up the portable TV from the kitchen in the bedroom and handed her the remote control. Donna drank the tea, snorted the coke. She fell back against the crisp white pillows and covered herself with the sheets, unable to sleep but out of pain, a million thoughts racing through her mind.

Danny finally arrived back at the flat around ten to find Donna watching the news in bed. The fire at Kings Cross tube station was raging out of control and the police had no idea how many were dead. It was a scene of complete carnage. As soon as he had finished with Tommy in the kitchen, he went through to Donna in the bedroom.

As usual words of remorse poured out of him as he stroked her swollen and bruised face, all the while begging for forgiveness. Donna could sense that he didn't really care, that these were all just so many platitudes, but she accepted his excuses and lies, if only because to do so bought her the time she needed to recover and plan her fight back. Where once there'd been overwhelming love for Danny, she now felt only steely contempt for him. She knew better than to argue with him, though, and when she saw the familiar crocodile tears she pulled his head to her bosom and said that everything was OK and it wasn't his fault.

Over his shoulder, she stared at the images unfolding on the TV and wondered about the injustice of it all. All those innocent people losing their lives while Danny was strutting about like the cock of the walk, without a care in the world. Good people who'd never hurt a fly dying so unnecessarily. It just wasn't fair that the likes of Danny got away with what he did. She thought of the WPC and what she'd said in the hospital. Danny continued to spout bullshit about how much he loved her, and Donna just let him ramble on. She hoped he was enjoying himself because it was the last time he'd ever get to pull a stunt like this. Next time there would be no going back, no pretending.

She continued to fix her eyes straight ahead on the TV, resolved that life was too short for her to waste hers with a monster like Danny Lester. Her belief that a new and better life was waiting for her, if only she could find the courage to make her move, gave her the strength to do whatever it took. She'd get the fucking cunt back.

When Danny grew tired of apologising he started to talk enthusiastically about a new business contact up North who went by the name of Fat Larry, and how doing business with him was going to catapult them into a new league. Donna smiled weakly. Like she gave a shit.

Chapter Eighteen

As the weeks passed Donna's health slowly improved, but she had been left with a squint to her left eye and constant discomfort in the pelvic area. On a return visit to the hospital for a check up, the doctors had found that she had venereal disease as well as an infection from shards of a Champagne glass embedded in her vaginal wall. They hinted, too, that unless she showed significant improvement over the next months, a bowel operation may be necessary in the future. Donna's damaged bladder kept her constantly on the loo and this too would require surgical repair unless matters improved significantly.

She desperately wanted her mum to hold her and for her family to help her through her ordeal, but knew there was no way she could tell her parents about what had happened without all hell breaking loose and them insisting she press charges and come home once and for all. In order to win through, she needed to keep her head down and keep on keeping on for just a little while longer. Getting the police involved would simply inflame Danny all the more and he was not a man who took well to goading. You couldn't push Danny Lester and not expect to suffer the consequences.

Knowing full well that he was narrowly escaping a

criminal conviction, and keen to keep Donna out of the NHS hospital that had alerted the police in the first place, Danny stepped in and offered to pay for her to attend a clinic in St John's Wood, even agreeing to let Nicola accompany her there. It was a big concession for him. For a while Donna thought that he was finally beginning to accept her best friend, but Danny was just using Nicola for his own convenience. The sooner he could get Donna fixed up, the quicker he could get her back to servicing his top clients. He wanted Donna to think he had come round to Nicola, and made a point of saying that a woman needed her mates round her at times like these. Donna and Nicola were ecstatic not to have to creep around and meet in secret. Not only was Donna getting speedy medical attention, she got to spend lots of time with her best friend.

By the end of November, she found herself in a luxurious room in a private hospital in St John's Wood where two reconstructive operations to her bladder and bowel were carried out. The surgeons ordered a month's rehabilitation which made Donna euphoric as it meant she would be out of commission for the string of Christmas parties Danny was organising. With most of the action now located at the house on Kings Square, and Danny travelling further and more frequently than ever, Donna had the flat to herself and could rest in peace and quiet.

The house in Kings Square had become a magnet for the drugs world. Danny's reputation as a man who could provide anything and everything spread far and wide, and with the burgeoning rave scene, Kings Square was where it was at for dealers looking to purchase upward of several thousand ecstasy tablets at a time. He had even made contact with a guy called Fat Larry and his hard-core gang in the North. Fat Larry's reputation as the baddest, biggest, filthiest bastard in the region only made him more attractive to Danny. Danny Lester was now a big-hitter and wanted to associate only with other big hitters. He was in the premier league now and determined to keep his place. Whatever he heard was on offer at Larry's, he would match or even top at Kings Square.

Despite numerous calls from neighbours to the police, little attention was paid to the loud noise and constant stream of people who came and went. Sometimes a single beat officer would call at the door and ask the party goers to lower the music, but it seemed the police had no interest in the house until they could get its owner good and proper. They didn't want Danny Lester for disturbing the peace, they wanted to put him away for a long time and that was going to take inside intelligence.

Danny meanwhile thought he had the world at his feet. It didn't bother him that Donna wasn't around for the parties for a while. He could always recruit new girls, grateful ones who would perform for the drugs and money that came from hanging around with Danny and his crew. The orgies went on, Danny fucked whoever he liked, male or female, and continued to have a great time. He felt untouchable. None of his gang of lads would ever dare question him – or so he thought. But Trippy was harbouring deep and secret reservations about the way his old friend conducted his life. For the time being, though, he too held his tongue and bided his time.

Donna and Nicola were in their element. With Danny absent most of the time, Donna healed well, and with Tommy at the flat, to fuss over both of them, they were enjoying a relatively quiet, peaceful time. Having Nicola by her side allowed Donna to gain strength and the conviction that her life would not always be like this. And yet still she played for time. Her little nest egg was building nicely in her knicker drawer and the bank. By the middle of December she had nearly two thousand pounds stashed.

Donna resumed her visits to the sun bed shop and the beauty parlour and had even joined a local gym with Nicola. She had convinced Danny that the gym was a good way for her to get back into shape, and after a steady diet and regular vitamins she soon began to look fit, well, and almost like her old self again. Danny was happy to let the pair of them continue like this as it kept them out of his hair.

He even found himself looking at Nicola in a new light after Freddie told him what a good fuck she was. Freddie didn't mention that this had all been years ago, when Nicola was a little girl and had been viciously abused by her uncle, father and brother. Why would he put his hands up to that? And so Danny was left thinking that if she could fuck her own brother, she could fuck anyone. That might come in handy.

Donna and Nicola had managed to meet up with Shaz a few times and include her in the plans they were making for Donna's escape. A lot of Shaz's family were indirectly involved with the Hackney boys, and her own fondness for a smoke kept her in the loop of the small-time dealers who liked to boast to her about all the goings on. She told the two girls that she had been invited to a select party at Kings Square but had politely declined, knowing damn well that it would be more than a rave.

'Don't ever go there, Shaz, promise me? No matter what they tell you, never go there. Ever.'

Shaz was cuter than Donna gave her credit for. She might look little but she knew all about the house at Kings

Square, and a lot more about Danny and Donna than she let on. Secrets weren't easy to keep in the East End.

With the three girls back in regular contact, a plan was starting to take shape. Donna's sister Jane had been contacted and given a very brief outline. She was horrified by what Donna told her and wanted to involve their parents immediately, but after much persuasion was sworn to secrecy. Jane had known for some time that things weren't right. She had listened to her mum weeping down the phone because Donna never got in touch, and the incident where Danny had picked Brandon up without informing anybody had tipped her off that this guy was one you had to watch. Jane's boyfriend David came up trumps, offering Donna a safe place to stay with his family in Newcastle. He also had friends in Glasgow who would be happy to put her up, no questions asked. Nicola, with a thirst for retribution, was keen to shop Danny to the police once Donna had been whisked away. Donna, more realistic and cautious after her time with him, knew that this would be seen as a wanton act of provocation on her part, and for that Danny would feel honour bound to hunt her down and make her pay. No unnecessary risks, therefore. No police. Not for now.

For all her plans and growing strength, Donna still had her fearful moments. Danny may not have been around so much but he still wanted to know what she'd done, where she'd been and with whom. He knew anyway, as his spies regularly radioed in with Donna's movements, but he liked to check, to see if she lied to him. One rare evening when he was at home he even asked, 'How's that little nigger friend of yours? 'Eard you met up with her recently. Ain't her name Shaz?' It was his way of letting her know that he knew everything. Donna just replied that her friend was fine, and that it had been nice to see her again, but her heart beat wildly in her chest as she answered him. What if he knew what she was really up to?

She knew now after the last beating she had received that he was capable of anything, and one evening in particular scared the living daylights out of her. It was the build up to Christmas. Unlike the previous year, when she'd put up a tree and festooned the house and bought presents for all the family, there was no sense of celebration in the air. She couldn't be bothered and he didn't care.

Danny came home in a bolshie mood, racked out the lines and poured some strong drinks. 'Take it and drink,' he ordered Donna. She obeyed as she knew she must, realising that such an occasion was likely to come and she would have no more absence of leave. Her official one month recuperation period after her op was up and Danny wanted to get her back to work. A sad-faced Tommy was dismissed abruptly.

'Fuck off, Tommy, you're not needed no more tonight.'

Once the door had closed behind him Danny turned to Donna and said, 'Time to find out if the money I spent on those ops were worth it. Now, get undressed and assume my favourite position. Take some more gear – I reckon you're as tight as a drum now, and it may hurt a little. But, trust me, babe, I'll go easy, promise.' Danny had a sickly smile on his face. 'Suck me first, bitch, and let's get that arse and fanny well lubricated. A nice little mixture of KY and coke spread all over for good measure . . . tell me ya love it?'

Donna grimaced as her mouth sucked his hard penis. Drawing back, she told him everything he wanted to hear. With all her strength she endured the assault, biting back tears of disgust. When he had finished, he fell down beside her and pulled her to him.

'See, you done well, girl. A bit more practice, just to get

you up to speed, then we can let Tommy join in, and maybe Stevie and Johnny. You need to get back into the swing of things. Everyone's missed ya, babe.'

He turned over and in minutes was snoring heavily. Donna made her way to the bathroom and stepped straight under the shower. Despite being sore, there were no signs of blood and she breathed a sigh of relief. She had made it through in one piece, but knew it wouldn't be long before she would be expected to return to the old routine. Time was running out.

The next morning Donna felt panicky and tried to call Nic, but there was no answer. She kept herself busy, cleaning, cooking, even sorting out her clothes in the wardrobe in readiness for her departure. Tommy was busy at the door, serving up to punters in the run up to Christmas, and when there was nothing left for Donna to do she dozed on the bed, reading magazines and drifting in and out of sleep, dreaming of escape and freedom. When Tommy knocked gently on her door to tell her that he'd finished and was off home, it was already dark.

'Call for you, too, babe, it's Nic.'

Donna rubbed her eyes and took the phone call in the front room, closing the door to try and keep the conversation as quiet and private as possible. She whispered to her friend everything about the previous evening and both girls agreed that the time was drawing near.

Donna agreed to meet Nic at the gym the following morning, and hung up. She went out into the hall and found Tommy standing there, looking sorry for himself.

'What's up, Tommy? You look like you've lost a fiver and found a pound.'

In a moment, he had her in his arms, kissing her and holding her tight.

'I can't stand the way he treats you . . . I love you so much, it kills me to see it.' Donna pushed him away. He was angry and tense. She had to be clever.

'I wanna kill him and wish I 'ad the fucking guts, but I know I can't and I feel miserable all the time when he's 'ere. He's been good to me, but the way he treats you . . .'

Donna placed her fingers over the boy's lips.

'Listen, I've got feelings for you, too, but we can't because that would put us both in danger. Do you understand, Tommy?'

He nodded sadly and made to turn away, then came back and pulled her close to him, pressing his erection against her leg.

'I want to make love to you, Donna.'

'Our chance will come, Tommy, really it will, but for now we have to keep it under wraps.'

Reluctantly he went to the door. After closing it behind him, Donna breathed a sigh of relief and thought to herself, They're all the fucking same.

Donna was walking on eggshells for the next few days, just waiting for Danny to pounce; what she didn't know was that he had designs, but they weren't on her. All he could think about was Nicola. After all, he'd been good as gold about letting her spend time with Donna after the operation. Now her beautiful blonde hair and striking fuller figure made him want Nic in every way possible. Donna would be his link to getting her well fucked by him, and if all went well, he would have Nicola and Donna together with Johnny and Stevie. The idea became all-consuming, and when he mentioned it to Johnny and Stevie, they loved the thought of getting hold of Nicola, especially as she was an angry type. The thought of her fighting back gave them all a stiffy and made them howl with laughter.

Soon he would tell Donna that Nic could stay overnight when he wasn't there. He'd make-up some cock and bull story, anything just to get her where he wanted her. The more Danny thought of Nicola and the fight she would put up, the more turned on he became. He had often fantasised about the rape and buggery of a woman who didn't want him and now the urges were getting stronger. The thought that Nicola hated him so much just made the eventual conquest of her even more enticing.

In the meantime Danny had a lot of business to sort out. His new association with Fat Larry was proving extremely profitable. Nowadays Danny's problem was not how to earn money, but how to stash it. He'd tried laundering it as best he could, spinning it through several cash purchases in shops which acted as a front for his activities, but there was more than he could cope with. Most of it was simply buried in the grounds around the house on Kings Square, watched over by trusted employees but doing little to earn him even more. Fat Larry had opened up a bigger market than Danny had ever had access to before, and he simply didn't know what to do with the profits.

Only occasionally would he have the vague feeling that he might be getting out of his depth, but a few lines of coke soon dismissed such concerns. Fat Larry, a bald eighteen-stone bruiser, was more hard-core than anyone he'd ever dealt with before and ran his own operation with a rod of iron. There were enough legends about him for Danny to know that enemies and traitors within his circle were dealt with ruthlessly. You were either with him or against him, no exceptions.

He was a huge great bear of a man with a foppish dress

sense, favouring smoking jackets, handmade shirts from Jermyn Street and cravats. Danny had met up with him when Larry had come to London to visit his tailor and order five new suits. Over a long lunch at the Café Royale, Larry encouraged Danny to smarten himself up a bit and use some of that spare cash he had swilling around on some fine gent's tailoring. Over the quails' egg starter he also told Danny about his taste for asphyxiation during sex, and how he had recently shot one of his employees in the head for fucking his ex-wife.

'I can't stand the bloody bitch, but with the amount of maintenance I'm shelling out, no other bugger's getting a sniff at it.'

Danny, having always believed himself to be a tough guy, suddenly felt like the Milky Bar Kid.

Danny had laid on a bit of post-prandial entertainment for Larry at Kings Square and they arrived in a cab around four to find Christine and Jen waiting for them and ready to perform. But even Christine had trouble pleasing him. Larry liked his sexual playthings naive and innocent, virgins ideally, and Danny knew he'd have his work cut out keeping this guy entertained.

On a subsequent visit to London, Larry found the time to attend one of Danny's Christmas parties – a series of raves at the Kings Square house that ran from the week before Christmas right up to New Year. Danny had sent him home with a sample bag of pharmaceutical goodies, after seeing to it that he'd been able to fuck a stream of good-looking young men that had been his preference that night. Men or very young girls, Larry didn't really discriminate, the main requirement was that they had to be tight. If Danny's plan worked, the fat ugly faggot would bring him in another fortune.

*

The New Year rolled around quietly: 1988. Donna feigned sickness and managed to sit at home and watch the telly while Danny raved away in Kings Square. He cared less and less what she did, and didn't seem in the least bothered whether she wanted to sleep with him or not. She was more trouble than she was worth these days, what with having to go easy after the operations, and with so many other willing girls on hand, why waste his time?

His main preoccupation at the start of the New Year was his burgeoning link to the North. When an invitation to go up and see Larry's operation arrived in the middle of January – 'Come and see a proper party, you Southern poofs!' – Danny wasted no time organising a trip for himself, Johnny and Stevie. Larry had suggested that they do business on the Friday afternoon and spend the weekend partying. The timing was perfect. Donna was safely tucked up, with Tommy minding her and Nicola being allowed to stay in the flat, and Danny left several lieutenants and his main man Trippy in charge in London as he raced up the M1 for the long weekend.

His new best friend Larry had organised a real Northern welcome. Danny thought he'd lived large and seen it all, but this was in a league of its own.

He had never laid eyes on so many nubile virgins outside a school playground, all seemingly willing and ready for the taking. He thoroughly enjoyed his first taste of a fourteen year old, desperate as she was to try drugs and be a part of the rave scene that had taken Manchester by storm.

His first night out started innocently enough at the Hacienda, but it was the warehouse party held down by the old canal after hours that really opened Danny's eyes. The said fourteen year old had arrived courtesy of her elder sister, heroin-dependent and an old hand at the orgy scene. Young girls were being passed around like canapés, and the heroin addict was happy to serve up her sister for a baggie. Flesh was traded for substances in a barter system that made Danny's London life look tame.

The rave scene in Manchester was well established. Along with innocent punters, out for a good time, came unscrupulous dealers who expected to be paid in any way they demanded. Danny had a little difficulty with the fourteen year old to start with. He had tried to sweet talk her and, when that didn't work, went for the more direct approach of trying to plunge his fingers inside her by pulling her school knickers to one side. But she started to fight back. This only encouraged Danny more. He didn't know at the time just how young she was, but didn't really care. When the little bitch started to scratch and claw at him, he pinned her to the sofa bed in a back room of the warehouse, determined to teach her a lesson.

He wasted no time in spreading her with gel and then pushing as hard as he could up her anus, unmoved by her screams and obvious distress. He called to Stevie for assistance and, although happily fucking a beautiful black girl at the time, he instantly withdrew and went over to help his mate out. 'Get Johnny to get some crack over 'ere, the little fucker is fighting like a wild cat.'

Johnny made his way over and forced the kid's head up by her hair, clamped her nose shut and got her to inhale as much of the crack as possible. Within minutes, the kid threw up then went limp.

With coke smeared all around her fresh arse and fanny, the three of them soon took control and before long she was out of her mind and being used by them all at the same time. She would come round briefly and try to put up a fight, but the volume of the music meant her screams for the rape and torture to stop went unheard. Danny and the boys, high as kites on coke and ecstasy, just thought it was funny until she went limp and unconscious. Johnny had been forcing his penis deep into her throat at the time. He didn't realise the only reason the kid had stopped screaming was because she'd stopped breathing.

Danny called out to Fat Larry who was sweating profusely, dripping beads of sweat over the naked arse of the young boy he was fucking. He glanced over, raised his hand to signal he would be a couple of minutes. When he'd finished, he walked over to the boys, his fleshy body drenched in sweat and semen. He unceremoniously lifted the girl's head by the hair.

'Well, you played too rough with her, the bitch is finished. Don't worry, it happens.'

Fat Larry called to two giant men, dressed incongruously in dinner suits amongst the bejeaned and T-shirted ravers, to get over to him quick. They showed no emotion as they picked up the girl's limp body. Vomit oozed from her nose and mouth; the rest of her was covered in blood and shit. 'Wrap that up and get rid of it,' Larry ordered them. Danny and the boys moved on, shaken but determined to keep partying. Only later, when they came round from their forty-eight-hour binge, would they pause for thought. In a small terraced house in Salford, a mother was wringing her hands and staring at the clock, waiting for her girls to come home.

Three days later, a man walking his dog discovered a young girl's body dumped on waste ground near a disused industrial estate. Cold and still as she was, the man assumed she was dead. When the police and ambulance arrived on the scene everyone was shocked to discover that the child still had a faint pulse. Rushed to Intensive Care she remained in a coma, the doctors unsure if she would ever regain consciousness. For the time being, the police decided to keep the child's discovery a secret. A few girls and some young lads had turned up dead recently, but no one had seemed to be able to give them any information as to where they had been or how they had ended up dead. The common link was that they had all been sexually abused.

The police were convinced the crimes were drug-related and in some way linked to Larry Sureman, but there was little in the way of evidence to link him to the dead kids. To launch a full-scale investigation would only tip him off, and the last thing they wanted was for him to go on the run. They needed to keep him where they knew they could find him once they got the evidence they needed. Larry was a master criminal who grassed up or killed any of his rivals or henchmen who threatened to endanger his liberty in any way. If people did have dealings with Fat Larry, they knew better than to speak about it. Silenced by fear of the potential repercussions for their families, nobody had as yet been willing to speak to the police. They had little to go on except the one slim chance that the girl would come round, not be brain-damaged, and be able to remember enough to put Fat Larry and his gang away for good.

Chapter Nineteen

With Danny away for the weekend, Donna breathed a deep sigh of relief and felt the weight of fear slide from her shoulders. But even with him away, there were games that had to be played – with Tommy, for example. Donna knew that she had to keep him sweet as he remained her only ally amongst Danny's friends and acquaintances – not that she could rely on him to stand up for her against Danny, but the feelings he had for her could be used to her advantage. Occasionally this meant pretending that these feelings were reciprocated and actually sleeping with him. Despite what he had learned from Danny's special parties, Tommy only really wanted straight face-to-face love-making; the least arduous of all the sexual acts she was required to perform. Besides, Donna had long ago learned how to disengage what was happening to her body from what was going through her mind.

As Tommy fucked her, kissing and caressing her and telling her he loved her, she just went far away in her mind, to a safe place where she felt nothing, wanting only peace and for everything to stop. Donna was so mechanical in her approach to sex now it was as if she was just an automaton, bent on finishing a task. The sooner it was over, the sooner she could get back to what was real.

With Tommy around to take care of business and run around after her like a puppy dog, she was free to spend as much time as she liked with Shaz and Nicola, and tried to act as openly as possible about this so as not to arouse any suspicion. Knowing that Danny's spies were thick on the street, they stuck to the normal activities of sun beds, trips to the beauty parlour or just mooching around the shops. Only when Tommy had finished for the day and packed away his scales would the real conversations take place.

Those few evenings alone in the flat gave the girls their first real taste of freedom for a long time, away from the watchful eyes of Danny's web of acquaintances. They helped themselves to a few wraps from company supplies, fixed drinks, played loud music and danced around the room laughing until their tummies hurt. Donna revelled in the warmth and companionship of her oldest friends after such a long period in the wilderness, a time when she'd foolishly thought she could survive on the dubious love of one man.

She was learning an important lesson: men could be great, but it was your girlfriends who never let you down. Loving Danny to the exclusion of everybody else had put her in the position she was today: beaten, raped, little more than a possession, to be passed from one abuser to the next as Danny decreed.

But she learned something else that rocked her world to its foundations. One night during Danny's absence, when Nicola was tucking Donna up in bed with Pookie before dashing back to her digs at the Savoy, Donna asked her rhetorically, 'How come you're so kind?'

Nicola gave her an answer she definitely wasn't expecting.

'Because I've been there, babe.'

'Been where?'

'Where you are now.' Nicola finally explained why she had been so against Danny from the outset. 'I could just tell, he had that edge about him . . . the same edge my Uncle Sean had.' She went on to describe what her life was really like when she was little, about the sexual torment she had endured at the hands of her dad and Uncle Sean from the ages of five to thirteen. Some days she had been so bruised and upset that she hadn't been able to go to school. Donna suddenly realised the real reason for Nicola's frequent absences and why she'd always had to work hard to make-up lost ground. She was amazed that her friend had kept it quiet for all these years.

'Why didn't you tell me, Nic?' asked Donna tearfully.

Her friend shrugged.

'Because you think it's your fault and that nobody will believe you anyway, don't you? My mum certainly didn't. Used to call me a little liar.'

Donna was dumbstruck, thinking back to their school-days and Nicola's often erratic behaviour, flying off the handle and laying into some other kid at the slightest provocation. A combination of Chinese whispers and character assassination had had her branded the school slag, a victim twice over. The Stewarts, without ever really knowing what was going on, had steadfastly stood by her, though. Like all good people, they believed that children were everybody's responsibility, not just the parents', and that if Nicola chose to spend all her time round their house, then by simple deduction life had to be hard for her at home.

Nicola squeezed Donna's hand. 'Thanks, Don, for sticking by me. And your mum and dad, of course. They're the closest thing to family I'm ever gonna know.'

In some strange transference of emotion, Donna cried then because Nicola couldn't.

'Yeah, but, Nic, you'll have your own babies one day and then you'll be able to put it right. You're going to be a brilliant mum,' she tried to reassure her. Nicola wasn't so sure, describing to her friend exactly what her childhood had been like.

It wasn't easy for Donna to listen to that catalogue of abuse, all those years of suffering as a little girl. Sure, Donna had had a bad time with Danny, but not even two years of it and she was at least an adult. Nicola had been just a scrap of a girl, and it had only stopped when Uncle Sean had been sent to prison on drug-related charges and her father had lost his nerve without his sidekick to goad him on. When Nicola had reached out to her own mother for help, she'd been told to go away and not make-up stories.

Her father and uncle never met with any punishment for their crimes, no retribution for the repeated acts of rape that left a little girl's life in tatters.

Nicola went on to explain calmly that Freddie, emboldened by what he had seen his father and uncle do, used to force himself on his little sister, too. During one incident she recalled she was being raped by Uncle Sean when Freddie had burst into the bedroom. She still could not shake off the memory of him leaning against the wall, watching her uncle thrust deep into her, and how he'd laughed and attempted to take over. At seven years of age Nicola had lost her virginity along with her ability to trust, and had blamed herself, thinking she was a bad girl. She bore the full load of other people's shame on her seven-year-old shoulders, thinking that she must be very bad to be punished in this way. She had grown up over-responsible, worrying about everybody's welfare but her own, and with the kind of finely tuned radar that could instantly spot a bastard like Danny Lester for exactly what he was. Only this time he wasn't getting away with it.

Donna felt nothing but relief at Danny's absence. It was only when the flowers arrived on Monday morning, announcing his imminent return, that the sick, cold sensation of fear came back. She didn't care that he had been with other women or taking drugs, it was the thought of what he had planned for her next that got the adrenaline pumping. Because there was no doubt that Danny would be looking to return the hospitality he had received up North, with dividends, and she would be enlisted to provide it.

Shaz and Nicola popped in on their way to college that morning. Shaz had heard rumours through some of the dealers connected to her family circle that a big rave was being planned at Kings Square in a few weeks' time. It was to be a Valentine's party with a difference. It came as no real surprise to Donna, though Danny hadn't thought fit to mention it to her himself. He knew the only way to get her to play ball these days was by stealth. They had long since passed the point where they could even pretend to be honest with each other, if indeed they ever had.

Nicola too had been forewarned by Danny himself who had hinted that he could show her a good time if she went along.

'Filthy fucker's 'ad me in the frame for weeks now. He only had the bloody cheek to ask me to go!'

'You didn't say anything to me?' Donna was shocked that her best friend had kept this from her.

'What was the point? You know what he's like. I just ignored him. But maybe this is the opportunity we've been looking for.'

Donna was horrified.

'Are you flaming mad or what?'

Nic shushed her. 'No, listen, it's not the gear talking or the drink now, it's first thing in the morning. If we all got ourselves invited and played along, you'd 'ave us there with you to get you out. Think about it, Don. You're not going to get away from Danny unless he's totally flying and busy elsewhere. The last thing he's gonna be expecting is for you to bolt in the middle of a party, not after last time, especially if me and Shaz are there. And he won't dare lay a finger on you there either – his reputation took a right hammering after he put you in hospital. Let's face it, babe, nobody looks up to a wife beater.'

Shaz and Donna looked at her open-mouthed, and then Shaz started to laugh at the audacity of what Nicola was suggesting. To take Donna from right under Danny's nose and make him look a complete cock in front of everybody.

'I don't know, it sounds too risky,' said Donna. 'Not after last time . . . and the number of those bloody cocktails he makes me down before we leave the house, I'd be too out of it to do it properly.'

'Yeah, but, babe, you didn't have us with you last time and you didn't have a plan. This could be your best chance, Don. At least think about it.' Nic was convinced that the best way to spirit Donna away from Danny was to do it right under his nose, when he'd be least expecting it. 'I know it's as chancey as fuck, but we could pull it off if we're really careful.'

Donna felt a shiver run down her back.

'What if it all goes pear-shaped? What if some big fucking animal gets their hands on one of ya? I'm not sure, girls. It don't feel right to me. You gotta remember, I've been there. Danny watches me all the time.' She paused, hands held together in a prayer position. 'No, I've got a better idea. We make out we're all going, get dressed at the flat, then tell Danny we're going over in your car, Nic, and we'll meet him there. Only we don't. We get in your car and you drive me to King's Cross so I can get the train up to Jane's.'

'And you think he'll fall for that?' asked Shaz.

'Well, he's not going to leave his own party, is he?'

'Provided he doesn't get wind of it first,' warned Nicola.

Donna weighed this up carefully before replying.

'No,' she said with emphasis, 'I still think we're better off getting the fuck out, early doors. No way will he leave when it's all about to kick off. Can you imagine Danny, cock of the walk, not showing up for his own party? He's got too much to prove to too many people. Pathetic really. And it's not even as it it's about me any more. He doesn't love me, how could he? It's all a face-saving exercise with Danny.'

'If you're sure, Don, then let's do it your way.'

Nicola put her arm across Donna's shoulders and left it there, a gesture of trust and support, and Shaz shrugged as if to say, All right by me.

Donna looked at her two friends and nodded her head. She was afraid to speak because she thought she might cry. What would she do without these two?

After a successful weekend where they declared themselves brothers-in-arms, Danny pulled off the deal of a lifetime with Fat Larry. Together with a huge order from the Hackney boys and his now regular deliveries South of the River, he was looking to net somewhere in the region of £300,000 for a week's work. Not bad for a boy who'd dragged himself up on the streets.

Locked away in the attic of Kings Square, he surveyed the piles of drugs ready for distribution. He was going to be a very rich man soon. He allowed himself a smile of deep satisfaction. He had come a long way from the skinny, knife-wielding kid he used to be, the one who'd had to fight for everything. Now he had it all: his empire, people's respect, and all the things he'd lusted for. He hadn't been back to the flat for over a week. Although he'd had some good times up North, his thoughts now turned to Donna and her oh, so special mate Nicola.

He thought about going back this evening to surprise Donna. He'd sent her the usual bouquet on Monday, so she'd know he was back in the area, and felt a little randy after testing the new gear. So, with a good fuck in mind, he left everything safe and secure with Trippy and made his way back to the flat earlier than usual to surprise her. But there was something in the way that Trippy looked at him as he said his goodbyes that made Danny pause. Was that a look of contempt he'd seen on his old mate's face? He wanted to fucking watch it if it was. Danny had made Trippy the wealthy man he was today. If he wanted to be a stay-at-home, pussy-whipped wife-pleaser, that was his fucking lookout. Danny Lester was his own boss.

As Danny approached the door to the flat he could hear voices and music inside. Quietly slipping the key into the lock, he pushed the door open and crept down the passage to the living room, where he peered in to watch Nicola and Donna, dancing and singing. Shaz had left earlier, knowing she had a course test the next day, but the other two had decided to party and chat on. There was a crackle of excitement in the air as Donna allowed herself the luxury of thinking that, in a very short time, she would be away from here. They had been talking in raised, girlish voices, shrill with adrenaline. Danny smiled as the two of them suddenly caught sight of him and froze in their tracks. He could hardly believe his luck; they'd obviously been drinking and almost certainly been at his coke, but rather than feeling angry he was pleased.

'Well, what do we 'ave 'ere then?'

Donna recovered her composure in a seamless act of looking pleased to see him. 'Hiya, babe, we were just messing around. You're early. Nic just offered to keep me company.'

Danny smiled, looking past Donna and fixing his eyes on Nicola.

'That's OK, babe, I'll join the party. You know me, always willing to be sociable. So, Nic, how's your love life?'

Nicola immediately bent down to pick up her shoes and slip them on. She made her way towards the door where Danny leaned against the frame.

'I'm sorry, guys, I should be going,' she said, but he blocked her exit.

'Don't be hasty, babe, stick around a while.' He glanced at Donna. 'You'd like that babe, wouldn't ya?'

Donna didn't know what to say and looked at Nicola helplessly. Danny puffed himself up, looking large and threatening.

'Sit down, Nic. Donna, get some gear out – the good shit, not the crap Tommy sells.'

He stared at Nicola and felt his mouth water at the prospect of what lay ahead. As Donna left the room, Danny was at Nicola's side in an instant. His hand slid up her short skirt. Within seconds, he'd spread her legs apart and started to finger her and pinch her clitoris.

'Now, Nic, it's playtime. And you *will* play, and do exactly what I ask. If ya don't, your little mate will really suffer. And don't forget, I mean what I say. Now you be a good little girl and strip off.' In a raised voice he shouted straight into her face: 'NOW!'

Donna returned to find her friend undressing. She felt her knees go weak but in an effort to protect Nic, dared to stand up to Danny.

'No, Danny, leave her out of things . . . please! I'll do whatever you want, but don't touch Nic. She doesn't like it.'

It came so fast she didn't see it, but the back of Danny's hand sent Donna reeling across the room. 'Make the fucking drinks, bitch, and line up the gear!'

Reaching into his pocket, he produced some ready-rolled joints. 'Trust me, Nic. Smoke this and it'll make things easier for ya.'

Nicola knew she was trapped and that there was no way out. Either fight and let Donna take the brunt of it, or go along with Danny and keep her friend safe. So she took the joint he offered and had a long slug on the vodka bottle. She'd done it before, she could do it again. Do your fucking worst, you piece of shit, she thought to herself, your Day of Judgment is coming. Her eyes met Danny's in a confrontational stare. He would get all the action he was after, but she was damned if she was giving him the satisfaction of seeing her fear.

After watching her finish the joint and swig back the neat vodka, Danny grabbed Nicola by her blonde curls and forced her face down into the lines of gear, spread out in their usual place on the coffee table.

'Sniffer!' he shouted to Donna, and quickly she produced the thin silver tube that she had bought him as a present so long ago. 'Go on, baby, sniff a few lines, you know you want to.'

Nicola sniffed the gear up both nostrils and felt the terrible stinging sensation at the top of them as she did. She had fooled around with coke plenty of times, but never stuff so pure that it burnt the inside of her nose. Her eyes started to water, and Danny forced another drink into her hand and made her gulp it back.

After a joint laden with crack, pure coke and the booze, Nicola was soon as high as a kite, flying through the air and not wanting to come down. Donna knew she had to follow the same rules. Soon she too was ready for the night ahead. Danny wanted to give Nicola a night to remember, and now the fantasy he'd created in his mind was about to come true.

As he laid her back on the sofa, he smeared her genitals and anus with a mixture of coke and KY. He inserted his penis into her and, as he slowly fucked her, whispered in her ear, 'I know what you like, Nic. Yer brother Freddie has told me how you used to beg yer uncle to fuck ya. Even 'ad a taste for Freddie, didn't ya? Well, now you'll 'ave a real man *and* a few surprises.'

He quickly pulled out of her and turned to Donna. 'Strap on the big black dildo and get started on her *now*.'

Donna hesitated. Her eyes said 'Sorry' as she started to fuck her friend while Danny inserted his penis into Donna's arse. 'It's a three-way fuck,' he shouted, and began to laugh as he pounded harder into Donna, forcing her to pound harder into Nic. At one point when Danny turned Nicola over the two girls' eyes met and, very slowly, almost imperceptibly, Donna nodded at Nicola. We'll get through this, she silently said.

Around eleven the next morning Tommy arrived for work to find all three of them crashed out in the front room. He sighed heavily before gently lifting Donna off the sofa and carrying her to the bedroom where he laid her on the bed and covered her naked body with the duvet. He found a sheet to cover Nic's naked body too and then gently shook Danny awake. With his customary lack of remorse, Danny stretched himself luxuriously before slapping Tommy on the back and telling him, 'You missed a fucking blinder last night! I'm off for a shower now, mate. Leave the slags to sleep it off. And, Tommy, next time I'll invite you!'

At the sound of the door slamming behind him, Nicola suddenly came to. Looking at the scene around her, tears pricked her eyes. Even though she didn't remember too much of the previous night, the state of the living room told the whole story. Tubes of KY Jelly lay strewn across the floor, a large dildo and harness had been left on the sofa, and her genitals and arse were bruised and raw. Cocaine floated in the particles of air, joint stubs lay in the ashtrays and empty vodka bottles lay on their side on the carpet. Her head was thumping. She held it in both hands in an attempt to stop the room from spinning.

Tommy appeared at the door then, holding a mug of coffee and a packet of painkillers. 'Here, take these, it'll help.' Nic took them and just stared at Tommy, who reassured her, 'Don't feel bad, mate, I've seen this so many times before. I'm gonna check on Don.'

Danny whistled as he skipped down the stairs, two at a time. Outside the flats he jumped into his car, feeling energetic and refreshed. A good shower, a strong coffee and a couple of lines had him restored to his usual good humour. The regular throwing up in the mornings was getting to be a pain, but the gear soon chased the sickness away. Anyway, he was only bringing up foamy shit, it wasn't as if he couldn't keep his food down. Just a bit of heartburn, probably.

Danny drove off, whistling and thinking what a fucking good night he'd had! He'd been wanting to knock that Nicola off for a while, and now he'd like to go there again. She was something special. She'd put up a bit of a fight, even scratched him, the cheeky cunt, but, boy, could she moan. He could still feel himself inside her, teasing her by going slow and easy then ramming her like a train, and, oh, that tight round arse made it all the better. That double fuck was one of the best moments he'd had in a long time. He'd got extra pleasure from seeing the two loving friends obey his every command. He'd felt strong, commanding, all-powerful.

Nicola would be a regular fixture on his party scene now; with her great big tits, fat firm arse and tight little cunt, she would be a very pleasing addition. A bit old for Fat Larry perhaps, but he was sure that Tyrone and Yellow Man would get a kick out of her. Danny could think of little else now except the return match for Fat Larry and his crew in a ten days' time. He was meticulous about detail and kept going over the arrangements, time and again.

This would be the party that made Danny Lester a legend and put him on the map for good.

The only fly in the ointment was the run of violent headaches he had been experiencing lately. At one point he'd accused Trippy of cutting the gear with something that was making him ill. In fact, his temper was on a very short fuse these days and Trippy in particular had started to notice a deterioration in him. Danny had always been a mad, impulsive bastard, but his explosions of temper were getting harder and harder to handle.

After the trip up North, he had met Trippy at their usual café, just the two of them, to talk privately. It was late afternoon and they huddled at the corner table, smoking a joint and drinking coffee. Trippy was looking forward to hearing about the increased volume of business that would now be coming their way. He and Maggie had been talking about buying a house together and he needed to make some proper calculations.

Danny, obviously strung out after a mad one, was bragging about the girl who'd had to be carried off because she couldn't handle the pressure.

'Can you fucking hear yourself?' Trippy broke in.

'What's your fucking problem?' Danny had replied, but Trippy came straight back at him.

'No, Dan, *you're* the one with the problem. What are

you, some kind of fucking animal, banging schoolgirls until they pass out?'

Danny went to reply but some deeper bond to Trippy prevailed. He just reddened with fury and shame, and took it out on Ali, the café owner, instead.

After a tense few minutes of silence between the two friends, Ali had approached their table and, when he'd asked if they wanted more coffee, delicately raised the subject of Danny's tab of several months' standing. It wasn't that Danny had forgotten; it was more the fact that he thought Ali should be grateful he even hung out here at all. Rather than pay up or fob him off with an excuse, he marched Ali into his own kitchen and pulled a knife on him, holding it close to his ear.

'I keep you and your fucking mates in drugs, don't I?' he demanded. Ali, frightened out of his wits, backed off immediately and Danny returned to the table.

Tricky, now doubly pissed off, just stared at him hard. Looking his friend square in the eyes, he said, 'You can't fucking handle it any more. You gotta cut down, man.'

Danny had just laughed and laughed at that. The idea that he, Danny Lester, couldn't handle his drugs was comic. Sure he dabbled – a bit of coke, bit of brown, bit of crack – but he was purely a recreational user. It wasn't like he was some kind of fucking addict, was it?

Danny arrived at Kings Square to check on the three guys he had permanently stationed there on a rota system. There were so many drugs and so much cash that he couldn't leave the place empty for a minute. His guys were always tooled up in case of trouble, but so far it hadn't come to that. Danny liked to turn up unannounced, to remind everybody who was still boss. Larry had given him that piece of advice.

'Stay on top of it, son. Keep your face around and let them be in no doubt about what will happen if they cross you.'

As pumped up as Danny felt, there was a nagging tension within him still. Despite his great night with those two ace fucking bitches, Donna and Nicola, he still felt agitated and unfulfilled. He needed a crack joint or something to take the edge off and so, once in the attic, he dragged hard on a joint until gradually he started to feel like his old self.

What Danny still didn't realise, though it was obvious to everyone else, was that the drugs he took daily just kept him ticking over. The headaches and mood swings were the come down if he didn't top himself up on a regular basis. To stop now was the only way to rescue his mental and physical well-being, but he never accepted this. He was Danny Lester, top dog, always in control.

His main boys turned up for work at the house, to relieve the night shift. Johnny and Stevie were weighed down with money after their twenty-four-hour round trip to Manchester, which had gone according to plan and without a hitch. Trippy had sorted the Hackney boys out, and a new recruit, Jason, a sharp little operator originally from Clapham, returned a little later on with the money from the South London boys. Trippy had a few more visits to make. He decided to get to the West End and back as soon as he could, in the hope of catching Danny alone later and having a serious talk with him then.

Trippy left when the others all started on the crack pipe. He sighed heavily. No stranger to drugs himself, he nevertheless was careful not to mix business with pleasure. He liked to chill out with Maggie in the evenings and smoke a joint or two, but he was always mindful that once a dealer was hooked on his own merchandise, the only way was down. It made you sloppy, and you couldn't afford to take risks in this game; the stakes were high enough when you had all your faculties.

Trippy privately conceded that Dan had gone past the point of no return. He'd seen it so many times before, only he'd never thought it would happen to his best mate. But there was no denying the fact that Danny was bang in trouble and had long since lost the luxury of choice: the mood swings, the outrageous sex, and the constant need to take something, anything, just to make himself feel normal. Danny had always been a monster consumer of everything, but now it was beginning to catch up with him and Trippy didn't want to be taken down with him when he met his Waterloo.

He still loved Dan, but he'd grown up and moved on, met the right girl and had recently started to think about kids. Maggie wanted his child and Trippy knew she was the only candidate as mother of his children. What he did for a living was wrong and illegal, but it was all he knew. Sure, Danny had made him a rich man, and for a long time he hadn't wanted to read the writing on the wall – who would, with all the free drugs, easy money and fast cars on offer?

Donna, though, what was to become of her? She was still a beauty if a bit ragged around the edges now. But her spirit was dimmed, as if Danny had snuffed her pilot light out. If they weren't careful, Danny would take them all to the wall.

That kid up North weighed heavily on Trippy's mind. There was no denying his old friend was no longer the man he used to be, but only Trippy knew the full extent of the problem.

Back at the flat, Nicola entered the bedroom to find Tommy slowly rocking an inconsolable Donna in his arms. She buried her face in his shoulder, unable to look at her friend's face. Nic sat down on the edge of the bed.

'Donna, it's all right and I'm OK. Look at me, Don,' commanded Nicola.

Gulping in air and struggling to compose herself, Donna straightened up and, with a tear-stained face, looked at her best friend.

'It's over, Donna. He got his way, but it was the only thing for us to do. Tommy, fuck off and do something. Me and Donna need to talk.'

Tommy tried to object, but Donna pushed him off the bed and told him to leave them in peace.

'I'm so ashamed, Nic. I don't know what to say or how to make it up to you, I'm so sorry.'

The sobbing started again, but in a flash Nicola was holding her friend tightly and gently kissing the top of her head. Trying to break the ice, she made a fleeting joke. 'What the hell? I've always fancied you anyway!' Donna looked at her friend in alarm. 'Joke, Don, joke!'

'Everything's such a mess, though. Now what do we do?' asked Donna.

Still holding her friend, Nicola replied, 'We stick to our plan to fight back and make sure we get you away from him forever. Look at it this way – Danny now thinks he has us both, but he doesn't. Yes, he can threaten you if I'm not here to play ball. If that happens and he wants me again, I'll do it. I know Danny ain't finished with me yet, he's the kind of man who wants it all and at the moment I'm his target, but playing him along just a tiny bit longer will get us where we need to be.

'We *will* go to the ball, Cinderella, only this time it's gonna be planned down to the last fucking detail and you are going to get out of this shit for good. Do you understand, Donna? We're gonna win.'

*

In the run up to the party, the girls got busy. Nicola had made all the arrangements. Donna's train was leaving King's Cross at eight-thirty and a call to Jane had provided her with a safe house once they had her out of London. Donna transferred all the money she had in the bank to her sister's account. For the first part of the plan to work, she was to make sure she did her damnedest to avoid the lethal cocktail that Danny always made for her before a party. If she played it well, she could just sniff a few lines for Dutch courage and drink watered down vodka to make him feel she was getting ready for action.

The tricky bit would be to get Danny believing that all three girls wanted to turn up at the house at Kings Square in special outfits they had planned for the evening as a surprise for him. But they were so good at acting they'd started to believe it themselves. One afternoon several days before the party, Nicola had acquired a bag full of sex-shop outfits: French maids, nurses, bunny girls and the like. The idea was to pretend to be trying them on in readiness for the party and to act all coy when Danny came back; tell him he wasn't allowed to look as it was going to be a surprise for him on Saturday. It worked like a charm. The girls all pretended to be hastily rearranging their clothing when they heard his key in the lock and began to stuff bags under sofa cushions, knowing he would catch them in the act.

'What's going on here, then?' Danny said with a smile.

'Go away, nosey, this isn't for your eyes . . . yet,' Donna goaded him. Danny took the bait immediately and yanked off a sofa cushion to reveal a pair of crotchless knickers and some nipple clamps. His smile stretched from ear to ear. Donna screamed at him playfully to get off and threw herself on the sofa to cover the items she was pretending she didn't want him to see. Danny tweaked her nipple and said, 'I hope this is all for my benefit?'

'It is, but not till Saturday, Danny, it's going to be a surprise.'

Shaz and Nicola joined in then, joshing with him to go away. Danny put his hand down the front of Donna's jeans and kissed her hard. 'I knew you loved it, you tart. You're my favourite little whore, you are, Don.'

She kissed him back, looked him in the eye and said, 'Well, then, you're just going to have to wait a couple more days, aren't you?'

'I've got to go out in ten minutes, can't you just suck my cock before I go?'

Donna nodded in the direction of her mates and said, 'Later, baby.'

Danny smiled at her, slapped her backside and went off to the kitchen, whistling, to get himself a drink. The three girls looked at each other as if to say, I think he fell for it.

Freedom was drawing so near Donna could almost smell it.

Nicola too knew that her life in the East End would soon be over. She was in too deep with Donna to stay around. With no one to worry over and no family that cared for her, Nicola viewed this departure as her chance to get herself a new life, away from all the miserable memories here: her uncle, her miserable low-life brother, and the parents who'd never stood by or protected her.

In some strange way Nicola could forgive Freddie his drug-induced assaults on her as he was barely more than a child himself then, but not her uncle or father. Uncle Sean, in particular, had made her perform like a puppet. She'd no choice but to do his bidding. It was only his prison sentence for dealing heroin that had saved Nicola from any more abuse, not Social Services or the police. Once her uncle was locked up, her father backed off. Didn't have the guts without an accomplice to egg him on, or possibly fearing that he might be the next one to go to jail. But it was her mother Nicola hated most. Why hadn't she protected her little girl, taken her away from it all? Why hadn't she believed her?

When Uncle Sean used to come and visit, Nicola's mother would hole up in the front room with the television playing really loud, so that she could not hear her daughter's screams. When Uncle Sean left, Nicola would go to her mother, eyes red from crying, her little nightie covered in blood, and still her mother would call her a liar.

Nicola had prepared herself well for her new life. She fancied getting a placement in a restaurant in Paris. She'd always been good at French and could re-enroll back in her old college if it didn't work out. Confiding her plans to her manager at work, she had already obtained a glowing reference from the Savoy.

Shaz, too, was looking for a fresh start. She loved her course but was sick and tired of the English climate and the dinginess of the East End. Always good with money, she had squirrelled away quite a bit and was now in a good position to take a long break.

Donna didn't care where she ended up eventually, but in order to go anywhere she needed money. Careful skimming of the profits had left her with a tidy sum from the daily buyers and Danny, awash with cash and usually off his face, was none the wiser. She had also managed to smuggle out some things of value, jewellery and expensive trinkets that he had bought her, to be stashed away with Nicola for safekeeping. She was ready.

Chapter Twenty

In a single room at the Manchester Royal Infirmary, a fourteen-year-old girl lay motionless. Beside her bed, her parents and sister prayed for her to regain consciousness. The sister sobbed uncontrollably, unable to believe that it had been she who had led this defenceless child into the world of drugs, drink and sex. Amy Postle was a student at Manchester University. At nineteen she was a heavy-set girl, never really part of the student 'in' crowd, and when she found herself being invited to parties by some of the local lads, grabbed this chance of becoming popular. She had been a studious girl, reading History and Law, until the party scene took her over.

When her little sister Hilary had begged to be taken along, she hadn't really seen the harm. The parties had been fairly tame to start with and Amy would always be careful that Hilary never saw her take the lines of coke she enjoyed. There wasn't much of it around, students being a poor lot, and when it did turn up at parties it was a real treat. Hilary would often stay on campus with Amy, loving the feeling of freedom and being grown up it gave her.

John and Mary Postle were just your average parents. Drugs had never been heard of in their house, and they put their younger daughter's frequent absences down to straightforward teenage rebellion, figuring no real harm would come to her if she was with Amy. John and Mary were convinced that if there were any drugs around , it was only likely to be a bit of dope, nothing major, nothing they need worry about. Hard drugs were only taken by pop stars and kids from broken homes, not their girls. Amy and Hilary had good heads on their shoulders and one day would make decent lives for themselves. So, not wanting to make a big fuss and alienate their little girl, they had allowed fourteen-year-old Hilary to visit her big sister. After all, what harm could come to her on campus? It had to be better by far than roaming the streets on her own.

With their loving, gentle ways, they couldn't understand how their little girl had ended up left for dead on a bit of waste ground by an industrial estate, raped both ways and full of drugs. They put their elder daughter's distress down to shock. Like many a naive girl before her, Amy had believed that if you kissed enough frogs you would eventually find your prince and settle down to a life of bliss. Heroin was just the medium that gave you something in common with the boys; a way of meeting men, if you like. She wouldn't get hooked, she'd always believed. She was too bright for that and came from a good home. It hadn't stopped her agreeing to bring Hilary to one of Fat Larry's notorious parties, in exchange for the fix she craved.

She knew, though, that soon she would be asked questions. That the last sighting of Hilary before her body was found had been with her elder sister. Rumour was already rife on the university campus and her fellow students feared answering questions from the police about Amy and Hilary and their patterns of behaviour. Already they were building a picture of the two girls, where they went, who they saw, and what kind of drug trouble they were in. Amy was known to be a frequent visitor to raves, her absences from lectures had skyrocketed, and it was obvious that she was deep in trouble.

Since the discovery of her sister's body, no one had wanted to be seen with her, her dealers had disappeared, and she was clucking for her next fix. Her parents put her continuous shaking down to shock and the fact that she probably hadn't eaten for days. But Amy was trembling with fear because she knew that Fat Larry and his henchmen would be out to silence her.

Danny paraded around the house making sure that all his final preparations were carried out precisely. The last party had been a huge success but he was the classic over-achiever. He needed to top each successive rave. The popularity of his parties and the difficulty in getting an invite had resulted in hundreds of wannabees queuing up to be part of the action. Danny was the man, the one to be in with or known by. He greatly enjoyed playing God, giving his yea or nay to all the names on the guest list. The beautiful Georgian house in Kings Square was by now infamous. The police were highly suspicious about the goings on in it, but no one seemed to complain any more and no one called to tip them off. Danny had silenced them all with money or, when that hadn't worked, by menace. The families in the Square just wanted a quiet life and to protect their own. None of them felt like playing the have-a-go-hero against a gangster of Danny's reputation.

He controlled his little patch of the East End like a Mafia Don, dispensing favours to the chosen few and terrorising the rest. Though he hadn't actually killed anybody, they all knew he had it in him, and his handiwork with a knife over the years had left plenty of people with permanent reminders of what happened if you challenged him.

With somewhere in the region of thirty guys on his payroll, all of them earning a good living, it was unlikely he would be knocked off his perch any time soon. Sure, sometimes one of his guys got arrested or some junkie was dragged in for questioning, but all of them knew it was preferable to do a bit of time than to grass up Danny Lester. Occasionally he would give way to paranoia and have dealers brought in to be questioned; some were tortured with obscene cruelty, their families threatened and silenced. With such increasingly erratic behaviour, no one knew what to expect from him on a daily basis. Sometimes he would be generous and kind, dispensing cash and favours like an East End king, but if crossed in only the tiniest way, a late delivery, a sideways look, he had no hesitation about using his knife to restore proper respect. The rule of fear was effective. So far, the police had nothing concrete on Danny. The King and his Empire were untouchable.

Chapter Twenty-one

On the Thursday evening, once Tommy had gone home and the two girls knew that Danny was busy at Kings Square, they went through the final arrangements. Nicola had already parked her car in a side street, barely a minute from the flat. They had packed only the barest necessities: a change of clothes, rudimentary toiletries and a few items of value locked in the boot – a purse with two hundred pounds and some items of jewellery that could be sold on quickly for emergency cash. Donna was fretting that Danny would recognise the car but, as Nicola pointed out, beaten up Ford Escorts were ten a penny in the East End, especially blue ones. There was a brief moment of panic when Donna realised that she hadn't packed Pookie. By this point Nicola had grown impatient and tried to persuade her that it didn't matter, but Donna was insistent. She ran all the way up the stairs, grabbed her old stuffed toy and sprinted back down to lock it safely away.

Settled back in the flat with a bottle of wine, they talked for hours, going over every possibility and contingency, time and again. Danny was over at the house, making his last-minute party preparations, and wasn't expected any time soon. Nicola raised her glass.

'Your last night in this place, eh, Don? Your time has finally come.'

''Bout fucking time too,' she replied. They both laughed.

That morning Danny had told Donna that he expected her and her friends to act as hostesses: greeting his guests, serving up drinks and generally keeping the punters happy. Danny himself would be busy. 'But anything they want, and I mean *anything*, you and your fucking mates make sure they get it,' he had warned Donna. 'I'll let you know when you can knock off duty and go and enjoy yourselves.'

As if servicing a bunch of strangers in the most degrading fashion possible counted as having a good time! Donna had just smiled at him. If all went according to plan the three girls would be long gone before the first pair of trousers was dropped and anyone noticed they were missing.

The following day, Tommy arrived for work at eleven as usual, pumped up and excited that he had been privileged enough to receive a much coveted invitation to Danny's party that night.

Donna gazed at him and felt a wave of true pity. Tommy thought he was a player now, thought he knew what to expect after his night at the flat with them both, but she winced at the prospect of what he was really going to discover. He had no idea what awaited him at the party, no concept of how these circles he longed to be a part of really lived. He was young and handsome; to the hard-core gay guys he would prove irresistible, and saying no would achieve nothing except to excite them even more. To try and warn him off could arouse his suspicions and put everything in jeopardy, though. Despite feeling a vague gratitude towards Tommy for the tenderness and care he had shown her at her lowest point, Donna was not about to sacrifice herself to save him. This was about her survival.

Danny phoned her several times at the flat during the day, to give instructions and ask her to make calls for him, tying up loose ends such as checking what time the drinks would be delivered. He'd obviously started early on the gear and spoke in a rapid, angry voice.

'I want it all iced by eight o'clock so that it's properly chilled by the time people arrive. Last time some of the Champagne wasn't cold enough and it really pissed me off, made me look like a fucking amateur!'

Donna was cheerful, compliant and reassuring, and when he asked if she'd received her flowers she gushed down the phone, telling him how lovely they were and how much she adored him.

Danny smiled to himself, thinking what a fucking silly little bitch she was. He suspected she'd hit the coke already but didn't care as long as she was there tonight, on time, on form, and ready to get stuck in. He told her he'd be home around tea-time to get bathed and changed and head back to Kings Square around seven. She was to make sure she was there by eight, no later, with her friends, dressed to kill.

Danny got no real pleasure from Donna any more. Her tits were saggy, she was thin and gaunt, but the repair work to her arse and fanny at that private clinic had tightened her right up again and he knew she was still a good dish to offer up to others, even if he'd lost interest himself. Tyrone and Yellow Man said that she felt like a well-fucked virgin, childlike in some ways, and they loved it. If it pleased them so much, they could have her.

His thoughts were all on Nicola at the moment: more womanly, full-bottomed, tight fanny and great tits that cried out for biting and pinching. He'd already earmarked her for himself that night, although Sean, the older guy from the South London gang, had heard talk of her and had already expressed an interest.

'I like 'em with a bit of meat on 'em, Dan. You know, something to grab hold of while I fuck the living daylights out of them.'

It certainly wouldn't hurt his business interests South of the River to share her. Besides, it would be good to watch her cope with a real onslaught – put her through her paces and see exactly how much she could take. He'd gone easy on her so far.

Inviting Tommy along had been a good move too. Tyrone had a huge henchman with a fetish for slender, pretty young men, and Tommy fitted the bill perfectly. Everything was lining up to be a night to remember. This would be the rave to end them all, one that would be remembered and spoken of for years to come.

Shaz and Nicola arrived at the flat just as Tommy was packing up around four o'clock and giggled with him about the night ahead. 'Honestly, I can't wait!' Tommy was on fire with anticipation.

'Oh, you'll have the time of your life all right,' said Donna, winking at Nicola as she said it. The girls had to go through the motions of pretending they were getting ready for their big night so Danny came home to find the three of them in various states of undress, with rollers in their hair and beauty masks smeared across their faces. Nicola, the most professional of the three, had painted her nails a daring shade of slut-red and was dusting her cleavage with sparkling powder when he walked into the bedroom.

'Well, well, well, what have we got here then?' he said with a leer.

'Getting ready to party, ain't I?' Nicola teased.

Danny slapped her bum playfully.

'You're a right sort, you are, girl. Me and you are gonna get down and dirty tonight.'

'I can take anything you wanna give me,' Nicola challenged him.

Danny smiled, slid off the bed and went to the bathroom.

By seven o'clock he was still hanging around the flat, showing no signs of leaving. He was racking out lines on the glass coffee table and inviting the girls to join him. They were having to appear to be taking ages to get ready. 'Don't you need to get going, babe?' asked Donna, as casually as she could.

'Nah, 's all right. Stevie's over at the house already. I thought we'd all go over together as soon as you lot are ready. What's taking so bloody long?'

'Oh, nothing,' said Donna in a deflated voice, looking to Nicola for help.

'Don, come and help me get these suspenders sorted out, they're driving me mad.'

Nicola was thinking on her feet. They retreated to the bedroom where Shaz was sitting in her dressing gown, applying lipstick for the sixth time. 'What's up?' she hissed.

'It's gone tits up,' said Donna, panicking.

'What do you mean?' asked Shaz.

'He says he's waiting for us all to go together,' Nicola told her.

'Well, can't you just tell him to go on without us?' asked Shaz.

'No,' Donna and Nicola replied in unison. 'He's not silly, he'll know something's up,' Nicola explained.

Donna sat on the bed, her head in her hands. 'Now what the fuck are we going to do?'

Nicola took control.

'Don't go all soft on me, Don, we'll just have to go to Plan B.'

'We don't have a fucking Plan B!'

'Yes, we do. Remember how we were going to leave from the party in the first place.'

'Yeah, but your car is parked around the corner. How are we supposed to get it over to the party? You know what Danny's like, he always wants to drive.'

'Leave it to me,' said Nicola, striding purposefully back into the front room. She reappeared in the bedroom five minutes later. 'Right, get those fucking silly outfits on, we're off. We're gonna freeze our tits off, but we'll go in my car.'

'Did he go for it?' asked Donna, amazed.

'He's off his face already so I told him I'd drive him, as a special treat. I had to rub his dick too, mind, but it did the trick.'

Shaz sniggered and even Donna had to smile at that one. 'You're a mad bastard, you are, but I do love you!'

'You got any of those tranquillisers left that you were given at that private clinic?' asked Nicola.

'Yeah, loads, they gave me hundreds.'

'Well, bring 'em, they might come in handy for slipping into drinks.'

With that the girls hastily dressed and threw their coats on over their skimpy outfits. Donna was never going to make her train, but together they thought they could manage to give Danny the slip once he got busy at the house and speed away in Nicola's car. They'd have to call Jane once they got on the road and tell her of their change of plan.

*

The girls were well aware that they would have their work cut out keeping any eye on each other that night. Before they came out of the bedroom to join Danny, Nicola said, 'We've just got to drug every fucker in sight. I know it means some of the innocent will suffer, but it's not like they won't wake up.'

Donna was impressed by Nicola's resolve and drew strength from it. On the short drive to Kings Square Danny rambled excitedly about the great night ahead of them all while Donna studied the determined set of Nicola's profile and took deep steadying breaths. They arrived all too quickly, parked up and walked the short distance to the house.

Danny was noticeably high when Stevie opened the door and they greeted each other enthusiastically. He was still in control, though. They wouldn't be able to take any chances just yet.

Donna was surprised to see Trippy there, this kind of scene was definitely not his speed, but she felt strangely reassured by his presence. He nodded by way of hello, clearly put out that Danny had made him hang around but sensible enough to know that, in his current volatile state, Danny could not be crossed.

The girls made their way to the kitchen where they prepared trays full of glasses of Champagne and poured crushed tranquillisers into the decanter of neat vodka which was cooling over ice. Nicola stood watch as Donna sprinkled more powder into the Champagne glasses while Shaz nipped unnoticed to the back door where she was able to turn the key in the lock.

At quarter to nine, Danny ordered the girls to take up their positions with the trays by the front door, ready for the first punters to arrive.

Donna smiled as she handed him a glass from her tray and said, 'Good luck, babe.' Danny downed it in one, placed it back on the tray and picked up another just as the bell rang and one of his monkey-suited heavies opened the door.

The first to arrive were Yellow Man, Tyrone, and a host of huge men and fat women who all eagerly swigged down the drinks. Donna walked through the back to the kitchen to get another tray and be ready with plenty of refills for everyone. As each girl's tray emptied, they went off to the kitchen to open more bottles and sprinkle in the contents of the tranquilliser capsules. Donna's palms were sweaty and the repetitive beat of house music was making her feel not loved-up, but anxious. For a moment she felt like her mum and wanted to scream at Danny to turn it down, she couldn't hear herself think.

Shaz was a cool little operator, though. She'd never been to a rave, let alone one where sex was the main item on the menu, but maintained a steady pace, back and forth, with the drinks, on the move the whole time, smiling at everybody but never pausing.

Nicola was the real pro that night, an actress of the first order. At one point she leaned across to Danny and whispered in his ear that she was expecting something a bit special tonight and she hoped he wouldn't let her down. Danny's grin was so wide you could have wrapped it round his head and still had some spare. Like a bride on her wedding night, he wore the air of someone whose whole life had been leading up to this moment – the finest hour, the one that crowned all that had gone before.

Only Donna was starting to panic as by midnight a lot of the guests still hadn't shown – this was 1988, after all, a time when it was commonplace to arrive at a party at three in the morning and still feel the night was ahead of you. But until the place was totally rammed she wouldn't be able to get away. Christine, Little Jen and a few heavily made up women arrived just after midnight, followed shortly after by an enormously fat, dome-headed brute who Donna knew had to be the bloke from up North. She flinched when she was introduced to him and recoiled from his gaze as if from a flame. She'd seen a lot in her time with Danny but had never before felt such certainty that she was in the presence of evil.

Fat Larry's entourage had at least twenty members of both sexes, some of indeterminate gender. The party was really hotting up now and all they were waiting for was the South London crew. By one they'd arrived and, seizing the moment before the party took off unaided, suddenly Danny clapped his hands.

The music came to a halt, the crowd stopped talking and everybody listened as Danny gave them a welcoming, if slightly slurred, introduction to the madness, encouraging his guests to 'have a night of total freedom'. When the lights went back down and the music blared out once more – 'Free at last, free at last' – there was nothing else to do but choose a partner and get on with what they had come for.

As explicit videos came on in the downstairs rooms, Danny swaggered over to the three girls and asked them to down trays and get stuck in. Donna and Shaz exchanged imperceptible sideways glances , unsure of how to act, but Nicola took the initiative by grabbing Danny's limp penis and rubbing it hard.

'Give us a bit more time, baby, we've got something special planned for you, and we girls take our work seriously. Go and get fucked and warmed up. I'll be with you when I'm good and wet.'

For a heartbeat Danny hesitated, not able to find the words – she was so fucking assertive, Nicola, it really turned him on. He recovered sufficiently to lean across and tell her, 'You fucking prick tease, I'll be waiting, don't be long.'

Nicola dodged the strange, metallic odour on his breath and made herself smile at him and lick her lips.

'Fuck me, that was close,' she whispered as she walked past the other girls taking her tray to the kitchen. Shaz, as feared, was having a job fighting off the dealer she knew, but Nicola told him no uncertain terms to back off, that she'd be with him when she was ready and not before. Donna could only stand in awe of her bravery and was finally starting to believe that they might pull it off.

Nicola's first moment of terror arrived when the doorbell rang and it was opened to reveal her brother Freddie. He was pathetic now, an emasculated junkie who could do her no harm, but the memory of being raped by him could still make her catch her breath. Freddie, for his part, looked sheepish. He wasn't there to fuck, it had been a long time since he'd been capable of it, but he needed his drugs and would do what he had to.

Danny, busy back-slapping and pumping handshakes with the boys from South of the River, motioned over to Nicola to come forward. Everybody had a drink, there was no one left to serve and no excuse to get her out of it. 'Nicola baby, I've a surprise for ya.'

Taking the tray from her hands and passing it to a stunned Donna, he frog-marched her into the drawing room. Nicola stared straight ahead of her in disbelief, winded by what her eyes beheld. He'd lost a lot of hair and thickened around the middle but it was definitely him.

Danny laughed out loud. 'You remember your Uncle Sean,

don't ya, babe? He's come all the way here with Freddie as well as the gang to give ya a blast from the past.'

Uncle Sean, with an expensive-looking suntan and piercing blue eyes, took in every inch of Nicola, grabbed her by the arm and pulled her to him.

'It's been a long time, Nic. You still as fuckable as ever, little girl?'

Donna looked on, frozen, as Nicola nervously surveyed the man she hadn't seen for years.

Danny instructed her to get on with it: 'The other two have work to do elsewhere, let's get you limbered up and ready for a family reunion.' Donna watched Nicola being dragged up the stairs, looking back over her shoulder in despair.

Where previously Nic had seemed bullet-proof, she was clearly terrified now. Donna didn't know what to do, this hadn't been part of the plan. She could only watch with Shaz huddled by her side. Both girls felt powerless to help.

On top of the sexual pounding she knew she had coming to her, Donna was concerned that Danny would force her to take drugs that would put her out of the game completely. They'd agreed that, whatever the night was going to bring, they would need a clear head to cope with it.

With Nicola out of the picture, the pressure was now building on the two remaining girls to get started, but with Danny preoccupied, Donna was able to feign a need for the loo and leave Shaz to duck and dive around the punters. She was so little she managed to slip around unnoticed. Donna locked herself in the downstairs toilet, dry-heaving at the thought of her friend in so much pain, both mentally and physically. Her mind raced. Everything now depended on Nicola getting out so they could escape.

Donna had no idea what was happening in that room or how many men Nicola was having to accommodate, but she felt compelled to act.

Donna splashed her face carefully with water, and opened the small window to catch some gulps of air, before pulling the chain and making her way back to Shaz. With everyone busy shagging and taking more drink and drugs, she pulled her friend to one side.

'I have to get Nic out of that room, fast. We need a diversion.'

Shaz thought quickly. 'There's some real hard-core stuff going on in there, they won't want to miss it,' she said, nodding in the direction of one of the downstairs bedrooms where Donna spied four guys all fucking Little Jen and two gay guys trying to get what action they could from the fringes. The poor kid was screaming, and knowing how Danny loved the torture side of sex, he wouldn't be able to resist taking a look. Maybe that was enough to get them to leave Nicola alone for long enough for the other two to get her away. Donna knew she was going to have to be bloody convincing.

Climbing the stairs to the first floor, she tried a few doors but came up empty-handed. She went up another floor and followed the sound of Danny's laughter, coming from the main attic bedroom. She took a deep breath and entered. Nicola was being fucked by her uncle with Freddie pathetically trying to get it up and shove it in her face. Danny was gulping down his drink, waiting not very patiently for his turn to join in. 'What the fuck d'you want?' Still staring at the fucking, he directed his voice at Donna.

'Dan, you just gotta come downstairs and see what's happening. Little Jen is being fucked and tortured by six blokes, you won't wanna miss it!'

Danny drained the last of his drink before looking at Donna and saying, 'You're kidding me?'

'Nah, honest, babe. Come and see for yourself, and bring the guys, it's hard-core.' Danny paused, looked at Nicola longingly and said, 'Hey, lads, leave 'er a minute, there's something 'appening downstairs that can't be missed.'

Uncle Sean came quickly and threw Nicola aside to follow Danny out of the door and down the stairs. Donna rushed to her friend.

'My God, babe, I'm so sorry . . . I didn't know who he was, I swear.'

Nicola, bruised and battered, told her, 'We gotta go now, Don. I can't take all this shit again. It's now or never.'

She hastily pulled what was left of her clothes around her, clutching Donna's arm for support as they went down the stairs.

At the bottom of the staircase, jammed around the doorway of a reception room, a small crowd had formed to witness the terrible abuse being meted out to Little Jen. They were cheering and clapping as the fragile young girl was pounded until she looked like she was going to pass out. Doing a quick scan, Donna couldn't see Danny and assumed he was inside the room getting a good close look. Shaz spotted the two of them and nodded towards the back door. The three girls passed through the crowd unnoticed and made it through the kitchen and out by the back door. Out in the garden they fumbled with the key before locking the door from the outside and wedging the bins against it to stop or at least delay anyone trying to get out.

Donna looked back briefly through the big sash windows to see the crowd dispersing. Whatever had happened was over now, and her thoughts went briefly to young Jen who had given them the few minutes they needed to get away.

'Fucking hell,' screamed Shaz. 'Danny's just clocked me through the conservatory. Run . . . for fuck's sake, run!'

The girls raced across fifty feet of lawn and made it to the door at the rear of the garden, only to find it locked. For several seconds they just stared at each other, waiting for someone else to make a suggestion. The fence was about eight feet high – they could probably do it.

Shaz cupped her hands together. 'C'mon, Nic, you first.' Looking over her shoulder, she could hear someone trying to force the back door open. ''Urry up, for Christ's sake, they're on to us.'

Donna insisted Shaz went next, she was too small to scale the fence alone while Donna was sure she could make it. With the two girls safely over, they screamed at her to hurry.

'You two, get to the car, I'm on my way over now, but if I don't make it, go without me. I'll be all right.'

Donna scaled the fence. Despite the rough woven lathes cutting into her and grazing her skin, she made it over. She could see Shaz and Nicola ahead in the distance. Kicking off her shoes, she broke into a run.

As she reached the street leading up to the square, she could hear voices behind her. Some of the guys had seen a game of Cat and Mouse developing before their eyes. They'd catch the girls and make them pay.

Nicola and Shaz made it to the car, but Donna had vanished from sight. Nic started the engine. 'Lock the doors and keep the windows up,' she shouted at Shaz. 'Let's see if we can spot her.'

Turning into the square from the side street, they could see the house with its front door standing open. Danny stood on the steps, screaming at some of his guys to get dressed, get out and search. Terrified of being spotted, the girls turned off the car engine and headlights and parked on the other side of the square, behind the small patch of grass at its centre. They slid down in their seats and watched and waited, hoping and praying that they wouldn't be seen – and that Donna had managed to slip away to somewhere safe.

Still in her red devil fancy dress, and with no shoes on her feet, Donna had made off down another side street once she'd realised the guys from the house would notice her if she tried to get across the square to the girls in the car. Logic told her that Nic and Shaz would have driven away as the guys came closer to them. She knew the girls were still close, but didn't know exactly where. She felt frozen with indecision but, with the voices getting closer, she knew she had to move quickly and find herself a hiding place.

Beyond the square stood a block of pre-war flats. Instinctively she headed in their direction. Her feet were cold and sore from running barefoot on the wet ground and she could feel her toes going numb. Her breath was coming in short bursts. She fought down an urge to scream for help – it would only lead them to her. Donna arrived at the block of flats, sweating and with her heart thumping.

'Fuck, God help me, what do I do now?'

Looking quickly around, she spotted the big metal doors leading to the huge circular bin bay that caught the rubbish from all the flats above. It was full to the brim with stinking detritus. Without hesitation, Donna got a foothold on the handle of the bin and managed to flip herself headfirst over the rim into the foul-smelling garbage. Instinctively she gagged and dry heaved, feeling a sharp pain in her foot as if something had sliced into it.

She heard the men's voices draw closer, Danny, Stevie, and another guy she didn't immediately recognise. Then more voices, maybe five more; desperately she tried to separate the voices and count them. There had to be about eight of them all told.

'Right, search all the floors, check the lifts and stairwells. The bitch is in here somewhere.'

The voice was familiar although very slurred. She knew it was Johnny.

Despite holding her breath and trying desperately to keep still, Donna's heart was beating so hard she was certain they could hear it. She heard the sound of steps rushing past then coming to a halt, a button being pressed for the lift and someone kicking its metal door. Then doors to the flats above being opened and some raised angry voices.

'D'you know what fucking time it is?'

'What the fuck's going on? Is it a police raid at number twenty again?' she heard someone say.

'Fuck off and mind yer own business,' was the reply, and the doors slammed shut.

Minutes passed with Donna desperately trying to steady her breathing and not gag on the stench. The voices became lower. It seemed that the search of the flats had come to an end. She made the mistake of allowing herself to believe that maybe she was safe, but as the gang of men began to drift away one noticed the door to the bin room was slightly ajar. A bright light went on and an involuntary gasp escaped from Donna's mouth. ''Old it, fellas, what's in 'ere then?'

Donna was dragged away, screaming, biting and fighting for all she was worth, but with at least eight men restraining her, she knew she had no chance. As her half-naked body was dragged back to the house in Kings Square, hands were clasped around her mouth and throat. Before they reached the house she had blacked out.

From their position in the car, Nic and Shaz saw every bit of what happened. As Donna was carried back into the house like nothing more than a sack of rubbish and the door slammed shut behind her, both girls started to sob. Neither of them could help her now.

At the police station the two terrified girls stood shaking in coats which barely covered their near-nakedness. Nicola had asked to see John Sillings and Paul Metcalf, the two officers she'd met at the hospital the last time Danny put Donna there. She refused to budge until she saw them. Luckily for the girls, the two officers were on duty out in patrol cars and within an hour had arrived back at the station to talk to them.

Taken into an interview room, she recounted the events of the last few months in frantic detail, trying to impress upon them how dangerous this was. She was pleading with them to get to the house and save Donna.

Two plainclothes officers entered the interview room then and asked her to go over the story again. Nicola could not control herself.

'For fuck's sake, get a car round there *now*. They'll kill her, don't you get it? We ain't got time for all this shit, and I've already told ya enough. My mate's life is on the line, please . . .'

She lost it then, sobbing from the sheer abject terror of what was happening to Donna.

The officers were gentle as they spoke to her. The elder of them, DCI Godson, explained that patrol cars had already been sent to the scene, but that he had to go through all the formalities and get the girls' statements. A female officer entered with coffee for everyone, and stayed in the room as the girls each spoke in turn of their ordeals that night, their plan to get Donna away, and her capture.

DCI Godson could barely contain his joy at the wealth of information they gathered. Danny Lester had been a thorn in his side for some considerable time, but no one had spoken out against him before. Now he finally had something to nail the bastard with. Danny Lester's reign was coming to an end!

Chapter Twenty-two

Donna regained consciousness in an unfamiliar place. She had been laid out on a filthy old linen sofa, and everywhere around was rubbish, dirt and grime. Bottles of vodka were littered about the place, some empty and some half full, spread out lines of coke had been abandoned on a glass table and unfinished joints were stacked in overflowing ashtrays. On a small armchair, a diminutive bloodied body was curled up, unmoving. When Donna tried to move to help, she realised she was bound by duct tape and rope. She had never been in this place before and had no idea where she was or to whom it belonged, only that it was old and had been unused for some time. Wallpaper was falling from the walls in strips, and the ceiling was cracked and yellow from smoke fumes. Spiders' webs hung from the single bulb that lit the room, and threadbare curtains kept out the sunlight that tried to filter in.

She at least knew she had made it to daylight, and that whatever else might have happened since her losing consciousness, she wasn't dead yet. Her thoughts went to Shaz and Nic. She prayed they were safe and away from harm. She also prayed that they were doing something to help her or to try and find her. In her heart she knew that neither of them would be able just to walk away and leave her. Her two friends were her only hope of rescue and survival. Donna felt an acute stab of longing then for her mum and dad, and their clean, warm, safe, home.

The door to the room opened and Danny, Trippy, Johnny and Stevie all entered. All four of them were off their heads but Danny was different from the others. He looked terrifyingly vengeful. Dropping on to the sofa, he glared at Donna. Placing his hands around her throat, he spoke through clenched teeth.

'I could squeeze the life outta ya right now, with my bare 'ands, but that'd be too easy. You're gonna suffer for what you've done, you fucking bitch.'

As he spoke, his hands tightened involuntarily around her throat and she began to choke. Donna had never seen Danny look so ugly, his face contorted with hate.

Reluctantly he released his grip.

'Johnny, Stevie, double fuck her as hard as ya can. Spare her nothing, I want her ripped apart. And when you've 'ad enough, I'll take over. Get them toys out, too, she's gonna get it like never before.'

Johnny and Stevie, though flying, were not so beyond human feeling that they didn't flinch at the sight of a badly beaten Donna, wrapped up in duct tape and rope. Now, rather than follow their first instinct to help her, they were supposed to make it worse. They looked at each other and at Danny as if to say, He's gotta be joking, ain't he?

But Danny's expression was murderous. He kept goading them until they dropped their trousers and lifted her rag-doll body off the sofa. With no painkilling drugs to help her, Donna could not contain her screams of agony as each of them penetrated her time and time again. Each time she screamed, Danny would punch her full in the face, until she felt it balloon like a football. Occasionally, when the guys stopped to gulp down drinks or sniff more gear, Danny would lift her off the sofa and throw her to the floor. As she hit it full force, she felt bones snapping in her body. Soon she was covered in blood. And still he didn't stop.

'She's had enough, Dan, leave it!' a voice ordered quietly from the corner of the room. Everybody froze as Danny turned his head to look at Trippy. Johnny and Stevie glanced at him too and shook their heads as if to say, No, mate, don't do it. Don't cross him.

But Trippy held his gaze and challenged Danny openly. Trippy had seen so much that he had travelled beyond fear to a place where anything had to be better than this. Their eyes locked on each other. Trippy said, 'It's over. Finished.'

Danny laughed, high and long, a brittle sound. He urged Johnny and Stevie to keep going, with the threat, 'Nothing's finished till I say it is. Fuck her again. Turn her over, make her fucking bleed. I wanna see blood.'

Trippy shook his head at him, disgust, contempt and pity threatening to overwhelm him. He turned to leave.

'You go now and that is fucking it, Trip, d'ya get me?' Danny dared him. 'You're either with me or you're against me, you know that, mate.' Trippy noticed just a hint of pleading in his voice that Johnny and Stevie would have missed, but it no longer cut any ice with him. He said firmly, 'Get her to the fucking hospital.'

'Hospital? For this slag? She tried to run away. *This* is what happens to people who run away, Trip, you watching?'

Danny picked Donna's head up by the hair with one hand and slapped her face with his free hand before pouring neat vodka on it. As the vodka seeped under her eyelids and burned her, Donna's eyes flickered.

'Can you see me, bitch?' Danny murmured in her ear.

As her eyes struggled to open he held his knife close to her face then calmly sliced her down both sides. She didn't even feel it. Next he yanked her long black hair, thick with filth and blood, and sliced off her left ear completely.

Throwing it on to her body, he stood up, laughing.

'Johnny, Stevie, I'm done with 'er. Get the bitch outta here and dump her in the bins at the back of Kings Square where we found 'er. She won't wake up this time. Goodnight, sweet Donna, love of my life.'

He forced a loud laugh as he looked at Trippy, but it was hollow. They both knew that even though he'd defied his friend by leaving Donna for dead, Trippy had in fact won. Wrapping the almost-dead girl in old blankets, the other two boys did what they were told. Danny sat down on the bloodstained sofa and swigged the bottle of vodka until it was all gone. Trippy watched him silently from the corner of the room, deciding that now was not the time. He'd come back for Danny. For now he just needed to get home and hold Maggie

Trippy wasn't the only one questioning Danny's antics. When Donna had been dragged back into the house at Kings Square, Sean and the South London lads took one look at her and decided they'd had enough. If Danny Lester could be like that with his own bird, then he wasn't a safe pair of hands for business. Trippy had noticed Sean talking to Fat Larry, and both of them shaking their heads. After they'd left, the other party-goers, sensing mutiny, quickly gathered their things and beat a hasty retreat.

Something nasty was going down and they didn't want to be around to discover how it was all going to play out.

At the police station, after all the formalities, Nicola and Shaz were examined by a doctor and then allowed to wash and get some clean clothes. News had reached them that when the police eventually raided Kings Square, they'd found the place empty of bodies but stacked with evidence in the form of abandoned drink and drugs. Whatever had broken the party up had happened quickly and dispersed the crowd with immediate effect. But Donna was nowhere to be found.

Nicola had given the address of the flat and details of as many of Danny's gang as she could. It was hard to be precise for she only knew nicknames and first names, apart from her brother Freddie and her Uncle Sean. She gave the address of her parents' home, where Freddie might be found, but all she knew about Uncle Sean was that he lived South of the River. His father, her grandfather, was called Sid, and the surname would be the same as hers, Rafferty.

The names were not unknown to DCI Godson. His liaison with the police South of the River had led to an address but the house was empty. It had been thoroughly cleared and appeared to have been unoccupied for some time. Whoever left it must have been in a hurry, though, moving so fast they didn't have time to pick up the three kilos of cocaine that the police found stashed on the premises.

With Sean Rafferty's previous record, he was a marked man. The police in South London and their mates from across the water were sure something would turn up on him soon.

Freddie's was the first arrest to be made. Completely off his tits, the *numero uno* lagging boat had been dumped in a cell to sleep things off until he was ready for questioning. With Freddie in custody, Nicola knew that once he came round and started clucking for the gear, he would sing like a bird and hopefully shed some light on Donna's whereabouts.

For Nicola and Shaz's safety, the officers offered them the protective custody of the station and the girls readily accepted. Neither of them knew where else to go, as both of them were now fresh targets for Danny and his gang, highly visible and totally vulnerable. Nicola privately believed that Danny knew already where they were.

With the house in Kings Square empty, he and the rest of the gang must have anticipated their trip to the police station. They'd left no shortage of evidence, though. Video equipment had been hauled off to the police labs. Tapes were being made and a roll-call of names investigated. It would hopefully account for everyone there that night, but most importantly the police were interested in the main gang members, who they were and where they came from. If they had form, they should be easy enough to track down.

Danny didn't stop after he'd ordered Donna's body to be dumped. He did not lie low but carried on pumping more and more drugs into his system. By now the guys were getting twitchy. Johnny and Stevie had dumped Donna's body as instructed, but as they came down and their minds began to clear they realised that they were in the frame now, probably for murder.

Twenty-four hours after the party, Danny was still right on one: unshaven, smeared with blood and looking like a madman as he paced the room. Trippy was nowhere to be seen. Probably at home, but Danny wasn't saying. He stared at Johnny and Stevie through a glaze of hysteria.

'I thought I told you I wanted clean clothes and a shower? *And* I need some money. Are you all fucking stupid?'

Pulling his knife, he wielded it wildly in the air, like a man possessed. 'And I told ya once before, get rid of that fucking useless bitch . . . NOW!'

Little Jen's body was covered over again with a blanket. Johnny and Stevie were twitchy now, but Danny wouldn't listen to Stevie's pleas.

'Dan, we all need to change our clothes, get clean and lay low for a few days.'

Danny didn't even hear him as he leant back on the sofa, hair thick with blood, hands smeared with congealed KY Jelly, semen and more blood. His clothes were soaked through with sweat and stale booze, his breath disgusting with the tang of metal that wouldn't go away these days.

At one point before they left the flat, a door slammed several houses away and Danny turned his head blindly and said, 'Trip, is that you, mate?'

Stevie cried in the car as they drove Jen away from the house, too tired and beyond it even to worry what Johnny might think. He didn't care, he felt the same.

Another pair of friends, another pair of tearaways, were heading towards the Regent's Canal with their roach poles to do some fishing. The boys were known in the area as little trouble-makers. They cut through the railway arches, clambered over the track itself, and shimmied down a large water pole at the far end to reach the best fishing area on the canal. With their packed lunches and bottles of squash they were set for the day.

They set up their rods, got themselves seated on the gravel path near the small bridge that crossed Bethnal Green Road, and cast their lines.

Within minutes the boys were both into their first bites and this continued as the morning went on. They had a fine catch of roach, bream and gudgeon by lunchtime.

The boys were used to the debris floating in the canal, but when young Josh spotted something big floating in the water, he knew it was no shopping trolley or bag of rubbish. The object snagged against a piece of metal junk jutting out of the water only a few feet away. As he called out to his mate Jimmy, the two of them stared at what they at first thought was a dummy, realising finally that it was a human corpse.

Stunned speechless, the boys make no movement at all. On the other side of the river, a man on a bike, with a fag dangling from his mouth, cycled by.

'Mister, mister!' croaked Josh. 'There's a body 'ere, in the water!'

The police arrived and the boys found themselves the centre of attention. Josh was jostling Jimmy out of the way, pushing himself forward, saying, 'I saw it first, mate, it was me that discovered it.'

The boys were led away while a police forensics team cordoned off the site and retrieved the body from the canal. After the lads' parents were notified, the two of them were allowed to go home. The body described by the pathologist was female, around fifteen, with no distinguishing marks. Her death had been caused by a cocktail of drink and drugs, horrendous rape and asphyxiation. She was sent down to the morgue. She had no name.

The dustmen arrived early the next morning. They were laughing and joking as usual but as one of them pulled the big metal bin on wheels out of the chute and saw what he thought was a bundle of rags, it suddenly went quiet. On closer inspection he felt horrified. Nearly puking, he called to his colleagues to phone the police and get an ambulance over as quickly as possible. The crew rushed the girl's inert body to the London Hospital, preparing her for emergency surgery as their vehicle screeched through the streets.

With no identification on her, the police were asked for details of matching missing persons. Without any doubt, the station believed they had found Donna.

Joyce and Ian Stewart travelled in silence on the way to the hospital, not knowing what they would find when they got there. In the emergency room they were finally able to identify the horrifically injured young woman as their daughter, though it was difficult to be sure. Virtually all her ribs had been broken and she had two fractures to her skull, a broken arm, a missing ear, totally disfigured face and major internal injuries. The surgeons took them to a quiet room and told them they were not sure they could save her. Donna had lost a lot of blood, and would require extensive surgery to get her back in one piece. For now, they needed to get her stable, repair the internal organ damage and get some blood into her. Whether she made it alive from the table was not just in their hands, it was in God's.

In another hospital in Manchester, a young girl opened her eyes for the first time in weeks. She had slept soundly, unaware that her parents had been keeping a bedside vigil while her sister Amy had been taken into custody for a brief period, to give some useful information about parties, dealers, and a man she had seen only a few times but was notorious by reputation, Fat Larry. She was released without charge but told to hang around until her sister woke up. They might want to talk to her again then, depending on what Hilary could tell them. If she could tell them anything, that was. The chances of her having permanent brain impairment were high.

Her mother dozed in a chair, holding her daughter's

small hand, when a slight squeeze on her fingers made her sit up with a start.

'Hilary, sweetheart, are you awake? My God! Nurse . . . Nurse,' shouted a jubilant Mrs Postle.

The doctors and nurses alike were overjoyed by the young teenager's return from her long sleep. Caring and looking after her had made them very fond of the mousey-haired, plain little girl who slept like a princess waiting to be kissed.

Amy, who was being detoxed in a clinic but holding it together, sank to her knees to thank God for His mercy in saving her sister. Challenging her demons, and struggling all the way, the thought of her sister being awake caused a dramatic upsurge in her determination to fight her addiction and win back her family and her life.

Hilary was still a very sick girl, but she was going to get better eventually. And with the help of the clinic staff and intensive therapy, Amy now had a new chance at life too.

The police were notified, but remained cautious in their attempts to question the child. On their first visit, a young WPC took Hilary's hand.

'Who was responsible for this, Hilary?' she said softly.

Faintly the child spoke two words, 'Fat Larry!' and fell back to sleep.

Back in the East End, the news spread like wildfire. Two bodies had been found, both young women. One was clinging to life, and the other, unidentified, was dead. Danny paced the floor of Johnny's little flat, both Johnny and Stevie awaiting instructions from him. Trippy was on his way, but they didn't know that yet.

The guys were unsure what to do. When they gave the news to Danny that Donna had survived, his fury knew no bounds. He realised it was only a matter of time before she spoke and then all of them would be arrested and imprisoned.

After an absence of two days, Trippy appeared at the flat, cool as a cucumber. Gently, he informed Danny that the police had all the video tapes as evidence and Fat Larry had closed his operation as the girl Danny and his mates nearly killed on his turf had regained consciousness and was likely to speak. Fat Larry was moving on to another area and wouldn't be back in touch. From one gang leader to another, he suggested that Danny did the same.

News was not good from Hackney or South London either, and even young Tommy was frightened to go to the flat, for fear the police would be there waiting.

Johnny and Stevie got twitchy and started talking volubly about getting out of town. Danny, washed, refreshed and clean, was as mad as could be. The silly little bitch he'd once loved had cost him everything. In order to get away, he'd need money, a safe place to stay, and a new area to re-start his business.

He had no fear of the police. Even though all avenues of escape were closing down with the disappearance of the other dealers, he knew the police would have a job finding him if he just jumped on a plane. But where to? Right now, he needed some gear to get him going so that he could make some decisions. Trippy looked on in concern as Danny cut up line after line of gear and started to roll a crack joint.

'Dan, leave out the shit, you need to be on top of all this.'

Danny just stared at his best friend for a few seconds, turned and glared at Johnny and Stevie, ordering them to get some shit up their noses. Trippy looked at the closest thing he'd ever had to a brother and thought back in time, remembering two skinny kids roaming the streets of Bow and Poplar, trying to duck and dive and make enough money to survive. Danny had been his one and only friend then, and the two of them had been inseparable since their early childhood.

Trippy felt powerless to help his friend now. What lay between them was bigger even than a pair of wise guys like them. Danny had never hurt Trippy. If anything, he had always protected him, from anything or anyone. Trippy had spent two days feeling torn but the decision had to be made. Finally, with Maggie's help, he made it. He knew this wasn't the real Danny before him now. He'd checked out some time ago.

Crazed with anger and the need for revenge, the man he had become ranted incoherently for hours, ordering Johnny and Stevie to visit the Hackney and South London boys. He wanted it known that he was still the king pin. He wasn't going on the run. Danny Lester wasn't afraid.

Chapter Twenty-three

Nicola stayed by her friend's side in the small private room at the hospital, leaving only for toilet breaks or a cup of vending-machine tea. Donna was gravely ill, the doctors said it was touch and go, but Nicola would not give up and kept chatting to her friend. At one point she even read her horoscope from the paper as if they were sitting round the kitchen table. The Stewarts filed in and out, but Joyce and Ian found it hard to see their daughter in such a state and Joyce had to keep excusing herself as sitting there, unable to do anything to help her girl, was too much for her for her to bear. The police called by occasionally to see if there was any further improvement, desperate to interview Donna but aware it would be some weeks before the young woman would be able to recall the details, if any, of how she got to be in such a state. The injuries to her head had been so severe the doctors warned her family to be prepared for potential brain damage, but Nicola refused to believe it.

Rightly or wrongly, she felt responsible for the state Donna was in and had gone over the events of that night again and again, thinking of what she should have done differently. She stuck fast to Donna's side. When Shaz turned up to visit they would talk of all the good things in their lives and their plans for the future to the sleeping Donna, hoping it would help her through the healing process.

Days passed. After more surgery and more sleep, Donna was gradually able to sit up in bed, come off the drips and eat solid food. The thrill of seeing her family and friends helped with her recovery, but she knew the time would soon arrive when the police would want to interview her. With Nic and Shaz Donna felt strong and purposeful, but when she was alone fear filled her body, and the slightest noise, even the sound of the door opening, made her jump out of her skin.

One afternoon, when a nurse had brought in some flowers, Donna started to scream and in a wild fit yelled at the nurse, 'Send me no flowers! Please, send me no flowers!' The nurse told her not to be a silly girl, they were only flowers, but in the end Donna had to be sedated and a note was made on her records not to allow any flowers into Donna Stewart's room.

When the time arrived for Donna to have her head bandages removed, the nurse in charge suggested that Shaz and Nicola might want to stick around to support her as it was bound to be a shock. She knew that her hair had been shaved off and that her ear had been badly damaged, but she didn't know that it had been sliced away completely until the doctors came in and started talking to her about prosthetics.

The nurses were careful and gentle and the doctors explained to Donna exactly what would need to be done. As the bandages came off, Nicola and Shaz each held one of Donna's hands, standing to either side of her and gripping tight. As the last of the bandages came away Shaz gasped involuntarily and tears rolled to the floor from her eyes, despite Nicola giving her a stern warning look. Donna asked for a mirror. Hesitantly the nurse brought one to her. Nicola held her breath as she waited for Donna's reaction to her reflection in the glass.

Two large scars ran down either side of her face like tribal markings. Stitches were still in place over two areas of her head. In between, her hair was starting to sprout in tufts over her skull. One eyelid was weak and half closed. As she turned her head to the side, she saw the red congealed mass that had once been her ear.

The room was quiet for several seconds until a stifled sob coming from deep inside Donna filled the silence. The others in the room looked down in a vain attempt to hold themselves together. Even the nurse welled up with tears. It was hard on all of them, but Nicola sniffed loudly and held her friend's hand tighter in an attempt to show moral support and squeeze some life back into her.

Danny never left Johnny's flat, which seemed to be fine as he and Stevie had gone on the missing list. In the wake of the party and the attack everybody had gone to ground. There had been no news from anyone. Johnny and Stevie had vanished completely from the area, leaving Danny exposed and vulnerable, lost and alone in a haze of continuous drug-taking and boozing. As a marked man, he could not leave the flat. The only visitor who came by was Trippy.

Danny saw day turn to night, taking more drinks and drugs and watching an endless stream of porno films on the old TV and video player. The king pin was no longer the bullet-proof Don but a spun-out junkie. Trippy came by every day, bringing Danny what he needed and keeping him company, as much as he could, until he passed out. Trippy had stopped serving up the hard drugs. At Maggie's insistence he had gone back to selling puff only. They wouldn't be rolling in it as they had been, but it was a decent enough living. Although known as a close associate of Danny Lester's, Trippy was still a free man and he wanted it to stay that way. He had done nothing on the night in question except keep out of the way. When the police questioned him, he pleaded ignorance and stayed tight-lipped. Besides, they were only focusing on those whose faces had appeared in the videos and had already pulled a few in for questioning. Nobody seemed to know where Danny had gone and the police knew they were unlikely to get anything out of Trippy.

Trippy's home life with Maggie was nearly perfect. She had recently discovered that she was now pregnant and a whole new world was opening up for him. All that remained of his former life was this last remaining tie to his best friend. Trippy knew what he'd have to do in the end, but decided to bide his time a bit longer.

The heat on the street was getting heavy. Local people were baying for blood. In light of the events of that evening and the countless other occasions when he had threatened or terrified some poor innocent, locals who had once spoken reverently of Danny 'The Knife' Lester were now disgusted by the reports they had heard. Crime was a way of life in the East End and few would judge Danny for the way he made his living, but brutality to women was not tolerated. People shook their heads over pints in the local pubs, speculating as to how one man had been able to exert such influence over the lives of so many for so long. Even if he came back a reformed character, he would not be forgiven.

There was never going to be any escape for Danny Lester. Everyone was praying for the day when he would be found and suitably punished.

A tired, frightened, middle-aged woman from the North of England was ushered into the morgue at the London Hospital. The mother of a young daughter reported missing, she had spent every day for the last few years leaning on the police about the whereabouts of her absent child. She had long believed that her girl had run away to London in search of her brother, but the police insisted they did not have the resources to go scouring the country for every teenage runaway. It was only the child's dental records that had led to a call for her to come to London and identify a girl's body.

Gaynor Bridgend, formerly Gaynor Lester, had little trouble identifying her daughter Jennifer, despite her horrific injuries. There was no mistaking the mole on the side of her face that had been there since girlhood or the way her little finger on her right hand was slightly bent after a netball injury had resulted in a broken bone.

When it came out that the kid was Danny Lester's half-sister, the bush telegraph went into overdrive. Now the knives really were out for him. To do all those things to a young girl was bad enough, but to your own sister . . .

The reporters from the local papers had a field day. When the news reached Donna she was dumbfounded. Like her, Little Jen had been tortured and left for dead, but unlike Donna she had not survived. Images of Little Jen filled her head. When she thought of what Danny had done to her, she wanted to be physically sick. The small, childlike girl who had been so brutally abused was Danny's own flesh and blood. He hadn't even known it, but she wondered if he'd have cared anyway.

Jennifer Bridgend was buried in a churchyard in Bow, close to where her mother and brother had been born and where she had returned in search of him, fleeing her mother's new husband, an alcoholic with a temper. Whether Jen ever knew that Danny was her brother was now a moot point, but Donna said a quiet prayer for her, wondering if Danny had any concept now of what he'd done.

With him still at large, Donna was in a permanent state of terror. Even though she had police protection, she knew it would count for little if Danny were really determined to find her. He had no regard for human life any more; hadn't done for a long time. When she thought of all the people he had been involved with and whose lives had been touched by Danny, she realised that no one had ever gained anything but misery from him.

There was no reception after the funeral, just the huddled figure of a lonely woman making her way to the station to take her train back up North. The search for Jennifer had ended, and with it her last hopes. Having lost her son long ago, she now had to go home and come to terms with the fact that her daughter was gone forever too. The lonely figure sat in the crowded carriage, staring out into the darkness, looking back over her life and her failure as a mother and wife. As the train thundered northwards the woman remained lost in memories and grief. When it pulled into Preston station, she made no move to get off, though it was her destination. She sat and thought of what kind of life she was going back to. A violent husband waited for her, a man who would care little for her grief. She had no friends, basically no life.

The train pulled out with her still in her seat. Gaynor didn't know where she would end up, but anywhere was better than home.

Trippy made his usual call to the flat. Johnny had been arrested for getting into a fight in the West End, and as the police checked his records and personal details the trail was leading straight back to Danny. His hideout was no longer safe. Trippy needed to sort something else out for his friend, and quick.

When he entered the flat it stank of stale booze, drugs,

filth and grime. The toilet was full of puke and shit. As he walked past the kitchen, he saw that cups filled the sink, rubbish lay strewn across the work surfaces and floor, and the whole place had an unholy feeling about it.

From the small hallway, Trippy could hear the TV. As he entered the front room, he saw Danny sitting with his trousers around his ankles, rubbing himself as he watched a hard-core porn film. His penis was red and swollen. Wet welt marks were starting to appear on it as it was obvious that, no matter how hard Danny rubbed, he would never come. Drugs and empty booze bottles were everywhere. Trippy gagged several times. The stench was almost unbearable. Danny didn't even notice his presence.

Retreating from the front room, Trippy leaned against a wall and looked heavenwards for strength and guidance in what he had to do. The man he had known and loved lived only in Trippy's memory. Danny was like a ghost of his former self, more animal than human, with no friends, eating scraps of food occasionally, but mostly getting as many drugs into his system as he possibly could, to send himself to oblivion. He had lost everything: respect, money and property, a beautiful girlfriend and a host of friends. The only one left standing, the only one able to do anything, was Trippy.

Having made the decision some time before, he knew that the moment had come. Walking back into the room he tried to talk to Danny but he just stared ahead before flopping forward, not hearing or caring who was there. Still Trippy talked to his friend. Snot oozed from his nose. His eyes were filled with tears. He wiped his nose on his sleeve and looked sorrowfully at his friend.

'I've come to a decision, mate. This can't go on, and there's nowhere for you to run, nowhere for you to go. You're not the main man any more, mate, and you've done things I can never forgive or forget. Little Jen was your kid sister, Dan, and yer killed her. You violated and killed her, and I have to live with the fact that I was there and did nothing to help her or Donna. It will haunt me forever. I'm only glad Donna escaped with her life and that one day she will be OK. I should have helped her, but I let you keep on and on and never said a fucking word, and when I eventually did, you shot me down and like a fool I let ya.

'Well, my life's moved on, mate. Maggie's pregnant and I'll protect that kid with my life. I'll never forget you, Dan, but it's over now.'

Trippy loaded up three syringes and, one by one, injected Danny with lethal doses of pure heroin. Danny was so out of it, he thought his mate was just fixing up for him and smiled. He was dead by the time the second syringe had been emptied. Trippy turned off the TV and cradled his friend in his arms, rocking him gently, the tears rolling in a steady stream down his face.

'Remember fishing over the canal, mate. Remember chasing that older kid and protecting me, always watching my back. And 'ere, remember in the Wimpy when we did that runner after eating two Special Grills and two Knickerbocker Glories. They were good times, mate, weren't they? Just you and me together, brothers-in-arms, always.'

He sat and talked like that for a long time, thinking back to the old days and all the things they had shared. When his arm grew numb from Danny's dead weight, he laid him out on the sofa and covered his body with a dirty sheet, kissing the top of his head and ruffling his hair into place. Placing the syringe in Danny's hand, choking back sobs, he said, 'It had to end, Dan, and I'm glad it's me standing here. See you again sometime, mate. I love ya, and God bless.'

The door slammed and Trippy made his way home to Maggie.

*

When the police finally arrived at the flat, three days had passed. As they forced their way in, the smell was too much for them all. They recoiled on to the balcony outside for some fresh air. Covering their mouths and noses, they re-entered to find the cold body of Danny Lester. An ambulance was called, but it was obvious that he had died almost instantly from an overdose of heroin and had been lying there for some time. They knew before the body was officially identified that they'd found their man. The hunt for Danny 'The Knife' Lester was over and everyone breathed a sigh of relief. The reign of terror was now over, especially for Donna Stewart.

The neighbourhood had an almost euphoric feel to it. Most of the gang members had scattered and ordinary people's lives were getting back to normal. Those who had known or been involved with Danny had either disappeared or stayed away, returning only once they knew that he was dead. No one fully realised the terror he had caused during his reign as king pin, but in a small café in the heart of the East End, a tall young man was busy with orders and the distribution of drugs. Surrounding him were two or three others, waiting for their deliveries. Tommy wasted no time in putting them through their paces and setting them on their way. He had picked up where Danny had left off and was now the principal dealer in the area. He often thought of Donna. Even though she was long gone there would always be a special place in his heart for the once-beautiful girl he had truly loved.

Recently released from hospital, Donna Stewart sat in her bedroom, back in the family home. By her side Pookie took pride of place on her bed, and her room felt familiar, clean and fresh. She had been offered the opportunity to return to the flat in Poplar, but had told her dad she would never go back there. Nicola had collected all she wanted from the flat. What was is left would be dumped, all the bad memories scoured away. Even in the safety of her room, in the certain knowledge that Danny was dead, she was still vulnerable to flashbacks. She remembered the last time she was in this bedroom, getting ready for her man, and the anticipation she used to feel.

The news of Danny's death had been shattering, if only because it finally drew a line under all her foolish dreams, but she could only admit to feeling relief. When she thought of the man she had once loved, it was not the brutal crazed junkie she recalled but the Danny who had loved her, taught her things and treated her like a princess. She knew that in reality she had lost that man a very long time before he died.

She sat in front of her dressing-table mirror. Her face still bore the two long scars but they were fading. Fortunately the other cuts to her face were superficial. With careful make-up they were easily disguised. She desperately wanted her hair to grow back, and tugged and teased it into some kind of shape constantly. But the doctors had done a wonderful job with her prosthetic ear and she was grateful just to look faintly normal.

As she stared at her reflection, she saw that a small glimmer of the old Donna was still there. An offer of plastic surgery had been made, to widen her damaged eye, and with time her internal injuries would heal. She would start to see the old Donna creep back then, not as she once was but as a changed woman, one with a history and a past that she wanted to forget.

She'd known in her heart when she was in hospital that she couldn't stay in the East End. Her life here was over. Despite offers from Jane and David to visit them up North, Donna had her sights set further afield.

*

Standing on the grass verge, Donna gazed down at two freshly dug graves. She hesitated then inched forward. A small wooden cross marked one plot, and an identical one the next grave to it. Rest in Peace, Jennifer Bridgend. Rest in Peace, Daniel Lester. She laid a single rose on each of the graves, and in place of the tears of recent months came a feeling of peace. She was pleased she had made this visit. She needed to draw a final line beneath everything.

She spoke aloud to Little Jen, wishing she had done more for the girl but deep down realising that it was Jen's and Danny's fates, not hers, that had led them both there.

In a different part of the cemetery stood a tall lone figure. Trippy stared at the young woman, watching as she bowed her head in prayer, wondering what she was thinking but hoping she realised that her real life started now.

His eyes filled with tears for all that had happened, for the lives lost, ruined and changed forever. He sniffed and wiped his nose again, turned on his heel and headed home to his new and wonderful family, a different man but one who would never forget his friend, the way he first knew him a long, long time ago.

The three girls are all together, the plans are in place. After months of soul-searching and discussion, the day has finally arrived for them to make the much-discussed move. With tickets in hand, bags packed and Ian waiting to drive them to the airport, the three giggling girls bundle into the car, waving goodbye, and promising to call as soon as they arrive.

The flight is short and quick. As they make their way by taxi to their new apartment, Shaz yells with delight.

'Look, everyone, it's the Eiffel Tower!'